Geoffrey's Victory
Or The Double Deception

By

Mrs. Georgie Sheldon

Geoffrey's Victory
Or The Double Deception
by Mrs. Georgie Sheldon

ISBN: 978-93-61429-83-5

Published by

DOUBLE 9 BOOKS

2/13-B, Ansari Road
Daryaganj, New Delhi – 110002
info@double9books.com
www.double9books.com
Tel. 011-40042856

ABOUT THE AUTHOR

Sarah Elizabeth Forbush Downs (1843–1926) was an American dime novelist". She wrote novels under her own name, as "Mrs. Georgie Sheldon" and "Mrs. George Sheldon Downs". Downs was born on June 5, 1843, in Wrentham, Massachusetts. Her parents were Edwin A. Forbush and Malvina F. (Ware) Forbush. She was educated at the Ladies' Collegiate Institute in Worcester, Massachusetts. In 1868, she married George Sheldon Downs. She wrote under a pseudonym based on his name. In 1869, she began her career by contributing to newspapers. Theodore Dreiser signed her to write for Smith's Magazine. Dreiser regarded her as one of the "three most popular authors in the world." Lost-A Pearl, also known as A Lost Pearle, was one of Mrs. Georgie Sheldon's early publications, appearing in 1883. This story revolves around a young lady named Margaret Pearle Radcliffe, who is engaged to Captain Richard Byrnholm. However, she abandons her joyful marriage owing to the unscrupulous ways of Adison Cheatham, her fiancé's adversary, who has incriminating information that will tarnish the name of Byrnholm if Pearle does not marry Cheatham. The tale follows Pearle as she quickly distances herself from Cheatham and attempts to avoid her new husband's menacing gaze, never forgetting the guy she once loved.

CONTENTS

CHAPTER I
A STRANGE ADVENTURE

It was a beautiful winter night. The sky was brilliant with millions of beautiful stars that glowed and scintillated as if conscious that their light had never before penetrated an atmosphere so rarefied and pure. The earth was covered with a glaring coat of ice above newly fallen snow.

Trees and shrubs bent low and gracefully beneath the weight of icy jewels which adorned every twig and branch.

Every roof and spire, chimney and turret, gleamed like frosted silver beneath the star-lit heavens, while the overhanging eaves below were fringed with myriads of glistening points that seemed like pendulous diamonds, catching and refracting every ray of light from the glittering vault above and the gas-lit streets beneath.

But it was a night, too, of intense cold. Never within the remembrance of its oldest inhabitant had the mercury fallen so low in the city of Boston, as on this nineteenth of January, 185-.

So severe was the weather that nearly every street was deserted at an early hour of the evening; scarcely a pedestrian was to be seen at nine o'clock, and the brilliantly lighted thoroughfares had a lonely and desolate appearance without their accustomed flow of life and humanity. The luckless policemen, who alone paraded the slippery sidewalks on their round of duty, would now and then slink into sheltered nooks and door-ways for a brief respite from the stinging, frosty air, where they would vainly strive to excite a better circulation by the active swinging of arms and the vigorous stamping of feet.

Even the horse-cars and omnibuses were scantily patronized, while the poor drivers, muffled to their eyebrows in fur coats and comforters, seemed like dark, grim specters, devoid of life and motion, save for the breath that issued from their mouths and nostrils, and, congealing, formed in frozen globules among their beards.

At ten o'clock on this bitter night, Thomas Turner, M. D., was arranging his office preparatory to retiring, and feeling profoundly thankful that he had no patients who demanded his attention, and believing, too, that no one would venture forth to call him, when, to his annoyance and dismay, his bell suddenly rang a clanging and imperative peal.

With a shiver of dread at the thought of having to leave the warmth and comfort of his home, to face the fearful cold, yet with a premonition that the summons would result in something out of the ordinary course of events, he laid down the case of instruments that he had been carefully arranging, and went to answer the call.

He found a lad of perhaps fifteen years standing outside the door.

Without a word he thrust a card into the physician's hand.

"Come in, boy! come in," said the doctor, pitying the poor fellow, whose teeth were chattering at such a rate it was doubtful whether he could have spoken if he wished.

He obeyed the invitation with alacrity, however, and made directly for the radiator, toward which Dr. Turner pointed, telling him to "go and warm himself."

The physician then stepped beneath the hall light to examine the card he had received.

It proved to be the business card of a first-class, though small, hotel in the city, and on the blank side of it there had been hastily written these words:

"Come at once to the — — House. An urgent case demands your immediate attention.

A. Payson, Clerk."

Dr. Turner frowned, and hung his head in thought for a moment.

He had had a hard day; he was very weary, and would have hesitated about answering a strange call even in mild weather, and the temptation to send the boy and his card to some one else, and remain in the genial warmth of his own home, was very strong.

Still, the man was conscientious. The summons was urgent, and it might be a case of life and death. Perhaps the delay of sending to some other physician might result in the loss of a human life.

This thought decided him.

He turned quickly on his heel and passed down the hall to his office, remarking to the waiting messenger as he went:

"Wait here. I will be ready to return with you in a few moments."

He looked into his medicine case to see that he had everything that he wished, wrapped himself in a long ulster with an ample cape, drew a fur cap down over his ears, and a pair of seal-skin gloves upon his hands, and then went forth with his youthful guide to face the penetrating air of this bitterly cold night.

When he reached the — — House, he was conducted directly to a handsome suite of rooms in the third story, and ushered into the presence of a magnificently beautiful woman, who was reclining upon a luxurious couch.

Dr. Turner had never seen a lovelier woman. She was, apparently, about twenty-one or twenty-two years of age. Her hair was very dark, almost black; her eyes were also very dark, with straight, beautiful brows.

She was deathly pale—the pillow on which she lay was scarcely whiter—but her complexion was faultless, her skin as fine and smooth as an infant's, while her features were remarkable for their delicacy and loveliness.

Beside her, in a low rocker, and holding one fair white hand in both her own, there sat another woman, some two or three years older, but scarcely less beautiful, although of a different type, and looking anxious and distressed.

A few direct inquiries enabled the physician to comprehend the nature of the case, after which he rapidly wrote a few lines upon a card, and, ringing for a servant, dispatched it to the clerk below.

An hour later a middle-aged woman, of respectable and motherly appearance, was conducted to the sick-room, and when morning broke there was still another presence in that chamber—a tiny baby girl, with rings of golden brown hair clustering about her little head, with eyes of heaven's own blue, and delicate patrician features, which, however, were not like those of her mother, who lay pale and weak among her pillows, and who, strange to say, had betrayed no sign of joy or maternal love at the coming of the little stranger.

Three weeks previous two ladies had arrived, late one evening, at the — — House, where the younger had registered as "Mrs. E. E. Marston and maid."

The clerk, as he read the entry, had glanced with astonishment at the lovely blonde who had been thus designated as "maid," for her manner and bearing were every whit as stately, cultivated, and prepossessing as that of her supposed mistress.

Both ladies spoke French and German, as well as English, fluently, and it was impossible to determine to what nationality they belonged. The younger seemed almost like a Spanish beauty of high degree, while her companion had more the appearance of an Anglo-Saxon.

Both were richly and fashionably attired, and evidently belonged to the wealthy class, for Mrs. Marston wore jewels of the purest water in the richest of settings. She selected the most elegant suite of rooms that were unoccupied, and ordered all meals to be served in her private parlor; consequently but very little was seen or known of either mistress or maid after their arrival, although the very fact of their so closely secluding themselves served to excite a good deal of curiosity on the part of the other inmates of the house.

After the birth of Mrs. Marston's little daughter, Dr. Turner made his usual number of visits to see that his patient was doing well, and then he discontinued them, although his curiosity and interest were so excited regarding the mysterious woman and her attendant that he would have been glad of an excuse to attend her even longer.

Three weeks passed, and he was considering the propriety of presenting his bill, since the lady was a stranger in the city, and would doubtless leave as soon as she could do so with safety to herself and her child, when, one morning, he received a note from Mrs. Marston, requesting him to call upon her at his earliest convenience.

That evening found him knocking at her door, his heart beating with something of excitement, and with a sense of constraint upon him such as he had never before experienced.

"The maid" admitted him, a dainty flush tinging her fair cheek as she encountered his earnest glance, and he thought her more beautiful than ever, while he was firmly convinced that she was in reality no servant, but connected by some tie of blood to the woman whom she professed to serve, although there was no resemblance between them.

Mrs. Marston arose to receive him as he entered.

He had never seen her dressed until now, and he was almost bewildered by her brilliant beauty.

She was tall, with a symmetrical figure. She was queenly and self-possessed in her carriage, and betrayed in every movement the well-bred lady, accustomed to the very best of society.

She was dressed in a heavy black silk, which fitted her perfectly, and fell in graceful folds around her splendid form.

She wore no colors, and might have been in mourning, judging from the simplicity of her dress, and she might not—he could not determine. Her only ornaments were several rings of great value, and an elegant brooch, which fastened the rich lace, fine as a cobweb, about her throat.

"I am very glad to see you, Dr. Turner," she said, graciously, as she extended her white, jeweled hand to him; "and I thank you for responding so promptly to my request. Nellie, please bring that rocker for the gentleman," she concluded, indicating a willow chair in another portion of the room.

The maid obeyed, and then quietly withdrew.

"You are looking remarkably well, Mrs. Marston," Dr. Turner observed, hardly able to believe that she could be the same woman who had been so pale and wan when he had first seen her.

Her complexion was almost dazzling in its purity, while the flush on her cheek told of perfect health and a vigorous constitution.

"I am very well, thank you," she responded, somewhat coldly, as if her physical condition were not a question that she cared to discuss with him— "so well that I am contemplating leaving Boston by the end of another week, and I have asked you to come to me in order that I may consult you upon a matter of great importance. But first, do you think I shall run any risk in traveling by that time?"

"If any one else had asked me that, I should have said at once, 'Impossible!'" returned the physician, smiling. "But you have so rapidly recuperated that I should not fear a change so much for you as for many others. It depends somewhat, however, upon where you are going."

Mrs. Marston flushed slightly at this, but, after an instant of hesitation, she said, composedly:

"Oh, I intend to go to a warmer climate. I shall probably spend the rest of the winter in the South."

"Then I think you may go with perfect safety, if you are quite sure you feel well and strong."

"As to that, I never felt more vigorous in my life; but——"

The lady bent her shapely head in thought, a shadow of perplexity and doubt crossing her beautiful face.

"Perhaps you fear to take the little one; the weather is rather severe for a tender infant," suggested the doctor.

"Oh, no. I do not intend to take the child at all," returned the mother, quickly, a nervous tremor running through her frame as she spoke.

"You do not intend to take your child with you?" repeated the physician, astonished, while he searched the downcast face before him with a suspicious look.

"No; and that was what I wished to consult with you about," replied Mrs. Marston, shifting uneasily for an instant beneath his glance.

Then she lifted her head proudly and met his eyes with calm hauteur.

"You wish to leave it out to nurse, perhaps, and desire me to suggest some proper person," observed Dr. Turner, trying to explain her conduct thus.

"No," answered the lady, coldly. "I wished to ask if you could recommend some institution in the city where I could put her, and where she would receive proper care."

Dr. Turner regarded the woman with amazement.

"Institution, madame! What kind of an institution?" he asked, aghast.

"Some public institution, or some home for homeless children," she answered, not a muscle of her beautiful face moving.

"I really do not comprehend you," the physician said, almost ready to believe that he was in the presence of a lunatic, for surely no mother in her right mind could think of abandoning her child in such a heartless way.

"Indeed, I thought I made an explicit statement," remarked Mrs. Marston, haughtily. "However the child is not to go with me. There are reasons—imperative reasons—that compel me to dispose of her——"

"Abandon her, do you mean?" questioned the physician, sternly.

The lady shrugged her shapely shoulders and made an impatient gesture, as if the subject and object were alike distasteful to her.

"If you choose to put it in that disagreeable way, I suppose I shall have to accept the term," she replied, coldly. "But you have not answered my question. Do you know of a home for orphans where she would be received and where I might safely leave her? I would make it an object for any such institution to take her."

CHAPTER II
A MONSTROUS PROPOSITION

Dr. Turner did not immediately reply.

He was so indignant, so overcome by the startling and unnatural proposition that he was rendered speechless.

The knowledge that this woman, so beautiful and gifted, and who had, to all appearance, unlimited wealth at her command, should desire to cast her offspring adrift upon the world, coldly throwing her upon the indifferent care of strangers, was simply horrible to him.

The mystery, which, from the first, he had instinctively recognized as attaching itself to this woman, was thickening about her.

There must, he thought, be some terrible secret connected with her life, which she was anxious and bound to conceal, or she never could have contemplated such an unfeeling act, and he could think of but one contingency that would compel her to adopt such extreme measures.

"Madame," he at last said, and speaking with dignified reserve, "I cannot refrain from expressing my surprise at your startling and—I am compelled to say it—heartless proposal. It would be a most unnatural—a most reprehensible proceeding. My whole nature recoils at the mere mention of it, and I can think of but one reason that would seem to make it necessary for you to abandon your child in the way you propose."

The physician paused a moment, as if in doubt as to the propriety of saying more.

"Well, and what may that be?" briefly demanded his companion, in a tone that should have warned him not to give expression to his thought.

"Perhaps your little one has come into the world unprotected by the tie of wedlock, and therefore you desire to conceal from every one the evidence of——"

She checked the words upon his lips with an imperious gesture.

A vivid crimson rushed to her brow, suffused her neck, and seemed to extend to the very tips of her fingers; then the color as quickly receded, leaving her patrician face ghastly pale.

She threw up her proud head with a movement of exquisite grace: an angry fire leaped into her dusky eyes; an expression of scorn curled her beautiful lips.

"How dare you say such a thing to me?" she demanded, in a passionate tone that had a thrill of pain in it as well. "But for your former kindness to me, I would never pardon you! You have a suspicion that I am not a married woman."

"I could think of no other excuse for what you proposed regarding your child," replied the physician, meeting her flashing glance calmly, and with a note of contempt in his voice, although he half regretted having spoken as he had.

He believed even now that she was acting a part.

She saw it, and again her face flamed scarlet.

Then she drew from the third finger of her left hand a superb solitaire diamond ring, and passed it to him.

"Examine that if you please," she commanded, briefly and icily.

He took it, and upon its inner surface found engraved in tiny characters, "C. to E. Sept. th, 185—. *Omnia Vincit Amor.*"

It had evidently been given to her in September of the previous year.

"An engagement-ring," he remarked, as he passed it back to her with an air that plainly said: "That proves nothing to your advantage."

Madame bowed and then quietly but proudly drew from the same finger a massive circlet of gold which she also handed to him.

A dusky red surged to the physician's brow as he received it and realized what he had done. He felt as if he had offered the fair woman an unpardonable insult.

This ring was marked "*C. S. to E. E., Paris, March 15th, 185—.*"

Both circlets proved an honorable engagement and a lawful marriage, the latter occurring some seven months subsequent to the former, and Dr. Turner felt that he had got himself into a very unpleasant predicament.

"I beg your pardon, madame," he said, with visible confusion, but in a grave, respectful tone; "but your very extraordinary preposition must be my apology for my unjust and offensive suspicion."

For a moment the lady regarded him gravely, but with a little gleam of triumph in her dark eyes; then with a shrug of her shapely shoulders, she replied:

"Perhaps it was but natural; let it pass. I became a lawful wife, as you have seen, nearly a year ago, and my child has had honorable birth: but, for reasons which I cannot explain to you, I can never acknowledge her, and it becomes necessary for me to make some other provision for her."

"But it is such an unnatural thing to do," persisted the doctor, with a deprecating gesture.

"Granted; but—it cannot be helped," replied the mother, firmly, an inflexible purpose written on her fair young face.

"Allow me to inquire if your husband is living?" Dr. Turner asked, after a moment of silence.

"Excuse me; I cannot answer that question," replied his companion with pale, compressed lips.

"Ah! there has been some trouble and a separation, perhaps," thought the doctor; then he asked:

"Do you think that he would uphold you in thus sacrificing your little one—his little one, to your selfish purpose—to abandon her, as you propose, to the doubtful charity of a cold world."

An icy shiver seemed to run throughout the woman's frame at this. She shifted uneasily in her chair, her white lids quivered, her hands were locked in a rigid, painful clasp.

"I tell you there are circumstances which make it absolutely necessary for me to give her away," she said, in a strained, unnatural voice, after an evident effort at self-control. "My husband would—is as helpless in the matter as myself."

"I can conceive of no circumstances which should make the well-being of your child of secondary importance, especially since you have assured me that you are a lawful wife, and it is evident that you have abundant means at your command. She is your own flesh and blood, and it becomes your duty, as a mother, to give her a mother's love and care. I care not what fancied or real obstacle stands in the way, it should be resolutely swept aside for the sake of both duty and humanity," Dr. Turner argued, with impressive earnestness.

"You simply do not know anything about the matter, sir," retorted his patient, with an angry flash in her eyes, "and, if you please, we will not discuss that point any further."

Dr. Turner bowed a cold assent; then, as he returned the wedding-ring, which he had retained until now, he remarked:

"The name you have given here does not correspond with your husband's initials upon this ring."

The lady's lips curled in a little scornful smile.

"Did you imagine that I would use my true name in such a venture as this?" she asked. "But that is neither here nor there," she added, with an impatient toss of her head. "Do you know of any institution in this city where my child would be received?"

"No: there is no public institution that would so far countenance your conduct as to open its doors to her, and I would not designate it if there were. Such places are for children who have no parents, or for those whose parents are too poor to care for them," the physician indignantly replied.

Then, after a short pause, he continued, with great earnestness:

"Let me make one last appeal to you, madame. You have given birth to a lovely little daughter, who bids fair to be a child of whom any parent might well be proud. It would be a continual delight to watch her grow and develop into womanhood, and she would no doubt be of the greatest comfort to you years hence, when you begin to descend the hill of life. Keep your child, Mrs. Marston, do not cast her off upon the doubtful care of strangers, to become you know not what in the future. Love and cherish her, nourish her innocence and purity, and do not, I beseech you, commit the irreparable wrong which you are contemplating."

The woman before him threw out her white jeweled hands in a spasmodic gesture in which impatience, pain, and anger were commingled.

"Spare your importunities, Dr. Turner," she said, coolly, "for I assure you it is only a waste of breath and sentiment on your part."

"Have you no love for your innocent babe?" he demanded, sternly.

"I have not dared—I will not allow myself to become attached to her," was the low, constrained reply.

"Have you no pity, then, that you thrust her thus remorselessly from your sheltering care?"

"I should become an object far more pitiable if I should keep her with me," returned the incomprehensible mother.

"I cannot understand it. Poor child! poor child!" sighed the sympathetic and perplexed physician.

"Doctor," said his companion, with a sudden start, her face lighting with eagerness, "have you children of your own?"

"No, madame. I should consider myself blessed, indeed, if I had," he sighed.

"Then will you adopt my daughter? I can assure you that there is not the slightest taint upon her parentage, and it is only the force of hard, obstinate circumstances that compels me to give her up. Your sympathies seem to have been enlisted for her. I am sure you are a good man, and I know that she would find a kind parent in you."

The man flushed, and tears rose to his eyes at this appeal.

"Mrs. Marston," he said, sadly, "if your child had been born six months earlier, and you had asked me this question at that time, I should have answered you with eagerness in the affirmative; but she who would have given the little one a mother's care is no longer in my home. She died five months ago this very day, and I have no one else in my family to whom I could commit the babe."

"Then what shall I do?" murmured the woman, with knitted brows and sternly compressed lips.

"I can think only of one alternative that I should be willing to suggest," replied the doctor.

"What is that?" she demanded, eagerly.

"Advertise for some young couple to adopt the child. You will then have an opportunity to select a permanent home for her, and escape the anxiety which her uncertain fate in a charitable institution would entail upon you. I should suppose the mere thought of it would be torture to you."

"It is," replied the mother, with a quick, indrawn breath, while a nervous shiver ran over her. "I will do it," she added, the look of care vanishing from her face, which had now become to the high-minded physician more like the face of a beautiful fiend than that of a tender-hearted woman. "I will advertise in the *Transcript* to-morrow morning, and will offer the sum of five hundred dollars to any respectable couple who will take the babe and promise to rear and educate her as their own. I wonder why I did not think of that plan myself," she concluded, with a sigh of relief.

"I should propose omitting the reward from the advertisement," observed the doctor, with a slight curl of his lips.

"Why so?"

"Because in that case you would be sure that whoever applied for her was actuated by a real desire to have the little one; while, if money were offered, cupidity might be the main object in the application."

"Perhaps you are right," Mrs. Marston observed, thoughtfully; "and yet I believe I shall offer it. I shall, at all events, give that amount to whoever adopts the child."

She then adroitly changed the subject, plying the physician with numerous questions regarding Boston, its attractions and advantages, and so effectually led his mind in another direction, charming him with her rare conversational gifts, her evident culture and familiarity with both America and Europe, that he spent a delightful hour with her, and temporarily forgot the contempt and repulsion which he had previously entertained for her.

When the clock upon the mantel struck four, he started up in surprise, at which a sly smile curved his fair entertainer's red lips, for she knew that she had held him by the magic of her fascinations, as she had meant to do.

But she arose also, and cordially extended her hand to him at parting, while she remarked, smilingly:

"I have neglected a very important item of business, and came very near forgetting it altogether. If you have, with you, the bill for your services to me, I shall be very happy to settle it."

Dr. Turner flushed, and began to search his pockets, without appearing to notice the proffered hand.

At length he drew a slip of paper from his diary, and handed it to her.

She smiled again as she noticed the figures upon it; but unlocking a drawer in the table near which they were standing, she took from it an elegant purse, in which there appeared to be a plentiful supply of both gold and paper money.

She selected a bill and extended it to him.

"I am not able to change that for you, madame," he said, as he glanced at it and saw that it was a hundred-dollar note.

"I do not wish it changed. Please take it. Even then I shall feel that I am deeply indebted to you," she returned, with an earnestness such as she had not betrayed before during the interview.

Again the dusky red rushed to the doctor's temples.

"If it is not convenient for you to hand me just the amount of my bill, you can send me a check for the sum later," he said, coldly.

She bit her lips with mortification, and then tears rushed into her eyes.

"Oh, it is perfectly convenient. Excuse me; I did not intend to offend you, but I am truly grateful for the kind attention you have bestowed upon me, and I shall always entertain friendly memories of you."

Dr. Turner returned a courteous bow for the promise of "friendly memories," but remarked, briefly:

"I have but done my duty as a physician, madame."

An angry flush mounted to her brow as she counted five golden eagles from her purse and laid them in his hand.

"I know," she said, "that you think I am a heartless monster in woman's form; but you would not, I am sure, if you could understand the strait that I am in."

Another bow was his only reply to this.

He could not gainsay her statement regarding his estimate of her character, and he would not presume to inquire further into the mystery surrounding her.

"I should be glad to retain your good opinion," she resumed, with a slight, deprecating gesture, "for you have been a good friend to me in my necessity, but a stern fate compels me to forego that. I trust, however, that I shall see you again before I leave your city."

And she again extended her hand to him in farewell.

"If you need me—if I can serve you in any way, command me," Dr. Turner returned, politely, but with an emphasis which plainly indicated that he should not voluntarily seek her society.

He bowed again, but barely touched the hand held out to him, and then went his way, wondering what mysterious circumstance, or combination of circumstances, could have forced this beautiful and gifted woman to abandon her child thus at the very beginning of its life.

CHAPTER III
THE LITTLE STRANGER ADOPTED

The next morning there appeared an advertisement in the Boston *Transcript*, offering five hundred dollars to suitable parties who would adopt a female infant, and stating that applications were to be made by letter, addressed to the office of the paper.

Of course a great many answers were received, for there were hosts of people who would agree to almost anything for five hundred dollars, while there were others who were really anxious to adopt the little baby girl that was to be so strangely thrown upon the world.

One alone out of these many epistles pleased Mrs. Marston. It was written in a clear, elegant hand, signed "August and Alice Damon."

It was from a young couple, and stated that only a month previous they had lost their own little daughter—a babe of a few weeks—and their hearts were so sore over their loss, their home so lonely and sad, that they would gladly take a little one to fill, as far as might be possible, the place of their lost darling, and if the child in question pleased them and there was nothing objectionable connected with her birth or antecedents, they would gladly adopt her without the payment of the premium that had been offered.

Mrs. Marston, after reading this communication, immediately dashed off a note asking the young people to call upon her at their earliest convenience—in case they were at liberty to do so, the next morning at ten o'clock; she would reserve that hour for them.

Promptly at that time a young gentleman and lady of prepossessing appearance were ushered into Mrs. Marston's private parlor, and one glance into their kind and intelligent faces convinced her that she had found the right parties to whom to intrust her child.

"Mr. and Mrs. Damon," Mrs. Marston said, graciously receiving them, and glancing at the cards that had been sent up before them to announce their arrival, "I am very much pleased to meet you."

She invited them to be seated, and then entered at once upon the object of their visit.

"I have appointed an interview with you in preference to all other applicants," she said, "because of the real interest and feeling evinced in your letter to me. But before we decide upon the matter under consideration, I would like to know something about you and your prospects for the future."

Mr. August Damon, a fine-looking young man of perhaps twenty-five years, frankly informed the lady that their home was in Boston; that he was a clerk in a large wholesale boot and shoe house; his salary was a fair one, and there was a prospect that he might become a member of the firm at no very distant date, if all went well with the business. He said that both he and his wife were very fond of children, and had been almost heart-broken over the loss of their own child. They had resolved, if they could find one to whom their hearts turned, to adopt another, and bestow upon it, as far as might be, the love and care that their own child would have received if it had lived. They had seen her advertisement in the *Transcript,* and had determined to respond to it, hoping thus to succeed in their object.

"Nothing could be better," Mrs. Marston eagerly said, in reply. "This is just the opportunity that I desire. I feel sure that you will give my little one the kindest care, and I shall relinquish her to you most willingly. I shall expect you will do by her exactly as you would have done by your own; that you will give her your name, educate her, and give her such advantages as your means will allow. This must be your part in our contract, while mine will be to renounce all claim upon her, and make over to you the amount which I specified in my advertisement."

August Damon never once took his eyes from the face of that proud, beautiful woman while she was speaking. They burned with a strange fire, an indignant flush mantled his cheek, and an expression of contempt curled his fine lips.

His wife viewed the apparently heartless mother with speechless wonder, her eyes fastened upon her in a sort of horrible fascination.

Her sweet, delicate face was colorless as the snowy ruffle about her white neck, and she trembled visibly as she listened to her abrupt and apparently unfeeling disposal of a human soul.

There was an awkward pause after Mrs. Marston concluded, and she seemed to become suddenly conscious of the very unpleasant impression which her strange words and proceedings had produced upon her visitors, and a rush of vivid color mantled her cheeks.

She could not fail to realize that her guests were well-bred, even cultivated people; the stamp of true gentility was upon them, and it was extremely galling to her haughty spirit to feel that they had been weighing her in the balance of their own refined and noble natures, and had found her sadly wanting in all those gentler qualities and attributes which naturally belong to a woman, and especially to a mother.

But she was impatient of all restraint and discomfort. She threw off the feeling with the usual shrug of her shapely shoulders, and raising her handsome head with a haughty air she continued, somewhat imperiously:

"Do you accede to the conditions that I have mentioned; and you, madame?" turning her great dark eyes full upon the gentle but shocked wife.

"Oh, how can you bear to part thus with your little one, the darling whose pulses are throbbing with your own life-blood?" exclaimed sweet Alice Damon, tears starting to her earnest, gray-blue eyes, her delicate lips trembling with emotion.

"That is a question that I cannot allow myself to consider," responded Mrs. Marston, with a peculiar gesture of her jeweled hands, which might have meant either pain or repugnance, "neither can I enter into any explanation upon that point; the fact remains, I must part with her, and it is my wish to make the best possible provision for her."

"We should be glad to see the child, madam," Mr. Damon gravely remarked.

"Of course. I will have her brought in immediately;" and Mrs. Marston arose to ring a bell.

A moment later a portly matron entered the room bearing in her arms a lovely babe about a month old, arrayed in a richly embroidered robe, and wrapped in the softest and whitest of flannels.

Alice Damon uttered an eager cry, in which the tenderest mother-love and the keenest pain were blended, as she caught sight of the beautiful child who recalled so vividly her own lost treasure.

Starting from her seat she glided swiftly over the soft carpet, and the next moment the tiny creature was clasped close to her aching heart, while a sob burst from her as she pressed her quivering lips to its velvet cheek. Then she turned to her husband with it still in her arms.

"Oh, August, she is lovely!" she murmured, in husky, unsteady tones. "And, dear, my heart longs for her!"

Mr. Damon stood looking down upon the two for a moment, while he seemed struggling with some deep emotion.

He took one of the little soft hands that lay outside the heavily wrought blanket tenderly in his own, and bent for a nearer view of the small face.

"Her eyes are blue," he said, under his breath.

"Yes, like our own darling's. Oh, August, we will take her, will we not?" pleaded his wife, eagerly.

A look of fondest love leaped into his eyes as they met hers, but he did not reply to her just then.

He turned again to Mrs. Marston.

"I have an important question which I feel it necessary to ask you?" he began.

"In a moment," she returned, and signed to the nurse to withdraw.

"Now, if you please," she added, as the door closed after the woman.

"Is your child legitimate? If you can assure me of that, and that nothing of dishonor can ever touch her in the future, and that, as far as you know, she inherits no taint of insanity or incurable disease, I see no reason why we should not accede to your conditions and adopt the babe as our own."

Mrs. Marston's face had grown crimson during this speech, and her eyes flamed with anger.

Twice that week she had been obliged to meet this humiliating suspicion, and it was more than her proud spirit could endure.

"Do you presume— —" she began, haughtily.

"Madame," August Damon interrupted, gravely, but with the utmost respect, "pray do not accuse me of presumption when I have only the well-being of your own child at heart. If you will but consider a moment you cannot fail to realize that it is both natural and proper I should wish to be assured that the child I contemplate taking as my own is of honorable parentage, and with no heritage of future misery hanging over her. We shall, of course, use every precaution to prevent her from ever realizing that she is not our very own; but there may come a time when unforeseen events will lead her to suspect the truth, and then she will demand to be told her history. I must have it in my power to tell her that no story of shame, no stain, was attached to her birth."

The gentleman's tone was firm but courteous, and the proud woman before him realized a pride as deep-seated as her own, and that she had no common character to deal with.

He had a perfect right to ask her these questions, she knew, and she was bound to answer them in all sincerity.

The anger died out of her eyes; the color left her face, and there was more humility in her manner than she had before displayed, as she replied:

"Mr. Damon, I assure you that you need never fear even a breath against the fair fame or parentage of my child. I was legally married to a noble, high-minded gentleman, on the 15th of last March, although the ceremony was not performed in this country. More I cannot tell you regarding my private history. As to the little one's constitution, she inherits no taint of disease or mental trouble that I am aware of. I have always enjoyed vigorous health, as my physique at the present time ought to prove to you.

"I know," she continued, after a moment of thoughtful silence, "that the giving away of my child, when to all appearance there is no necessity for such an unusual act, appears like a monstrous proceeding; but I am so situated that I cannot help myself; the need is imperative—a relentless fate compels me to the unnatural act. I can tell you nothing more; if you see fit to adopt the babe, after hearing this, well and good; if not, I must reply to some other application, and make other arrangements for her."

"I am satisfied with what you have told me, and the child shall come to us. Alice, she is yours if you so wish," said the young husband, turning with a fond smile to his fair wife.

"I do wish it, August. I could not give her up now. See! how content she is!" and the sweet woman looked lovingly down at the little face lying so peacefully upon her bosom.

"You are willing to make the gift a legal one, I suppose," said Mr. Damon, turning again to Mrs. Marston, who, with a look of intense relief upon her face, was closely watching the young couple.

"If you mean by that that I will sign papers to ratify the bond, I must say, No!" the woman replied, with decision.

"Of what use would such papers be," she went on, "since I could not place my real signature upon them, and the name, by which I am known to you to-day, would amount to nothing, legally. I can only give her to you here, now, in this informal way. Take her—she is yours; and may she be a great comfort to you during your future lives."

"I see," replied Mr. Damon, "papers of adoption would amount to nothing;" but, nevertheless, he did not appear very well satisfied with this conclusion.

"And here is the future little Miss Damon's dowry," continued Mrs. Marston, with a smile, as she took a roll of bills from the same drawer whence she had paid Dr. Turner, "and I cannot begin to tell you how much of gratitude goes with it."

"Madame, I cannot accept your money," August Damon said, flushing hotly, as he drew back from the proffered bribe; for such it seemed to him.

"I am rich; I wish you to have it," said the lady.

"It is the child that we want, for her own sake, not for what you offer as an inducement to adopt her," returned the young man, with dignity.

"But I must insist," Mrs. Marston replied. "If you have no immediate use for it, put it at interest somewhere for her, and let it accumulate for a marriage portion. You will have to name her," she resumed, with a glance at the little one. "Call her whatever you wish, and may she prove a real blessing to you."

She approached Alice Damon as she spoke, laid the roll of bills between the soft, pink hands of the now sleeping babe, bent over her and imprinted a light kiss upon her cheek, then turning quickly away, she bowed to the husband and wife and walked abruptly from the room.

A half-hour later the mysterious little stranger was sleeping peacefully in the dainty cradle that had once held Alice Damon's namesake, while two tender, earnest faces bent fondly over her, as husband and wife prayed that she might long be spared to be a comfort and a blessing to them, and never realize the shadow that rested upon her birth.

The next morning, at an early hour, Mrs. Marston and her "maid" quietly left the — — House, and the city, leaving no address, nor any clew to their destination behind them.

CHAPTER IV
A CHANGE OF RESIDENCE
AND AN ADVENTURE

Thus the stranger's child found a home, with loving hearts and willing hands to care for her.

But August and Alice Damon Huntress had for certain reasons withheld their surname from the mother of the child they had adopted.

"I shall never put myself in the power of this woman," he had said to his wife, while discussing the question. "If we adopt this little one we must so arrange matters that she can never be taken from us; so that she can never even be found by those who give her to us, or be told that she is not our own flesh and blood."

So he had called himself August Damon, which was the truth, as far as it went, but no one in Boston knew him by any other name than Huntress, and he did not intend that the mother of the little one should ever know what became of the child after it was given into his hands.

They gave her the name of Gladys, for, as Alice Huntress said, she began to brighten and gladden their saddened hearts and lives from the moment of her coming to them.

The Huntresses lived in a very quiet way, on an unpretentious street in the city of Boston. Mr. Huntress had a good salary, but they were people of simple tastes, and had more of a desire to lay by a snug sum for declining years than to live extravagantly and make a show in the world.

For several years nothing occurred either to entice or drive them out of the beaten track; then, all at once, August Huntress conceived a brilliant idea, put it in practical use, secured a patent, and became a rich man.

No other children came to share the love and care bestowed upon Gladys, and the hearts of her adopted parents were literally bound up in her.

Every possible advantage was lavished upon her, and at the age of twelve years she was a bright, beautiful little maiden with glossy brown hair, lovely dark blue eyes, and regular features, and gave promise of rare beauty when she should reach maturity a few years hence.

About this time it appeared necessary for the interests of the house with which Mr. Huntress was connected, that he should remove to New York city.

Accordingly, the beginning of Gladys Huntress' thirteenth year found the family established in a well-furnished mansion in Clinton avenue, one of the pleasantest portions of Brooklyn, while Mr. Huntress' office was located in Dey street, New York.

Here Gladys at once entered the high school, having passed her examinations most creditably, and giving promise of becoming a brilliant scholar.

She dearly loved study, and asserted that as soon as she should complete the high school course, she should "make papa send her to Vassar for another four years, to finish her off."

And now there occurred an incident destined to have a wonderful influence on the young girl's whole future life.

One afternoon in May, after school was over for the day, Gladys persuaded her mother to allow their coachman to drive her over to New York to meet and bring her father home to dinner.

She had not, as yet, ever been allowed to go out alone in this way; but Mrs. Huntress could not accompany her that day, having an important engagement with some friends; but she knew her driver was perfectly trustworthy, he was very fond of the young girl, and she was sure that no harm could befall her, so the desired permission was given, and the youthful maiden drove off in high glee, and full of importance at being permitted to go by herself to the great metropolis.

The Fulton Ferry was safely crossed, and the carriage was rolling slowly up toward Broadway, when Gladys' attention was arrested by a group of street gamins, who had surrounded a boy whom they appeared to be jeering and tormenting in a cruel manner, and who seemed completely dazed by his position, and greatly distressed by the ill-treatment to which he was subjected.

He was a peculiar looking boy, having a slender though perfect form, a delicate, rather aristocratic face, and a finely shaped head, crowned with masses of light, waving hair, in which there were rich tints of gold and brown.

He was very pale and his full, large blue eyes had a strange expression in their depths—half wild, half pathetic—which went straight to our young heroine's heart.

He was neatly but plainly clad, though his garments had become somewhat disarranged by the rude handling of his tormentors, and he was making ineffectual efforts to recover a very good-looking straw hat that had been snatched from his head and was being ruthlessly tossed about by the vicious gamins, who were triumphing in his distress with a sort of fiendish joy.

"John, what are they doing to that poor boy?" Gladys asked, leaning forward, and speaking to the coachman.

"They're a set of imps, miss, and as usual up to some of their infernal tricks," replied the man. "It looks to me as if the lad is half-foolish, and they're making game of him."

"It is a shame," cried the little lady, flushing indignantly. "See what a nice-looking boy he is—so different from those coarse, rude children. Stop John, and let us help him to get away from them."

"Indeed miss, I can't: it wouldn't be at all proper," returned the dignified driver. "It's the business of the police to look after such cases, not for a young lady in your position."

At this instant a mischievous ragamuffin seized the strange lad by the hair, giving it such a savage pull that he cried out with fright and pain, while a shout of mocking delight rang out from the motley crew about him.

Gladys Huntress sprang up in her carriage, an angry flush surging over her pretty face.

"John, stop!" she cried, imperiously. "Stop!" she repeated, laying her gloved hand upon his arm, with a touch which he involuntarily obeyed, and, drawing his reins, his well-trained horses came to a stand close beside the group we have described.

"Boys, what are you doing? Let him alone. Aren't you ashamed to torment a boy who is weaker than yourselves?" the young girl exclaimed, in a tone of authority and scorn which for a moment arrested their cruel sport, while they gazed open-mouthed with astonishment at the elegant equipage and its fair occupant, who had so nobly espoused the cause of their luckless victim.

But it was only for a moment.

Everybody knows what lawless creatures the street urchins of New York are, and the next instant a derisive shout rent the air at this strange and unlooked-for interference.

"Hi!" cried one, who appeared to be the leader in the fray. "Mr. Chalkface must be some prince in disguise, and 'ere comes the princess with 'er coach and span to the rescue."

Another shout more deafening than the preceding one rent the air at this sarcastic speech, and Gladys shrank back with a look of disgust on her young face.

"Pretty little Miss Uppercrust," the young rascal insolently resumed, encouraged by the applause around him. "I guess it'll take more'n you and your fine feathers to squelch Nick Tower. See 'ere now, how d'ye like that?" wherewith he gave the poor boy a brutal punch in the ribs which elicited a shriek of agony from him.

Gladys' eyes blazed wrathfully. For a moment she gazed straight into the face of the impudent urchin, her beautiful lips quivering with contempt, while every eye was fixed upon her with wonder and curiosity.

It was a new departure for a young and delicate girl to face them like that. It was their experience to have every one of the better class shrink from them in disgust, and get out of their way as soon as possible.

Gladys saw that their attention was all concentrated upon her, and that the boy, upon whom they had been venting their malice, was for the time unheeded.

She saw, too, that he was stealthily edging his way toward the carriage, and a sudden bright thought flashed into her mind.

She bent forward as if to speak again, and the interest deepened on those youthful faces beneath her.

Quick as a flash she turned the handle of the carriage door, threw it open, and with a significant gesture, she cried out, in clear, ringing tones:

"Come here, boy, quick! quick!"

The lad needed no second bidding.

With one bound he was outside the circle of his tormentors; another brought him to the side of the carriage, and the next instant he had sprung within the vehicle, where he sank panting and trembling upon a rug at the young lady's feet.

The door was immediately shut and fastened. Gladys' face was glowing with triumph over the success of her ruse, while, at an authoritative chirrup from the coachman, who, sooth to say, had keenly enjoyed the spirited and courageous attitude assumed by his young mistress in defense of the persecuted boy, the horses started on, leaving the group of gamins speechless and spell-bound with amazement at this unexpected master-stroke.

It was only for a minute, however; the next rage, at having been outwitted by a girl, and that one of the hated favorites of fortune, superseded their astonishment, and a succession of frantic yells burst upon their ears, while as with one mind they stooped to gather mud from the gutter, rolled it into balls, and then sent their filthy missiles flying after the receding carriage and its occupants.

Gladys did not pay the slightest heed to this attack, though one vile mass came plump against her pretty sunshade where it adhered for a moment and then rolled into the street, but leaving an unsightly stain where it had struck upon the rich, glossy silk.

The irate little wretches would have followed up their assault had not a policeman suddenly made his appearance upon the scene, when they took to their heels, scattering and disappearing around a corner, like a flock of frightened sheep, quicker than it has taken to relate the occurrence.

Gladys gave a sigh of relief as the noise and pelting ceased, and then she turned her attention to the luckless waif whom she had befriended in his hour of need.

"Get up, boy," she said, kindly, "they cannot hurt you now."

But as he still crouched, trembling and frightened, at her feet, she turned to the coachman and said:

"John, help him up, he is too frightened to move."

"Come, my lad, you've nothing to fear now," the driver remarked, encouragingly, and reaching over the back of his seat he took the boy by the arm and lifted him from the floor, placing him opposite his young mistress.

He glared wildly about him at first, but as his eyes fell upon Gladys' sympathetic face the fear faded from them, and he seemed reassured.

Then all at once he put his hand to his head in a distressed way, and called out:

"M'ha! m'ha!"

"What does he mean, John? Can they have hurt him, do you think?" Gladys asked, looking perplexed, and regarding the boy's blank, though beautiful, face with anxiety.

"I don't know, miss; perhaps it's his hat he's troubled about."

The lad turned quickly at the word hat, nodded his head emphatically, and showed two rows of white, handsome teeth in a broad, satisfied smile.

"M'ha! m'ha!" he repeated, and then there followed a lot of gibberish that was wholly unintelligible to his listeners.

"How strangely he appears!" Gladys exclaimed, regarding him curiously.

"He do, indeed, miss. The poor chap is an idiot, or I'm much mistaken."

"An idiot! Oh, how dreadful! Poor boy," cried Gladys, pityingly. Then she added, soothingly: "Never mind your hat, papa shall buy you another."

The young stranger nodded contentedly, as if he understood her, while his great blue eyes were fixed earnestly and confidingly on her face.

"What is your name and where do you live?" continued the young girl, wondering what she should do with him now that she had rescued him from his persecutors, if he could not tell where he belonged.

The only answer to this query was a senseless smile, accompanied by a low crooning sound of contentment.

"Oh, dear! can't you talk at all? What is your name? you must tell me or I shall not know where to take you," said Gladys, beginning to look greatly disturbed, and wondering what would be the result of this strange adventure.

The boy reached out a white, slender hand and touched the girl caressingly on the cheek, at the same time making a sound indicative of pleasure and admiration, but uttering no intelligible word.

It was evident that he was not only simple-minded, but that there must be some paralysis of the vocal organs as well, that prevented his talking.

A flush sprang to the young girl's face, and a strange thrill pervaded her at the touch of those delicate fingers.

"He is the most beautiful boy I ever saw," she said, "but, oh! how dreadful for him not to know anything! I wonder who he is, John!"

"I'm sure I can't say, miss," replied the man, looking perplexed and somewhat annoyed.

"How old do you think he can be?"

John gave a long look at the young stranger.

"He's small of his age, miss, but I reckon he must be older than yourself."

"Older than I! Oh! I do not think that can be possible," Gladys exclaimed, attentively studying the strangely attractive yet vacant countenance before her.

"What shall we do with him, John?" she inquired, after a moment of thoughtful silence.

"I think we'd best take him straight to the office, tell the master all about him, and he'll settle the matter."

"Yes, I believe that will be the best plan," Gladys returned, looking greatly relieved. "Papa will know just what to do. But," bending forward and laying her hand on the boy's arm to attract his attention more fully, while she spoke slowly and very distinctly, "can't you tell me where you live, boy? Do try, and then we can take you directly to your home."

The lad looked up with a most confiding smile at her, gently took her hand from his arm, clasped it tenderly in both his own, and murmured, in an exceedingly rich and mellow tone, some strange sounds.

"Oh, how sorry I am for him!" Gladys said, with starting tears: "I wonder if he has any father or mother, brothers or sisters. It would break my heart to have a lovely brother like this, and not have him know anything. Hurry on, John, please; I am anxious to know what papa can do for him."

CHAPTER V
A GRAVE CONSULTATION

Arriving at Mr. Huntress' office in Dey street, Gladys alighted, bidding John detain the boy in the carriage until she could bring her father.

She ran lightly up the stairs, and found that gentleman just on the point of leaving to return home, but evidently very much pleased to have his daughter come for him.

She related what had occurred on her way over to the city, and he listened attentively to her story; but his face grew grave as she proceeded, for he was so fond and careful of her, that he could not endure the thought of her running into any danger.

"I fear you have been unwise, my darling, in taking this boy into the carriage with you," he said, drawing her fondly toward him, and bending down to kiss the bright, eager face upturned to him. "He may have come from some fever-infested locality; you should have given him into the care of a policeman."

"But, papa, there was no policeman near at the time, and the poor boy was so frightened and distressed I hadn't the heart to make him get out of the carriage, at least until we could get beyond the reach of those rude boys. I supposed, of course, he would tell us where he lived, so that we could take him home, but we could not understand a word that he said."

"Perhaps he is some foreigner," suggested Mr. Huntress.

"No, I think not, for he seemed to know what we said to him. He isn't like those other boys—he looks as if he must belong to very nice, respectable people. His clothes are very plain, but as clean as can be—even his hands and nails are as white and clean as mine, which is not usual in a boy, you know. Come and see him, papa. I know you will pity him," pleaded Gladys, with a very sweet and sympathetic face.

She slipped her hand within her father's arm and drew him with gentle force out of his office and down the stairs to the carriage, where John sat, looking a trifle anxious and as if he feared a reproof for allowing a strange child in his master's elegant equipage with his idolized daughter.

Mr. Huntress was struck with the refined, even aristocratic appearance of the boy the moment his eyes fell upon him.

He instantly recognized the wonderful beauty of his face, remarked the shape and color of his eyes, which, had they been lighted by the fire of intelligence, would have been his chief charm. His frame was slight, but he was finely formed, with shapely hands and feet. His head was rather massive for his body and of that square structure, with a broad, full brow and an unusual height above the ears, which generally proclaims a large brain and rare intellectual capacity, and yet he was unmistakably an idiot! One look into those blank, expressionless eyes but too plainly told that.

Mr. Huntress entered the carriage, after assisting Gladys to her seat, and spoke kindly and cheerfully to the boy.

He made no answer, but fixed his great eyes earnestly upon the gentleman's face while he shrank close to Gladys, as if he instinctively realized that she was his stanch friend, and would protect him against all evil.

"I do not wonder that you were interested in him, Gladys," said Mr. Huntress, regarding the stranger gravely, "he is peculiarly winning in appearance, though evidently very simple in mind."

"Do you suppose he was always so, papa?" Gladys asked.

"It does not seem possible, for, aside from that vacant look in his eyes, his face has a wonderfully intelligent expression, especially when it is in repose. Can't you make him say anything?"

"No, sir; he tries to talk, but I cannot understand what he means."

"Ask him a question, Gladys," said her father.

"Boy, you have lost your hat—would you like a new one?" the young girl questioned.

"M'ha! m'ha!" he instantly answered, putting his hand to his head, thus showing as before that he had comprehended something of what was said to him.

Mr. Huntress' face lighted.

"Try something else," he commanded.

"Where do you live, boy?" Gladys inquired.

This query, like the previous one, only elicited a perfect storm of unintelligible sounds.

"Do you wish to go home to your friends?" Gladys continued, making another effort.

But the only response was a short, sharp ejaculation of pain, while the lad seized her hand and laid his cheek affectionately against it, looking appealingly into her face, as if thus to signify that he did not wish to leave her.

"I cannot understand him at all, papa, only it seems as if he wishes to stay with me," said Gladys, with a sigh.

Mr. Huntress thought a moment, then he turned to the coachman and said:

"Drive home, John."

"Oh, papa, are you going to take him home with us?" cried Gladys, eagerly.

"Yes; for to-night. I find myself strangely interested in him, and I have not the heart to turn him adrift upon the street. He evidently belongs to a good family, and has probably strayed from home and got lost. We will care for him until we can learn who his friends are, and can return him to them," Mr. Huntress replied, and they then proceeded directly home with their strange *protege*, where Mrs. Huntress received them with considerable surprise, although her sympathies were also soon enlisted in behalf of their charge, and she bestowed the kindest of care and attention upon the unfortunate waif so singularly thrown into her family.

Mr. Huntress caused an advertisement to be inserted in the papers the next morning, inquiring for the friends of the wanderer.

But a week passed and he received not one word in reply, and thus his identity remained a profound mystery.

Meantime, the object of these inquiries was so docile and tractable, so affectionate in his manner toward every member of the household; he was so trustful, appearing to recognize instinctively that they were kind friends; he was so exceptionally nice about his person and habits, and so gentle in his manner, that they all became greatly attached to him, and they felt more and more convinced that he belonged to some family of good blood and high position, in spite of the very common clothing which he wore, and his imbecile condition.

There was nothing about him to give the least clew to his identity. Every article he had on was thoroughly examined to try to find some name; every pocket was searched with the same purpose, and at last Mr. Huntress began to believe that he must have been brought from a distance to New York by some person or persons, and there willfully deserted for some secret reason, with the hope, perhaps, that the authorities would care for him and have him sent to some institution for weak-minded people.

This view of the affair made him very indignant toward the supposed perpetrators of the deed, and tenfold more tender toward the unfortunate victim of such an inhuman transaction, and one day, upon returning from his business in New York, he was accompanied by one of the most skillful physicians in the city.

To him the pitiable but interesting innocent was submitted for examination.

The noted M. D. at once became absorbed in and enthusiastic over the peculiar case.

"He would be a remarkable boy but for the torpidity of his intellect," he asserted. "He was not born so. His present condition was caused either by some acute disease of the brain, or by some injury to it—the latter, most probably."

"Possibly a great wrong has been perpetrated, and he has been deserted in this mysterious way to conceal the deed," suggested Mr. Huntress, gravely.

"I should not be at all surprised," returned the physician. "He may be the heir to some large property, and jealousy has brought him to this pass. Everything about him, save his idiocy, betrays that he came of a refined parentage. His physical condition is sound, although he is not fully developed as he should be, but that is owing undoubtedly, to his mental incapacity. He is evidently about fifteen years of age."

All this was the result of but a superficial examination. A more critical one confirmed one of the doctor's theories: there proved to be a depression of the skull which must have been caused by some accident to or violent blow upon the head.

"It was done a number of years ago," the learned man affirmed, "and that produced a paralysis of the brain and also of the nerves that control his organs of speech."

"Is there any help for him—can he be restored?" Mr. Huntress inquired, eagerly.

"Possibly, by an operation; but it would be attended with considerable risk."

"Would the risk be so great, that were the boy your own son, you would hesitate to attempt it?"

"No; I should have it done at once. Still, the trouble is of such long standing that I could not answer for the success of the operation in restoring the boy to his normal condition, even should he survive the shock to his system; and yet— —"

"Well?" almost impatiently questioned Mr. Huntress. He was becoming greatly excited over the matter.

Somehow a conviction had taken possession of his heart that such an operation would result favorably, and he longed to have his hopes confirmed.

"It would be a great triumph of science if the trial could be made, and he should have his reasoning powers restored," returned the physician, gravely.

"Would he be able to talk? Would his power of speech be regained?"

"Yes, I believe so. I suspect that a portion of the skull, which was broken at the time of his injury, is pressing upon his brain, causing not only loss of memory, but also a partial paralysis of the hypoglossal nerve. If this pressure can be relieved, and the piece of skull lifted to its place, or removed altogether, and the aperture trepanned, I see no reason why he should not recover the full use of all his faculties," the doctor explained.

"I wish it might be done. Doctor, I wonder if it would be right for me to assume the responsibility of ordering this operation to be performed," said Mr. Huntress, reflectively.

"It would be a great blessing to the boy."

"Yes; provided all went well."

"And an otherwise inexplicable mystery might thus be solved; he would doubtless be able to tell who he is, and thus you could restore him to his friends."

"Dr. Scherz, will you share the responsibility—simply that—of this matter with me?" Mr. Huntress gravely asked, after thinking deeply for several moments.

"I feel rather delicate about giving you an affirmative answer to that question," the physician replied, "if I am expected to have charge of the case. I might be severely criticised and accused of a desire to experiment for the benefit of my profession, if there should be a fatal result."

"Yes, perhaps; but, on the other hand, you would acquire fame if the boy was restored."

"Undoubtedly." And the eminent physician's eyes glowed with eagerness.

"Well, the matter stands like this," said Mr. Huntress, after another thoughtful pause. "I have done my best to find the lad's friends, but there is evidently no one, at least in Brooklyn or New York who will claim him. I am unaccountably interested in him. I will not send him to an insane asylum. I cannot cast him forth again upon the street to wander about at the mercy of the rabble. I have resolved to care for him as I would wish a son of mine cared for under similar circumstances, and yet his presence, in this imbecile state, is a constant pain to me. What shall I do?"

"If you intend to give him a father's care, I see no reason why you should not exercise a parent's judgment and authority in the matter of his possible restoration," Dr. Scherz responded, thoughtfully.

"Then will you take charge of the case and treat it as your judgment and skill dictate? The expense and risk shall all be mine, yours the reward and fame if a cure is effected."

Dr. Scherz did not reply to this request for several minutes. He appeared to be considering and reviewing the matter in all its points, and evidently regarded the undertaking as one of grave responsibility and importance.

At length he looked up, and Mr. Huntress was more encouraged by the expression on his pale, thoughtful face, than he had yet been over anything that he had said about the case. He felt sure that the man would act conscientiously, and exert himself to the extent of his skill.

"I think I will attempt it," he said, slowly. "But before I do, I would like to consult with a friend in the profession, and get his opinion upon the undertaking. I will see you again in a few days; meantime, do your best to build up the boy's strength with a nourishing diet."

With this, the two men separated.

CHAPTER VI
THE DEVELOPMENTS OF SEVERAL YEARS

A full week passed before Mr. Huntress heard anything further from Dr. Scherz, and it was a week of anxiety and unrest for him.

At the end of that time the physician went again to see the Huntress *protege*, taking a noted hospital surgeon with him.

After another protracted and critical examination, the two gentlemen decided to undertake the operation together.

The boy was removed to a hospital where diseases of the brain were treated, and there the delicate and hazardous operation was performed.

The result proved that Dr. Scherz had thoroughly understood the case—that his theory was the correct one.

A severe blow upon the head, years previous, fractured the skull, a portion of which was crowded in upon the brain, the pressure causing temporary paralysis and idiocy, also loss of energy in the hypoglossal or lingual nerve.

This piece of bone was removed, the brain relieved of the unnatural pressure, and the result was both wonderful and startling.

Before the patient had fully recovered from the effects of the ether which had been administered to him, memory and speech both reasserted their functions by completing a sentence which had evidently been interrupted at the time of the accident which had deprived the boy of their use.

"——tell my papa!" were the words which fell upon the ears of the startled surgeons, while the large blue eyes of their patient slowly unclosed and gazed up into the faces bending over him, the light of reason once more gleaming in their azure depths.

"What will you tell papa?" asked Dr. Scherz, in a quiet tone, while the other surgeon drew quickly out of sight.

"Jack struck Margery," was the instant reply.

"Who is your papa, my boy?"

"Why, he's papa; don't you know?—my good papa," was the response, while a puzzled look shot over the lad's pale face.

Dr. Scherz knew from his manner of speech that he must have been very young—not more than five years of age—at the time of his injury, and when that great darkness had so suddenly enveloped him.

"Yes, your good papa," said the doctor, soothingly. "Now go to sleep like a man."

"I'm Margery's little man—where is Margery?" he questioned, drowsily, and closing his eyes, he was soon in a profound slumber.

The two physicians watched him in silence for a few moments, then they looked up into each other's face; eye held eye for an instant with an eloquent glance, the next their hands met in a prolonged and hearty clasp across their patient, for they knew that, if all went well, they had succeeded in an operation that would give them a famous reputation for all time.

When the boy awoke again he called lustily for "Margery," and a kind and motherly nurse was at once appointed to care for him.

He seemed to know, however, that she was not "Margery," although he appeared to take to her and was content to have her attend him.

"Where's Jack?" he asked of Dr. Scherz, who still remained with him, determined to watch him most carefully.

"Jack who?" he asked.

"Why, Margery's Jack; but he isn't good like Margery," from which the physician inferred that "Jack" must have been Margery's husband, and not an over kind one either.

"Oh, Jack has gone away," he answered, carelessly. "What is your name, my boy?"

"I'm Geoffrey, sir."

"Geoffrey what?"

"Why, Geoffrey Dale—don't you know? I'm papa Dale's own boy."

"Where is papa?"

"Gone away off," was the reply, accompanied by a grieved look, "and he won't come again for ever so long."

Dr. Scherz would not press him further; he knew that they must be patient. Memory had lain dormant for so long, and the child had been so young at the time of losing it, that it was doubtful if they could ever learn very much regarding his history.

Weeks passed, and Geoffrey was at last pronounced well enough to return to the beautiful home awaiting him in Brooklyn.

He had recovered without a single drawback. The light of reason gleamed in his eyes, and he had the full use of all the organs of speech.

But, although the doctors had decided that he must be fully fifteen years of age, notwithstanding his growth had been somewhat stunted by the effects of his injury, mentally he was little better than an infant.

He talked like a child of five years, and acted like one.

But very little could be learned of his previous life. It was evident that he had been living with a woman named Margery—who, probably, was his nurse—and a man named Jack, possibly the woman's husband.

Margery he had loved, and he often called for her now. Jack he had feared, and looked frightened whenever his name was mentioned.

Of the injury which had deprived him of his memory he seemed to be able to tell nothing, although he affirmed that Jack had struck and tried to choke Margery, and he wanted to "lick the naughty man."

Of his mother he knew absolutely nothing; his father was not much more than a name to him, although he spoke of him as his "good papa," while he could not tell anything whatever about the place where his former home had been, and knew nothing of the circumstances of his being in New York.

He was very quick to comprehend, however, now that he once more had his reason, and readily adapted himself to his new surroundings.

Mr. Huntress resolved to adopt him legally, and do all in his power to atone for the long interval of darkness and mental incapacity to which he had been so strangely doomed.

Geoffrey began at once to regard his new friends with the greatest confidence and affection, while toward Gladys he manifested the most devoted love.

She, on her part, regarded him with tenderest compassion and sympathy, for, in spite of his remarkable beauty and natural ability, he was truly a pitiable object, with the simple mind and manners of a child five years of age in a body of fifteen; for he soon began to develop rapidly, physically, after his restoration, and bade fair to be a man of splendid physique.

He was not long in realizing that he was far from being like other boys of his age, and he began to be very sensitive over the fact—to grow grave and thoughtful, and sometimes positively unhappy.

"Why can't I be like other boys?" he once asked of Mr. Huntress, with a perplexed look on his fine face, and the gentleman kindly explained that, when he had been very young, some one or something must have struck him a blow on the head which had injured his brain, so that for years it had been the same as if sound asleep, and had only just waked up again; that his body had grown, but his mind had not.

"Oh, I know," Geoffrey returned, with a startled look, a new light coming into his eyes. "Jack threw a great stick of wood at me."

"What made him do that?" Mr. Huntress asked, eagerly.

The boy bent his head, and seemed trying to recall the events of that dim past.

"He came into the kitchen with a dreadful red face," he said, "and he was very ugly to Margery—I can't think about what. He put his hands around her neck, and she screamed. I ran up and struck him, and told him I'd tell my papa, and—that's all I know," he concluded, with a sigh.

Mr. Huntress could imagine that the man was intoxicated, and being in a frenzy, he had perhaps seized a stick of wood from the hearth, thrown it at the child, and knocked him senseless.

"What was Jack's other name?" he asked.

"Jack—Jack—" Geoffrey began, then shook his head hopelessly. "I can't tell," he concluded; and Mr. Huntress felt that it only annoyed him, and it would be useless to try to find out anything definite from him, so he let the matter drop.

One day, after Geoffrey had been with the family some three months, he came in from the street looking flushed and angry.

Seeking Gladys he besought her most piteously to teach him to read.

Upon inquiring what prompted the request, she found that Geoffrey had been attracted by a glaring placard that had been pasted up somewhere on a building, and had asked some boys what it was.

This had at once betrayed his woeful ignorance, for if he had even known his letters, he could at least have made out something of the nature of the bill, and they had tormented him unmercifully for being a simpleton.

Gladys at once procured a primer and set herself at work to teach him.

He proved to be a most diligent pupil, with great perseverance and a wonderful power for memorizing, for in a month he had mastered the whole of its contents.

Mr. Huntress was astonished at his progress, and wanted to put him at once into school.

But Geoffrey, who was developing rapidly in every way, shrank from the proposal, and begged his Uncle August, as he had been taught to call Mr. Huntress, to allow him to study at home.

"They will laugh at me at school, for I shall have to go into classes with little boys only five or six years old," he pleaded, with a crimson face.

"But you must go to school some time, and you will have to begin with boys younger than yourself," Mr. Huntress replied.

"Won't you keep on teaching me, Gladys?" Geoffrey asked, appealingly. "I will study hard and never trouble you by not having my lessons, and perhaps I can catch up with big boys by and by."

Gladys said she would keep on with him. But she was not allowed to do so, although she often gave him help in many ways.

She had her own studies to attend to and was working hard at them, therefore Mr. Huntress would not allow her to tax herself any further, and so a tutor was engaged to come to the house every day to attend to Master Geoffrey's lessons.

The boy was true to his promise. He studied diligently, and his tutor never had occasion to utter a word of complaint over ill-prepared lessons. Geoffrey seemed to realize more and more how far behind other boys of his own age he was, and with his pride and ambition thus aroused, no task seemed too difficult to accomplish, if it would only serve to help him to overtake them.

Another thing troubled him exceedingly. He had learned that Gladys was two years younger than himself, and yet she was nearly half through the high school, while he was simply learning his alphabet. The thought overwhelmed him with shame and pain.

"Gladys is a girl younger than I, and I am years and years behind her, when I should be ever so far beyond her," he said one day to Mrs. Huntress, when he had become almost discouraged over one of his lessons, and had gone to her for help and sympathy.

"But Gladys has always been at school and you have not, Geoff," returned his aunt, kindly. "Go and ask her to show you about these problems; she can help you much better than I, for they are fresher in her mind."

But the proud boy had all at once grown keenly sensitive, and would not seek the young girl's aid. He preferred to fight the battle out by himself, rather than be coached by a girl younger than he was.

Of course this was the better way; he gained in mental strength and self-reliance by it, and he accomplished more in three years than the ordinary school-boy would in six.

Aside from his pride and sensitiveness in this respect, he was ever ready and eager to be with Gladys.

Wherever she went, after school hours, he was her constant and devoted attendant, and no service was too hard or disagreeable to be performed for her.

And she enjoyed having him with her. He was outgrowing the delicate, almost effeminate look which he had had when he first came to them; an air of manliness and strength had taken its place, while there was a natural gallantry and manliness about him that made him a very agreeable escort.

Another year passed, and he made even more rapid strides in his studies than before; still it was a great trial to him that he had only completed the studies of the second year of the high school course, and Gladys was ready to graduate.

He was present at her examination, and also at the exercises of the class when it graduated, and it was evident, from his flushed cheek and glittering eye, that some bitter struggle was going on within him.

He watched the beautiful girl's every movement, he eagerly drank in every word that she uttered, and was as proud of her as he could be, yet all the time miserably conscious of his own deficiency.

That evening he shut himself within his own room and fought a terrible battle out with his pride and wretchedness.

"I am nineteen years old, and she is seventeen," he said, bitterly. "I am two years behind her, and I should be two years in advance—there are four years of my life lost; no, not lost, either," he added, with sudden energy, "for I will make them up, I will gain them. Can I do six years work in four? Harder work, too, than I have ever done before? Yes, I will!"

He sat down to his table and began to look over his books, making calculations as to how much ground he could get over in a given time, while every few moments he would consult some catalogues that lay beside him.

The next morning he walked down to the Fulton Ferry with Mr. Huntress, and on the way he remarked, with more than his accustomed gravity:

"Uncle August, Gladys is going to Vassar next year, isn't she?"

"Yes; she is ambitious to take an advanced course, and there is no reason why she should not do so, if she desires."

"Will you allow me to continue my studies during the summer with Mr. Rivers, and enter some institute in the fall where I can advance more rapidly?"

Mr. Huntress turned and looked searchingly into the young man's flushed face, as he asked this question.

He was a tall, manly fellow of nineteen, strong and stalwart of frame, his fine, massive head crowned with waving hair a few shades darker than it was when we first saw him; his eyes full of fire and intelligence, his whole face glowing with strength of character, and a certain something which gave one an idea of great reserve power, and it was no wonder that the countenance of Mr. Huntress lighted with a look of pride, as he realized that, under God, he had been instrumental in giving to the world this noble specimen of manhood.

Then a sudden smile broke over his face.

"Why, Geoff, are you envious of Gladys, because she is going to college?" he asked, in a bantering tone.

A deeper flush suffused the young man's handsome face. Then he replied, in low but intense tones:

"I hope I am not envious of any good that comes to her; I am more proud of her than I can express, and I would not have her anything but just what she is, the kindest, the smartest, and loveliest of girls; but I can't quite stand it to be so far behind her, to have her look down upon me and despise me for being so ignorant."

"I do not think that Gladys would ever be guilty of anything so unkind. Geoff; she loves you far too well for that," returned Mr. Huntress, gravely, but still closely watching his *protege*, for he could well understand the pain he was suffering.

Geoffrey's face kindled, and his companion could see his temples throbbing as the blood coursed more quickly through his veins at his words.

"Thank you, Uncle August, for assuring me of Gladys' affection; but I want her respect as well," he said, with a slight quiver in his tone.

August Huntress started at that reply, for it betrayed a great deal.

It told him that the devotion and affection which he had manifested for Gladys from the first had now grown into a strong, deep passion, which would either make or mar his whole future, and he was strangely moved by this discovery.

How would it be with Gladys if she should discover it? Would her heart respond to this wealth of love? Would she ever be willing to link her fate with his?

She was far in advance of Geoffrey, mentally, but he was making such rapid and resolute strides after her, that, at the rate he had been gaining on her of late it could not be very long before he would reach the plane on which she was standing, even if he did not distance her altogether.

Well, well, it would be a romantic ending to the story of their lives, he thought, if these two, so strangely thrown upon his care—with so much of mystery surrounding their birth and parentage, and likely always to envelope them—should some day unite their fates and wed each other.

But he allowed nothing of all this musing to appear; he simply said, with his accustomed kindness and genial smile:

"You are worthily ambitious, Geoff, but I don't know how you will stand it to apply yourself so closely all summer and then go right on in the fall. I cannot allow you to sacrifice your health to your love for study."

"But I am well and strong as a giant; will you let me try, sir?" he pleaded, earnestly.

"Yes, indeed, with all my heart. It is a pleasure to give you advantages when you improve them so eagerly. I will make it an object to Mr. Rivers to remain with you during the vacation, and then we can decide later where you will go in the fall."

"Thank you, Uncle August, you are like a dear father to me, and I could not love you better if you really were. I hope some day to prove, in some tangible way, how grateful I am for your goodness," Geoffrey said, with deep feeling.

"Tut, tut, my boy, don't burden yourself with any sense of obligation. I am getting my pay as I go along, in the enjoyment I get out of having a fine, manly fellow like yourself in the house. I don't believe I could be prouder of my own son than I am of you, and, taking us all in all, I imagine there isn't a happier family in all Brooklyn than the one residing at No. — — Clinton avenue. Eh, Geoff?"

CHAPTER VII
GEOFFREY ENTERS COLLEGE

August Huntress and his gentle wife, Alice, deserved to be happy, for they had devoted the best of their lives to the work of rearing the two children who had been so strangely thrown upon their care.

Of course it was but natural that their love for Gladys should be deeper, stronger, and more sacred than for Geoffrey, for they had taken her to their hearts as their very own when she was but a tiny babe, and having had no other children sent them to share their affection, their every hope had long been centered in her.

But they felt very tenderly toward the hapless boy who had first aroused their sympathy for his misfortune, and subsequently won their love by his gentleness and confidence in them.

Mr. Rivers, Geoffrey's tutor, was very glad of the opportunity to remain with his pupil during the summer vacation, for it was simply a pleasure to teach one so eager for knowledge; while, too, being in limited circumstances, he needed the pecuniary benefit accruing from the arrangement.

Mr. Huntress sent them both into the country upon a farm, where they could have fresh air and country living to strengthen their bodies, while storing their minds with knowledge.

Mr. Rivers was most faithful in fulfilling his duties as a tutor, while Geoffrey was indefatigable as a student. He applied himself early and late; he dug to the very root of every problem and question, while he possessed the power of concentration to such a degree that he got over the ground much more rapidly than most students.

At the beginning of September he was pronounced qualified to enter a private institution for young men, where the principal, after learning the circumstances regarding his early misfortune and inability to study, allowed him special privileges.

Here he remained for a year, overcoming every obstacle with an iron will and unflagging perseverance, and surprising every one by his progress.

He developed in other ways also, becoming more mature physically, and acquired a dignity and thoughtfulness almost beyond his years, yet at the same time possessing a peculiar gentleness and courtesy of manner that won every one.

At the end of the year he was qualified to enter college.

Mr. Huntress told him that he might remain where he was if he felt the least sensitiveness about entering a university; but he was ready and eager now to take his place in the world with young men of his own age. Geoffrey had a consciousness within him that he could hold his own anywhere, and he decided that he would go to Yale.

He passed his examinations, and was received without a condition, and he could not help experiencing a feeling of triumph that at last he was on the "home stretch," so to speak, for the goal toward which he had for years so longingly and enviously looked.

Now he was only one year behind Gladys, and he hoped to be able to lessen the distance between them before he was through with his course. At all events, if his health was spared, he would now have a finished education, and would not need to feel that he was beneath her in point of intellect.

As for Gladys herself, she was as proud as she could be when Geoffrey told her of his success.

"Just to think of it," she cried, with shining eyes and flushed cheeks, though a little mischievous smile played over her red lips; "only six years ago I taught you your letters, and now you are almost at the top of the ladder! Oh, Geoffrey, I'm afraid you are very smart!"

"Afraid, Gladys?"

"Yes, and please don't drive your chariot too fast, even now. Why, if you had had the opportunities that have fallen to my lot, you would have been so far above me by this time that I should never have dared so much as to lift my eyes to you," the young girl returned with mock humility.

He bent and looked earnestly into her eyes.

"Gladys," he cried, under his breath, "I am sometimes almost glad that I was cast adrift upon the world."

"Glad! Why, Geoff!" she exclaimed, astonished, and wondering at his intense mood.

"You think that rather an extravagant statement," he said, smiling, "but if my life had run along smoothly in my own home, like that of other boys, I might never have learned what mettle there was within me, and besides, I might never have known you—you who have been my good genius and my inspiration."

Gladys shot one startled glance up into those earnest eyes looking into hers, then her own quickly dropped, and a vivid scarlet shot up to her brow.

Geoffrey had never spoken like this to her before, and the suppressed passion in his voice betrayed volumes.

The unexpected glimpse of his heart set her own to beating with strange emotions.

She had always been fond of him in a sort of tender, compassionate way, which of late had developed into something of pride for his smartness, and the character he exhibited; but she had never dreamed that she could ever learn to regard him other than as a dear friend or brother, or that he would ever entertain but fraternal affection for her.

She was strangely affected by this discovery of a deeper sentiment.

Geoffrey entered Yale the first of September, and began his four years' course there with the greatest of enthusiasm.

He had been hard at work at college a little over a week when, one evening, while he was deeply absorbed in the preparation of the morrow's lessons, there came a quick, sharp rap upon his door.

He glanced up as the door opened, and was astonished to see half a dozen fellows from the sophomore class enter and station themselves at different points in the room, while one, who appeared to be the leader of the company, slowly advanced toward him.

In an instant it flashed upon Geoffrey that he was about to be subjected to that terror of all freshmen—hazing—it being before the days when the practice fell into such disfavor as at present.

For a moment he was indignant at this intrusion; then he said to himself:

"If they are not unreasonable I'll make the best of it, and let them have their fun."

He arose from his table and turned to meet the young man approaching him, a genial smile on his handsome face.

But, as if suddenly arrested by some supernatural power, both young men stopped transfixed, and gazed at each other with undisguised astonishment, while expressions of wonder passed from lip to lip among those who were looking on.

And it was no wonder, for those two standing in the center of the room might well have been twin brothers instead of utter strangers, for they appeared to be exactly alike in form, and feature, and bearing.

Both were fair, with nut-brown hair and blue eyes.

Both were tall and well-developed, with a proud bearing that would have made them conspicuous anywhere, although a critical observer might have noticed that Geoffrey was more firmly built, more muscular, perhaps; thus showing greater strength than the other.

The intruder was the first to recover himself, however, and remarked, with a toss of his fine head and a long-drawn breath:

"I say, Huntress, this is downright queer! We came to give you a little surprise party, and you've completely taken the wind out of our sails to begin with. I could almost swear that I was looking at my own reflection in a glass. Who are you, anyway? Give us a history of your antecedents."

"Gentlemen, you have the advantage of me," Geoffrey politely returned, as he glanced from face to face. "You appear to know me by name—be good enough to tell me whom I have the honor to entertain, then I shall be happy to answer your questions."

"Well, I must say you're a cool one for a 'fresh,'" returned the other, with a light laugh, "but we can't stop for formal introductions all round. Since I am master of ceremonies for the evening, I will introduce myself as Everet Mapleson at your service. I am a Southerner by birth—son of Col. William Mapleson, of 'Vue de l'Eau,' Virginia. Now, for your genealogy, young man."

Geoffrey colored.

Young Mapleson's tone was offensive in the extreme, while his manner said as plainly as manner could say, "I belong to one of the F. F. V's—beat that record if you can," and Geoffrey's first impulse was to refuse to comply with his authoritative demand.

But he had heard something of the indignities which sophomores sometimes heaped upon unlucky freshmen, and after a moment of thought he quietly replied:

"My genealogy is not a remarkable one. I am an orphan, having lost my parents at a very early age, but I have been reared and educated by an uncle, Mr. Huntress, of Brooklyn, New York."

"Is that so?" drawled the young Southerner, with languid insolence. "Then it's a very singular coincidence, our being the double of each other. Why, one would be almost tempted to swear that the Mapleson blood flows in your veins; but since my governor and I are the very last of our race, that can't be possible, and it can only be accounted for, I suppose, as a strange freak of nature."

Geoffrey simply bowed in reply to these remarks; his blood began to boil at his visitor's assumption of superiority, and his fingers began to tingle to take him by the collar and walk him out of the room.

"However," young Mapleson resumed, rubbing his white hands and winking at his comrades, "we must not be diverted from the object of our visit. We have called upon you, Mr. Huntress, to test your powers of oratory; you will kindly favor us with a speech. Be seated, my fellow sophs."

Everet Mapleson helped himself to the easiest chair in the room, and waved his hand toward his companions as a signal for them to do likewise.

Geoffrey saw by the expectant faces around him that there would be no reprieve for him, and though he inwardly rebelled against having his privacy thus unceremoniously invaded, and at being peremptorily ordered about by a conceited fellow younger than himself, as Mapleson evidently was, yet he knew he would get off easier if he made light of his uncomfortable situation and indulged their caprice, at least to a reasonable extent.

CHAPTER VIII
THE HAZER HAZED

Accordingly Geoffrey smiled and bowed, remarking, in an off-hand way:

"I fear that my powers as orator will be somewhat disappointing to you, gentlemen; nevertheless, I will favor you to the extent of my ability."

Assuming a somewhat exaggerated attitude of dignity, he began reciting one of Cicero's orations, rendering it in the original with perfect ease and fluency, while his audience listened as if spell-bound to the smoothly rolling sentences.

But this display did not satisfy Mapleson. He insisted that Geoffrey should give a recitation in a reversed position—the speaker standing on his head.

This proposal was received with shouts of "Shame!" "No, no!" "You are going too far, Everet!"

Geoffrey's eyes glowed with indignation, and a spot of vivid scarlet settled on each cheek. He saw that the young Southerner intended to degrade him.

"I think you have made a serious mistake," said Geoffrey, boldly approaching Everet Mapleson, "if you expect to humiliate me. If you are *sure* that these gentlemen will not be satisfied until they see how I would look standing in a reversed attitude — —"

"Quite sure, and we'll soon prove it if you don't get about it," was the satirical interruption.

"Then I will give you a text from the ancient Phœdrus, and at the same time gratify your friends—by proxy."

Geoffrey made a sudden spring as he uttered those last words, seized the young Southerner about the waist, whirled him to the floor quick as a flash, and grasping him by the legs, held him aloft in this reversed position with a grip of iron, while he repeated, in a voice of thunder, that Latin maxim:

"*Sæpe intereunt aliis meditantes necem.* Often they who plot the destruction of others become the victims of their own machinations."

Then he released his hold upon the young man, politely assisted him to rise to his feet, and making a profound bow before him, gravely remarked:

"I think I have satisfied all requirements. I have shown your friends, if not you, how I should look standing on my head, while I have given you a quotation which may prove useful to you in the future."

It had all been done so quickly and so resolutely that there had scarcely been time for the others to interfere had they been so disposed; hardly time, even, for Mapleson himself to resist, he had been so completely taken by surprise, while every one was amazed at the wonderful strength and dexterity that Geoffrey displayed.

But once more on his feet, Mapleson flew into a white heat of rage.

All his hot Southern blood was up, and he dashed at Geoffrey with blazing eyes, crimson face, and with fists clenched and uplifted as if to smite him to the floor.

But Geoffrey caught him by the wrists, with a grip that rendered him instantly powerless, while he said, with the utmost good nature:

"Mr. Mapleson, you are no match for me; I measured you well before I touched you; my muscles and sinews are like iron from long gymnastic training, so I advise you not to waste your strength. I am sorry to have offended you, but this affair was none of my seeking, and you tried my patience altogether too far. I have simply acted in self-defense."

But Mapleson had lost his head entirely, and blustered and swore in the most passionate manner, while his comrades were so struck with admiration for Geoffrey and his masterly self-control in the face of such excessive provocation, that not one of them was disposed to meddle in the quarrel.

"Let go! you cold-blooded Yankee!" Everet Mapleson cried, hoarsely, through his tightly locked teeth.

"I will release you, Mapleson, but you must not try the same thing again," Geoffrey returned, with quiet firmness, and instantly loosed his hold upon the young man's wrists.

With another violent oath, quick as a flash, and before any one suspected his intention, Mapleson whipped out a pistol from an inner pocket, cocked and pointed it at Geoffrey.

What might have been the result no one can tell, if a young man named Abbott had not dashed forward, and thrown up his arm.

The next instant he had wrenched the weapon from his grasp.

"Are you mad, Mapleson?" he cried; "we shall have the whole faculty down upon us if you trifle with such a plaything, and then there will be a fine row."

The other sophomores now gathered around and tried to pacify their enraged leader, but he only grew the more furious and vowed that he would yet have the Yankee's heart's blood for his insolence in laying hands upon him.

"No, no, Mape, you drove him to it," interposed one; "you can't blame him, and you would have done the same had you been in his place."

"Who ever heard of a 'fresh' getting the upper hand of a half-dozen 'sophs' before?" he retorted, angrily. "You're a set of cowards, every one of you."

Two of the students seized Mapleson by the arms, and he was forced from the room, muttering threats of vengeance as he passed out.

When Geoffrey was at length left alone, he closed and locked his door, and then sat down and fell into troubled thought.

He was sure that he had made a bitter and lasting enemy of the young man, and he regretted it, for Geoffrey Huntress was one who loved to be at peace with all mankind; but he could only wait patiently to see how the matter would end, and having reached this conclusion, he resumed his interrupted studies. But he could not put his mind upon them, for all at once the remarkable resemblance between himself and the young Southerner began to haunt him.

Could it be possible that any of the same blood flowed in their veins? If so, how?

Why was Everet Mapleson the favored son of a proud and wealthy father, while he had been a poor, demented outcast, abandoned in the streets of a large city and left to his fate.

CHAPTER IX
A STRANGE ENCOUNTER

Several days went by, and Geoffrey heard nothing more either of or from the sophomores who had attempted to haze him.

Neither did he happen to meet any of them on his way to or from his recitations, and he hoped that the occurrence would gradually be forgotten and occasion no more trouble.

He did not mention it to any one, and he bore none of the actors any ill-will, for he well knew that hazing had been an established custom in many colleges, and that every freshman was liable to be subjected to the ordeal.

But the affair was destined to be more serious, eventually, than he imagined an occurrence of that kind could ever become.

Young Mapleson realized, as soon as his passion began to cool somewhat, that he should be obliged to relinquish all thoughts of retaliation for a season, for none of his comrades would bear him out in any plan for revenge; but he vowed in his heart that there should yet come a day of reckoning between himself and Huntress for the indignity to which he had been subjected before his companions.

He was furious with them for not having come to his release, and he raved over the affair all the way back to his room after leaving Geoffrey's.

But they made light of it, and tried to pass the whole thing off as a joke. This only enraged him the more, although he began to see the wisdom of keeping still about it, since he could get no sympathy from them.

There is no telling what rash act he might not have committed if he had been allowed to go and come as usual while this fierce mood lasted. But he had wrought himself into an excessive perspiration, and then going out into the chill night air afterward, he had taken a violent cold, and for three weeks he was confined to his room with a threatened fever.

At the end of that time, although his anger had not abated one whit toward Geoffrey, and he was no less determined to have his revenge, he had come to see the wisdom of refraining from all rashness which might rebound injuriously upon himself, and he resolved to conceal his purpose in his own breast and watch his opportunity to strike his foe down at some time in the future, when the blow would be felt with bitter force.

So, upon recovering his usual health, he resumed his studies and his intercourse with his fellow-students as if nothing had occurred to ruffle him, and those who had participated in the hazing of Geoffrey Huntress imagined that the unpleasant affair had blown safely over and become a thing of the past.

Thus the fall and winter passed.

Meantime Gladys was winning golden opinions for herself at Vassar.

Study was a perfect delight to her, consequently excellence in every department was but a natural result.

The name of Gladys Huntress became the synonym for all that was learned and brilliant in her class, and there was not one who did not predict that the first honor should be conferred upon her at the end of the course.

No one appeared to be jealous of her, either, on account of it, for she was a general favorite with both teachers and scholars, always having a pleasant word and a kind smile for everybody.

During the recess, which occurred between the winter and spring terms of her second year at Vassar, she was in New York city for a few days with her chosen friend and roommate, Addie Loring.

There was considerable shopping to be done to prepare for the warm weather, dress-making to attend to, besides a gay round of social duties, and the two girls were all the time in a delightful flutter of business and pleasure.

One morning, after a long siege of shopping, feeling both weary and hungry, they entered an up-town cafe to obtain a lunch and rest a little before going home.

At the cashier's desk near the door, as they stepped inside, there stood a tall, handsome young man in the act of paying for his dinner.

Gladys caught sight of him in an instant, and she started and flushed a vivid crimson.

Then a smile of joy illumined her whole face as she sprang forward, and, laying her hand lightly on the young man's arm, exclaimed in delighted tones:

"Why, Geoffrey, where did you drop from? I imagined you a solitary recluse at Yale, and hard at work over Latin and Greek, 'to gain time' as you wrote in your last letter."

The young man turned quickly as the sweet, lady-like voice fell upon his ear, his whole body thrilling at that light touch upon his arm, and found himself face to face with the most beautiful girl he had ever seen.

A tall, slender, perfect form, clad in a bewitching suit of modest gray, stood before him. Her small head was proudly poised on a pair of graceful shoulders, and crowned with a jaunty turban of gray velvet in which there gleamed a scarlet feather. The face was delicate in outline, with lovely features and a complexion of pure white and rose. Her eyes of dark blue were lighted with surprise and gladness, her lips wreathed with a tender smile of welcome which parted them just enough to reveal the small, milk-white teeth between.

A look of admiration shot into the young man's eyes, and then they began to gleam with amusement.

He raised his hat with all the gallantry of which he was master, and bowed low, as he replied:

"You have made a slight mistake, lady. I do not answer to the name by which you have addressed me, although I might be tempted to do so, perhaps, if I could thereby secure the pleasure of your acquaintance. Allow me," he concluded, drawing a card from his pocket-book, and respectfully presenting it to her.

At the first sound of his voice Gladys was conscious that she had made a dreadful blunder, and she was instantly covered with confusion.

She knew at once that this man could not be Geoffrey, and yet who was he? So like him in face and form, with his very eyes and hair, and that familiar way of throwing up his head when suddenly addressed!

"Everet Mapleson, Richmond, Virginia," she read upon the card that he had given her, and instantly the startled thought shot through her mind: "Can it be possible that he and Geoffrey are related?"

"I beg your pardon, Mr. Mapleson," she said, recovering herself somewhat, while she searched his face for something by which she could distinguish him from Geoffrey. "I perceive that I have made a mistake, but you so strangely resemble my—Mr. Geoffrey Huntress that I mistook you for him."

She had been about to say "my brother," but suddenly checked herself, for, since Geoffrey had shown so much of his heart to her and she had begun to analyze her own feelings toward him, she had been very shy about calling him brother.

"Ah! Mr. Geoffrey Huntress," repeated Everet Mapleson, with a quick flash from his eyes, while his keen mind at once made a shrewd guess, and argued therefrom that this beautiful girl must be either the sister or the cousin of his enemy. "I have met that gentleman, for I also am a student at Yale," he continued, "and—pardon my boldness—I presume I now have the pleasure of meeting his sister, Miss Huntress."

"No, I am not his sister, Mr. Mapleson," Gladys replied, her color coming and going in soft, little sunrise flushes, "but we are members of the same family, and I am Miss Huntress."

"Ah, yes—excuse me—you are cousins, I presume. Huntress once told me that he was reared by an uncle. I am sorry, upon my word," he went on, with an appealing look, "if our singular resemblance has caused you any annoyance to-day; pray think no more of it since it was a very natural mistake. We are often addressed by each other's name—indeed, we are known at Yale as 'the mysterious double.'"

All the time the young man was speaking he was closely observing the young girl.

He had noticed her fluctuating color when she spoke of Geoffrey; he remarked the tender inflection of her voice as she uttered his name, and how eager she had been to correct his mistake in supposing them to be brother and sister.

"They are cousins—perhaps not first cousins, either, and the girl loves him," he said to himself. "Of course he returns her affection—no fellow in his senses could help it. I wonder how it would work if I should try my own luck in this direction. I have never paid off that old grudge against him, and this would be a fine way to settle it."

But Gladys, all unconscious of this secret plotting against her own and Geoffrey's happiness, looked up with a merry smile at his words to her, and remarked:

"The resemblance is surely very striking, although your voices are unlike. I knew the moment you spoke that I had made a mistake, and my apparent rudeness must have been quite startling to you," she concluded, coloring again as she remembered how eagerly she had approached him and laid her hand upon his arm.

"No, indeed; you are very hard upon yourself, Miss Huntress. Believe me I shall consider the incident a most fortunate circumstance if I may be allowed to consider it as a formal introduction to you, and thus secure the pleasure of your acquaintance."

He was so gentlemanly and affable, so refined in his language and manner, that Gladys thought him very agreeable, and, since he claimed to know Geoffrey, she thought there could be no possible harm in receiving him as an acquaintance.

Still she was not quite sure that it would be proper, and this made her a little guarded in her reply.

"I am always glad to meet any of Geoffrey's friends," she said, with one of her charming smiles; but if she could have known how he cringed under her words, and what venomous hatred was rankling in his heart against him who was her ideal of all manly excellence, she would have fled from him in dismay.

But nothing of this nor of the miserable plot which was rapidly taking form in his mind appeared on the surface, while before he could frame a suitable reply Gladys turned quickly and drew Addie Loring to her side, saying:

"Allow me to introduce my friend—Miss Loring, Mr. Mapleson."

He lifted his hat in acknowledgment of the presentation while he was still inwardly chafing over that last guarded speech of hers.

"She wouldn't look at me if she knew the truth," he thought, "and that clever cousin will be letting it all out when he learns that we have met. Never mind. I'll make hay while the sun shines, and do my best to ingratiate myself with her before he finds it out; she's dusedly pretty and it would suit me finely if I could cut him out."

He detained the young ladies for a few moments longer—for he had the power of making himself very agreeable when he chose—then Addie Loring pulled forth a little gem of a watch and remarked, with a look of surprise:

"Gladys, dear, we promised mamma to be at home by four, and it is nearly three now, while we have flowers yet to get for Mrs. Brevort's reception."

Everet Mapleson's heart gave a great bound at these last words, for the friends at whose house he was visiting also had cards for Mrs. Brevort's reception, and he mentally resolved that he would grace that lady's elegant drawing-room with his presence that evening, although he and Al Vanderwater had previously planned for something entirely different.

He took pretty Miss Loring's hint, however, begged pardon for having detained them so long, then made his adieus and passed out of the cafe, while the young girls moved forward to an empty table, where they chatted over the strange encounter as they ate their cream and cake.

CHAPTER X
MRS. BREVORT'S RECEPTION

Gladys Huntress was very beautiful that evening when she entered Mrs. Brevort's drawing-room, leaning on the arm of Mrs. Loring, who was to present her to their hostess, while Addie and her mother followed close behind.

Her dress was blue, of elegant surah, which fell in soft, graceful folds around her, its long train making her most perfect figure seem almost regal.

It was cut, front and back, with a V shaped bodice, and this was filled in with a profusion of soft filmy lace, gathered close about her white throat, and fastened with a string of rare, gleaming pearls.

Her beautiful arms, round and as smooth as marble, were also covered, but not concealed, by sleeves of lace.

Her nut-brown hair, which shone like finest satin, had all been drawn up and coiled around the top of her head like a gleaming coronet, while a few soft, silken rings curled charmingly about her pure forehead.

There was not a flower nor an ornament about her anywhere excepting that string of pearls, but the very simplicity of her toilet was artistic and just adapted to enhance her beauty of face and form.

Everet Mapleson saw her the moment that she entered the room, indeed, he had been watching her for a half-hour or more, and his eyes glowed with admiration.

"She is a hundred fold more lovely than I thought her this afternoon," he said, under his breath. "I shall love that girl, if I allow myself to see much of her. And why not? I believe I will set myself regularly at work to win her; thus I shall not only secure a charming little wife, but accomplish my revenge, also, for the indignity that I have received from *his* hands."

He watched Gladys, while she was presented to the hostess, and was charmed with the ease and grace of her manners.

"She belongs, evidently, to a good family; she has been well reared," he continued, "even my critical and aristocratic mamma could not fail to be satisfied with her as a daughter, although she is not particularly partial to Northern women. She reminds me of some one, too. I wonder who it can be? There is something strangely familiar in the proud way that she carries herself."

He moved toward another portion of the room, as he saw Gladys and her friends pass on, and, seeking Mrs. Vanderwater, who, by the way, was the mother of Albert Vanderwater, Everet Mapleson's chum and especial friend at Yale, he asked:

"Do you know the party of people who have just entered—that gentleman with three ladies?"

"Oh, yes; they are the Lorings. Mr. Loring is a wealthy Wall street broker. His wife is a daughter of the late Colonel Elwell, and their daughter, Miss Addie, is a charming young lady, not to mention the fact that she is the only child and the heiress to a great deal of money."

"Introduce me, will you?" asked Everet, eagerly.

"To be sure I will; but is it the money or the beauty that attracts you most?" queried the lady, roguishly.

"I will tell you later," retorted the young man, in the same vein; "but you did not say who that young lady is who accompanies them," he concluded, as if his attention had but just been drawn toward her.

"No, I do not know myself; she is a stranger, but a very lovely one, is she not? Really, I do not believe there is another lady in the room so beautiful. Come, I have a curiosity to know who she is myself, and we will beg Mrs. Loring for an introduction."

Thus Everet Mapleson managed to secure a formal introduction to the Lorings and Gladys through one of the leaders of New York society.

He knew that there could be no exceptions taken to any one whom Mrs. Vanderwater vouched for, and therefore the young girl would have no excuse for avoiding him on the score of not having been properly presented to him.

But she received him very graciously, even referring in a laughing way to their previous meeting earlier in the day, thus showing him she would not have been the least bit prudish about recognizing him, even without Mrs. Vanderwater's reassuring presence.

He soon after searched out his friend Al, whom he presented to Miss Loring, and then left him to be entertained by her while he devoted himself exclusively to Gladys.

They danced together several times, and he managed to secure her company during supper, while afterward they had a social chat in Mrs. Brevort's charming little picture-gallery, where there were several works of rare value.

But the only picture which Everet Mapleson seemed to consider worthy of his regard was an exquisite face, framed in lustrous brown hair, with the bluest eyes that he had ever seen, and whose every expression only served to wind the silken chain of his bondage, the chain of love, more closely about him.

Gladys, on her part, was strangely moved by the young man's presence.

He was Geoffrey and yet he was not.

Several times she almost forgot herself and was on the point of addressing him in the old familiar way which she had always adopted toward her father's *protege*, and only restrained herself in season to prevent herself from appearing bold and forward.

Everet Mapleson found her eyes fixed upon him with great earnestness several times, and he knew that she was measuring him by her estimate of Geoffrey Huntress.

It nettled him exceedingly, for he was only too conscious of his own inferiority.

"Well, Miss Huntress, are you, like many others, trying to solve within yourself the mystery of my resemblance to your cousin, that you observe me so closely," he asked, with an amused smile, upon finding her gaze riveted upon his face instead of the picture before which they were standing.

Gladys blushed slightly.

"I shall have to plead guilty, Mr. Mapleson," she confessed. "I trust you will excuse me if I have appeared rude, but, really, to me it seems the strangest thing imaginable."

"It is, indeed," he said, and added to himself: "and dusedly uncomfortable to *me*, too."

"I wonder if you are not in some way related," Gladys said, musingly, and more to herself than to him.

Everet Mapleson's face darkened.

"I do not think so," he answered, curtly. "He is a Northerner—I was born at the South. *My* father is a Southern *gentleman*, and has always resided near Richmond, Virginia, excepting during the war, when he was in the field or camp most of the time, and a year or two that he spent traveling in Europe."

Gladys was conscious of a slight feeling of resentment toward her companion during this speech. The emphasis which he had, perhaps unconsciously, expended upon his personal pronouns, and the fact of his father being a "Southern gentleman," implied a sense of superiority which grated harshly upon her ear.

"Is your mother also a native of the South?" she asked.

"Oh, yes; and my mother is a most magnificent woman, too, Miss Huntress," the young man returned, with a kindling face.

Gladys' heart softened a trifle toward him at this. If he loved his mother like that there must be some good in him, she thought.

"Have you brothers and sisters?" she inquired.

"No, I am the only child. I was born within a year after my parents' marriage, and there have been no other children."

"Do you resemble your father or mother?"

"My father. My mother has often told me that I am very like what he was at my age; but there is a portrait of my grandfather Mapleson at home, which, but for the ancient style of dress, you would believe had been taken for me; the resemblance is every bit as striking as that between Huntress and me."

"Has your father no brothers or sisters?" Gladys asked.

Everet Mapleson looked surprised.

He knew that she was trying to account in some way for Geoffrey Huntress' likeness to himself; but, surely, he thought, she must know all about her cousin's parentage and their connections, and it was a little singular that she should be so persistent in her inquiries regarding the Mapleson genealogy.

"No," he replied; "my father was an only son. He had a sister, but she died while very young. The only other connections that I know anything about were an uncle who made my father his heir, and a distant cousin—a very eccentric sort of person. Both, however, are long since dead, and both died single. The Mapleson family was never a numerous one, and it is now almost extinct. I see, Miss Huntress," he added, with a slight smile in which Gladys thought she detected something of scorn, "that you are trying to account for this resemblance upon natural principles; but it is simply impossible that we are in any way connected. The fact can only be attributable to a strange freak of nature."

"Possibly," Gladys returned, thoughtfully, and yet she was impressed that there was more in it than Mr. Mapleson appeared willing to allow.

She did not feel well enough acquainted with him to speak of the mystery surrounding Geoffrey's parentage and his early life. It is doubtful if she would have told him, under any circumstances, because of Geoffrey's sensitiveness upon the subject, still she was strangely impressed by their resemblance.

The evening was one of keen enjoyment to Everet Mapleson, and when at length Gladys withdrew with her friends, he accompanied her to the carriage and assisted her to enter.

"I have rarely enjoyed a pleasanter evening, Miss Huntress, and I hope we shall meet again before I leave the city," he said, as he handed her the extra wrap which hung over his arm and stood a moment beside the carriage door.

"Then come and call upon us, Mr. Mapleson; the young ladies will be together for a few days longer," said Mrs. Loring, who had overheard this remark; and having learned from some source that he belonged to one of the F. F. V's, she was anxious to cultivate his acquaintance for Addie's sake.

CHAPTER XI
MARGERY

Everet Mapleson availed himself of Mrs. Loring's invitation, and called the second morning after Mrs. Brevort's reception, to pay his respects to the young ladies.

He was fortunate enough to find them both at home, and both were charmingly entertaining.

Addie Loring was a merry little body, and no one could ever be dull when in her society.

Gladys was more reserved and dignified in her bearing, but she possessed a peculiar fascination which instantly attracted everybody, and, taking the two together, it would have been difficult, go the world over, to have found a more entertaining couple than they.

Everet Mapleson was beguiled into a call of a full hour—a delightful hour it was, too, to them all—and looked his dismay when finally, glancing at his watch, he found how the time had slipped away.

Addie Loring laughed merrily, when she saw the expression on his face, and caught his well-bred, "I had no idea it was so late."

"Pray, Mr. Mapleson, do not look so disturbed," she cried; "there is no fine for such an offense, and you are absolved even before confession, for this time."

"But I have overstepped all bounds. I have been here a whole hour, and this my first call, too."

"How dreadful!" laughed the little lady, roguishly. "Pray, tell me, what is the Southern rule for first calls?"

"Twenty minutes, or half an hour, at most."

"I am glad I do not live at the South then. Why, one would hardly get through talking about the weather in that time."

"Miss Loring, I protest; there has not been one word said about the weather this morning," retorted the young man, thinking that she was very nearly as pretty as Gladys, as she stood before him in that graceful attitude, her head perched saucily on one side, a mocking smile on her red lips.

"True; but this wasn't a formal call, you know, for which we both feel very much obliged to you, I am sure. People usually begin upon the weather when they make ceremonious visits, and that is about all there is to say. It is really refreshing to have had such a breezy hour as this. Pray come again, Mr. Mapleson, and don't bring your watch next time; at least, don't look at it if it is going to make you uncomfortable," replied Miss Loring, with charming cordiality.

"Thank you; you are so indulgent and your invitation is so alluring that I am sure I shall not be able to resist it," he answered, as he shook hands with her. Then he turned to Gladys, and added: "May I assume that you indorse all that your friend has said, Miss Huntress?"

"It has, indeed, been a very pleasant hour, Mr. Mapleson—if an hour has really slipped by since you came in—and I shall be happy to meet you again, although I remain only a very few days longer with Miss Loring," she replied.

Mr. Mapleson's face clouded at this.

"Surely your vacation is not nearly over yet?" he said.

"Oh, no; but I only promised Addie a week; there are but two, and papa and mamma will want me at home the other."

"Allow me to ask where is your home, Miss Huntress?"

"In Brooklyn."

"True; I had forgotten. I remember that Huntress told me he resided in Brooklyn," Everet said, aware that the "City of Churches" was quite convenient to New York, and that he could run over there as easily as to come way up town to the Lorings.

"We are not going to give Gladys up until Saturday, Mr. Mapleson," Miss Loring here interposed, "for Thursday evening we give a reception in her honor; the cards were issued several days ago. It is rather late to offer you one, but if you will accept it, we shall be glad to see you with our other guests."

Everet Mapleson was only too glad to get it, even at that late date, and, with thanks, he took the envelope which Miss Loring proffered him, and expressed the pleasure it would afford him to accept her invitation.

He then bowed himself out, more than ever in love with beautiful Gladys Huntress, and more than ever determined to win her love in return.

He took a car down town, leaving it near Grace Church, on Broadway, to go to a certain club-house, where he was to meet his friend Vanderwater.

On his way thither he passed a flower-stand behind which there sat a woman who appeared to be about fifty years of age.

She was an unusually tidy and respectable looking person to be a street vender of flowers, and she had a rare and choice collection for that season of the year, and they were arranged in a really artistic manner.

It was this arrangement which attracted Everet Mapleson's attention, for he was a great admirer of flowers, and was rarely seen anywhere without some bud or spray in his button-hole.

He had worn heliotrope to-day during his call, but it was wilted and discolored, and he paused now before the stand to replace it with something else.

He selected one exquisite rosebud nestling between its dark green leaves, and taking out a piece of silver, he tossed it over the vases into the woman's lap, and then would have passed on without waiting for his change, but that she had put out her hand to detain him.

She had given a start of surprise and uttered a low cry the moment he had stopped before her, but he had not noticed it, and she had not taken her eyes from his face during all the time that he was making his selection.

As she looked she began to tremble, her lips quivered, her eyes filled with tears, and she breathed with difficulty, as if overcome with some powerful emotion.

Her face was wrinkled and sad, showing that she must have passed through some terrible grief. Her hair was very gray, and there was a white seam or scar above her right temple, the mark of an injury received years before.

"Oh," she cried, putting out her hand to detain him as he was turning away. "Oh, Geoffrey, have you forgotten Margery?"

Everet stopped short, looked back, and attentively scanned the woman's face.

"'Margery!'" he repeated. "I never knew anybody of that name, and mine isn't Geoffrey, either, my woman," he said, somewhat brusquely, for it nettled him whenever he heard that name, which he had grown to dislike so much.

"Surely my eyes can't deceive me," returned the flower vender, earnestly. "I could never forget the dear boy that I nursed and tended during the first five years of his life. *Can't* you remember me, dearie? Have you forgotten the chickens and the rabbits—old Chuck, the dog, and the two little white kittens. Ah! *try* to think, Master Geoffrey, and tell me what became of Jack after he gave you that dreadful blow and then ran away with you when he left me for dead, so many years ago."

"What under the sun is the old creature talking about?" murmured Everet, with a perplexed look.

"I'd readily forgive him for the hurt that he gave me," the woman went on, unheeding him, "and overlook the past, if I could only set eyes on him once more and feel that I wasn't all alone in the world in my old age; it's hard not to have a single soul to care for you. Sure, I *can't* see how *you* could forget Margery, when you were so fond of her in those old days."

"I tell you my name is not Geoffrey," repeated Mapleson. "You are thinking of some one else. I do not know anything about Jack, or his striking anybody, and then running away, and I never saw you until this moment."

The poor woman was weeping now, and moaning in a low, heart-broken way that made the young man pity her, in spite of his irritability.

"You *must* have forgotten," she responded, wiping her fast falling tears. "Perhaps the cruel blow Jack gave you hurt your memory—and whatever could he have done with you after he took you away from the old home that night? It breaks my heart that you don't know me, dearie, for I served your poor mother so faithfully when you were a wee baby. She was the sweetest little body that the sun ever shone on—so gentle, and kind, too, with a face like a lily and eyes as blue as heaven. Poor boy! You never realized your loss when she died, for Margery promised to care for you as if you were her very own, and she did. You were the pride of my heart during all those five blessed years."

"You have made a mistake, my good woman," Everet said, more gently, for her grief and pathetic rambling touched him.

He believed that he had run across an old nurse of Geoffrey Huntress, for he remembered now that he had said he lost his parents when very young, and he did not wonder that she had mistaken him for her former nursling.

But it angered him so to talk of his enemy that he would not take the trouble to tell her anything about him, and he never dreamed how near he was to discovering what had been a sealed mystery for many long years.

"*My* name is Everet," he went on, "and my mother is not dead, neither has she a face like a lily—she is dark, with a rich color and brilliant black eyes."

The woman appeared still more perplexed and troubled by this statement.

She wagged her head slowly from side to side, as if she could not reconcile his assertions with her belief.

"Your mother's name was Annie——" she began.

"No, my mother's name is Estelle."

"Estelle," she repeated, searching his face keenly; "that might have been her other name. Didn't she have bright, beautiful brown hair, and a sweet, gentle way with her?"

"No; her hair is as black as a raven's wing, and no one would ever think of describing her as 'sweet and gentle,'" the young Southerner replied, with a smile, as a vision of the magnificent woman who reigned in his home arose before him, "but proud and imperious. She is like some beautiful queen."

"And is she your own mother?" questioned the flower vender, eagerly.

"Yes, my own mother, and I am her only child."

"Well, well, it is *very* strange," sighed the poor woman, tears of disappointment again filling her eyes. "I was so sure that I had found my boy at last. I've been hunting for him these eighteen years. It isn't much wonder that I mistook you, though, for you couldn't be more like him if you were his twin; and yet he mayn't look like you at all, now that he's grown up. Ah, Jack, peace to your soul if you've gone the way of all the earth, but where under heaven did you leave the child?"

She dropped her head upon her breast and kept on with her muttering, apparently convinced at last that she had made a mistake.

Everet Mapleson stood irresolute a moment, half tempted to tell her where she could find Geoffrey, and yet obstinately averse to doing anything for one whom he so disliked.

He was in a hurry, too, for it was already past the time that he had appointed to meet young Vandewater, and he was unwilling to be detained any longer to answer the questions of a garrulous old woman, so he went unheeded on his way.

All the way to the club-house she was in his thoughts. Without doubt, he reasoned, she had been a servant in the Huntress family, and probably after Geoffrey's adoption by his uncle she had lost track of her charge, perhaps by a change of residence on her part or his.

He could not seem to understand her reference to the dreadful blow that Jack had given the boy, nor to his running away with him afterward and leaving his wife, as he evidently believed, dead.

The more he thought it over the more strange it appeared, and the more interested he became regarding the matter. Possibly there might be something connected with Geoffrey Huntress' history which he might be able to use against him in his future scheming.

"I will go back by and by and question her some more," he muttered, as he reached the club-house, ran up the steps, and entered the elegant vestibule.

He did not return that day, however, but the next he made it in his way to pass the spot where Margery had had her flower-stand the previous morning.

But she was no longer there. Flowers, stand, and vender had all disappeared, and although Everet sought her several times after that he did not see her again during his stay in the city.

He was greatly disappointed, for the more he considered the affair the more he became convinced that there was something which he might have learned of Geoffrey Huntress' life and parentage that would have been to his own advantage, and he blamed himself severely for having neglected his opportunity.

CHAPTER XII
THE RECEPTION

Mrs. Loring's reception on Thursday evening proved to be a very brilliant one.

It was given nominally in honor of Gladys, but it really was as much for the sake of the daughter of the house, who was the pride and darling of her fond parents' hearts, and her taste was consulted, her lightest wish gratified, in every arrangement.

The elegant mansion was beautifully decorated for the occasion.

A platform had been extended fifty feet from the broad south balcony and inclosed like a pavilion for dancing, while one of the finest bands in New York had been secured to discourse sweet music to entice tripping feet, and an elaborate supper had been ordered from Delmonico's.

Mr. and Mrs. Huntress were, of course, among the invited guests, and Geoffrey had also been sent for and pressed to honor the occasion with his presence, for Gladys' sake.

He had sent a telegram in reply, saying that he would come if possible, but at nine o'clock he had not appeared, and Gladys turned eagerly toward the door at every fresh arrival, hoping to see him enter.

Mr. Mapleson had not failed to present himself at an early hour, when he immediately constituted himself Gladys' most devoted attendant, and was so persistent and marked in his attentions that the young girl began to feel a trifle uncomfortable and anxious, lest matters should grow more serious than she desired.

"Papa, where do you suppose Geoff is?" she inquired, with a troubled face, as Mr. Huntress came up to her, while Everet Mapleson was doing his utmost to be agreeable.

Mr. Huntress had been introduced to the young man earlier in the evening, and had been startled, as everyone else was, by his singular resemblance to the boy whom he had reared, and he had resolved to make some inquiries of him regarding his connections, hoping thus to gain some light upon Geoffrey's early life.

"I do not know, dear," the gentleman replied to his daughter's question; "it is surely time that he was here. Possibly something detained him at the last moment, and he could not leave."

"Oh, I hope not; the evening will be spoiled if he does not come," Gladys cried, in a tone that made the blood surge angrily to Everet Mapleson's brow, for it told him how little hope there was of his retaining Gladys' companionship if his fortunate rival should make his appearance.

"I shall be sorry myself not to see Geoff; he needs the change and recreation, too, for he is working very hard," responded Mr. Huntress, glancing wistfully toward the door himself. "But you must try to enjoy yourself, all the same, if he does not come. Mr. and Mrs. Loring will be disappointed if their reception does not prove a pleasant one, after all their effort."

Gladys' glance was bent upon her fan, with which she was nervously toying: her cheeks were flushed, her brow slightly clouded, her lips compressed, and it was evident that she was greatly disturbed.

All at once she turned her gaze again toward the door. She gave a sudden start.

"Why! there he is now! Oh! I am so glad," she cried in a joyous tone, her beautiful face growing radiant with undisguised delight, as she saw Geoffrey, looking more handsome and manly than ever, just entering the room.

She instantly darted toward him without even thinking to excuse herself to her companions, thus leaving Mr. Huntress and young Mapleson to entertain each other.

The latter watched that graceful figure, a lurid fire in his eye, his lips compressed until they were colorless, his heart throbbing with jealous anger.

He saw her steal softly up to Geoffrey, who was looking in another direction, and slip one white hand within his arm, while she looked up at him, with a rogueish but happy glance, and addressed some bright words of welcome to him.

He saw, too, how Geoffrey's countenance lighted, how his eyes glowed as he turned to look down upon that fair, upturned face, while the glad smile that wreathed his handsome mouth, told something of the joy which this meeting afforded him also.

Everet Mapleson read these signs as plainly as he would have read a printed page, and he knew that the young man loved the fair girl with all the strength of his manly nature, and the knowledge made him grind his teeth in silent rage.

But Mr. Huntress spoke to him just then, and he was obliged to turn his glance away from those two central figures, which were now moving out of the room together, and answer him.

Mr. Huntress was more and more impressed every moment that there must be kindred blood in the veins of these two young men, and he was resolved to learn the truth.

But he was destined to be disappointed, for Everet Mapleson repeated about the same story, with some additions, that he had already told Gladys, and there seemed no possibility of there being any relationship between them.

"My father was a colonel in the Confederate Army during the war," Everet said, in reply to his companion's query, "and my home, with the exception of a short residence abroad, has always been in the South."

"And is your mother also a Southerner?"

Everet smiled, for he knew well enough what these questions meant.

"Oh, yes; she and my father were second cousins, and they were married in 1853."

"Ah! in '53," remarked Mr. Huntress, reflectively; "and was that Colonel Mapleson's first marriage?"

"Yes, sir; and it was a somewhat romantic affair. They had an uncle who was very wealthy, and when he died it was found that he had made a very singular will. He divided his fortune equally between them, but expressed a wish that they should unite it again by marriage; indeed, he made the possession of it conditional, and in this way. My father was about twenty, my mother seventeen, at the time of his death. Both were to come into their share of the property at once, but if either married some one else before my mother reached the age of twenty-five, he or she would forfeit that portion and it should go to the other. If both refused to carry out the conditions of the will and married contrary to his wishes, or remained single after my mother, who was the younger, reached the age of twenty-five, the whole fortune was to be made over to a bachelor cousin of the testator, and who was also a very singular character."

"That was an exceedingly strange will," observed Mr. Huntress.

"Very, though it was not more eccentric than the man who made it; but my father and mother chose to fulfill the conditions of the will; thus the property was all kept in the family."

"And are you their only child?"

"Yes, sir. I never had either brother or sister."

"It is very strange," murmured Mr. Huntress, musingly.

Everet Mapleson regarded him curiously.

"You are thinking of my resemblance to Mr. Geoffrey Huntress," he said, somewhat stiffly, after a brief pause.

"Yes, I am."

"Surely you can have no idea that we are in any way related."

"I—do—not know, of course; but——"

"You do not know!" interrupted the young Southerner. "Why, you surely ought to be able to trace his genealogy, since he is your nephew."

"But he is not my nephew."

"How?"

"I never saw the boy until about eight years ago."

Everet Mapleson turned a look of blank astonishment upon his companion, while a strange pallor settled over his own face.

Mr. Huntress then related to him the circumstances which brought Geoffrey to his notice, telling of his unaccountable interest in him, of the experiment which had resulted in the restoration of the boy's reason, and of his subsequent adoption of the lad.

Everet Mapleson grew very grave as he listened, and a hundred conflicting thoughts came crowding into his mind.

Could it be possible, after all, that this young man whom he had so disliked, and was fast learning to hate from a feeling of jealousy, was in some mysterious way connected with the proud family of Mapleson?

He did not know of a relative by that name, and yet there might be.

He resolved that he would sift the matter the very next time he went home.

"And you know absolutely nothing about him previous to that time?" he asked of Mr. Huntress.

"No, nothing; while he was evidently so young at the time he received the injury which deprived him of his reason that there was comparatively little that he could remember about himself. Of his father or mother he knew nothing; 'Margery' and 'Jack' are the only names that he has been able to recall, while his memories of them are very vague. I imagine, however, that the woman Margery must have been a sort of nurse who had the care of him."

Everet Mapleson started and colored as he heard these names.

He instantly recalled the incident that had occurred a few days previous, on Broadway, when the poor old flower vender had detained him, believing that she had at last found the boy whom she had nursed so many years ago.

His first impulse was to tell Mr. Huntress of this adventure, but he checked the inclination, resolving that he would himself try to find old Margery again and glean all that he could from her regarding Geoffrey's early history.

He began to realize that there was something very much more mysterious about their strange resemblance than had at first appeared.

It might not be so much a "freak of nature" as he had tried to think it, and if there was any important secret connected with the affair, he meant to ferret it out alone, and possibly it might give him an advantage over his rival in the future if he should stand in the way of his winning Gladys for his wife.

A little later, when he went in search of her, and found her pacing up and down the great hall leaning on Geoffrey's arm, chatting with him in a free and unrestrained way, and saw both their faces so luminous and happy, and knew that already they had become all in all to each other, he ground his teeth savagely, and vowed that he would destroy their confidence and peace before another twelve months should elapse.

He stationed himself behind some draperies where he could see without being seen, and continued to watch them, although it drove him almost to a frenzy to see how happy and unreserved Gladys was with his rival.

Her face was eager and animated—it never had lighted up like that when in his presence—her eyes glowed, her lips were wreathed with smiles, and she chattered like a magpie. She seemed to have forgotten where she was, by whom surrounded, everything, save that she was with Geoffrey.

He knew well enough when she began to tell him about encountering his double in the cafe, for he saw Geoffrey start, change color, and then grow suddenly grave.

"Is Everet Mapleson here in New York?" he heard him ask, as they drew near where he was standing.

"Yes; and oh, Geoff, he is so like you. Even I could hardly detect any difference."

Geoffrey smiled at the reply.

It implied a great deal; it told him that *she* could distinguish between them if any one could, and that her eyes, sharpened by affection, had been able to detect something unlike in them.

"Do you think you would always be able to tell us apart, Gladys?" Geoffrey eagerly asked.

"Of course I should, you dear old Geoff," she affirmed, with a toss of her bright head.

"How?"

"Why, I only need to look into your eyes to know you," she said, with a fond upward glance.

At this reply, Geoffrey hugged close to his side the small hand that lay on his arm, and his heart thrilled with a sweet hope.

"What is there in my eyes, Gladys, that is different from Everet Mapleson's?" he asked.

She blushed crimson at the question, for she knew that it was only in their expression that she could detect any difference.

"Perhaps strangers could not tell you apart," she admitted, with drooping lids; "probably it is because we have lived together so long that I know your every expression; then, too, there is a certain little quiver about your lips when you smile that he does not have. Your voices, though, are entirely different."

"Yes; any one could distinguish between us to hear us speak," Geoffrey assented; but his heart was bounding with joy, for he knew well enough that only the eye of love could have detected the points that she had mentioned.

Yet, in spite of all, he experienced a feeling of uneasiness over the fact that Everet Mapleson was spending his recess in New York and was cultivating the acquaintance of Gladys.

He had never mentioned him in any of his letters—had never spoken of that hazing experience, simply because his mind had been so engrossed with other things that he had not thought to do so.

"There is the band, Geoff," Gladys exclaimed, as the music came floating in from the south balcony. "Mr. Loring has had the loveliest pavilion erected for dancing, and you know that I cannot keep still a moment within ear-shot of such enticing strains. Come, let us go out."

"Which means, of course, that I am to have the first set with you," he said, smiling.

"It does mean just that. You know I always like to dance with you, for you suit your step to mine so nicely. There! I'm so glad you asked me, for here comes Mr. Mapleson, this minute, doubtless to make the same request," Gladys concluded, under her breath, as she saw the young man step out from among the draperies, where he had been watching them, and approach them.

CHAPTER XIII
"FIRST IN TIME, FIRST BY RIGHT!"

Everet Mapleson advanced toward the young couple with all the assurance imaginable.

He nodded indifferently to Geoffrey, simply saying, in a patronizing tone:

"How are you, Huntress?" and then turned to Gladys with his most alluring smile. "The signal for dancing has been given, Miss Huntress; may I have the pleasure of doing the opening set with you?"

Gladys' cheeks were very red, for she resented his manner toward Geoffrey. What right had he to assume such insolent superiority over him, who she knew possessed by far the nobler nature of the two.

But she said politely, though with a little secret feeling of triumph in refusing him:

"You are a trifle late, Mr. Mapleson, as I have already promised the first dance; but if you will come to me later, you shall write your name upon my card."

The young man frowned slightly, for he could never endure to have his wishes denied, but he was obliged to bow acquiescence, and turned away to seek a partner elsewhere.

But he managed to station himself where he could watch the young couple incessantly, and not a movement, not a smile or glance escaped him.

"They love each other," he muttered, "at least he loves her, and it would not take much to make them acknowledged lovers. I shall be both watchful and diligent. I wish I knew the secret of the fellow's life. It can't be possible that he is anything to our family, and yet I am dusedly annoyed by the mystery."

When he went later, to claim Gladys' promise to dance with him, he exerted himself more than he had ever done to be entertaining and agreeable.

He told her about his Southern home, and the life he led when there. He described the luxuriant beauty which surrounded "Vue de l'Eau," his father's estate, and so called from the broad, sweeping view which they had of the beautiful James River, which lay right beneath them. He told her something of his courtly father and his stately, beautiful mother, and was really eloquent in his description of the spot that had given him birth.

"I wish you could come to 'Vue de l'Eau' sometime, Miss Huntress; I am sure you would agree with me that there is nothing finer in the way of scenery, even on your far-famed Hudson," he said, in conclusion.

"Thank you, Mr. Mapleson; your descriptions are surely very enticing," Gladys replied, with a smile. "I suppose your parents are both natives of the South?"

"Yes, they were both born in Richmond, and my father was a colonel in the Confederate army at the time of our civil war; but, as it happened, his estate was not harmed, and it has since increased greatly in beauty and value."

"Do you remember much about the war?" Gladys inquired.

"No, I knew very little about it at the time, of course, I was very young — only about eight years of age — and besides, my father sent my mother and me abroad, where we remained until the war was over."

"I suppose some of your people still feel antagonistic toward us Northerners?" Gladys remarked.

"I presume there is a feeling of bitterness to some extent among the veterans, but, as to the generation that has been growing up since, I think we all feel that we are one nation, and our interests are with and for the Union. But if I had been ever so bitter toward Northern people, that feeling could not have possibly continued to exist after my present experience with them," and Everet Mapleson's glance told the young girl that for her sake alone he would have been willing to waive all past grievances, however aggravating.

Her cheeks flushed, and her eyes drooped.

"It is better to put aside all bitterness — the war was a terrible thing, and there were mistakes on both sides, and now that peace has been restored, it is far better to let by-gones be by-gones. Have your parents ever been North?"

Gladys tried to speak in a general and unconscious way, but it was very hard with those admiring eyes fixed so earnestly upon her.

"No; they have been in Europe, and my father has been on the Pacific coast several times, but they have yet to visit this portion of the country."

"Without doubt, then, they will improve the opportunity to do so when you leave college. It would be natural for them to desire to be present when you take your honors."

"Those will be very few, I fear," young Mapleson replied, with a flush. "I am not a good student."

He did not love study, although he was quick to learn, and brilliant in recitation, when he chose to apply himself.

"I do not believe you really mean that," Gladys said.

She could not believe that anybody could be a poor student who so closely resembled Geoffrey, who excelled. She imagined that he must be like him mentally as well as physically.

"Do you think it pays to get a reputation for good scholarship?" he asked.

"Perhaps not the reputation alone, but the knowledge pays. If I was a college boy I believe I should strive to attain the top round of the ladder."

"It is not every one who can do that."

"True, but every one can at least try to excel, and even if one does not, he has the satisfaction of knowing that he has done his best."

"Are you going to be first in your class at Vassar, Miss Huntress?" Everet Mapleson asked, studying her eager face earnestly.

Gladys flushed again, and laughed.

"I am doing my utmost, Mr. Mapleson, to come forth from my school an honor to my class; and Geoffrey is bending all his energies toward the same object; indeed, I surmise that he is trying to gain a year, by his being so zealous for study during the recesses."

A startled look shot into Everet Mapleson's eyes.

If Geoffrey Huntress did gain a year he would graduate at the same time with himself, and the thought was anything but pleasant to him.

"He will have to be very smart to do that," he said, with a skeptical curve of his lips.

"Geoffrey is smart; he has achieved wonders during the last few years, and I predict for him a brilliant college career. I am very proud of him."

The beautiful girl's face glowed, and her eyes gleamed as she said this, while her glance rested more fondly than she was aware, on the manly form that was standing beside his hostess, quietly conversing with her while they watched the dancers.

Her companion was so nettled by this, that for a moment he could not control his voice to reply.

"I should judge that the young man must be a prodigy," he said, at length, with a covert sneer.

Gladys lifted her eyes searchingly to his face.

His tone was not pleasant to her, but he looked as innocent as if he had spoken in all sincerity.

"Why!" she said, after a moment's thought, "if Geoffrey does gain a year he will take his degree when you take yours!"

"Yes."

A little ripple of roguish laughter issued from the fair girl's red lips.

"Then let me warn you," she said, with a merry glance, "to look out for your honors, Mr. Mapleson, for Geoffrey is bound to go to the front, and I have fully made up my mind to hear him deliver the valedictory at Yale two years hence."

Again the young Southerner had to pause for self-control; it was very hard for him to conceal the rage that was well-nigh overmastering him.

But all at once he bent toward Gladys, and, speaking in a low, resolute tone, said:

"Miss Huntress, you have inspired me with an ambition which I never before possessed. I would give more than you can conceive to merit such praise from your lips as you have just bestowed upon another, and from this hour, my purpose shall be to 'go to the front,' as you have expressed it. I shall deliver the valedictory two years from next summer."

Gladys laughed gleefully.

She never dreamed of the fierce enmity and jealousy that lay beneath all this, and she was delighted to think that she had aroused his desire to excel in his class.

"It will be a worthy contest," she said; "and I honor you for your resolution. I shall watch the rivalry with a great deal of interest, I assure you."

"Will you wear my colors if I succeed, Miss Huntress?" the young man asked, in a low, almost passionate tone.

"That depends——"

"Upon what?"

"Upon whether Geoffrey takes his degree at the same time; if he gains his year and leaves with your class, I think I shall have to be loyal to him, even though he should suffer defeat," Gladys replied, though in her heart she felt sure that he would not fail to do himself honor.

"That is hardly fair," urged her companion; "'to the victor belongs the spoils,' you know."

"Yes; but you will have your own friends to rejoice with you, and I could not desert dear old Geoff, though he should fail a hundred times," she returned, a tender glow overspreading her face.

"Happy Huntress!" sneered the exasperated young man, for a moment forgetting himself.

"Why, Mr. Mapleson, I hope you are not offended with me," Gladys said, with surprise, and not once suspecting that this venom was aimed at the object of their conversation; then she added: "Perhaps, however, his colors and yours will be the same, and then I can honor you both."

Everet Mapleson was glad that supper was announced just at that moment, which saved him the necessity of replying.

The mere thought of sharing any honors with his rival made him white with anger, and her praise of him had driven him nearly frantic.

He saw Geoffrey approaching them, and surmised that he contemplated taking Gladys in to supper.

He resolved that he should not; so, turning to her with a smile, as he laid her hand upon his arm, he remarked:

"That is no doubt a pleasing announcement to everybody. Shall we follow the hungry crowd?"

"Thanks; but I see Geoffrey coming for me; pray find some one else, Mr. Mapleson; I have already occupied more of your time and attention this evening than I ought," the fair girl responded.

"I could not bestow it more acceptably to myself anywhere else," he replied, in a low, earnest tone, and detaining the hand which she would have withdrawn from his arm.

At that instant Geoffrey bowed before them.

"Excuse me for interrupting your chat," he said, courteously; "but are you ready to go into supper, Gladys?"

"Excuse me, Huntress," young Mapleson interposed before Gladys could reply, and bestowing a haughty glance upon his rival, "but I must claim the privilege of taking Miss Huntress in by virtue of the old saw '*prior tempore, prior jure*'—'first in time, first by right.'"

Geoffrey colored more at his tone and look than at his words, but returned, with a genial smile:

"That will apply to my case exactly, Mr. Mapleson, since I secured Miss Huntress' promise, more than an hour ago, that she would give me the privilege you claim."

"But possession is nine points in law. Miss Huntress," said Everet, addressing Gladys, and ignoring Geoffrey entirely.

"Really, Mr. Mapleson, you will have to excuse me. I have given my promise, as Geoffrey says, and since he leaves for New Haven again to-morrow morning, I must say all I have to say to him to-night."

Everet Mapleson instantly released her, with a low bow of acquiescence.

"Your wish is sufficient," he said, with significant emphasis, and he turned abruptly away to seek some one else; but not before he had shot a revengeful glance at his successful rival.

"He shall have his pay some day," he muttered, as he moved down the room; "he maddens me beyond all endurance with his assumption of affability and his high-bred civility. He goes back to New Haven to-morrow, does he? Well, I'll improve the remainder of this recess to cultivate to the utmost my acquaintance with *ma belle* Gladys."

He found a young lady to whom he had been introduced early in the evening, and solicited her companionship during supper, but he was careful to station himself where he could watch every look and movement of the girl whom he was fast learning to adore.

After supper Gladys and Geoffrey stole away to a quiet corner, where they could have a little confidential chat before they separated, for each had much to tell the other about school and various other matters.

Geoffrey had been much disturbed inwardly to see how devotedly attentive young Mapleson appeared to Gladys.

He did not bear him any ill-will on account of the hazing to which he had been subjected so long ago, but he instinctively felt that he could not be a very noble-minded man to allow himself to be so controlled by passion as he had been at that time, and Gladys was too precious a treasure to be willingly yielded to one unworthy of her.

He wondered what opinion she had formed of him, and he meant to find out before he left her; and after they had chatted awhile he asked, smilingly:

"Well, Gladys, what do you think of my double?"

"I think it the most remarkable resemblance in the world; but why have you never written us anything about him?" she asked.

"I have had so many other things to write and think about, that I suppose it escaped my memory; besides, I seldom meet Mapleson, as he is not in my class. I am very glad, though, that he does not belong in New York," Geoffrey concluded, with a wistful glance at his companion.

"Why?"

"Because I fear you might often make the same mistake that you did the other day in the cafe, and—I think I should hardly like to share your favors with him."

Gladys shot a quick, inquiring glance into the young man's face, and saw it was clouded.

"Isn't he nice, Geoff?"

"I have heard that he belongs to a good family, and feel that I have no right to say one word against him; still, where you are concerned, Gladys, I feel very jealous lest any ill should come to you," he returned, earnestly.

"I think I could never again mistake him for you," Gladys said, thoughtfully.

"What makes you think that?" was the eager query.

"There are certain expressions in your face that I do not find in his, and *vice versa*; while somehow a feeling of antagonism, a barrier, almost amounting to distrust, comes between us when I am with him. Perhaps it is because I do not know him as well as I know you; it would be natural to differently regard one who had always been like a brother," Gladys replied, gravely.

A painful thrill shot through Geoffrey's heart at those last words.

"Does she feel nothing but sisterly affection for me?" he thought; "and I love her—oh! not with a brother's love; Heaven help me if I fail to win her by and by! She is dearer than my own life, and yet I dare not tell her so; I have no right to win the heart of the child of my benefactor until I can make a name and position worthy of her acceptance."

But he allowed nothing of this conflict to appear. He changed the subject, and they chatted pleasantly of other matters until Mr. and Mrs. Huntress came to tell him that they were going home.

He then bade her good-night and good-by, and went away, loving her more fondly than ever, but with a heavy burden on his heart.

CHAPTER XIV
A CONFESSION

There was not much sleep for Geoffrey that night. He lay through the long hours thinking of his love for Gladys, and half believing, yet hardly daring to hope, that she was beginning to return it.

Her manner toward him during the evening, her glad, even joyful greeting when he entered Mrs. Loring's drawing-room, her shy, sweet glances, while talking with him, and the ever ready color which leaped into her cheeks beneath his fond gaze, all thrilled him with the blissful conviction that she was not indifferent to him.

And yet this only increased his unhappiness—to feel that he might win her, and yet could not without being guilty of both treachery and ingratitude toward the man from whom he had received such lasting benefits, and who had stood in the place of a father to him.

"But my life will be ruined if I cannot win her," he said, a sort of dull despair settling down upon his heart at the mere thought. "I have always been determined to make the most of my advantages for her sake—that I might be worthy of her; I have resolved from the first that no one should excel me, and that when I should be through with my college course I would battle, with all the energy I possess, for a high position in the world to offer her. But what will it all amount to if, in the meantime, some one else steals my darling from me!—if, while my own lips are sealed, from a sense of honor, some other man wins the heart I covet, and I have to see her become his wife? Good heavens! I could not bear it—it would destroy my ambition—it would make a wreck of me."

He tossed and turned upon his pillow in an agony of unrest and apprehension, the future looking darker and more hopeless to him with every waning hour, and when at last morning dawned he arose looking haggard and almost ill from the conflict through which he had passed.

When the breakfast bell rang he shrank, with positive pain, from going below to meet his kind friends with this burden on his heart.

But he stopped suddenly while in the act of crossing the threshold of his room, his eye lighting, a vivid flush rising to his brow, as some thought flashed upon his mind.

"I will do it," he murmured, resolute lines settling about his mouth. "I will go directly to Uncle August and confess my love for Gladys in a manly, straightforward way, and if he does not oppose me—if he betrays no repugnance to such a union, I will no longer conceal my feelings from her, although it may be years before I shall dare to ask her to share my fortunes. I know if I can have before me the hope that she will some day become my wife, that no goal will be too difficult for me to attain. I shall be able to remove mountains, for her dear sake. But if he shrinks in the least from giving me his only child, I will sacrifice every hope—I will go away and hide myself and my despair from every eye, rather than he should think me ungrateful for all that he has done for me."

Having made these resolutions, a new hope seemed to animate him, the clouds cleared from his brow, his heart grew lighter, and he descended to the dining-room looking more like himself.

Still Mr. Huntress noticed his paleness and the unusual gravity of his manner, and wondered at it, for he had seemed remarkably cheerful, even gay, the previous evening at Mrs. Loring's.

"The boy is working too hard," he said to himself, anxiously: "he has too much ambition for his strength," and he resolved to caution him anew before he left.

As they arose from the table Geoffrey looked at his watch.

"Uncle August," he said, a hot flush mantling his cheek, "I have an hour just before I need to go. Can I see you alone for a little while on a matter of business?"

"Business, Geoff!" laughed his uncle. "I imagined that your mind was filled with literary pursuits, to the exclusion of all else. I had no idea you could combine the two."

"I should not have called it business; the matter upon which I wish to speak is far more vital than any business could possibly be," Geoffrey replied, gravely.

"I'll wager the boy is borrowing trouble over his resemblance to that chap whom we met last evening; he doubtless believes that he is on the verge of some important discovery, and wants me to help him ferret out the truth," Mr. Huntress mused, as he led the way to his library.

"Now, Geoff, I'm ready to listen to whatever you may have on your mind," he said, seating himself comfortably, and motioning the young man to another chair.

"Uncle August," Geoffrey began, after pausing a moment to collect his thoughts, "you know, do you not, that I am truly grateful to you for the unexampled kindness which you have shown me ever since you found me, such a pitiable object, in the streets of New York?"

"Why, my boy!" said Mr. Huntress, looking astonished over this unexpected speech, "I have never stopped to think whether you were grateful or not; you have always shown that you loved me and desired to please me, and that was enough."

"I have loved you—I do love you; if I should ever discover my own father I do not believe that I could give him the deep affection which I cherish for you. But, Uncle August, I have a confession to make to you this morning which may cause something of a change in your feelings toward me."

"A confession?" repeated Mr. Huntress, looking up quickly and anxiously. "Surely, Geoff, you haven't been getting into any trouble at college?"

"No, sir; what I have to tell you, you may regard as far more serious than any college scrape—it may alienate your affection for me far more, but——"

"Out with it, Geoff, don't beat about the bush; I fancy you won't find me very obdurate, no matter what you have done," Mr. Huntress interrupted, although he believed Geoffrey was making a mountain out of some molehill.

"I will, sir; confession is the only honorable course open to me, and yet if I offend you I shall dread to look my future in the face."

"Good heavens, Geoffrey! you begin to frighten me; speak out—what have you been doing that is so dreadful?" exclaimed his friend, now looking thoroughly alarmed.

"I have dared to—love Gladys, sir."

"You have dared to love Gladys! Well, of course, who could help it?" said August Huntress, his astonishment increasing, and not, on the instant, comprehending the full import of the words.

"But—but—Uncle August, you do not understand; I love her as a man loves the woman whom he wishes to make his wife," said Geoffrey, with a very pale face, for the die was cast now, and he waited the result with fear and trembling.

"Humph! and this is your confession?"

"Yes, sir; I hope you will not regard me as a viper that turns and stings the hand that nourishes it," the young man pleaded, with emotion.

August Huntress did not reply for a moment. He thoroughly comprehended the situation now, and a great sigh of relief came welling up from his deep chest, for he had imagined from Geoffrey's grave looks and ominous words that he had got into some difficulty at college which might hamper him through the remainder of his course. But it was only a love affair, after all, and he had long ago surmised that some such result might follow the intimate association of these two who were so dear to him.

His eyes began to twinkle as he regarded the handsome fellow, sitting there before him with downcast eyes and troubled countenance, and yet he knew that the struggle which had driven him to this confession must have been a severe one, and he appreciated, too, the sense of honor and the nobility which had also prompted it.

"Have you told Gladys anything of this?" he asked.

"No, sir; it was my duty to come to you first, for your approval or rejection of my suit. I could not forget that I am a nameless waif, whom your goodness alone has redeemed from a blighted life. I could not forget, either, the fact, that when I shall have finished my education I shall have nothing to offer her whom I love, save my heart, an empty hand, and a name that is mine only by adoption."

Mr. Huntress was touched by his frankness and honor.

"I can vouch for the heart, Geoff," he said; "it is large, and generous, and noble. Empty hands are no disgrace if they are honest and willing hands, backed by energy and a resolute spirit, both of which I know you possess. As for the name, it is above reproach, but not more so than the manly fellow upon whom I have bestowed it, and of whom I am very proud; I know he will never dishonor it."

"Thank you, Uncle August," Geoffrey replied, with a suspicious tremor in his voice: "but heart, hands, name, and even life itself will not amount to much with me if I am denied the love I crave—the world would be nothing to me without Gladys."

"It would be rather dark to all of us without her; she has been the light of our home and the pride of our hearts for a good many years; and, Geoff, to speak the truth, I believe nothing would please me better than to have you two marry, if you love each other well enough."

Geoffrey looked up with a transfigured face.

"Oh, Uncle August, do you mean that?" he cried.

"Of course I mean it, or I should not have said it. Your confession, although it startled me a trifle at first, as it would any father, to be asked to give away his only child, was not wholly unanticipated, for I have not been blind during the last few years, and it has proved your nobility better than almost anything else could have done, and if you can win Gladys, I shall give her to you with my sincere blessing. You have grown very dear to me, Geoff. I have been building great hopes upon you ever since I adopted you as my son, and now nothing would satisfy me so well as to have you become more closely allied to me, and thus cement even more strongly the bonds that already unite us."

"But," Geoffrey began, then stopped short, a burning flush rising to the roots of his hair, although his heart had thrilled with joy to every word his uncle had uttered.

"Well, out with it; surely you are not going to argue against your own cause, when you can have everything your own way—that is, as far as I am concerned," Mr. Huntress said, laughingly.

"But I wish you to consider the matter in all its bearings," the young man responded, very seriously. "You must not forget that you are utterly ignorant of my parentage. I may even be the child of some unfortunate woman, that was cast adrift in order to conceal the story of her shame. If we should ever make such a discovery, and you should then regret having given me my heart's desire, it might make misery for us all in the future."

"Geoffrey," August Huntress responded, in just as serious a tone, "I confess that such a discovery would pain me exceedingly, but more on your account than my own. Still, if I knew at this moment that you could honorably call no man father, if I knew that your mother had committed an irremediable error, it could not detract from my affection for you nor my pride in you. I hope, however, if such is the story of your origin, that you will never know it. The name that I have given you will be sufficient to aid you to an honorable position in the world; it is your character, what you are yourself, that is chiefly to be considered, and I could give you Gladys— provided she was willing to give herself to you—without a demur. Heaven bless you, Geoff! Go and win your bride, if you can!"

He held out his hand as he concluded, and Geoffrey seized it in a transport of joy.

"Uncle August, you are a royal gentleman," he cried, earnestly; "and now you have crowned all your past goodness to me with this great, this priceless gift, I am the happiest fellow in Christendom!"

"Well, then, don't come to me with any more confessions," returned his companion, jocosely, though there were tears in his eyes. "I declare my blood actually ran cold when I looked into your solemn face and thought, perhaps, you had been sent home from college in disgrace for some unheard of misdemeanor. Still," he added, more seriously, "I might have known better, for you have been studying too hard to have much time for mischief."

"Indeed I have; and, Uncle August, I am going to gain my year without any difficulty," the young man said, with shining eyes.

"Well, I like to have you smart, only don't work so hard that you will break down; I'd much prefer to have it take you a year longer to get through than to have you injure your health."

"I shall not; I am as strong as a giant, and now, with this new hope to brighten my life, I believe I could accomplish almost any thing. I want to get through with my course in the next two years, and then I must turn my mind to business, for I have my fortune yet to make, you know."

"Yes, I should advise you to choose something to do when you got through college; it is better for every man to have some business or profession, no matter how much money he may have. I may as well tell you, Geoff, and I do not believe it will do you any harm to know it, that I have made a handsome provision for you, and if you desire to get into something promising by and by, I shall be glad to anticipate my will and help you do it. I have plenty, my boy," he continued, confidentially, "and if it were not for this habit of business that is on me, like a son of second nature, I might retire and take my ease for the remainder of my life."

"I think you deserve to take your ease," Geoffrey replied; "you at least might have a few years of travel and sight-seeing."

"I should enjoy that if I could do all my traveling by land. I don't take to the water very well, and perhaps, by the time you and Gladys are through college, we will all like to run about a little. But," he added, looking at his watch, "if you're going on that nine o'clock train you will have to be off, and," with a sly smile, "since you are absolved from all your sins, you can go with a light heart and an easy conscience."

Geoffrey smiled and flushed.

"I think, Uncle August, I can manage to spare another day," he said, "and if you do not object, I believe I will run over to New York again, and escort Gladys home. She said something about returning to-day."

August Huntress laughed aloud at this change in the young man's plans.

"You do not intend to lose any time in your wooing, I perceive," he said, then added, more thoughtfully: "As a rule, I should say it was better not to mix love with Latin, Greek, and the sciences; but you and Gladys are so set upon your studies, I imagine it won't hurt you to season them with a little sentiment. Go along, you rogue, and good luck go with you! However, I imagine you need not tremble very much for your fate."

"Do you think that Gladys cares for me?" Geoffrey asked, eagerly.

"Go and find out for yourself. I'm not going to betray any of Gladys' secrets," Mr. Huntress retorted, with an assumption of loyalty, but with such a mischievous gleam in his eyes, that Geoffrey set off for New York with a strangely light heart.

CHAPTER XV
A DECLARATION

Arriving at Mr. Loring's, Geoffrey sent his name up to the young ladies, and a few minutes later Gladys came down alone.

How his heart bounded as she came tripping into the room, looking as fresh and lovely as the morning itself.

She was dressed in a morning robe of white flannel, relieved by quilted facings of pale blue silk, and fastened at the waist with a cascade of ribbons of the same hue.

Her hair was carelessly knotted at the back of her head, where it was pinned with a small shepherd's crook of silver, while a few light rings clustered lovingly about her forehead.

In spite of the dissipation of the previous evening, her eyes were bright as stars, her cheeks flushed, and her manner animated.

"Dear old Geoff," she cried, springing forward with a glad smile to meet him, "I imagined you were on your way back to New Haven, to bury yourself in Greek verbs and Latin nouns! What good fairy has sent you here instead?"

"Love!" was on Geoffrey's lips as he gathered both her hands in his, but he restrained the word, and replied:

"Oh, I wanted to have a little talk with Uncle August, and so concluded to remain over another day. I have come to act as your escort home."

"How good of you! I was dreading to go alone."

"How is your friend this morning?"

"Addie? poor child! she is laid up with a wretched headache; the dancing and excitement were too much for her. Mrs. Loring was obliged to go out early to her dressmaker, and as Addie is compelled to keep very quiet in a darkened room, I was having quite a solitary time of it when you were announced," Gladys explained.

Geoffrey was secretly delighted at this, although sorry for Miss Loring's indisposition.

The coast was clear, so to speak, for him, and yet, now that everything seemed so propitious for his suit, he almost feared to put his fate to the test.

"I regret your friend's illness," he said, "but you are as bright and fresh as if you had not lost an hour of sleep."

"Yes, I do not feel in the least wearied," Gladys returned, "and I had a most delightful time. But the best of all was to have you here, Geoff. I began to fear my evening was to be spoiled, you were so late."

"Was my presence so necessary to your enjoyment?" the young man earnestly questioned, a quick flush rising to his brow, as he searched her lovely face.

"Indeed it was; I had set my heart upon having you here—it was almost my first appearance in society, you know. How did I behave, Geoffrey?— like a novice?" Gladys asked, archly.

"No, indeed; you were quite the woman of the world, and entertained your admirers as composedly as if you had been accustomed to such homage for many a season. Do you imagine that you would enjoy a fashionable life, Gladys?"

"I think I would enjoy social life, to a certain extent, but I would not care to devote all my time to keeping up style, or to live in a fashionable whirl continually," she replied, thoughtfully.

"And yet you are eminently fitted for just that kind of a life," Geoffrey said, thinking how few there were who could compare with her.

"How so?" she asked, flushing slightly.

"You are beautiful and graceful; you have winning manners and a cultivated mind; you would shine anywhere," he answered, an earnest thrill in his voice.

"Flatterer! not one of my 'admirers,' last night, paid me such a tribute as that," retorted the fair girl, with a merry laugh, "and it is quite unusual, I believe, for one's brother to be so complimentary."

"You forget, Gladys, that I am not your brother," Geoffrey returned, gravely, and wondering that she should have spoken thus, for she had very rarely assumed that there was any kindred tie between them.

She could not have told herself what made her use the word, and she remembered how she had repudiated Mr. Mapleson's assumption of such a relationship; but somehow, though her own heart thrilled to Geoffrey's assertion that he was not her brother, a sort of perverseness took possession of her, and she continued, in the same strain, with a half-injured air and a bewitching pout:

"One would think that you were rejoiced over the fact, to remind me of it in such a way."

"I am rejoiced over the fact."

"Why, Geoff! After all these years!" and Gladys looked up in genuine surprise, for the restraint that he had been imposing upon himself had made his tone almost stern.

"Yes, after all these years; Gladys," he went on, eagerly, feeling that the supreme moment of his life had come, "can you conceive of no reason why I should be glad? As a boy, before I realized what you would become in the future, I was proud and happy to be allowed the privilege of regarding you as my sister; but as a man I exult in the fact that no kindred ties bind us to each other, for in that case I should have no right to love you as I do, and my life would be bereft of its sweetest hopes."

Gladys darted one quick, searching glance into his face as he uttered these impassioned words; then a burning blush suffused her face, and her eyes drooped in confusion before the ardent light in his.

"Have I startled you, my darling, by this confession?" Geoffrey went on. "Have you never suspected how I have been growing to love you day by day? At first, as I told you, I regarded you in a brotherly way. I was delighted with your beauty, I was proud of your intellect. I loved and reverenced you for your goodness and gentleness to me, and your patience with me as an ignorant, simple-minded boy; but, as I grew older, a deeper, more sacred love took possession of me, until I came to realize that my future would be a miserable blank unless I could win your own heart's best love. I do not forget that I am nameless, dear, that I am only a stray waif whom your father rescued from a hapless fate. I have nothing to offer you save my great love and an energy and resolution which will enable me to overcome every obstacle for your dear sake. Does your heart respond to my plea, my darling? Can you give me a deeper and holier love than that of a sister for a brother, and some day, when we are both through with our studies, when I can obtain a position worthy of your acceptance, become my cherished wife?"

He reached out, took the hands that lay clasped upon her lap, and drew her gently toward him.

She lifted her sweet face to him for one brief instant, and their glances met, soul answering to soul.

"Geoffrey! you have fairly taken my breath away," Gladys whispered, "and yet—and——"

His clasp tightened about her hands.

"'And yet'—Gladys—what?" he breathed, eagerly.

Her bright head drooped lower to hide the crimson in her cheeks, but there was no shrinking from him, as there must have been had not her heart responded to his appeal.

"And yet, I know that you are far dearer to me than a brother could ever be," she confessed.

He dropped her hands, and the next moment his arms were around her.

He drew her close to his wildly bounding heart and laid her head upon his breast.

"My own darling! that means that you love me even as I love you! Oh, Gladys, how I have longed to hear this confession from your lips, and yet I have never dared to betray the affection that has become a part of my very life."

"Haven't you, Geoff?" Gladys asked, a mischievous smile wreathing her red lips, which, however, he could not see.

"No; for I felt that it would not be right to do so. I feared that Uncle August would feel that I had betrayed his confidence, and taken an unfair advantage of his kindness. Besides, it galled me to feel that I had nothing to offer you save my nameless self, without any definite expectations for the future."

"You imagine that you have been exceedingly circumspect, don't you, dear?" and now a pair of merry eyes were raised to meet his.

"Have I not? Have you suspected anything of this before, Gladys?" he asked, quickly, a vivid crimson suffusing his face.

"I shall have to confess that I have—in a measure," she replied.

"When? What made you?"

"Just before you went to college, when you told me that you were glad you had been cast adrift upon the world."

"I remember—when I said but for that I should never have known you. It was very hard for me, then, not to tell you how well I loved you, but I believed I did conceal it. Did it trouble you, Gladys?"

"N—o; still I was taken by surprise. I had never thought of loving you in that way, or of your regarding me other than as a sister," Gladys replied, gravely.

"Then it set you thinking and you have been learning to love me since that time?" Geoffrey asked, fondly.

"Not exactly 'learning to love,' Geoff, but I began then to realize the fact that I did love you," the young girl confessed, with brilliant cheeks.

Geoffrey bent and kissed her red lips.

"Darling, I am glad I did not dare tell you then—I should have been very premature," he said, tenderly.

"How does it happen that you have 'dared' even now?" she asked, roguishly.

"Because I confessed everything to Uncle August this morning, and he bade me come and win my bride if I could," was the smiling retort.

"Geoff! did papa say that," cried the young girl, growing crimson again.

"Yes, those very words. Uncle August is a kingly man, and his permission to let me speak to you has raised me from the depths of despair to the very heights of joy."

"Oh, Geoffrey, what an ardent figure of speech!" laughed the happy girl.

"Indeed it is not a figure at all, you sweet, brown-eyed fay. I did not sleep a wink last night for wretchedness of mind."

"And all for nothing, Geoff."

"It was the fear of losing you, my darling. When I saw you so admired in these very rooms last night, I said to myself, 'some one else will win her before I shall have any right to speak so,' after lying awake all night, I desperately resolved to make a clean breast of everything to Uncle August. If he had told me he was unwilling to give you to me I should never have come to Brooklyn again."

"Geoffrey," cried Gladys, clinging to him, "you would not have left us like that."

"I should, dear," he answered, firmly; "I could not have remained in the same house with you and know that I must never, by either word or look, reveal the love I bear you. But all that is past. Uncle August seems even happy in the prospect of our union. You love me—you are sure you love me well enough, Gladys, to become my wife, with no regret for—anything?" he pleaded, bending to look searchingly into her eyes.

"Yes, I am sure, Geoffrey. I have never tried to analyze the affection which I have always cherished for you, but I know, now, that it has not been of that calm nature which a sister would feel for her brother. I have been happier at your coming, I have been lonely and have drooped whenever you went from home, and I can understand now why it has been so," Gladys answered, dropping her head again upon her lover's breast.

"My own darling! How wonderful it is that this priceless boon should be granted me to crown all the other good gifts that I have received," he said, in a thrilling voice; then added: "But, Gladys, I must remind you, as I have already reminded your father, that you will have to become the wife of a nameless man. Will that never trouble you?"

"Surely, the name that my father has bestowed upon you will do very well, will it not?"

"That was just what he also said, dear; but will the mystery that enshrouds me never make you uncomfortable or unhappy?"

"No; I am well content with you just as you are."

"But—have you never thought that there may be some story of wrong— of shame, even—connected with my early life? If we should discover it to be so, some time in the future, would you not regret having given yourself to me. Gladys, dear as you are to me, I could better face a separation now, than such a regret by and by."

"Such a story of wrong could never harm you, dear Geoff. All the shame or guilt, if any, would rest upon others—the perpetrators of it. But I have no fear that you will ever be troubled by any such discovery. I believe you will yet learn your parentage and feel honored by it. However, it will never change or mar my love for you," Gladys replied, with grave earnestness.

Geoffrey's face was luminous.

"This noble spirit is just what I might have expected from you, Gladys; yet, I confess, I am very sensitive over the mystery of my birth, and I should never have been fully satisfied without knowing just how you feel about it. Oh, my love, the future looks very bright before us, though the next two years will seem very long to me."

"Why, Geoff! I thought study was a positive delight to you," Gladys returned, in surprise.

"And so it is, but it frets me to feel that, even after I get through college, it will perhaps be years before I can attain a position that will warrant me in asking Uncle August to give you to me finally."

"What kind of a position would satisfy your conscientious scruples, Geoffrey?" Gladys asked, demurely.

"I would not feel willing to take you from a home of affluence to one of poverty—you must never miss the luxuries to which you have been accustomed," he said, thoughtfully.

"Do you expect to find the treasure of a Monte Cristo somewhere?" his companion asked, in the same tone as before.

"Oh, no; I expect to provide a home and competence by my brains and hands; but it will take time——"

"How much?"

"Years perhaps."

"How many?"

"Five or six, maybe, if I am successful; more if I am not; I shall start off to 'seek my fortune' just as soon as I can take my degree."

"Meantime, what is to become of your humble servant?"

"You?—why, Gladys, you will have your home and friends the same as now."

"And you will be out in the world, somewhere, working for me?" she said, sitting erect and turning her gaze full upon him.

"Of course; that is to be expected; doesn't it please you?"

"No. I am no hot-house plant that requires a tempered atmosphere in order to thrive and grow! Do you think that I can afford to let you spend the best years of your life away from me, toiling to give me luxuries, while you deny yourself even the comforts and companionship of a home? My father and mother began life in an humble way, and built up their fortune together. I am of no finer clay than they or you; if I am not calculated to share your burdens as well us your pleasures, I am not worthy to be your wife at all," Gladys concluded, with an energy and decision that made Geoffrey regard her with surprise.

"Why, Gladys, what would people think of me if I should ask you to marry me before I could provide you with a comfortable home?" he asked.

"I do not expect you will do that; but comfort and elegance are not necessarily one and the same. With the comfortable home provided, we will begin life together, and win our luxuries and elegance hand and hand; it is not a mutual love where one gives all and the other nothing."

"My darling, I had no idea there were such intensely practical ideas in this small head of yours," said Geoffrey, laughing, but with a very tender face.

"Had you not? Well, then, perhaps, I may astonish you again some time," she returned, laughing, too. "But," she added, "I think we are both rather premature in our plans, considering that we have two years more of school before us. Besides, it is time I was getting ready to go home with you, and we must not sit here talking longer."

Later in the day the lovers returned to Brooklyn, where they were received with many smiles and significant glances, for both August Huntress and his good wife were greatly delighted by the prospect of a union between these two, upon whom all their fondest hopes had so long been centered.

CHAPTER XVI
OUT OF COLLEGE AT LAST

Two years sped rapidly away, but they were improved to the utmost by both Gladys and Geoffrey in their efforts to secure a solid education. They saw but comparatively little of each other during this time, for Geoffrey was so bent upon gaining his year that he made the most he could of every recess and vacation.

But they corresponded regularly, each hearing from the other every week, and their letters were a source of great comfort and joy to them.

Everet Mapleson, too, worked harder during these two years than he had ever done before.

His ambition had been fired by what Gladys had said to him that evening at Mrs. Loring's reception, and he had determined then that he would bend all his energies toward securing the first honors of his class.

He was more strenuous in this, perhaps, than he would have been if Geoffrey Huntress had not succeeded in gaining his year; for when the juniors became seniors our young hero took his place in the class with a record to show that he would be no mean antagonist.

Young Mapleson flushed an angry red the first time they met in the class, and returned Geoffrey's courteous greeting with a haughty, supercilious nod.

They had not met until then since the evening of Mrs. Loring's reception, and the present year did not promise anything very pleasant in the fact that they would be members of the same class.

During these two years Everet Mapleson had seen considerable of Gladys, for he had resolved that he would cultivate her acquaintance upon every possible occasion.

During his long vacations he had managed to follow the Huntresses to the sea-shore or mountains, where, mingling in the same circles, they had been thrown much together. His shorter recesses always found the young Southerner in New York city, where, being a favorite in society, besides diligently cultivating Miss Loring's acquaintance, he managed to see a good deal of the beautiful girl upon whom he had set his affections.

But as yet he had not succeeded in establishing himself upon very intimate terms with her.

Gladys always treated him courteously and in a friendly way, but still managed to hold him at a distance, and he had, as yet, never presumed to address one word of love to her.

It chafed him that he had not been able to do so. It galled him to think that he could not conquer her unvarying reserve, and make her yield to the fascinations that had never failed to win wherever he had made up his mind to win.

He still cherished his secret hatred for Geoffrey, and was always on the alert for some way to vent it upon him; but no opportunity had presented itself, and he was forced to conceal his feelings as best he could.

He had tried several times, when in New York, to find the flower-woman, Margery. Indeed he never passed a flower-stand now without peering beneath the hat or bonnet of the vender in search of that sorrowful and wrinkled visage. But he had never seen it since that first time on Broadway, and he began to fear that she was dead, and thus he would never be able to learn the secret of Geoffrey Huntress' early life.

The first of April drew near.

There were now only about three months before commencement at Yale, and every ambitious senior was doing his best to acquit himself honorably.

Geoffrey, however, had not been obliged to work nearly so hard this year as during the two previous ones; those had been the test of his course, and he had strained every nerve.

It had been a little doubtful at the close of his last year about his entering the senior class.

The professors, fearing for his health, had advised him to relinquish his purpose to do so. Mrs. Huntress, too, was anxious about him, for he had been losing flesh and color for several months, but Geoffrey very quietly remarked, in the presence of the professors, that he would do his best during the summer vacation to prepare for his examinations for the senior class, and if he failed in them he would cheerfully remain the extra year.

Mr. Huntress would not curtail him in any of his privileges, and so again sent him to a pleasant spot in the country with a tutor, a boat, and a couple of saddle-horses, and the coaching went on as faithfully as ever.

The result was that Geoffrey passed his examinations without a condition, and then felt that his hardest work was over; he would need to burn no more midnight oil, and when there came a recess he would feel at liberty to enjoy it as others did and gain a little of the rest he so much needed.

He was not idle, however.

Gladys had told him that she would expect great things of him, and "great things" he meant to accomplish, if it were possible, for her sake.

At the beginning of the year Huntress and Mapleson were dubbed "the twins" of their class, and not long afterward it was whispered that they stood about equal in the race for first honors. Some were inclined to think that Huntress would win the day, others that Mapleson would be the favored one.

When the verdict was finally rendered in favor of Geoffrey, Everet Mapleson swore an angry oath, although his own name stood second on the list.

"He has seemed like some bad spirit pursuing me with some evil purpose in view, ever since he entered college," he muttered, distorting facts that would have seemed just the reverse to any one else. "If I could only find out the secret of his life I might ruin him, even now, before the year is ended. I'd give half of my expectations if I could find that old woman; but I'm afraid she's dead, and all that mystery buried with her.

"Well, I must calmly submit to his good fortune in excelling all his competitors," he continued. "I've done my best to win and I stand next, which is some comfort. If I could have stood first I would have gone to Gladys and told her that I worked for her sake, and perhaps she might have listened to me. I wonder if she will stand first in her class. I must run up to Poughkeepsie to see the little lady graduate; the commencement there comes a few days earlier than ours this year."

However much Everet Mapleson inwardly regretted the loss of the first honors, he betrayed it to no one else—he appeared to take the appointments as a matter of course, and spared no pains to make his own oration worthy and brilliant. But underneath all this outward calm there lay a relentless purpose to some day have ample revenge upon his rival for his disappointment.

As soon as Geoffrey learned of his good fortune he hastened to telegraph the news to Gladys.

"I shall not disappoint you—the first honor is mine," were the words which went flying over the wires to the beautiful girl at Vassar.

Gladys had just come in from a walk when she received it, and the principal, as he handed it to her, marveled at her exceeding beauty.

The rich glow of perfect health, deepened a little by exercise, was on her cheeks; a happy smile wreathed her lips. Her hair had been tossed about a trifle by the breeze, and lay in a light, fluffy network low on her brow, which gleamed white as ivory beneath it.

Her hand trembled a little as she took the telegram and opened it, but as she caught sight of the cheering words within she seemed almost transfigured.

Her eyes lighted and sparkled with unusual brilliancy; the vivid color ran swiftly up to her temples and she laughed a clear, musical, happy laugh, that rang through the great hall like some sweet silver bell.

"You evidently have some good news, Miss Huntress," the principal remarked, his usually grave face involuntarily relaxing into a sympathetic smile at her delight.

"Indeed, I have, sir;" she returned. "My—a friend has taken the first honors for this year at Yale."

She flushed again, for she had almost forgotten to whom she was speaking, and nearly said, "My dear old Geoffrey," but checked herself and called him a friend.

"You need not have corrected yourself," replied the professor, with a twinkle of his eyes. "If the 'friend' is your brother you should not allow your modesty to prevent your acknowledging it."

Gladys' eyes drooped half guiltily at this.

She could not explain that Geoffrey was not her brother, but something far dearer, and yet her sense of truthfulness made her shrink from giving a wrong impression.

"You will be able to send him as pleasant tidings in return, will you not? You have also been appointed valedictorian, I believe?" the gentleman continued.

"Yes, sir."

"I am almost inclined to think that two valedictorians out of one household are more than a fair allowance, especially for one year; your parents must be very proud over two such brilliant children. Are there any more of you to keep up the credit of the family?" the principal inquired, laughing.

"No, sir, Geoffrey and I are all there are," Gladys answered, and then tripped away to reply to Geoffrey's telegram with a jubilant letter.

"I am delighted with you, dear Geoff," she wrote. "Your telegram has made me the happiest girl at Vassar, though my heart failed me a trifle before I opened it, fearing that it might contain bad news. How proud I am of you! for you have climbed mountains of difficulties to attain your goal.

"Now let me whisper a little bit of news in your ear. I have won my spurs, too—if I may be allowed to use that expression—and as I shall graduate a few days before you take your degree, can't you come to Vassar to honor the occasion with your presence? Papa and mamma will be here, but the day will not be complete without you."

Geoffrey replied that nothing should keep him away; that he would be with her bright and early on commencement day, but would have to return to New Haven at three in the afternoon, as he still had much to do to prepare for the final exercises of his own class.

But notwithstanding his promise, the train on which he left New Haven was delayed two hours, and he did not arrive at Vassar until after the exercises were opened, and so had no opportunity to see Gladys before, as he intended to do.

An usher led him into the crowded room, but the only available seat was far in the rear, and so situated that he could scarcely see or be seen.

One of the graduating class was singing as he entered, and for a few moments his attention was arrested by the young amateur who gave promise of becoming something more by and by.

But presently his eyes began to wander about in search of Gladys, for she, of course, was the center of attraction for him.

She was sitting near one end of the platform, at the head of her class, and looking fairer than he had ever seen her, in her virgin white.

Her dress was of finest Indian mull, sheer and fleecy as a summer cloud. It was very simple, yet daintily made, one gauzy thickness alone shading her snowy neck and rounded arms, which gleamed fair as alabaster beneath.

She wore no ornaments save a string of costly pearls around her neck and a bunch of snowballs in her silken belt.

Her face was slightly flushed, her eyes glowed with excitement, and her lips were like polished coral.

Ever and anon her eyes wandered wistfully over the sea of faces before her, as if in search of some one.

All at once they rested upon a familiar face and form. She gave a slight start, her countenance lighted for an instant, then she gave utterance to a sigh of disappointment, although a little smile curved her lips and she bowed in a friendly way to some one in the audience.

She had seen Everet Mapleson, and at the first glance had thought he was Geoffrey, but catching his eager look of recognition, she realized her mistake, and felt almost angry with him for being there, while she feared that Geoffrey would not come at all.

She did not catch sight of her lover until just a moment before she was called up to deliver the farewell address to class and faculty.

Geoffrey saw that she was anxiously looking for him, and shifting his position he leaned forward and fixed a fond, magnetic look upon her.

She seemed to feel it, and turning her glance in that direction, their eyes met; a rosy flood swept up to her brow, a brilliant smile wreathed her lips with one glad look of welcome, and the next moment she was standing before the audience, her whole being thrilling with delight, and with the determination to do her best for Geoffrey's sake.

And she did; her effort was the crowning achievement of the day. The rapt and breathless attention of the hundreds before her testified to that, and when she concluded a perfect storm of applause showed their appreciation and how completely she had swayed them by her eloquence.

More than this, numerous floral tributes were borne forward and laid at her feet. These she acknowledged with blush, and smile, and bow; but when at the very last an exquisite bouquet of lilies of the valley followed the more pretentious offerings, she eagerly stretched forth her white-gloved hand and took it from the bearer.

They were her favorite flowers, and she knew that Geoffrey had sent them, even without the evidence of the tiny note that lay twisted in their midst and concealed from every eye but hers.

Everet Mapleson's card was attached to an elaborate basket of japonicas, roses, and heliotrope. Mr. Huntress had sent up a harp of pansies and smilax, and two or three of Gladys' admiring classmates had contributed lovely bouquets, but her little bunch of lilies, tied with snow-white ribbon, was prized above them all.

It was all over at last; diplomas were presented, the usual remarks made and advice given, and then admiring friends crowded about to offer congratulations and express their pride and pleasure in their loved ones.

In the midst of this confusion Gladys stepped aside a moment to ascertain what her little billet contained.

"My darling," she read. "I would not have missed this hour to have secured a fortune, and yet I came very near it. I will be in the reception-room below after the exercises are over. Come and receive my verdict there.

Geoff."

CHAPTER XVII
A DISAPPOINTED LOVER

Gladys stole away from the crowd as soon as she could do so without attracting attention, and sped down to the reception-room to find her lover.

He was there and alone, fortunately, as nearly all the guests were still in the hall above, and his face lighted with a luminous smile as she sprang toward him, gladness beaming through every feature.

"Dear old Geoff!"

"My darling!" was all the salutation that passed between them, and then for an instant Gladys was folded close to her lover's breast in a fond embrace.

"Oh, Geoff, I thought you had not come; I never got a glimpse of you until almost the last minute, and was so disappointed that I was about ready to break down," Gladys said, with a little nervous shiver, as she remembered how nearly her courage had failed her.

"I was late, dear, and I knew you would feel it; but I do not believe you would have failed even if you had not seen me at all," he answered, as he fondly smoothed back the clustering rings of hair from her throbbing temples.

"No, I do not think I should, really; but I could not have done as well; it was like a sudden inspiration to me when I found you at last."

"Then I am thankful I was here, dear, for your effort was the grand event of the day," Geoffrey said, smiling.

"You are very good to say so, Geoff," Gladys replied, modestly.

"Very good to say so," he repeated, laughing. "Why should I not say it, when your praises are on every lip, and a pin might have been heard, if one had dropped, while you were addressing the faculty and bidding your classmates farewell. Poor girls! the crystal drops were plentiful over the thought of parting."

"It is a little hard to leave school, Geoff, and all the pleasant friends one has made; don't you think so?"

"Perhaps," he replied. "I presume it is harder for you than it will be for me, because I am so eager to make a place for myself in the world, and a nest for somebody else."

Gladys blushed at this reference to coming events.

"Did I not see Mapleson here?" Geoffrey asked, after a moment.

"Yes; and at first I thought he was you; but I soon discovered my mistake."

"I wonder what he is here for?" mused the young lover.

"To see me graduate, of course," Gladys responded, roguishly.

"Did you invite him?"

"No. A long time ago he asked me to exchange tickets with him for commencement, and I think he has spoken of it every time that we have met since; so, of course, I could hardly help sending him one."

"You have seen a good deal of him during the last two years, haven't you, Gladys?"

"Yes, he has appeared at almost every place that we have visited the last two summers, and he was always in New York during the shorter recesses. I met him constantly in society, and I didn't like it very well, either."

"Why?"

"Because it rather annoyed me to receive his attentions," Gladys confessed.

"Then he *has* been attentive to you?" the young man asked, studying the face he loved very closely.

"Yes, quite so," Gladys answered; then noticing her lover's grave, anxious look, she added: "You do not like it, either, do you, Geoff?"

"No, dearest, I do not," Geoffrey replied, frankly, then continued: "Pray, do not misunderstand me—do not suppose that I am disturbed by a petty feeling of jealousy, but there are some traits in Mapleson's character which make me feel that he is not a proper companion or escort for you."

"Then, Geoff, I will never accept any attention again from him," Gladys said, quickly. "He has never been very congenial to me in any way, and somehow I have always resented his resemblance to you."

"Why should you?"

"I do not know—I cannot account for the feeling, but I have always had it. It may be because I have detected something not quite true in him, and did not like to have him look like you on that account, while it almost seems sometimes as if he were usurping a place that rightfully belongs to you."

"That is impossible, dear, and I am afraid, a sort of morbid fancy," Geoffrey replied, with gentle reproof. "I have never had such a thought, nor envied him either his high position in the world, or the immense wealth which I have heard will some time be his."

Gladys raised herself on tiptoe and softly touched her lips to her lover's cheek.

"How noble you are!" she whispered, "and I'd rather have my Geoff without a penny!"

"You will have your 'rather,' then," the young man returned, laughing, although he fondly returned her caress, "for he hasn't even a penny that is rightfully his own. But," he added, drawing himself up resolutely, "that shall not be said of me long—another year, I trust, will find me established in something that need not make me ashamed to take my place among other men."

"Oh, Geoffrey! who is indulging in morbid fancies now?" queried Gladys, chidingly.

"I do not mean to do so," he replied, cheerfully, "but I long to begin to do something for myself and for you, my darling. But I must not keep you here—people will be wondering what has become of the fair valedictorian. There!" as steps were heard approaching the door, "I'll venture that some one is looking for you now."

It proved to be even so, and Gladys was in great demand during the next few hours. Indeed, Geoffrey saw but comparatively little of her after that one interview, for he was obliged to leave at an early hour in order to reach New Haven that night.

There was to be a brilliant reception that evening for the graduating class, and it was quite a disappointment to Gladys that Geoffrey could not be present, but she strove to make the best of it, knowing that they would meet again in a few days; besides Mr. and Mrs. Huntress were to remain to accompany her when she should leave the next day.

Everet Mapleson also remained.

He had hardly been able to get a word with Gladys all day, and when he found that Geoffrey was obliged to leave, he resolved that he would attend the reception and devote himself to the fair girl whom he was learning every hour to love more devotedly.

When he presented himself in the evening before her a slight frown contracted her brow, and for a moment she was tempted to pass on and leave him to himself. But he made that impossible by instantly taking his stand by her side, and devoting himself exclusively to her, and thus it was out of her power to avoid him without being positively rude.

"Well, all this will soon end," she said to herself, with a sigh of resignation, "and for once I may as well surrender myself to the inevitable; after he leaves college we shall probably not meet again, and I should not like to have it on my conscience that I had been rude even to him."

She introduced him to several of her classmates, and tried thus to attract his attention from herself and slip away unobserved; but at her first movement he was at her side.

During the latter part of the evening he managed to draw her into the circle of promenaders who were pacing up and down the main hall, to the delicious strains of a fine band, where, after a few turns he led her, almost before she was aware of his intention, to a balcony at one end, and out of the hearing of the crowd within.

"Perhaps I am taking a great liberty, Miss Huntress," he began, before she could utter a word of protest, "but I must bid you good-night presently, and I have something very important which I wish to say to you first."

Gladys shivered at his words, although the night was intensely warm, for instinctively she knew why he had brought her there.

But she could not help herself now, and she thought perhaps it would be best to have their future relations definitely settled once for all.

"I am obliged to return to New York on the midnight train," the young man continued, "but I could not go without first telling you what has long been burning on my lips for utterance. Gladys, I love you, and all my future happiness depends upon my winning you to be my wife. Will you give me your love in return? will you give me yourself?"

It was a manly, straightforward declaration, and worthy a better man than Everet Mapleson was at that time.

It impressed Gladys as being earnest and genuine, and she was grieved to know that she must wound and disappoint him.

"I cannot tell you how sorry I am, Mr. Mapleson, that you should have said this to me," she returned, in a low, pained tone, "for I cannot respond as you desire; my answer must be a decided refusal of your suit."

"Do not say that!" he burst out in an agonized tone. "Oh, my darling, you must not ruin my life with one fatal blow. Let me wait—ever so long, if I may only hope that some day you will be mine."

"I cannot let you hope," Gladys replied, greatly agitated, "what I have said must be final. I do not love you—I can never become your wife."

"Perhaps you do not love me now, but you can learn to do so; I will teach you. I will be very patient; I will not press you. Oh, Gladys, my beautiful, brown-haired darling, do not break my heart! do not ruin my life!"

A quivering sigh burst from the young girl's pale lips. No one can tell how painful the interview had become to her, for she saw that he was a lover in deadly earnest, and that his affection for her was deep and true.

She impulsively reached out her hand and laid it upon his arm.

"Mr. Mapleson," she pleaded, "pray do not importune me further; for, truly, I can give you no other answer; my feelings can never change; I do not love you—I can never love you."

He seized her hand in an eager, trembling grasp, and bent his proud head until his forehead rested upon it.

"Why do you say that?" he cried, "that you can never love me? You do not know. I will serve for you—I will prove my devotion; oh! give me time, Gladys, before you discard me utterly, and no slave ever served more faithfully for the coveted gift of freedom, than I will serve, in any way, to win you, my fair love."

"No, no; please say no more, it is useless," she murmured, brokenly.

He raised his head and looked eagerly into her face.

"There can be but one reason for such a persistent refusal, such a decided answer," he said, in a low, concentrated tone; "you have given the wealth of your love to another!"

Even by the dim light of the moon which came struggling in upon them through the network of vines upon the balcony, he could see the vivid color which shot up over her cheek and brow, and dyed even the fair shoulders, beneath their gauzy covering, at this direct charge.

He grew pale as death.

"It is true! I know it must be true!" he said, in the tones of one who has suddenly been calmed or benumbed by a terrible shock.

"You never could have resisted an appeal like mine," he went on, between his tightly shut teeth, "if it were not so. Tell me," he continued, growing excited again, "is it so? have I guessed rightly?"

There was so much of concentrated passion in his voice, and such an authoritative ring in his tone, that it aroused something of resentment and antagonism in Gladys' heart, in spite of her sympathy for him.

She turned and faced him, standing straight and tall and calm before him.

"You have no right to speak in this way to me, Mr. Mapleson," she said, with quiet dignity, "and I am under no obligation to explain why I do not favor your suit. The chief reason in any such case, I think, is that persons are not congenial to each other."

"Do you mean to tell me that I am not congenial to you, Miss Huntress?" the young man interrupted, almost fiercely.

"You have it in your power to be a very pleasant friend, Mr. Mapleson; but more than that you could never be to me under any circumstances," Gladys answered, coldly. Her tone more than her words drove him almost to despair.

"Tell me, is it because you love another?" he persisted.

"I could not truthfully give that as *the* reason."

"That does not answer me. *Do you love* some one else?"

"Yes," answered the beautiful girl, briefly and proudly.

"Are you betrothed?"

Gladys lifted her head haughtily.

"Mr. Mapleson," she said, "I question your right to interrogate me in this authoritative manner, but if a plain answer will convince you that there can be no change in my decision, I am willing to acknowledge to you that I am pledged to another."

"To Geoffrey Huntress?" Everet Mapleson demanded, hoarsely.

"Yes, to Geoffrey," she repeated, with a tender intonation of the name that betrayed how dear it was to her.

At this confession the young man dropped the hand that he had clung to in spite of her efforts to release it, as if it had been a coal of fire, all the evil in his nature aroused by this triumph of his enemy over him.

"That low-born beggar!" he hissed.

"Sir!"

He shrank for an instant beneath the word as if she had smitten him. Then his passion swept all before it once more.

"He has opposed and thwarted me from the first moment of our meeting. He offered me an indignity once, which I have never forgotten or forgiven; he has robbed me of my honors at college and now he has robbed me of you! *I—hate—him!* and he shall yet feel the force of my hatred in a way to make him wish that he had never crossed my path."

CHAPTER XVIII
A LONG AND INTERESTING CONVERSATION

It is impossible to convey any idea of the anger, malice, and venom contained in these fiercely uttered words, and before Gladys could collect herself sufficiently to make any reply—before she was even aware of his intention—he had sprung past her and disappeared within the hall, leaving her alone upon the balcony, and she saw him no more that night.

"Mercy! what a volcanic nature," she murmured, with a sigh of relief over his departure. "I should pray to be delivered from a life with such a person, let alone trying to learn to love him. No, there can be no relationship between Geoffrey and Everet Mapleson, as I have sometimes imagined there might be. My Geoff is a noble-hearted gentleman; he could never forget himself and give the rein to passion as this fiery young man has done to-night. I hope I shall never meet him again."

She sat down a moment on the low railing of the balcony to recover herself a little more fully before returning to the company.

"I wonder," she mused, "what he meant by Geoffrey thwarting him, and what imaginary indignity—for it could have been nothing more than that—he offered him; and how could he have robbed him of his honors at college? I will ask him when we go to New Haven."

A little later she rejoined her friends, but all enjoyment had been spoiled for her, and seeking Mr. and Mrs. Huntress, she intimated that she was very weary after the excitement of the day, and they were quite willing to retire with her, knowing well that she needed rest.

The next morning Gladys bade a long farewell to her classmates and teachers, and then, with Mr. and Mrs. Huntress, left for New Haven to attend the commencement exercises at Yale.

We cannot linger over these, or even particularize much. Suffice it to say that Geoffrey acquitted himself most nobly, and Mr. Huntress was as proud of him as if he had really been his own son.

His oration was one that was long remembered by his class with great pleasure, and was highly commended by the faculty.

Everet Mapleson also shone upon this occasion. He had worked harder during this last year than he had ever worked before during his college life. A feeling of antagonism against Geoffrey, and a desire to win Gladys' favor, had spurred him on to strive for the post of honor in his class, and the disappointment at his failure was a bitter one.

It created a good deal of surprise and comment that two young men so nearly resembling each other, and yet in no way related, should stand so high in their class, and be such brilliant scholars.

Mrs. Mapleson, who had come on from the South to be present upon the occasion, was strangely impressed by the circumstance.

Colonel Mapleson had been called out West on business, and could not return in season to accompany her, so she had been forced to come alone.

She was a magnificent-looking woman; tall, with a stately figure, a brilliant brunette complexion, with dark hair and eyes, and beautiful teeth, such as a youthful belle of twenty might envy.

"It is the strangest thing in the world, Everet," she remarked to her son after the exercises of the day were concluded. "I mean this wonderful resemblance between you and that young man. If I had not known the Maplesons all my life, and that our family is the last of the race, I should be tempted to believe that he belonged to us in some way."

"Pshaw! mother, that is all nonsense!" her son replied, a hot flush of resentment rising to his brow. "Don't, for pity's sake, suggest that any of our blood flows in his veins!"

"Why, Everet? He appears like a fine fellow—handsome, manly, and he is certainly extremely clever," returned Mrs. Mapleson, with some surprise.

"Granted; though that may sound rather egotistical, since we are considered the counterparts of each other; but for all that he has been a thorn in the flesh and a marplot to me ever since he entered college, and I detest him!"

"That is not a very good spirit, I'm afraid, Ev.," Mrs. Mapleson said, abidingly. "But who is he? Geoffrey D. Huntress, I believe, was the name on the programme, but where does he belong, and what is his family?"

"Nobody knows who or what he is; there is a queer story connected with his life. I heard, while I was in New York, that this Mr. Huntress found him several years ago wandering in the streets of the city in a demented condition. He became interested in him, took him to some hospital, and had an operation performed—a piece of bone was pressing upon the brain, and was removed, I believe, and he recovered his senses immediately, but appeared more like a child five years old rather than like a boy in his teens."

"How very strange!" exclaimed Mrs. Mapleson, deeply interested; "but could he tell nothing about himself after his mind was restored?"

"No, nothing of any consequence; all that he could remember of his previous life was that he had lived with some people named Margery and Jack, and that his name was Geoffrey Dale——"

"Dale! Dale!" repeated Mrs. Mapleson, with a start. "There used to be a family of Dales living near Vue de l'Eau before I was married; at least there was a widow and her daughter, a girl named Annie. They were poor people; they lived in one of those cottages near the old mill, and after the mother died the girl suddenly disappeared, and was never heard of again."

"Mother, what is this you are telling me?" cried young Mapleson, a strange look flashing over his face. "The girl went away and never came back?"

"Yes."

"Where did she go? She must have had some especial place in view when she started."

"She said she was going to Richmond to serve as governess in some family; that was the last I ever heard of her."

Everet Mapleson's eyes glowed.

"Aha!" he thought; "who knows but what I have at last found a clew to the fellow's birth?

"Dale, Dale," he, too, repeated thoughtfully, "wasn't that the name of that queer old codger who was to have had Uncle Jabez's fortune, if you and father didn't fulfill the conditions of his will?"

"Yes, Robert Dale. He was a cousin of Uncle Jabez, and considerably younger than he, and I suppose he would have had all the money, if your father and I had been contrary."

"It was the most eccentric will I ever heard of," said Everet, musingly.

"It was indeed."

"What could have prompted him to make it?"

"Your father was his brother's only son. and the last of the Maplesons. I was a favorite niece, the daughter of his sister, and I suppose he did not wish the wealth which it had taken so many years to accumulate, to be divided, yet he desired to have it benefit his relatives, and so took this way to accomplish it."

A little sigh escaped Mrs. Mapleson as she concluded.

Her son noticed it, and shot a searching glance into her face.

"Mother," he said, as if some strange thought had suddenly come to him, "it has never occurred to me before, but were the conditions of that will obnoxious to you?"

Mrs. Mapleson colored a vivid red at this unexpected question.

"You are touching upon rather delicate ground, Everet, and this is hardly the time or place for the discussion of such a matter," she replied, gravely; "but since you have asked the question, I will tell you the truth about it."

"You need not tell me anything if the subject is painful to you," interrupted her son, whose love for his mother was the noblest trait in his character.

"No, the pain is all a thing of the past, if, indeed, there ever was any connected with my marriage with your father. When the conditions of the will were first made known to us, neither of us were willing to carry them out, not that we had any especial dislike to each other; we simply did not seem to be in perfect sympathy, we had no real affection for one another, and on that account we both shrank from assuming the intimate relations of husband and wife. William Mapleson was a handsome and noble gentleman, and I admired and liked him in a cousinly way. His own feelings were similar to mine, so you perceive it was not easy to comply with the wishes of your Uncle Jabez. The property, as you perhaps know, was divided equally between us, and we were free to use the income of it as we chose, until I should be twenty-five years of age, provided neither of us married any one else before that time; in that case, whichever of us violated the conditions of the will was to forfeit his or her share, and it was to go to the other, who was then free to marry, and would have the whole fortune. If both of us remained single after I reached the age of twenty-five, than all was to go to Robert Dale."

"It was an abominable will!" Everet Mapleson exclaimed, indignantly.

"Yes, it was, and it made me very antagonistic at first. I was extremely high spirited as a girl, and I resented the presumption of any one choosing my husband for me," Mrs. Mapleson replied, a flush dyeing her whole face at the memory of her girlish indignation.

"Of course, any one would. Besides this, Robert Dale had plenty of money of his own, hadn't he?"

"Yes, he was worth a great deal. He was a bachelor and a sort of miser and hermit."

"What if he had died before you were twenty-five?"

"That would have ended all our difficulties—the money would have been ours without restrictions."

"What finally induced you to change your mind?" Everet asked, searching his mother's handsome face earnestly.

She did not reply for a moment, and seemed to be struggling with an inward emotion.

"I shall have to confess, Everet, that it was the love of money," she at last said, with a sigh, although a slight smile played over her brilliant lips. "I had known what poverty was as a girl, and I hated it. I had struggled during my youthful years for even the necessaries of life, for, as you know, my father was poor and an invalid. After I came into the possession of my share of Uncle Jabez's money I enjoyed every luxury and was enabled to provide all the family with comforts such as they had never known before. Do you think it would have been easy to have gone back to the hardships of my early life?"

"I suppose it would not have been easy."

"Your father was situated somewhat the same. He had been dependent upon Uncle Jabez's bounty ever since the death of his parents, and, although he was as indignant as I, at first, over this will, and vowed he would not submit to any such arbitrary conditions, yet, after years of luxurious living, when he began to realize what it would be to be deprived of it, he came to me and asked if I was willing to revoke my early decision, and become his wife."

"But, mother, was there no one else in all the world whom you would have preferred to marry?—no one whom you had met and loved? Was there no romance in either of your lives that would conflict with such a proceeding?" Everet anxiously asked.

"No, there was no one whom I loved better—no one whom I would have been as willing, even, to marry."

"That seems very strange! How old were you at that time!"

"Twenty-four—it was my last year of grace," replied Mrs. Mapleson, with a little laugh.

"Have you never met any one since who has made you regret the step?"

"No, Everet; and if I had, I had too much respect for myself and for your father to ever have yielded to any such sentiment. More than that, I have become deeply attached to my husband, and our life, as you well know, has been a remarkably peaceful and uncheckered one."

"And father——" the young man began, and then hesitated.

"He told me frankly when he asked me to marry him, that he had no other attachment," interposed Mrs. Mapleson; "in fact we mutually confessed that, although we did not possess any romantic love for each other, such as lovers usually entertain, we had none for any one else; that we did admire and esteem each other, and we believed that a marriage would, under the circumstances, be best for us both."

"It is the strangest union I ever heard of, and I believe it was a very dangerous thing to do."

"Dangerous? Why?"

"You might have met some one later, whom you would have learned to love, and unhappiness must have resulted from it to all parties."

"That was hardly probable, for we had both been much in society and had seen a great deal of the world. At all events we have been a very contented couple. Our early admiration and simple liking have ripened into a deep and lasting affection, and we have been as quietly happy as most married people, I believe."

The young man regarded his mother curiously. It seemed very strange to him that such a beautiful woman as she was and must have been in her youth, should have missed that sweetest of all experiences—youthful loving and being loved.

She was just the person, he thought, to have inspired the most ardent passion in the heart of some strong, true-minded man; and just the woman to have loved such a man most fervently and devotedly.

He almost wondered that his father had not fallen madly in love with her at the very outset, and yet he could understand how the spirit of antagonism had been aroused in them, from the fact of not having been allowed to choose for themselves in a matter so vital to their interests and happiness.

"You say that this cousin, Robert Dale, was an old bachelor?" he asked, after a few moments of thought.

"Yes, and he was every bit as eccentric as Uncle Jabez himself."

"Are you sure that he never married? Somehow, what you have told me has created a suspicion in my mind that this Geoffrey Dale Huntress, after all, may be in some way connected with these Dales at home."

Mrs. Mapleson gave vent to a silvery ripple of amusement at her son's question.

"I am very sure that Robert Dale was never married," she said. "He despised all women, even disliked to eat what a woman's hands had cooked."

"How old was he when he died?"

"Forty, I should judge."

"Do you imagine that he could have had a secret alliance with any one, and that this Geoffrey Dale is a descendant of his?"

"No, indeed!" Mrs. Mapleson returned, her face dimpling all over at this suggestion. "If you could have seen him you would never ask such a question. No woman would have dared approach him; no woman would have lived with such a creature, or as he lived. He built himself a small stone house in the woods a few miles from Vue de l'Eau. It was as rude as it could be, and furnished with only what was actually necessary, and there he lived a kind of hermit's life, with an old negro servant, who was cook, housemaid, and everything else you may choose to call him."

"But during his earlier life he may have been different—he may have loved some one, and been secretly married, and then disappointed in some way in his hopes, which might have embittered him and made him the woman-hater he was," responded Everet, thoughtfully.

"No, I do not think that is possible; and even if it were, this young man could not be a son of his; he is not old enough; he belongs to the same generation as yourself."

"True. I did not think of that. How long did Robert Dale live after you were married?"

"Just one month."

Everet looked up quickly into his mother's face. "Before your twenty-fifth birthday?"

"Yes."

"And were you sorry that you did not wait a little longer? You would have been free from the conditions of that will, and could have kept your money."

"No, Everet, I have never regretted my marriage," Mrs. Mapleson calmly replied. "I think I have been far happier than I should have been had I remained single."

"What became of Robert Dale's money?"

"That has been a mystery to everybody, and one that has remained unsolved to this day. He was known to have given twenty thousand dollars to a blind asylum in Philadelphia several years previous to his death; but what became of the remainder of his fortune, which must have been very large, has been a question that has puzzled all who knew him. I think, however, he must have given away large sums at different times, and it was all distributed before he died, for no papers of any kind and no will were ever found."

"Was Miss Annie Dale a relative of this eccentric old bachelor?" Everet inquired.

"Yes; she was his niece, his own brother's child; but he never had anything to do with the family. There was some trouble between himself and his brother during their youth, and he never forgot or forgave the grudge. Even after the girl's father died, he refused to have anything to do with either mother or daughter, although I have heard that they were at times very needy."

"Did you ever see the girl?"

"No; my home, as you know, was in Richmond. I was not married, and did not go to Vue de l'Eau until some three years or more after she disappeared."

"Do you know the name of the family to whom she went as governess?"

"No."

Mrs. Mapleson seemed to grow somewhat weary of the conversation.

"It is very strange what became of her," her son murmured, reflectively. "Do you imagine there was any foul play about her disappearance?"

"Oh, no, indeed. She probably met some clever young man who fell in love with her and married her. I do not know much about the matter anyway, only that she was entirely alone in the world, and I do not know as there was anything so very remarkable about her going off and never coming back again. But, mercy! Everet, I do not care to sit here all day and talk about the Dales, even for the sake of making out your handsome orator to belong to them, which is not at all probable. Come, I want to look about a little."

Mrs. Mapleson arose as she spoke, thus putting an end to their long talk, and her son dutifully attended her wherever she wished to go; but he became more and more convinced that Annie Dale, who had so mysteriously disappeared many years ago, and Geoffrey Dale Huntress were in some way connected with each other.

He knew that there was some Mapleson blood in the Dale veins, although it was a good way back, and he believed that accounted for Geoffrey's singular resemblance to himself.

"I'll wager that there is some story of shame at the bottom of Annie Dale's disappearance," he thought; "and if I can ferret it out and fasten it upon him, Gladys Huntress will never marry him. I'll look into this matter as soon as I go home."

CHAPTER XIX
EVERET MAPLESON RETURNS
TO VUE DE L'EAU

Everet Mapleson conducted his mother to Sheffield Hall, thence to the Divinity Colleges, the Marquand Chapel and Library, and finally to the Peabody Museum.

In this latter place they lingered for some time, examining various objects of interest, Mrs. Mapleson appearing to be greatly attracted by the valuable collection of curiosities on exhibition there.

While they were standing before a cabinet of curious stones, one of Everet's classmates came to him and drew him aside for a moment of private conversation.

He then turned to his mother and excused himself, saying that he was wanted elsewhere upon a matter of class business, but would shortly return to her.

"Very well," she replied. "I will look about by myself until you come back, and you will find me here."

She wandered leisurely from case to case, looking over their contents, until suddenly her attention was attracted by a peculiarly pleasant voice, and, glancing up, she saw her son's "double" standing near her, with a beautiful girl leaning upon his arm.

She knew that it was Geoffrey Huntress from some trifling difference in his dress, although, even to her keen mother's eye, it was almost impossible to otherwise distinguish him from her son.

But after a passing glance at him, her attention was riveted upon the exquisitely beautiful girl at his side, whose face was all aglow with health and happiness.

"They are lovers," Mrs. Mapleson said to herself, as she saw how oblivious they were of all save each other. "I wonder who the young girl is? How graceful she is in every movement! how animated! and I have rarely seen such a lovely complexion, or such beautiful, expressive eyes!"

She stood beside one of the cabinets, partially shielded by it, and watched the young couple all the time they remained in the room, and would gladly have followed them as they passed on to another, so interested did she become in them, if she had not promised that she would remain where she was until Everet returned.

When at length he did come back to her, his face was pale and lowering. He had passed Gladys and Geoffrey on his way, and the sight of them together had wrought him up to the highest pitch of passion and suffering.

"What is the matter, Everet?" his mother asked. "Are you in trouble?"

"No," he answered, briefly, and then added: "Have you seen enough here?"

"Yes, I have been ready to go for some time; I have only been waiting for you. I have been quite interested in a young couple who have just gone out—your 'double,' as you call him, and a lovely young girl. Perhaps you met them."

"Yes, I passed them as I came in."

"Who is she?"

"She is the daughter of the man who adopted him; her name is Gladys Huntress."

"Gladys? What an appropriate name. She is a veritable sunbeam. Do you know her?"

"Yes; I have met her a great many times in New York society," the young man returned, but with a face so pale and pained that his mother could not fail to notice it.

"Everet, I believe that you have fallen in love with her, yourself!" she said, in a startled tone.

"It would not be a very difficult thing for any man to do, would it?" he asked, trying to smile, yet with a ring of pain in his voice.

"Is the family a good one?"

"They stand well; they are received in the best society in New York, and I have been told that Mr. Huntress is a wealthy man."

"Well, he has a charming daughter, anyway. I'd like you to win a pretty girl like that for a wife, Everet," said Mrs. Mapleson, wistfully.

"I assure you it would give me a great deal of pleasure to gratify you, *ma chere*," he responded, his lips curling with a bitter smile, as he thought of how he had tried and failed; then he abruptly changed the subject. "But time is flying, and if we are to be in New York to-night, we must be thinking about trains, while I have some packing to attend to yet."

Mrs. Mapleson signified her readiness to go, and they passed out of the museum and repaired to Everet's rooms.

That evening they were en route to the great metropolis, whence they were to go to Newport.

Mrs. Mapleson had arranged to spend the greater portion of the season at this fashionable resort, where she expected to meet some friends, who were also coming from the South.

But Everet had other plans for himself.

He attended his mother to Newport, saw her comfortably and pleasantly settled there, and then informed her that he was going home to Virginia.

She was amazed at this information, and protested indignantly against his departure.

"Why, I am a total stranger here, Everet," she said, "and it is too bad of you to desert me in this unceremonious fashion."

"But the Ainslies and Worthingtons will be here in a day or two, and then you will have plenty of company," he told her.

"But I want you for an escort. I do not like to be left alone."

"Then I'll try and persuade father to come on, if he is at home when I reach Vue de l'Eau," Everet returned, but without relenting in the least from his purpose.

"But what is your object? It seems inexplicable to me. I supposed, of course, you were going to remain with me," his mother said, searching his face curiously, and with some anxiety as well.

"I have an object, but— —"

"But you do not wish to tell me what it is," she interposed. "Everet, you shall! I suspect it is some love affair."

He colored crimson, and then was enraged at himself for doing so.

"Well, and what if it is?" he demanded, somewhat defiantly.

"Who is there at home in whom you are so deeply interested?"

"No one; I am going to trace out that Annie Dale's history, if you must know. I believe Geoffrey Dale Huntress is in some way connected with her, and," he burst out excitedly, "I am going to know!"

"Nonsense! What good will it do you? Everet," she added, as a sudden thought came to her, "you are in love with that girl, Gladys Huntress, and you are jealous of *him*."

"Well?"

"You have conceived the idea that Annie Dale disappeared because of some wrong that she had done, and that this Geoffrey Huntress may be her child, and not of honorable birth. You believe, if you can prove this, that Miss Huntress will never marry him, and you will then be able to win her."

Mrs. Mapleson had said this looking straight into her son's eyes, and seeming to read his soul like an open book.

"Mother, your penetration is something remarkable. I could almost believe you to be a mind-reader," he replied half guiltily.

Then, after a moment of thought, he continued, excitedly:

"Yes, I may as well confess it—I am madly in love with Gladys Huntress, and have been for more than a year. I have vowed that I will win her if it can be accomplished, even though I know that she loves this fellow, who has been nothing but a stumbling-block in my path since the day I first met him. I am going to Richmond, as you surmise, to trace Annie Dale's history from the time of her disappearance, and I fully believe that I shall discover that this Geoffrey Dale is her son. If he is a child of shame, I do not believe that Gladys Huntress will marry him, and I may yet be happy."

Mrs. Mapleson looked deeply troubled over this confession.

"Everet," she said, gravely, "I am afraid that you are building upon a false foundation, and your hopes will come to naught. If this girl truly loves that young man, and he is worthy of her, she will marry him, or I am very much mistaken in my estimate of her character."

Everet Mapleson's brow darkened.

"I am going home, anyhow," he said, doggedly.

"It will be a wild-goose chase, I warn you," returned his mother.

"I cannot help it. I shall go mad if I sit idly down, and Gladys is lost to me forever," he retorted, with quivering lips.

Mrs. Mapleson seemed very unhappy.

She loved her son as she loved no one else in the world, and she could not bear to think that he had learned to love unwisely, and was risking his future happiness in pursuit of an *ignis fatuus*.

She did not believe he would ever win Gladys Huntress. The young girl's face had haunted her ever since she had seen her with her lover, in the museum at Yale, and she knew, by the way she had looked up into Geoffrey's eyes, that she loved him with her whole soul, and that no dishonor, save that of his own making, would ever alienate her from him.

"Oh, Everet, pray give up this foolish infatuation," she pleaded, laying her hand beseechingly on his arm.

"Foolish infatuation, indeed!" he retorted, with an angry flush. "What can you know about it—you who never knew what it was to love a man as I love this peerless girl?"

Mrs. Mapleson crimsoned to her brow, then grew white as the snowy lace about her neck; her lips quivered painfully, and hot tears rushed to her eyes.

"Are you not somewhat harsh in your judgment of me, Everet? Surely, whatever else you may say of me, you cannot accuse me of lacking in affection for my son," she said, sadly and tremulously.

"Forgive me, mother," he pleaded, conscience-smitten, "but, indeed, it nearly drives me distracted to think that I may not be able to win Gladys; while he, that beggar without even a name, has won her without an effort."

"Has won? Then they are engaged?"

"Yes."

"What folly, Everet? I would respect myself too much to cry after a girl who was already pledged," said Mrs. Mapleson, scornfully, and with flashing eyes.

His face flamed angrily.

"I tell you, you cannot understand!" he cried. "At all events, whether I win or not, I will do my utmost to separate them. I detest him so thoroughly, I will never allow him to triumph where I have failed."

He stole from the room with these words, and that night he left Newport for Vue de l'Eau, where he arrived three days later, and found his father at home keeping bachelors' hall in fine style, with half a dozen servants to attend him.

Colonel Mapleson greeted his son with a heartiness which testified to the deep affection which he bore him, though he expressed some surprise that he should have returned at that season, when he might have been enjoying the cool breezes of Newport, and had his pick of the fashionable belles who thronged the place.

"I have not been at home for a long time, you know," Everet responded, carelessly, "and somehow had a peculiar longing to get back to the old place. Mother rebelled at being left, but I promised to send you on to take my place."

Colonel Mapleson shrugged his shoulders.

He was not particularly fond of gay society, and was never anxious to dance attendance upon his fashionable wife, although he was proud of her beauty, and the admiration and attention she received wherever she went.

"I have not been in Newport for a good many years," he remarked, as he passed his coffee-cup to be filled for the third time; for they were at breakfast.

"Surely you would enjoy the trip then," Everet replied. "Newport has changed greatly; it has become, literally, an island of palaces. You ought to run up there for a little change during mother's stay."

"Well, I'll think about it; but you will be lonely if I run off just as you come home."

"Never mind me; mother needs and wants you, and I have been in so much excitement of late that I shall be glad to be quiet for awhile," the young man remarked, carelessly.

This was such a strange desire on the part of one who had been accustomed to frequent all the gay resorts during the summer holidays, while, too, he was looking far from well or happy, that Colonel Mapleson shot a searching glance into his son's face, and began to suspect that he had been disappointed in some affair of the heart, and had come home to conceal it.

"That is a new freak, isn't it?" he asked, quietly.

"You can call it so if you like; but I have been working pretty hard this last year, and am tired. Besides, I have not had a really good chance to fish, hunt, and ride since I entered Yale, and I mean to improve my opportunity now to my heart's content. By the way," he continued, after a slight pause, "isn't there a place called the 'Hermitage' somewhere in this vicinity, where a relative of ours, who was a sort of recluse, used to live? In some of my roamings I may like to visit it."

"Yes; Robert Dale, a distant cousin, built it and lived there for years. I suppose your mother has been telling you about him; she always invested him with a great deal of romance," his father replied, with a slight smile of amusement. "He was a queer old codger, too, and lived a regular hermit's life for nearly a quarter of a century. The house is still standing, about ten miles from here, in a lonely spot surrounded by a dense growth of pines. He kept one servant—Uncle Jake, he was called—who was housekeeper and steward all in one—cooking, washing, and ironing, taking care of their one horse and cow, and the chickens. He also attended to all the marketing and errands, and his master was rarely seen."

"How did Mr. Dale occupy his time?" Everet inquired.

"With reading and writing. He had a choice library, the only luxury of which he was guilty; and he left piles of manuscripts, some of which were quite valuable, treating chiefly upon geology and ornithology. He had always been a great student of those subjects."

"What became of his library and manuscripts?"

"One of the trustees of Richmond College claimed that they had been promised to that institution, and although there was no writing of any kind found after his death to verify that claim, the books and papers were all made over to the college."

"What of his servant, Uncle Jake?"

"He died only a few months after his master. He lived on at the Hermitage in the same way, refusing to leave the place, and was found dead in his bed, one day, by some sportsmen, who stopped there to fill their canteens with water. He was buried there in the woods, the house was shut up, and has remained so ever since."

"This Robert Dale was a relative of yours, wasn't he, father?"

"Well, yes, I suppose he was, though the relationship is very distant. He was own cousin to my Uncle Jabez, who was my father's half-brother, if you can make that out," said Colonel Mapleson, laughing.

"Humph! There was another family of Dales, who lived somewhere in this region, if I remember right, that is, I remember hearing something about them," Everet remarked, after another pause.

Colonel Mapleson bent a look of questioning surprise on his son.

"It appears to me that you manifest an unusual interest in the Dales this morning," Colonel Mapleson said. "What has aroused it? I did not suppose you were even aware of their existence."

"Mother related something of their history to me. But you have not answered my question."

"Yes, there was another family of Dales; at least, there was a widow, and her daughter, who lived in a cottage not far from Vue de l'Eau, a good many years ago. They came here in a very destitute condition, after Mr. Henry Dale's death, and supported themselves by teaching and sewing."

"And yet this old hermit, Robert Dale, had plenty, and let them toil for the necessities of life," said Everet, indignantly.

"They were his own brother's wife and child, too; but——" began Colonel Mapleson, musingly, while he seemed to be busy with some memory of the past.

"Well, mother told me they were bitter enemies. What was the cause of it?" asked the young man, eagerly.

"Robert and Henry Dale both loved the same woman when they were young men. Henry won her, and Robert hated him ever afterward; that is the secret of his leading such a singular life, I suppose," explained his father.

Everet flushed.

He was thinking of two other young men who loved the same woman, one of whom hated the other for having won, where he had failed.

"What became of the two women?" he asked, wishing to hear his father's version of Annie Dale's disappearance.

"Mrs. Dale died many years ago, and the daughter, I believe, went somewhere to be a governess. But, gracious! Everet, it is nearly ten o'clock!" suddenly interjected Colonel Mapleson, looking at his watch in surprise, "and I promised to meet Major Winterton in town, at a quarter before eleven, to look at his sorrel mare. I am talking of buying her for a saddle horse. I must be off at once. Will you come with me?"

"Thanks, no. I think I will lounge about home for to-day," the young man replied, but feeling somewhat disappointed at having their conversation so abruptly terminated.

Colonel Mapleson bade his son good-morning, and hurried from the room to order his horse, while Everet sat musing upon what he had learned, and wondering what his next step would be to ascertain what Annie Dale's fate had been, after going to Richmond to seek her fortune.

CHAPTER XX
AN INTERESTING DWELLING

Colonel Mapleson received a letter from his wife, a day or two after Everet's return to Vue de l'Eau begging him to come to Newport to join herself and friends.

She wrote that she was an odd one in the party, and although every one was very kind, she felt rather embarrassed to be without an escort, which marred her enjoyment very much; if he could not come she should return home.

Everet urged his father to go, and the colonel, feeling that it would be too bad to have his wife's holiday spoiled, decided that he would gratify her, packed his portmanteau, and started off at once.

Everet accompanied him to the station, and gave a sigh of relief as he watched out of sight the train that bore his father northward, for he felt that he could now pursue the investigations he was contemplating independently, and without fear of criticism.

With his thoughts full of this purpose, he turned his horse's head again toward home, but on his way he made a detour, taking a road which would lead him around by the old mill.

He had not traversed this way since he was a boy, and had almost forgotten how the place looked, though he used to row upon the pond and play about the dilapidated wheel, which once had turned the mill, while he had followed the stream that fed it for miles, in search of the pretty speckled trout that lay hidden in their dark haunts beneath the tangled roots of the overhanging trees.

The day was excessively warm, but the trees with their luxuriant foliage made a perfect arch above his head, and afforded a delightful shade, through which the sunlight only came in checkered gleams, making quaint shadows on the grass-grown path beneath. Hundreds of birds on every hand made the woods ring with their sweet melodies; myriads of flies buzzed lazily about; the beetles hummed among the bushes, and gayly painted butterflies fluttered among the many-hued flowers that grew by the wayside. Now and then a squirrel would spring out, chattering from some gnarled and moss-grown trunk, and dart across the path or along the zigzag Virginia fence on either hand, while occasionally a nut-brown partridge, startled from its covert, darted deeper into the forest, followed by its timid and clamorous mate.

It was a perfect summer day, and remote from the busy haunts of men, with the tender blue of the sky above, and the waves of golden light, that streamed softly on him between the interlacing branches over his head, Everet thoroughly enjoyed his solitary ride, and the lazy, peaceful life of bird and insect all about him.

By and by he heard the rushing of the brook that fed the pond farther on, and presently he came to the shallow ford where, as a boy, he had often played and sailed his miniature boats.

He rode his horse into the middle of the stream, where he gave him the bridle, and let him drink his fill, while he absently watched the ripples and eddies which he made with every swallow.

Then he passed on, and coming up on the opposite bank, he saw not far distant the smooth, glassy pond, and the old mill still standing on its margin.

It was an ancient and dilapidated building, black from age and neglect, but picturesque withal, for it was almost covered with a luxuriant growth of glossy, dark-green woodbine, intermingled with the deadly nightshade, whose bright purple blossoms made spots of rich color here and there among the foliage.

Passing this, he came to the miller's house, which was also empty and falling to decay, while still farther on he came upon a small cottage fairly embowered in vines, and brilliant with great clusters of the scarlet trumpet-honeysuckle and purple wisteria.

This also appeared to be deserted, and there was no sign of life any where about it; still it was not dilapidated like the other buildings which he had passed, and it looked as if, from time to time, some careful hand had trained and pruned the vines, and kept the place from falling to ruin.

It had originally been painted white, with green blinds, and a neat fence surrounded the spacious garden; but time and the elements had robbed it of its once spotless coat, and but for the vines it would have looked naked and forlorn.

Everet rode up to the hitching-post, dismounted and tied his horse to it, unfastened the low gate and walked up the grass-grown path to the broad veranda that ran entirely around the house.

Every window was curtained, and every curtain was down, and the front door was securely fastened.

The young man stood irresolute a moment as he observed this.

"It cannot be that any one lives here," he muttered; "I am quite sure that this must be the Dale cottage, and yet it looks as if it were inhabited."

He walked slowly around the veranda, trying to peer in at the side of the curtains as he passed the windows, but not a glimpse of the interior could he obtain.

There was another door at the back of the house.

He tried this also, but it was evidently bolted on the inside, for he could hear the bolt rattle in its socket.

He shook it gently back and forth a few times, in an impatient way, for he was very anxious to know what was behind all those closely drawn curtains, when, to his surprise, the door suddenly yielded and opened.

The iron had rattled from its place.

Stepping within, he found himself in what appeared to be a kitchen, for there was a cooking stove under the mantel; a dresser filled with dishes stood on the east side, and there was a small table, with one or two chairs opposite.

There was a door on his left.

Crossing the floor, which was covered with dust, and showed the print of every step, he passed into a small bedroom.

A faded carpet lay upon the floor. A bed, covered with a canopy of musquito netting, which once had been blue, but was now faded and discolored with age and dust, stood in one corner.

Pretty lace draperies fell over the window shades, and were looped back with broad satin ribbons, which were also blue. A cherry table and a couple of wicker chairs completed the furnishing of the apartment.

A second door led into another room from this. This stood open, and, passing through, Everet found himself in what must have been the parlor, for it extended the whole width of the house, and had been both richly and tastefully furnished, although, of course, everything was now faded and covered with dust, and had a look of neglect that was forlorn and cheerless.

There were pretty easy-chairs and tempting rockers scattered about; a luxurious sofa in one corner, and a handsome table in the center of the floor, covered with a richly embroidered cloth, evidently the work of a skillful pair of hands, and the young man wondered if Annie Dale had wrought the beautiful thing. There was a small piano between the two front windows, a book-case, filled with books by standard authors, in a corner, and at one end there was a lovely writing-desk, containing numerous drawers and pigeon-holes, and every convenience for writing. A small work-basket, on an elaborate stand, stood beside a pretty rocker by one of the low front windows. It was a dainty affair, lined with crimson satin and garnished with bows of ribbon to match; and Everet Mapleson could imagine just how the graceful figure of the fair girl to whom it had belonged, had looked as she sat beside it, intent upon some delicate bit of sewing or embroidery.

He turned again to the writing-desk, as if he instinctively felt that this was more likely than anything else to contain some information regarding the former occupants of the pretty house.

It was not locked.

He opened it, laying the cover out flat, and then began pulling out the drawers and peering into the various pigeon-holes and compartments.

They were all empty—so far there had not been even a scrap of paper to tell who, in days gone by, had made use of the convenient and elegant affair—and he shut them up again with a sigh of impatience and regret, while a feeling of gloom began to oppress him; there was something very dreary in this house, so completely furnished, yet so silent and deserted.

A sensation of guilt, too, began to intrude uncomfortably upon him. It almost seemed as if the former occupants of this home, although perhaps long since dead and passed beyond all things earthly, were yet spiritually present at that moment, and were viewing, with a reproachful eye, this wanton invasion of the place that had once been sacred to them.

He put up the cover, and was pushing in the little side rests that had held it, when a scrap of paper, wedged in beside one of them, caught his eye.

Something very like an electric shock ran along his nerves at this discovery.

He tried to dislodge the paper, but it was very firmly caught, while the ragged edges did not protrude sufficiently to allow him to grasp it with his fingers.

He drew forth his knife, and, working very carefully, finally succeeded in detaching it from its position.

Upon examining it he found it to be a portion of a letter that had probably been caught some time, when the slide was being pushed in, and the other part had been hastily torn away, doubtless by some one trying to remove it from the crevice.

He smoothed it out with an eager, trembling hand, while his face grew white from the excitement of the moment.

"Can it be possible that I have found a clew at last?" he muttered, in a repressed tone. "I am afraid it will prove but a faint one, but it may be something to begin upon."

The following is what he read from that torn sheet of paper, which had been torn lengthwise in a very irregular manner:

"My dear An

regret that I have
your mother. Of cour
you alone, and that the
for life only must now cea
unprovided for. My poor lit
nothing to comfort you, for I kno
cold words are at such a ti
heart is with you. I sorrow with
sible I would come to you
you in this sad hour. But
favor of you, Annie. We hav
life, and surely you will

"I want you to remain in
your home for the future
past. It is yours without

"You must not, however, stay there
not be safe, and I want you to
panion; some one older tha
be a sort of protector to you.

expense, Annie, for you know
I have a right to care for you
"Inclosed you will find che
your present necessities, and
will make some perman

for you. Write me at once

anxious until I hear from

"Ever y

Such was the fragment which Everet Mapleson found, and he read it over several times, his face growing whiter, graver, and more thoughtful with each perusal.

"At last!" he cried, striking his clenched hand upon the desk before him. "I have felt it coming, and now I will follow it up. I will leave no stone unturned until I get to the bottom of the whole matter. How tenderly affectionate this letter must have been," he continued, with curling lips. "He sorrows with her, and would have come to her 'had it been possible'. He evidently wanted her to remain here after her mother died until he could come. Meantime he advises a companion and protector, and does not wish her to 'mind the expense,' because he has a 'right to care' for her, and incloses a check as substantial evidence of the fact.

"Why didn't she stay here, I wonder?" he pursued, musingly. "Why did she go to Richmond to look for a situation as governess, or was that only a blind to cover her flight—to deceive him. There is a mystery about it. Can it be possible— —"

He sprang to his feet with the sentence unfinished on his lips, and began pacing the floor with a clouded brow, and his mouth drawn into a stern, resolute line.

"She is dead, though, if she was Geoffrey Dale Huntress' mother—and I'm as certain of that as that I am the heir of Vue de l'Eau—for that woman, Margery, said that he could not realize his loss when she died. But who was his father?—why was he named Geoffrey Dale? by whom and why was he abandoned in the streets of New York? There is some dark secret connected with Annie Dale's life and her disappearance from Richmond, and I shall never rest until I know the whole story from beginning to end."

He continued his pacings and mutterings for a long while, growing more and more excited over the matter. His face wore a dark and troubled look as ever and anon he raised that scrap of paper which he still held in his hand and scanned those disjointed lines.

At last he folded it very carefully and put it safely away in his wallet.

"It may come handy some day even if the other half is wanting," he said, an evil smile curling his lips.

Then he set about finishing the exploration of the little cottage.

There was a little hall leading from one end of the parlor and a flight of stairs conducted to the second story.

Ascending these Everet found two comfortably furnished chambers above, one of which had evidently been used for a servant's room.

Retracing his steps he came to the front door, which he found fastened with a spring lock. He then went back to the kitchen, where he securely bolted the door, after which he passed out the front way, the lock springing into place with a sharp snap after him, as if in vigorous protest at his intrusion upon the mysteries which it had guarded for so many years.

Passing out of the little gate, he fastened it after him, then mounted his horse and rode slowly and thoughtfully back to Vue de l'Eau.

CHAPTER XXI
AN OCTOGENARIAN INTERVIEWED

The following morning, bright and early, Everet Mapleson was en route to Richmond.

His object was to visit an old lady who resided there, and who knew all about the Maplesons for the last three generations, for he believed she would be able to throw some light on Annie Dale's history.

She resided in a quiet, old-fashioned street, and her family consisted of one servant, her cat, dog, canary and parrot.

Everet found her in her dining-room, surrounded by her pets, and looking as contented and benignant as if she had been in the midst of as many children.

"Aha!" she exclaimed, looking at his card as Everet followed the servant into the room, "you must be the son of William Mapleson; he married Estelle Everet, and I see they have combined the two names: quite a good idea, young man, and not a badly sounding title, either. And how is my friend, the colonel, your handsome lady mother, too?—at least she was handsome the last time I saw her."

The young man informed the loquacious old lady that both his parents were well, and were at present enjoying the gayeties of a season at Newport.

"And they've left you at home to look after the plantation, eh? That is rather reversing the order of things, isn't it? Most young people think they must have the good times, while the old people stay at home."

"No, I have not been left; it was my own preference to remain," Everet told her. "You know, Miss Southern, I have not been at Vue de l'Eau very much during the last four years, and so it is quite a relief to be at home for a little while."

"Vue de l'Eau is a grand place, Mr. Mapleson, and I think anybody ought to be happy there," the old lady observed; "and I'm sure," she added, with an appreciative glance, "it was very good of you to call upon your father's old friend. I do not see many young people nowadays."

Everet colored slightly at this reference to his visit, and it made it a trifle awkward for him, since he did not like to tell her outright, after that, that a selfish interest alone had brought him there.

He bowed, and murmured something about being partial to elderly people; and then, after chatting a while longer upon indifferent topics, he asked her, casually, if she had known the Dales, with whom the Maplesons were distantly connected.

"Bless your heart! yes; I knew them as well as I knew my own brothers and sisters," replied Miss Southern, her eyes lighting with interest. "I suppose you are more particularly interested in Robert Dale, who was to have had the whole of the Mapleson fortune if your father and mother had not married according to the conditions of Jabez Mapleson's will."

"Well, yes. I am interested in him; but he had a brother named Henry, hadn't he?" Everet asked.

"Yes; Robert and Henry Dale were brothers, and were left orphans when they were about twelve and fourteen years of age. After completing their education, they both started in life with a comfortable fortune, for their father died a rich man. Henry was all business, and went at once to speculating, determined to increase his patrimony; while Robert, who was a great student, settled quietly down to his studies, content with what he had. But, unfortunately, both fell in love with the same girl, Nannie Davenport, and she was about the sweetest girl that I ever knew. She, however, preferred the gay, dashing Henry, and Robert never forgave neither his brother for being his successful rival, nor her for marrying him. It just ruined his life, for he withdrew from all society, made a recluse of himself, in fact, and finally ended his days in a little stone hut not far from your own house, young gentleman."

"Yes, so I have been told," Everet replied, "and I intend to visit the place some day soon. But what became of the other brother?"

"Poor Henry was unfortunate in his speculations; he lost every dollar of his money, and though he struggled along for a few years, he finally died, broken-hearted, leaving his wife and child almost destitute."

"This child was a daughter, I have heard, and there is some romantic story connected with her, I believe," interposed Everet, who could hardly restrain his impatience to learn Annie Dale's history.

"Yes, yes; I will tell you all about it, only you must let me do it in my own way, if you please," returned Miss Southern, who, like many other garrulous old ladies, did not enjoy being interrupted.

"Nannie Davenport," she resumed, "was, as I have told you, a very beautiful girl, and her little daughter inherited all her mother's loveliness, which was of the golden-haired, rose-and-lily type, and much of her father's energy and love of business. Jabez Mapleson, whose mother was a sister of Annie Dale's father, supported them after Henry Dale's death until the girl was fifteen years of age, when she insisted that she and her mother were able to take care of themselves, and they opened a small private school, to which some of the wealthiest families of the section where they lived sent their children. In this way the mother and daughter managed to get a comfortable and independent living. But this proud spirit on their part offended old Jabez Mapleson, who never left them anything at his death, but made that queer will, which you, of course, know all about."

"Yes," Everet returned, with a slight smile.

"It was the most absurd and arbitrary affair that I ever heard of," Miss Southern asserted, indignantly, "to divide his great fortune between those two young people—one the son of a sister, the other a daughter of a brother—giving them a taste of the luxuries and pleasures of life for several years, and then dooming them to poverty again if they refused to marry each other at the end of a given time. It all turned out well enough, though, as it happened, only I always thought it a little queer that your father and mother fought shy of each other until almost the last moment, when they concluded to comply with the terms of the will. They were wonderfully suited to each other; there was no question about that; and they made a handsome, noble couple; but I've always wondered if there was really any true love between them, or whether they had become so accustomed to the life of luxury they were living that they could not give it up, and so married to secure the fortune."

This last seemed to have been uttered in an absent way, as if the old lady were simply musing upon what had always been a mysterious question with her.

Everet colored resentfully at the implied reflection upon the love of his parents for each other; but he saw that she had spoken thoughtlessly, as if hardly aware of his presence, and, respecting the infirmities of age, he concealed his feelings, although he hastened to set her right upon the matter.

"My mother once told me," he said, a trifle coldly, "that her married life has been a very happy one, and that there was no one else whom she would have preferred to marry at the time she was united to my father. There was something rather mysterious about the disposal of Robert Dale's fortune, was there not?" Everet asked, anxious to change the rather delicate subject, and determined to find out all that he could about the Dale family.

"You are right," replied the old lady; "and it is a matter that has never been cleared up to this day, and is never likely to be, according to my way of thinking. He died very suddenly, and that may perhaps account for it, for I believe the old miser hid his money, and it has been rusting itself away all these years and doing nobody any good. He gave quite a sum to some charitable association, I've been told; but that could not have been a tithe of his possessions, for, the way he lived, his income must have accumulated very rapidly."

Everet Mapleson looked interested at this view of the mystery. He had never thought of such an explanation.

"I say it is a shame!" the old lady continued, excitedly, "that his brother's widow and child could not have had the benefit of some of his money. Charity begins at home, and he had no business to give even a blind asylum his thousands and hide away the rest, while they were toiling early and late for the bare necessities of life."

Everet thought of the richly and daintily furnished rooms that he had visited only the previous day, and came to the conclusion that perhaps Miss Southern did not know just how they had lived.

"Did they own the cottage where they resided?" he asked.

"Bless you, no! Old Jabez Mapleson owned that; didn't you know it? And it fell to your father, with the rest of the estate, after he died."

The young man started at this information.

He had never known just the extent of his father's estate.

He had been at the North in different schools during the last eight years, and previous to that he never had felt interested enough in the property to ask any information about the boundaries of Vue de l'Eau.

Colonel Mapleson, in speaking of the Dales, had said they lived not far from that place; but now it appeared that his estate included the little vine-clad cottage, the old mill, and other buildings in that vicinity.

Did the furniture of that little house also belong to him, or had he simply let it remain there after the mysterious disappearance of Annie Dale, thinking, perhaps that some time she might return to the home she had so strangely left? Or had the writer of that letter, a portion of which he had found, had something to do with the rich garnishings of that cozy home?

The mystery seemed to be thickening, rather than being explained.

"I have been at home so little that I have had no opportunity to learn much about the estate," Everet remarked, in reply to Miss Southern's look of astonishment. "But do you know how old this girl was when her mother died?"

"Annie was in her eighteenth year. Poor child! She seemed to be entirely alone in the world then, and came here, to Richmond, to try to earn her living. She made me a call, while looking about for a situation, and I pitied her from the bottom of my heart," said the old lady, with a sigh.

"Where did she make her home while searching for a place?" Everet inquired.

"With her old nurse—a free colored woman, who was very fond of her. Mauma Gregory was her name. I begged her to come to me, and would have been glad of her company, for her mother and I were great friends during our youth; but she feared to hurt her nurse's feelings, while she hoped to obtain a situation in a few days, and thought it best not to change her address."

"Is that old nurse living now?" Everet eagerly asked.

"I am sure I cannot tell. If she is, she must be very aged, and I think it doubtful."

"Where did she live at that time?"

Miss Southern told him the street and number, directing him, as well as she could, how to find it.

"I never saw the girl again," she went on, sadly. "After her call I did not hear anything of her, and, feeling interested to know how she had succeeded, I went one day to see Mauma Gregory, and make inquiries about her. The woman was herself in deep trouble on account of her. She told me that Annie had remained with her about two weeks, and during that time she received two applications to go into families as a governess, and about the same time she also received a letter that appeared to agitate her considerably. A day or two later, she told Mauma Gregory that she was going to a situation out of town—she would not tell where, but said she would write about it as soon as she was settled in it. But she never did—at least, her nurse had not heard anything from her at the end of another year, and in great grief told me she was sure that Miss Annie must be dead, or she would never have treated her so."

"It seems very strange that a young and beautiful girl should drop suddenly out of the world like that, and no one ever learn her fate," Everet remarked, thoughtfully.

"It does indeed," said Miss Southern, "and yet she had no near friends to interest themselves for her; there appeared to be no one, save her nurse and myself, who had any special interest in her, and what could two weak women do, with no tangible facts to work upon? I have a theory of my own about the matter, however, though it may be far from the truth."

"What is it? Tell me, please," the young man urged, eagerly.

The old lady regarded him curiously.

"You seem strangely interested in a generation of the past," she dryly observed.

"I am," he acknowledged, frankly. "I have only very recently learned this story about the Dales, and their connection with my own family. Yesterday, while I was out riding, I came to a small cottage which attracted my attention. I dismounted and went to peer in at one of the windows, but every curtain was down. I finally forced an entrance by a back door, and found the house furnished just as its occupants had left it many years ago. I was convinced from what I had already heard that it was the Dale cottage."

"Was it a small white cottage, standing near an old mill, and not far from the pond? Was there a low ornamental fence around the yard, and a veranda entirely surrounding the house?" Miss Southern asked.

"Yes; you have described it exactly."

"And is it still furnished?"

"I should judge it remains just as they left it."

"That is strange, for it is more than twenty years since Annie Dale left it to come to Richmond," mused Miss Southern. "It was very good of Colonel Mapleson to leave it so," she added; "perhaps he disliked to disturb anything, hoping that the wanderer might some time return."

Everet did not say what he thought, but his face wore a troubled look.

"You were going to tell me what your theory is regarding Miss Dale's disappearance," he remarked.

"I think there was a lover in the case," she replied. "I believe she must have made the acquaintance of some young man, who was enamored of her beauty, and who, having won her heart, enticed her to go away with him to some place, promising to marry her, and who then—betrayed her confidence."

"Then you think she was never married?" said the young man, flushing with excitement to find how like her theory his own was.

"If she had been a lawful wife I think she would have written of the fact to her nurse; for she promised to let Mauma Gregory hear from her when she was settled, and there has never come a word from her."

"She may have written and the letter miscarried," Everet suggested.

"In that case she would have written again, for Mauma could write, and if Annie did not get an answer to her letter she would have sought a reason. Besides, what you have told me confirms my suspicion; if she had been a happy wife, with a home of her own, she surely would have wanted the articles of furniture belonging to her, and which must have been sacred to her because of their associations. No; I firmly believe that the poor girl met with some crushing sorrow and has either died of a broken heart, or is still hiding herself and her misery from all who ever knew her."

Miss Southern wiped a tear of regret from her eyes as she concluded.

Everet Mapleson felt that he could have settled the fate of the unfortunate girl for her by telling what Margery, the flower vender, had told him; but he did not care to say anything about it then, and believing he had learned all that Miss Southern could tell him, he changed the subject, and after a few minutes took his leave, promising to come again to see his father's old friend upon another visit to Richmond.

He went immediately to seek Mauma Gregory, but learned that the faithful old nurse had died nearly two years previous.

He was deeply disappointed in having his way thus hedged about, for he was puzzled to know what step to take next.

He regretted more than ever that he had neglected to question Margery at the time of his encounter with her in New York. Had he done so, he felt as if he might have now held the key to this perplexing riddle.

He turned his face homeward, more miserable and troubled over the matter than he would have cared to own.

CHAPTER XXII
A REMARKABLE DISCOVERY

"I shall hunt up that old hermit's retreat to-day," Everet Mapleson said, as he awoke the next morning. "I want to see for myself just how and where he lived. I begin to find these researches into the past somewhat interesting, if perplexing. I enjoy real romances, but not unfinished ones. I like to be able to complete a story, and have all the characters definitely disposed of. It begins to look, though, as if Miss Annie Dale was a lost heroine, and like the celebrated 'Lost Chord,' never likely to be recovered or accounted for.

"So this queer old character, Robert Dale, was her mother's lover?" he resumed, as he began to dress. "How strangely things get mixed in this world. Why can't people always love the right ones, and escape all this jealousy and disappointment? Nannie Davenport's story is likely to be repeated in this generation. Oh, Gladys, why couldn't you have loved me instead of that mysterious personage who seems to have won your favor? I could have given you an honorable name, wealth, and a proud position in life, while he has literally nothing to offer you. But," his face assuming a stony expression, "I will not give you up even now! I will move mountains to accomplish my purpose, and you shall yet be Gladys Mapleson!"

After breakfasting, the young man ordered his horse to be saddled, and after inquiring of the groom the way to the "Dale Hermitage," as the recluse's home was called, he mounted and rode away toward the forest, in the depths of which Robert Dale had spent so many years of his life.

It was a long ride, though a delightful one, through the spicy pine woods and over the grass-grown cart-path, where only mule teams passed now and then in hauling great logs to market.

It was nearly noon when Everet came in sight of the Hermitage, and he found it not such a rude affair, after all, as he had pictured in his imagination from the descriptions he had heard of it.

He saw that it must have been quite an expensive structure, for it was built mostly of stone, while every bit of the work had been done in the most thorough manner.

It made quite a pretty picture, standing there beneath two huge pine trees, and with the glossy ivy climbing thickly all about its rough walls, hanging in graceful festoons from the overlapping eaves and the mullioned windows.

It was composed of but one story, and a couple of granite steps led up to the one door, which was set in the center of the structure. This was not locked, and entering, Everet found himself in a narrow hall, which divided the building through the middle, and was lighted by a window at the other end.

On each side there were two rooms.

On the right was what appeared to have been the cooking and eating-room, for a great dresser had been built upon one side; a wide fire-place, with andirons and an old-fashioned crane, was opposite the entrance, and a small table, with two chairs, stood in the center of the room.

Back of this there was a smaller apartment, probably the servants' quarters, and on the opposite side of the hall there were two similar rooms.

In the front one there stood a plain but solid desk, and a large arm-chair before it. Near it was an iron safe, but the door was swung partly open, and Everet could see that it was empty, and he thought that it had probably been used as a receptacle for the valuable manuscript of which his father had spoken. A couple of book-cases, reaching from floor to ceiling, had been built into the wall upon two sides of the room, like the dresser in the kitchen. Back of this there was another bedroom, its only furniture consisting of a single bedstead of iron.

The walls were all of rough stone, the crevices being filled in with cement, while all the floors were of red brick, laid in zigzag pattern.

The furniture was of solid oak, but plain to clumsiness, and everything about the place betrayed how utterly indifferent to the comforts and elegancies of life the owner had been, and Everet could not help contrasting it with the luxuries that were stored away in that little cottage which he had visited only a few days previous.

The book-cases alone possessed any claim to elegance. They were also of oak, like the other articles of furniture, but somewhat ornamented, and glazed with heavy plate glass, showing how tenderly the recluse had guarded the books that he had loved so well.

There was a spacious fire-place at one end of the room, in which there were a pair of rude andirons, and a clumsy pair of tongs, with a shovel, stood beside it.

The apartment was light and pleasant, for there were four windows in it—two on the front, which looked toward the east, and two more on the south.

It was just the nook for a student and a recluse, and, in spite of its isolation from all the world, there was a sort of charm about the place, even to the gay and society-loving Everet Mapleson.

At the back of the house there was a small wooden structure, now fast falling to decay, and a yard fenced in, where, evidently, Robert Dale had kept his one horse, cow, and hens, while beyond this there was a patch of cleared ground, which, doubtless, had once been a kitchen garden.

Everet sat down in the great chair before the desk, after completing his round of investigation, and fell to musing upon what he had seen.

He tried to imagine what the appearance of Robert Dale had been— what his temperament and disposition.

Bitter and vindictive he must have been, to have so hated his brother that he allowed him to die in poverty, and his family to struggle on for years afterward for a mere pittance, while he had thousands lying idle and useless; surly and churlish, too, he surmised, to have hidden himself away from all society there in the depths of the forest.

The place seemed invested with an unearthly mystery, and it was not strange, taking into consideration the life its owner had lived, and the death he had died, leaving no trace behind him of the vast possessions that had been his.

"If he did not dispose of his wealth while he lived, and made no will before his death; if there is money concealed anywhere and should ever be found, it would belong to Annie Dale's heirs, for she was his nearest kin," Everet Mapleson murmured, as he leaned both arms on the desk before him, and looked thoughtfully out of one of the south windows.

"If Geoffrey Dale Huntress proves to be her son, as I am more and more inclined to believe, he will be the heir to Robert Dale's missing thousands. This place would be his, anyhow, if the relationship could be proved. I wonder how much land belongs with it! Zounds! I wish I knew what has become of the old chap's money! The more I seek to penetrate this mystery, the more tantalizing it becomes; but I swear that I will never rest until I get to the bottom of it!"

He struck the desk a terrific blow with his fist, in the heat of his excitement, as he uttered this vow; and the weight and force of it jarred it so that something was displaced, and clattered noisily to the floor.

The young man leaned forward to see what he had done, and found that a panel, about twelve inches long and six wide, had fallen from one end of the desk.

"Well, I should think it was about time for this truck to be falling to pieces, solid as it is," he said, as he stooped to pick it up.

Upon examining it, he found that there were some hinges upon one end, and that time and dampness had caused them to rust until they had fallen apart, while upon the opposite end there was a socket for a spring.

"Aha! a secret compartment!" he exclaimed, his face lighting with eagerness.

Bending to inspect the place from which the panel had fallen, he saw that his surmise was correct.

There was a cavity, about four inches deep, in the end of the desk, just under the molding that ran around the top of it, with the other portions of the hinges attached to the top, and a small spring at the bottom.

"Ye gods! there is something in it, too!" he cried, in a startled voice, and his hand actually trembled with nervous excitement as he drew forth a small black morocco case, and a package of papers, tied with red tape, which lay underneath.

The case was an old-fashioned miniature case, and doubtless contained a likeness.

Everet instinctively shrank from opening it for a moment, for he felt as if he were trenching upon some secret almost too sacred to be revealed.

"There must have been a soft spot somewhere in the old fellow's heart, to have kept a thing like this," he muttered, turning it over and over in his hands.

"But, 'to the victor belong the spoils;' I have made this discovery after everybody else has failed, and so I have a right to know what I have found."

He touched the spring and the case flew open, revealing the likeness of a young girl of exquisite beauty.

"Nannie Davenport! I'll wager a ten-dollar note," he ejaculated, in a breathless tone.

The face was a pure oval, crowned with a wealth of hair that was twined in a massive coronet about the small, beautifully-shaped head. The eyes, Everet felt sure, must have been a deep, dark blue, and their expression was lovely beyond description; the nose was small and straight, with delicate nostrils, the mouth full and sweet, with a slight smile just curving the tender lips.

"What a bewitching little fairy she must have been. No wonder Robert Dale buried himself here and ate his heart out with grief and jealousy at losing her. Poor old man! I reckon I know something of your feelings, but I shall never sit tamely down and bear it. I'll conquer or die in the struggle," he concluded, between his set teeth.

Then he grew deadly pale.

"Perhaps he didn't give up either until after she was married," he said, "and then he couldn't help himself. Bah! Gladys Huntress shall never marry Geoffrey Dale!"

He shook himself impatiently, as if these reflections were too painful and disagreeable to dwell upon, closed the miniature with a snap, and turned his attention to the package that he had also found.

He carefully untied the tape that bound it, removed the wrapper, and several certificates, representing a large amount of bank stock, fell out.

Examining them closely, Everet found that they were dated several years previous to his own birth, and all were made out in the name of Annie Dale.

"Good gracious! she was his heiress!" he exclaimed, in amazement. "The old chap had to give in at last. He loved that woman to the death, though he was too proud to show it by helping her while she lived, and so left his money to her child.

"Let me see," he went on; "these are dated just about the time the girl's mother died, I should judge, or a little before; so it is evident he did not mean she should have anything until he was gone. How strange! these papers have lain here all these years and no one the wiser for it, while, of course, the stock has been accumulating all that time. It is remarkable that the directors of the banks represented have not taken measures to find the holder of the certificates. Possibly they have, and failed to do so. I wonder father has not been applied to; but, then, Robert Dale was such a secretive character, he may never have revealed his residence, and it would have been a very easy matter to give orders to let the stock accumulate until called for."

He fell to musing again over his wonderful discovery, until all at once he gave a violent start, and a vivid flush mounted to his brow.

"Blast it!" he muttered, "if my theory is correct all this money belongs to Geoffrey Dale. What in thunder am I going to do about it, anyway?"

CHAPTER XXIII
EVERET MAKES A NEW ACQUAINTANCE

Everet Mapleson spent the next week mostly in hunting and fishing, occupying, however, a portion of one day in looking over the Hermitage again, although without the slightest return for his labor in finding anything new.

At the end of that time he began to grow very restless, and a feeling of depression and loneliness took possession of him.

A few days more of the same kind of life and he declared he could stand it no longer.

Still, he could not make up his mind what he really wanted to do, and was miserable and discontented.

He would have been glad to go to Brooklyn, ascertain where Gladys had gone for the summer, and then follow.

But he reasoned that Geoffrey would be with her this year, and knowing it would be simply maddening to see them together, he felt it was best that he should keep away.

But something he must do to kill time and amuse himself; he had an unaccountable distaste for gay society, and yet longed for some excitement.

"I believe I will take a Western trip," he suddenly said, one morning, after having read in his paper an interesting account of a certain route taken by a party of travelers going to California and the Yosemite Valley.

Acting upon the impulse of the moment, he packed his portmanteau, dashed off a few lines to his mother informing her of his project, and was westward bound before noon.

He reached Chicago the second morning after starting, and took a room at the Palmer House, to rest for a few days while he was deciding what direction he would take from that point.

The following day, after a good night's sleep and a fine breakfast, he strolled into the smoking-room with a morning paper to idle away an hour or so and read the news.

There were several people in the room, but he paid no attention to them more than to cast a sweeping glance around; then, seating himself by a window, he lighted a cigar and was soon buried in the contents of his paper.

He looked through one-half of it, and then laid it aside, taking up the other, when a deep, gruff voice just behind him remarked:

"I say, stranger, could you spare a part of that there paper? I've read yesterday's *Inter-Ocean* about through, and would like something a trifle fresher."

Everet turned to see who was addressing him, and found a man, every bit as rough looking as his voice had sounded, sitting near him.

He was evidently a miner or ranger, but had an honest, open face which at once attracted the young Southerner.

He passed him that portion of his paper which he had read, receiving his brief thanks with a courteous bow, and then resumed his interrupted reading.

He sat there for perhaps an hour longer, until he grew tired of keeping still, and was contemplating going out for a stroll, when the man addressed him again:

"I take it you're a stranger in these parts," he remarked, with a keen, comprehensive glance over the young man.

"Yes, I am from the South," Everet replied, politely.

"Travelin' for pleasure?"

"Y-e-s—partly."

"Any special route laid out?"

"No; I thought I'd like to see something of the far West. I think I shall visit the principal cities on my way, and the chief points of interest, and perhaps take a look at some of the mines; I've always had something of a curiosity regarding mining."

"Have you now?" asked the man with delighted emphasis, his face brightening with pleasure. "Perhaps I can be of use to you in that line then, for I've been a miner all my life and know all the ins and outs about as well as any man living. I'll be glad to give you any points about the business."

"Thank you," Everet returned, looking interested. "What mines have you been connected with?"

"I've been in Nevada, Colorado, New Mexico, and California," answered the man, with an air of pride.

"Indeed, you have surely seen a good deal of that kind of life," remarked Everet, smiling. "When were you in New Mexico? I know a man who once owned stock in some mines there."

"I went to New Mexico in 18—," replied the stranger, in answer to Everet's question, "and did tip-top for ten years, and after that I tried Nevada. What was your friend's name, sir?"

"Mapleson."

"Mapleson?" repeated the miner, reflectively. "I don't think I ever heard the name before, leastwise not in the diggings. What mine did he work?"

"He had some shares in the Moreno mines on the east side of the Rocky Mountains."

"Wall, I wasn't located in the Moreno mines myself. I was rather up among the mountains, though I've been there; but I never met a man by the name of Mapleson; though there's nothing strange about that, where so many people own shares. I worked for a man named Dale——"

"Dale!" interrupted Everet, with a sudden shock.

"Yes, and a fine man he was—handsome chap, too; altogether too much of a fine gentleman to be roughing it as a miner, I used to think."

"Where did he come from?" the young man inquired, trying to repress the eagerness that possessed him.

"I couldn't tell you. I was in Santa Fe one day looking for a job and he was looking for a man, to sort of superintend a claim. We took to each other, struck a bargain on the spot, and I went back to his diggings with him that very night. He couldn't or wouldn't wait till the next day, though I'd been glad to, and afterward I found out the reason—he had the trappiest little wife up there that I ever set eyes on—a sweet, white-livered little thing, with eyes as blue as the sky and hair as bright as the gold we dug out of the bowels of the earth."

The miner was waxing eloquent over the reminiscence.

"'Tisn't often that a man cares to take such a dainty piece of humanity into such a wild, outlandish place as a miner's camp, and goodness knows that it's rare enough for a rough set like us to see a beautiful woman, let alone having her right among us all the time. But there wasn't a soul that wouldn't have risked his life to defend her from any evil or danger, for she always had a kind smile and a gentle word for the worst of us."

Everet Mapleson sat suddenly erect and looked the astonishment he felt.

His face had grown as white as his shirt front, while his companion was speaking, and his heart was beating with great heavy throbs that almost suffocated him; for a wild suspicion had suddenly taken possession of him.

"You say the man's name was Dale?" he asked.

"Yes, William Dale——or Captain Dale, as we all called him. You see he was only newly married, and had just brought the little woman there, and that was the reason he didn't like to leave her alone over night in that wild region," the miner explained, beginning to notice his listener's strange manner.

"You are sure that they were married—that she was really his wife?" said Everet, in an excited tone.

The miner looked the surprise he felt at such a question.

"Why, yes; at least everybody supposed she was his wife; he said she was; while they seemed to set the world by each other, and the poor captain grieved like one bereft of his reason when she died."

"Died?" gasped his listener.

"Yes, poor little lady! she was in the camp just one blessed year, then the little shaver came, and the mother never got up again."

"There was a child!" ejaculated Everet Mapleson, losing his self-possession more and more.

"Strange," said the man, with a curious stare, "you seem wonderfully moved over my story—did you ever hear of these people before?"

"I'll tell you by and by. But go on—tell me about this child," Everet eagerly urged.

"Well, there was a fine boy," continued the miner, "and he was the pride of the camp; you see it was a rare thing for a set of rough miners to have a baby among us, and every man Jack of us took as much interest in him as if he'd been our very own; but it cast a gloom over the whole lot when it came to be known that the gentle little mother had to go. I never saw a fellow so upset as Dale was over it; he went about with a face as white as a sheet, and all bowed down like an old man. Not one of us dared to speak to him he looked so awful, and we all kept out of his way as much as we could. It came at last—the final blow; the captain's lovely wife—pretty Annie Dale—was dead, and the only baby in the place was motherless.

"Annie Dale!" breathed Everet Mapleson, actually growing dizzy as he caught the name.

"Yes, that was her name," the man answered, with a sigh, "and I shall never forget the day they buried her. They had a parson over from Fort Union, a grave-spoken but pleasant-faced man, and he almost took us right into heaven where that sweet woman had gone, with the beautiful, solemn words he spoke. The coffin was solid rosewood, and came from Santa Fe, with another great box of sweet smelling flowers. The captain never showed himself that day; he just sat alone by the coffin in the front room of his house and never made a sound until the men went in to take it away, when he gave a groan, that I shall never forget as long as I live, and fell on his face to the floor where he was picked up in a dead faint. Poor fellow! he was worn-out with watching, to say nothing of his grief. I tell you that was a sorry day for the camp, for there wasn't more'n a half-dozen women in the place, and most of them were none of the best; though after the captain's wife came there they seemed to take more pride in being kind of decent. Well, she was buried under a great cypress tree where she loved to sit on warm days, and the captain had it all fenced off, after a while, and put a white stone up by the grave with just her first name on it, and the miners rough as they were, never let the flowers wither on that grave as long as I staid there. I don't know how it was afterward, for it's more than twenty years since the poor thing died."

The man had to stop and use his handkerchief vigorously just here, and Everet could see that he was deeply moved over the memory of that sad time.

"What became of the child?" the young man asked, after a moment.

"Well, when the Dales first went there to live, they hired a girl to serve Mrs. Dale, for she was delicate, and the captain wouldn't permit her to do any work, and she—the girl had the care of the boy after the mother died. But they didn't stay long in the place, only about a month. The captain didn't seem to have any heart for anything; appeared wretched and half crazed, and finally, when the girl was married to a man named Jack Henly, who was going to California, to be a farmer, the cottage was shut up, its furniture sold, and they all went away together."

"What was this girl's name?" Everet demanded.

"Margery something. I can't remember her other name just now," said the miner.

Even though Everet Mapleson had been expecting just this reply it gave him a shock when he heard that name pronounced.

He had, at last, he believed, traced Geoffrey Huntress' birth! It was proved that Annie Dale was his mother. When she left Richmond she had doubtless gone to the man whom she loved, and who had enticed her, with smooth words and fair promises, to go with him to that wild mining region where they had lived together as husband and wife.

That they were not really so, Everet felt quite sure, else the man would never have taken the girl's name, instead of giving her his own.

"What did they name the child?" he asked.

The miner looked perplexed.

"I'll be dashed if I can think," he said, after a moment's reflection, as he scratched his head. "'Twas a sort of queer, high sounding name—Jeff—Gof—or something after that sort with a tail to it."

Everet had heard enough to confirm all his suspicions, but he did not enlighten his companion, as to the rest of the name; he did not care to seem to know too much.

"Did Captain Dale ever return to his mine after that," he inquired.

"Not while I was there; an agent came once or twice, to act for him, and finally bought him out. I've never seen him since, though I've often wondered what became of the little motherless chap that we were all so fond of."

The young Southerner sat with bowed head and thoughtful mien for several moments, then taking a case from his pocket, he opened it, and held it before the miner.

"Did Annie Dale look anything like this?" he asked.

The man gave his companion a look of questioning surprise as he took the picture, and turning it toward the light, examined it critically for a moment.

"It does, and it doesn't," he said, at last. "It ain't so delicate like as she was; the eyes are a little smaller, and the face fuller and rounder. I should say this might be a sister or some relation, but it ain't the captain's wife. I say, youngster," he added, looking Everet full in the eye; "it's mighty queer that you should have this picture, and it strikes me that I've been firing arrows at a mark I'd no notion of hitting. Who be you, anyway?"

"My name is Mapleson," Everet returned, "and the name of the young lady, whose picture I have shown you, was Miss Nannie Davenport. She married a man by the name of Dale, a distant connection of my father's family. They had one child, a daughter, whom they named Annie. After her parents' death, she suddenly left the place where she had lived, and no one ever heard anything of her afterward, and her disappearance was a matter of mystery to all who had ever known her."

"You don't say! Well, I am beat!" exclaimed the miner, in astonishment. "Things do come about queer enough sometimes, and I reckon there ain't much doubt that the woman I've been telling you of was the daughter of the one in the picture. But—you say her *own* name was Annie *Dale*?" he concluded, looking puzzled.

"Yes."

"That's queer, too. Then who was *Captain* Dale?"

"I do not know; possibly some relative," Everet said, not caring to destroy the man's romance by arousing his suspicions that there had been a story of shame enacted in that mountain camp.

Further conversation developed the facts that the stranger was in comfortable circumstances, the owner of two or three mining claims in New Mexico, and was on his way there to try to dispose of them.

Everet Mapleson manifested a great interest in New Mexico, and intimated his desire to accompany his new acquaintance thither.

The stranger gladly assented, and said: "I can give you some points about the country, and the mining business, too, that you couldn't find out for yourself."

"Thank you; but if we are to be traveling companions, it would perhaps be pleasanter for both of us if we could know each other's name. Mine is Everet Mapleson, and I am from Richmond, Virginia," and the young Southerner smiled as he thus introduced himself.

"Well, I'm beat! Here I've been talking to you for more'n an hour and never told you who I be!" said the miner, looking blank. "There ain't nothing high-sounding about my name, but Bob Whittaker is an honest one, and I'm not ashamed of it; and I'm from most anywhere, just as it happens. I guess now we can hitch hosses and go along without any more ceremony."

CHAPTER XXIV
EVERET MAKES A STARTLING DISCOVERY

It was settled that Everet Mapleson was to accompany Bob Whittaker, the miner, to the mines of New Mexico, and two days after the conversation related in the previous chapter found them on their way thither.

Arriving at their destination, about a week later, they found that what had been a small camp in those early days, when Bob Whittaker had worked for Captain Dale, was now a thriving village, or "city," as the place was designated in that region, and the miner could hardly realize that it was the same place which had once been so familiar to him.

Everet looked about the town with a great deal of interest, after which he visited the tiny plot where, overshadowed by a venerable cypress tree, all that remained of beautiful Annie Dale rested.

There was no sign of any grave there now; every trace of it had disappeared. There was nothing save a simple head-stone of pure Italian marble, with the single name "Annie" inscribed upon it, standing in the center of the inclosure, to mark the spot where she had been laid.

Two or three varieties of ivy had been planted by some loving hand beside the fence which surrounded it, and a luxuriant growth now almost concealed it from view, and embowered the little plot of ground in a frame-work of living green.

The small house, where the beautiful girl had lived during that short, happy year, and where her child was born—where, as Everet Mapleson firmly believed, Geoffrey Dale Huntress was born—stood near this spot, and was still empty.

No one had ever lived in it since the poor young mother died, one of the older inhabitants of the village told him. It was believed that the same gentleman owned it still, though he had not been seen there for years, and would not allow any one else to occupy it. It seemed as if he deemed the place too sacred to be invaded by strangers, and so had preferred to sacrifice it to desolation and decay.

Everet passed through the small yard, now thickly overgrown with vines and brambles, to the tiny porch, and looked in through the side-lights of the front door.

The doors on each side of the small hall were all open, and the place was bare and forlorn in the extreme, and in strange and gloomy contrast with that luxurious little nest near the old mill at home, that had been Annie Dale's former home.

He went around the house, peeping in at each window; but there was nothing to be seen save bare floors, and walls from which the rich paper, that had once adorned them, was falling away, while every nook and corner was infested with dust and cobwebs.

He came back again, after a time, to the front porch, where he sat down upon one of the steps, wondering where he should turn next to pick up the thread which seemed to have suddenly broken and vanished from sight again here.

He sat there a long time pondering the mystery—who was the man who had called himself William Dale?—whither had he gone after leaving that place, and which way should he—Everet Mapleson—turn now to hunt him down?

But he could arrive at no definite conclusion; there was only one thing that he could think of to do to satisfy himself regarding the truth of a suspicion that haunted him continually, and that he shrank from with a feeling that was akin to horror; while it might result in nothing save making a fool of himself and becoming an object of ridicule and scorn.

He arose at last, with a sigh of weariness and discouragement to return to the public house where he was staying and to seek his new friend, Bob Whittaker.

But, owing to the cramped position in which he had been sitting, one of his feet had "gone to sleep," and he found he could not walk a step.

He stamped vigorously, and impatiently, too, for the intense prickling sensation with which circulation began to reassert itself irritated him, when, without the slightest warning, the step on which he was standing gave way and he was unceremoniously precipitated into the rank grass and among the brambles which grew all about it.

He picked himself up, after giving vent to a somewhat unrefined expression of annoyance, rescued his hat, which had lodged in a prickly cactus nearby, and then turned to see how much damage he had done.

The step was a complete wreck, the top board being split entirely across, while the rotten supports beneath were wholly demolished, and lay in a crumbled heap on the ground.

He gave the mass a kick with his foot, scattering it right and left, when suddenly a gleam of light from something among it, flashed into his eye.

He stooped to see what had caused it, when, to his intense surprise, he found a small ring, the gold all blackened and tarnished, but with a beautiful diamond, clear and brilliant as a drop of dew in the sunlight, set in its delicate crown.

"Well, I imagine I have found a treasure now," Everet exclaimed, eagerly, as he turned it over and over to examine it more closely.

He saw that there was some inscription upon its inner surface, but it was so blackened with age and so filled with dirt that he could not make it out.

"Aha!" he cried, exultantly, "I'll wager almost anything that I have at last found the end of the broken thread that will unravel the mystery."

He sat down again upon the upper step of the porch, deliberately drew a cigar from his pocket, lighted it, and began to smoke.

The first ashes that he detached from it he carefully saved upon a piece of wood, and, using his handkerchief, began to polish the discolored ring with them.

It was not long before his efforts were rewarded—the inner surface of the ring began to take on its original color and the inscription to stand out more plainly.

"It is evidently an engagement-ring with only some initials and a date engraven upon it," the young man murmured, as he held it up to inspect it more closely.

The next instant he lifted his head with an air of triumph, though his face was as white as a sheet.

"It is the key to the whole mystery," he said. "This will take me straight to the heart of the secret."

While Everet Mapleson was following the trail of the mystery that possessed such a power of fascination over him, August Huntress and his family were luxuriating at Saratoga.

Mr. Huntress had obstinately insisted that Geoffrey should have a long holiday after the close application of the last three years, although the young man himself would have much preferred, and was very eager to begin the real business of his life at once.

"It is time that I was at work for myself," he had pleaded, "and if you will only use your influence, Uncle August, to help me into some good position, my conscience would be easier."

"Your conscience needn't trouble you, and I won't hear a word about business for three months to come," replied his friend, decisively. "You've given yourself no rest during all your college course, and now, my boy, I'm determined that we shall all have a jolly good time together to celebrate your own and Gladys' release from school-life."

So, by the middle of July, they were settled for the summer in pleasant rooms at the Grand Union, and were as happy and united a party as ever visited that resort of gayety and fashion.

Gladys was very much admired from the first; her beauty and charming manners winning her legions of friends.

But none of them were to be compared to Geoffrey, and the lovers managed to be much by themselves, in spite of the fact that "that delightful Miss Huntress was such a favorite with everybody."

One morning they were leisurely strolling through one of the shady avenues of Congress Park, when they saw a distinguished-looking gentleman advancing toward them.

He did not appear to notice them, however, until he was almost upon them, when, suddenly looking up, he gave a violent start of surprise; then he advanced, with an eager smile and extended hand, exclaiming:

"Why, Everet Mapleson! Where on earth did you drop from? I should as soon have thought of seeing the Emperor of Russia as yourself this morning."

Geoffrey lifted his hat and bowed politely to the speaker, as he replied:

"You have made a slight mistake, sir; I am not Everet Mapleson, although this is not the first time that I have been taken for him."

"Nonsense; don't try to play such a joke on me—I've known you too many years for you to palm yourself off as any one else," returned the gentleman, laughingly, while he shot an amused glance at the young man's companion, as if he suspected that she was the cause of his wishing to remain incog.

"I assure you, sir, I am speaking the truth. I am not Everet Mapleson," Geoffrey reiterated.

The stranger's face grew suddenly overcast.

"Then who in thunder are you?" he demanded, in sharp, excited accents.

"My name is Geoffrey Dale Huntress, at your service, sir," Geoffrey responded, courteously, although he had flushed hotly at the curt question.

"Geoffrey Dale! Good heavens!" cried the man, shrinking back as if he had been dealt a violent blow, and growing deathly pale.

Geoffrey himself turned white at this.

He was ever on the alert to gain some knowledge of his parentage, and this man's strange manner made him think that perhaps he might know something of his early history.

"Yes, sir; I perceive that the name affects you strangely. Did you ever hear it before?" he asked, earnestly, searching the stranger's face.

"Ah—years ago—a friend—excuse me—I am very much overcome," the man murmured, incoherently, as he staggered to a rustic bench near by, where, sinking upon it and bowing his head upon his hands, he groaned aloud.

Geoffrey stood transfixed, his face plainly betraying anxiety, dread, and perplexity, while he was inwardly so excited over this strange meeting that Gladys, as she leaned upon his arm, could feel him trembling in every limb.

"Will you explain yourself, sir?" Geoffrey said at length, and feeling that the silence and mystery were becoming intolerable. "Do you know aught of me—of any person named Dale?"

The gentleman shivered, as if the question had jarred upon some sensitive chord.

"Yes," he answered, after a moment of hesitation, while he lifted a haggard face to his questioner; "years ago I had a friend by that name; but—but——"

"Will you relate the history of that friend to me?" Geoffrey asked, with white lips, and speaking with an effort.

Something seemed to tell him that he was standing on the very threshold of the revelation which he had longed for so many years.

Again the stranger shrank as if he had been smitten.

"Why do you ask me that?" be huskily demanded.

"Because," Geoffrey returned, with grave earnestness, "there is a mystery connected with my own life—because, when I was a child I was abandoned in the most cruel manner, and but for the goodness of the man who found me an outcast in the streets of New York— —"

"New York! How came you there?" interrupted his listener, amazed.

"That is more than I can tell you, sir. This gentleman found me in a state of imbecility, took me to his home, cared for me until I was restored to my right mind, and then adopted and educated me as his own son; but for him I should still have been an imbecile, and more pitiable than the lowest paupers that wander about the streets of that city."

"What! what is this that you are telling me? An imbecile! I cannot understand," cried the man, looking bewildered.

"I do not know how I came to be in such a state," Geoffrey continued; "the physicians said it was caused by some injury while I was very young, so my life before that time has remained a mystery to myself and those who have befriended me. If you can throw any light upon it, sir, I entreat you to do so."

The man quickly arose from his seat at this appeal, but staggered like a person who had been drinking deeply, and seemed like one who had sustained a terrible mental shock.

"I cannot tell you anything now," he said, putting his hand to his head. "I shall have to ask you to excuse me. I cannot think; I must have time to recover myself."

"I do not understand your excessive emotion, sir. I do not understand your desire to avoid explaining your very strange words and manner," Geoffrey interposed, looking both pained and anxious; "but I am terribly in earnest about this matter, and if you know anything about my family or antecedents, I beg that you will not keep me in suspense."

"Some other time I will talk with you again," murmured the stranger, turning aside, and striving to keep his eyes averted.

"When? name any place and hour, and I will come to you," said Geoffrey, eagerly.

The man thought a moment, then said:

"Come to me at five o'clock this afternoon, at the 'United States,' and inquire for room forty-five."

He turned abruptly away, and would have passed on, but Geoffrey detained him.

"What is your name, please?" he asked.

"That you shall know when we meet again," was the evasive reply.

"Tell me one thing," pleaded the young man, greatly agitated; "did this—friend of yours, have a son bearing the name that I have given you?"

A groan of pain escaped the man.

"Come to me at five this afternoon. I am not fit to talk more with you now," was the tremulous reply, and the man moved weakly away, seeming more like a person eighty years of age than like the upright, distinguished-looking individual of fifty, whom the young couple had met a few moments before.

CHAPTER XXV
GEOFFREY PICKS UP A THREAD

"Who can he be? How strangely he acts," Gladys said, as she gazed after the retreating form. "One would almost believe he has some personal connection with your history, he was so agitated on learning your name."

"I am sure that he has, Gladys; I believe that man is my father!" Geoffrey replied, with quivering lips.

"Oh, Geoff!"

"I do, dear; and I fear, too, that there is some miserable secret connected with my early life."

"Do not think that," the beautiful girl pleaded; "I will not believe it without the strongest proof; and even if it should be so, the fact cannot harm you."

"Gladys," Geoffrey said, in a stern, repressed tone, while his face was dreadful to look upon in its ghastliness, "if there is sin connected with my life—if I find that my birthright is one of shame—I can never ask you to share it."

Gladys clasped both hands closely about her lover's arm.

"Geoffrey, surely you will not ruin both our lives by any such rash decision?" she pleaded, lifting her troubled face to his. "It is you whom I love, not an illustrious pedigree. As far as my future with you is concerned, I care not who or what your parents may have been. Do not let anything of that nature come between us; it is false pride, and unworthy of you."

The young man regarded her with exceeding tenderness, but he was still greatly disturbed by his recent interview with the stranger, and could not readily regain his composure.

He believed that he was on the verge of an important discovery, and he was at the same time impressed that it would only bring him shame and sorrow.

"Gladys, would you not shrink from marrying a man whose mother had never been—a wife?" he asked, a hot flush mounting to his brow.

"I could never shrink from you, Geoffrey, and I would not accept the proudest position in the land in exchange for your love. I might deeply regret such a circumstance, on your account; but, dear, my affection for you is far too strong to be weakened by a mere accident of birth. Let us put all such dismal thoughts away from our minds. I will not believe that dishonor has ever touched you or yours," Gladys concluded, looking up with a fond smile.

"Dear little comforter," murmured the young man, trying to return it, though it was but the ghost of one.

"Do not go near that man, Geoff," Gladys continued. "Let us be happy as we are, and not trouble ourselves about the past."

The poor fellow sighed, as if it would be a great relief to let it go, to consign it to oblivion, but the anxious look did not leave his face.

"I cannot, Gladys," he said, with pale, compressed lips. "I shall never rest until all the dark mystery of my past life is explained. I must keep my appointment with that man this afternoon, and I will not leave him until I have wrung from him every scrap of information that he may possess regarding me and mine, and if— —"

"Geoff, what?" cried the young girl, breathlessly, alarmed by his unusual tone, and the look upon his face.

"If I find that that man is my father, and that he wronged my mother, he shall have reason to regret both those facts for the remainder of his life," was the stern reply.

"Geoffrey, surely you will do nothing to compromise yourself?" Gladys pleaded, anxiously.

"No, dear, for your sake as well as my own, I will do nothing to make myself disagreeably conspicuous. But he will not forget if I find my suspicions are true. You will say nothing to Uncle August or Aunt Alice regarding this encounter, please, until after I have seen him."

"No, certainly not, if you prefer I should not tell them," Gladys readily promised.

They turned to retrace their way to the hotel, both too much disturbed by the occurrence of the morning and by forebodings regarding the afternoon's appointment, to care to prolong their stroll.

They parted at the ladies entrance, Gladys going up stairs to her mother's apartments, where she tried to busy herself with some fancy work until lunch time, although her heart was in a continual flutter of apprehension and miserable suspense.

Geoffrey shut himself up in his own room, alone, for a season, but was too wretched to remain there inactive, and soon went out again.

When the family went down to luncheon he was still absent, and his seat vacant.

This was such an unprecedented occurrence that Mr. Huntress left the table to ascertain the reason.

He soon returned with the information that Geoffrey had gone out, but had left word with the clerk, in case inquiries should be made for him, that he might not be back for several hours.

Mrs. Huntress glanced at Gladys as her husband made this report, but she gave no sign of either surprise or disappointment. She had noticed an unusual reserve and quietness about her, ever since her return from her walk, and a suspicion crossed her mind that perhaps there might be some misunderstanding or lover's quarrel, that had caused this unwonted break in the family party.

She kept her suspicions to herself, however, resolving to await further developments.

It was after six o'clock when Geoffrey returned. Gladys was watching for him, at one end of the veranda, and sprang from the chair to go to meet him, as he came up the steps and then stopped short as she caught sight of his face.

It was as colorless as marble, and there was a look in his eye that actually made her tremble.

He did not speak, or even smile, as he came up to her, but quietly drew her hand through his arm, led her within the house, and to a small reception-room, carefully shutting the door behind them.

Then he turned again and faced her.

"Gladys," he said, in a hollow, unnatural tone, "it is as I feared——"

"Geoffrey!" she cried, in a shocked voice, all her own bright color fading.

"The worst is true," he concluded, not heeding her interruption.

"Have you seen him?—did he tell you so?" she asked.

"No, I have not seen him."

"Then how do you know?"

"He has fled."

"Fled?"

"Yes. I went to the 'United States' at five this afternoon. I called a servant to show me the way to room number forty-five, and was told that the gentleman who had occupied it left at twelve to-day."

"How very strange!" said Gladys, astonished.

"No, it is not strange," Geoffrey returned, bitterly; "the man is a miserable coward, and he dare not meet me; his history is doubtless one of shame and wrong—he knew that I would force it from him, and he fears to remain and confess it. But, Gladys, I shall find him yet—some day I will compel him to face me and own the truth. I will hunt him down! he shall not escape me!"

"Oh, Geoffrey, pray do not let it trouble you so—there may have been some other reason for his going," said the young girl, laying her hand sympathetically on his arm.

"No—I tell you he was afraid to meet me, and his guilt is evident in his flight; he never would have run away like this, if there had been no guilty secret in his life which he was anxious to conceal from me."

"Did you learn his name?" Gladys inquired.

A deep flush arose to Geoffrey's brow, and he gave a start of annoyance.

"No," he said, "I was so wretched and angry that I never thought to ask his name. When the servant told me he was gone, I turned on my heel and walked out of the house and have been walking ever since, trying to recover my composure."

"That was an oversight, dear," said his betrothed, gently; "you should have secured his name and address."

"You are right; I will go back immediately and ascertain it."

"Oh, Geoffrey, perhaps it will be better for you to leave it all just here," the fair girl urged. "'Where ignorance is bliss'—you know the rest."

"But I know too much already; I can never rest until I sift this matter to the very bottom. Could you, darling? If you were not Uncle August's own child, and knew there was some mystery connected with your birth, would you be satisfied until you knew the truth?"

"No, Geoff, I don't believe I should," Gladys replied, thoughtfully, "and—I know that such a discovery would make me very unhappy," she concluded, with starting tears.

Geoffrey stooped and kissed her fondly, then turned abruptly and left the room.

The young girl sighed wearily as she slowly followed him.

"I am afraid there is trouble in store for him, for my heart is heavy with forebodings," she murmured.

Half an hour later, Geoffrey returned, and there was now a savage glitter in his eyes, although his face was pale and full of pain.

He found Gladys watching for him as before.

He went up behind her chair, leaned down, and whispered in her ear:

"The man's name is—William Dale, and he registered from Fort Union, New Mexico."

Gladys looked around, a startled expression on her face.

"William Dale!" she repeated; "then he must be——"

"My father, and—a parent to be proud of, surely," the young man interposed, with exceeding bitterness. "Oh, Gladys!" he continued, in an agonized whisper, "I feel as if I should go mad—I can bear anything better than dishonor."

Gladys turned and laid her soft cheek for an instant against the hand that was resting on the back of her chair.

The involuntary and sympathetic caress comforted him more than any words could have done, for it seemed to say, no matter what lay away back among those early years before she knew him, nothing could change her love for him, and he would always be the same to her.

"I wish I could know the story of my mother's life," Geoffrey continued, with a sigh, while a moisture gathered in his eyes. "Poor woman! I am afraid that her fate must have been a sorrowful one. Darling, I believe I shall go to New Mexico and see what I can learn about this man who registered from Fort Union."

"Oh, Geoff, I fear it will only be chasing a 'will-o'-the-whisp!'" Gladys said, looking distressed.

"I cannot help it. I must go. I shall be wretched and good for nothing until I learn all there is to know. I am going now to tell Uncle August about it."

He sought Mr. Huntress, and laid the whole matter before him, making known his desire, too, to go to New Mexico to see if he could gain any further clew.

Mr. Huntress sympathized heartily with him, and favored the project. He could well understand how restless and miserable Geoffrey would be until he had used every possible means to discover his parentage.

So he did all that he could to hasten and facilitate his departure, and even offered to accompany him; but Geoffrey frankly told him that he preferred to go alone.

He felt that if he must learn that any stigma rested on his birth, he could not bear to have any one, not even his kind friend, witness the struggle that must come with the knowledge. He could fight it best by himself.

He left the next day but one, but owing to delays both by rail and coach, he did not reach Fort Union until ten days later.

He made inquiries here for a man named William Dale, but for several days could gain no intelligence whatever regarding such a person.

At last he fell in with an old miner, by the merest accident, who had known a man by that name many years previous, and who directed him to that mining village already described.

Thither Geoffrey hastened at once, reaching it one evening just at sundown, and only a week after Everet Mapleson's visit to the same place.

Here he learned something of Annie Dale's story, for Everet's inquiries and interest in the same person had revived memories regarding that sad romance, and it had become a common theme since.

Annie Dale's grave, and the house where she had lived, were pointed out to Geoffrey, and he went by himself to visit them.

He came to the dismantled home first, and walked round and round it, as Everet Mapleson had done, peering in through the windows, noting the position of the rooms, and wondering if he should ever know if this had really been the home of his mother, and under what circumstances she had lived there; whether she had been a loved and honored wife, or whether her early death had been caused by some secret sorrow that had broken her heart.

He knew there had been another visitor there before him—although he had been told nothing regarding the stranger's visit of the week previous—for the broken step and the trampled grass gave ample evidence of that fact.

He wondered if it could have been the man who had so suddenly fled from Saratoga after meeting him, who had, perhaps, been driven there by sorrow and remorse to look once more upon the ruin he had wrought.

He grew more and more fearful that the story of his birth must be a sorrowful one, for it was evident that no one bearing the name of William Dale had ever resided in Fort Union.

He would not have been able to trace the man beyond that point at all, but for his accidental meeting with the old miner, who had worked in the mines where he had owned an interest, and thus been able to direct him to this remote village.

If William Dale had never lived at Fort Union, why had he registered from that place? If he was now living at Fort Union, and his name was not William Dale, why had he used that address again after the lapse of so many years?

There was something very mysterious about the whole matter, and it began to seem like a hopeless puzzle to the young man.

He finally left the house and bent his steps toward that small inclosure where, in the gathering dusk, he could just see the pure white head-stone gleaming among the vines that grew all around it.

He entered the place and approached the spot, noting that here, too, there were signs of a recent visitor, and knelt down to read the name that had been inscribed upon the spotless marble.

"Annie," he read, and the single name sent a thrill through every fiber of his being.

Here, too, there seemed evidence that there was some sad tale of wrong and suffering connected with the life of the girl who had been buried there, for had she been a wife and with nothing to conceal, would not a fond husband have wished the name that he had given her also chiseled there?

"Oh, if I could only know!" Geoffrey groaned within himself, as he bowed his head upon the stone, feeling completely baffled, and as if all trace must end here. "Was this woman my mother? She was something to William Dale, and William Dale is something to me, or he would never have betrayed so much emotion upon meeting me, and then fled from me. Was she his lawful wife? Am I her child, and had I honorable birth?

"Good heavens!" he added, aloud, "there must be some way to solve these questions. Oh, if the Fates would but guide me to some one who could tell me how to unravel this mystery!"

"Ahem! Well, youngster, I shouldn't wonder if I was yer man. What'll ye give to hear a prettier love-story than ever was writ?"

CHAPTER XXVI
A THRILLING STORY

Geoffrey started to his feet as if electrified, as these unexpected words fell upon his ears, and found himself face to face with a man of perhaps fifty years, his face seamed and browned by hardships and exposure, rough in appearance, uncouth in dress, and with an anxious, alert air about him, which conveyed the impression that he feared being identified and apprehended for some reason or other.

"Who are you?" Geoffrey sternly demanded, for he knew that country was not the safest place in the world, and it flashed upon his mind that the man might be a robber, and had followed him there with some evil intent.

"I'm all right. I've no wish to harm ye, sir," was the reassuring response, as the new-comer appeared to read his thought, "and I guess it don't matter much who I be, provided I can tell ye what ye seem to want to know about this here grave."

"No," replied Geoffrey, his suspicions instantly vanishing. "If you can give me the history of the poor lady who lies here, and tell me where I can find the man who brought her here, I'll pay you well, and ask no further questions about yourself. But how came you to follow me to this place?"

"I didn't foller ye. I was sittin' yonder, behind that clump of spruce, when ye hove in sight. I didn't mean to show up at all, but when I saw ye so eager by this here tombstone, I was kind o' curious to know what yer game was, and crept on ye unawares. But, I say, youngster," the man added, suddenly taking a step forward, and peering eagerly into Geoffrey's face, "who are you?"

The rough fellow had actually grown pale, and his breath came in gasps through his tightly locked teeth.

"I am an Eastern man," answered Geoffrey, evasively.

"Is—is your name Geoffrey?" the man demanded, in a hoarse whisper.

"Yes."

"Ha! Geoffrey Dale?"

"Yes."

"Great Christopher! I—I thought so. Something about yer sent a chill over me the minute I laid eyes on ye," said the man, trembling and terribly agitated. "Boy—boy," he continued, in a tone of fear, "how on earth came ye and me to turn up together here, of all places in the world?"

Geoffrey was amazed at his words.

Evidently the man knew something about him, and with that knowledge there was connected some incident that caused him personal fear.

Instantly the young man's mind reverted to the condition in which Mr. Huntress had first found him—a poor abandoned imbecile. Had this rough creature known of that, or had anything to do with it?

His next words enlightened him somewhat.

"You're all right, too, in the upper story, and ye can talk," he muttered. "Where ye been all these years?"

"All these years, How many years?" queried Geoffrey, with a rapidly beating heart.

"It's eight years ago, last spring, since I set eyes on ye, and little thought I should ever see you again; never with that look on yer face. Where ye been, I say?"

"Eight years ago, last spring," began Geoffrey, gravely, while he closely watched every expression on his companion's countenance, "I was one day wandering, a poor, demented boy, in the streets of New York city. My strange appearance and actions attracted a mob of urchins, who began to make sport of me. They were in the midst of their cruelty when a carriage stopped near me, and a beautiful little girl beckoned to me, at the same time opening the door of the carriage. I darted away from my tormentors, sprang in beside her, and the next moment was driven away in safety, much to the rage of the boys. The girl's father took an interest in me, consulted a physician, who made an examination of my case, and reported that my demented state had been caused by a heavy blow on the head several years before."

Geoffrey saw the man shudder, as he made this statement, while a low exclamation of pain or fear escaped him, and a dim suspicion began to dawn on his mind.

"It was found," he resumed, still watching the man, "that my skull had been fractured, and that a portion of the bone was pressing on my brain, which caused temporary paralysis, and made me an imbecile."

Another shudder, more violent than the other, strengthened his suspicion.

"This physician and another," he went on, "believed that an operation might be performed which would improve my condition, if it did not fully restore me to my right mind. Mr. Huntress, the man who had taken me under his protection, authorized the doctors to undertake the operation. They did so—it was successful, and I was restored."

"Heaven be praised!" ejaculated his listener, heartily but tremulously. "I haven't that quite so heavy on my conscience any longer."

Geoffrey started, and his face brightened.

He was gaining light, little by little.

"The first words that I uttered on coming to myself," he continued, "were something about a woman named—Margery——"

At the sound of that name, the man before him bounded from his feet as if he had been shot.

"Margery!" he repeated, in an agonized voice, his face twitching, his hands clenching themselves convulsively, while his eyes rolled in every direction, a look of wildest fear in them. "Do you remember Margery!"

He leaned breathlessly toward the young man, while he awaited his answer with trembling eagerness.

"I remember only this—and it is only a confused remembrance, too," Geoffrey replied, "that some one by that name was kind and good to me— that she was called Margery, and I loved her. I have a dim recollection that something happened to her—that she was hurt or struck——"

On hearing this, the man stretched out his hand with a quick, appealing gesture.

"Don't—don't," he pleaded, hoarsely. "Do—do you remember anything—any one else?"

"Yes, I recollect that there was a man named Jack"—another violent start confirmed Geoffrey's suspicions—"who was not always good to me, and whom I feared and—you are Jack!"

This was something of a shot at random, but it told instantly.

The man sank to the ground, trembling and unnerved, his face blanched with fear, while great beads of perspiration started out upon his forehead.

"Good Heaven! I am lost! Have I come back after all these years, just to get caught like a rat in a trap?" he cried, brokenly. "But," he went on, crouching lower among the tall grass and weeds, "I never meant ye any harm, Master Geoffrey. It was the drink that did it; it crazed my brain, and

I never really knew I done ye such injury, or that I'd killed the girl I loved, till hours after 'twas all over."

Geoffrey grew pale now, at this revelation.

It was far more than he dreamed of extorting when he had charged the man with his identity.

He was so excited that it was with difficulty he could compose himself sufficiently to speak. But after a moment or two he said:

"Well, Jack, since it is you, and we have recognized each other, you may as well make a clean breast of the whole story. Owing to the kindness which I had received, the injury which you did me has not resulted so seriously as it might have done; but poor Margery!"

"Boy—boy—ye will drive me crazy if ye talk like that," Jack cried, in a voice of horror. "I tell ye, I loved the girl, and I'd never have lifted my hand agin her—I'd have cut it off first, though we didn't always agree—but for the drink; and if I could only look into her good face once more, and hear her say, 'Jack, I forgive ye!' I'd be willin' to lay down in the grave beside her, though Heaven knows I've never even seen the spot where she's buried."

Great sobs choked the man's utterance, while tears rolled over his weather-beaten cheeks and dropped upon the ground.

Geoffrey pitied him sincerely, while at the same time a feeling of horror crept over him as he began to realize that the man had been making a confession of murder.

Had he killed Margery, and attempted his life also? And was that the secret of his having been abandoned in the great city of New York?

He was burning with eagerness to learn all the truth.

"I do not wish to pain you, Jack," he said, "but I want you to tell me all there is to tell. Begin at the beginning, here in this peaceful spot, where no one will come to disturb us, and ease your conscience of its burden."

Jack looked up quickly as he referred to that sacred inclosure.

"How came ye to know where to find yer mother's grave?" he asked.

Geoffrey's heart bounded within him at this question.

"Annie" had been his mother, then. It was a great thing to have that point settled, and he felt sure now that the rest would all be explained.

"Never mind that just now, Jack," he replied, with what calmness he could assume; "when you have told me all your story I will answer any question you may ask."

"Ye'll not give me over to the officers, lad?" the man pleaded, pitifully.

"No, Jack, you need have no fear of me; as far as I am concerned, you may go free for the rest of your life; if you have wronged any one else, you will have to settle that with your own conscience. All I ask of you is to tell me the history of my early life, and what you know regarding my father and mother."

"Thank ye, Master Geoffrey," returned Jack, humbly. "I don't deserve that ye should be so considerate. I've had to skulk and hide for more'n twenty years, and though there ain't much in the world that I care to live for, yet a feller don't exactly like the idee of bein' put out of it afore his time. I'll tell ye all I know about yerself and your folks, and welcome."

"Come over to yonder log and let us sit down," Geoffrey said, indicating a fallen tree, but he was very white, and felt weak and trembling as he moved toward it.

At last he believed the mystery of his life was to be revealed.

"I came here to work in the mines about a year afore Captain Dale— that's your dad—bought his claim," Jack began, after they were seated. "He bought out old Waters all of a sudden, and, about a fortnight after, he brought the prettiest little woman I ever set eyes on to live in that house yonder——"

"His wife?" eagerly queried Geoffrey.

"Of course, lad—leastwise he said she was, and she was called Mrs. Dale; and if ever a man set his life by a woman, the captain was that one. He dressed her like a doll, and wouldn't let her do a thing except make little fancy knickknacks, and was forever pettin' and makin' of her as if she was a child. Wal, they kep' two maids—at least after a while—one in the kitchen and one to wait on Mrs. Dale, who was kind of ailin'. Margery Brown was the waitin' maid, and she and me had been keepin' company for quite a while, and it was agreed between us that we'd marry afore long and try our luck together in California, for I'd scraped together a snug little sum and was tired of mines. But after she went to the cap's house she began to put me off—she grew so fond of his wife that she wouldn't hear a word about marryin' and leavin' her. At the end of a year ye were born—a cute little nine-pounder ye was, too, and a prouder man ye never see than the captain was after ye came. But it didn't last long, for yer mother began to fail afore ye were a month old, and in another week or two she was dead.

"It just broke the captain's heart. He seemed half crazed, didn't pay any heed to his business, and finally said he couldn't stay here where everything kept his mind stirred up with the past. He told Margery he was goin' to break up, only he didn't know what he should do with you, for he hadn't any place or any folks to take you to.

"I thought my time to speak up had come then, and I told Margery she must take me then or never, and if the captain were willin' we'd take the baby along with us, until he could do better by it. This pleased her, and she said she'd speak to the master about it. He was glad enough to let ye come with us, for he knew my girl loved ye and would take better care of ye than any stranger. He said he'd pay well for it until ye were old enough to go to school, when he'd take you to some good one to begin yer edication.

"Well, Margery and I were married, and went to California to live on a small farm I'd leased, just out of Frisco, which I worked part of the time and let out the rest, at odd jobs, to get a little ready money. The cap shipped all his fine furniture off somewhere to be sold, shut up the house yonder, and left for parts unknown, though for the first two years he came every six months to see how his boy was gettin' on. After that he didn't come so often, though he sent money regular.

"Ye were the smartest little chap I ever did see. Margery couldn't have loved ye any better if ye'd been her own, and she made more on ye than I relished, and I got jealous sometimes. We got on finely for three years, then hard times came, the crops didn't turn out good, odd jobs gave out, and I lay idle for weeks at a time. I wasn't long gettin' into bad company those times, and I came home wild with drink sometimes, and Margery would cry and beg me to mend my ways. But I didn't; and at last she got riled, and threatened to give me the slip, which only made me wicked and sullen.

"One night I came home worse than ever—Heaven forgive me! I'd been at the bottle all day long, and the very Old Boy had got into me. I staggered into the house ugly enough for anything. Margery had the table all laid, the kettle was steaming in on the stove, and she was settin' with yerself in her arms—ye were about five then—laughin' and playin' with ye as happy as a cat with one kitten. The sight angered me somehow; I couldn't get reconciled that we'd no tots of our own, and I gave ye a cuff on the ear with an oath.

"Margery sprang up, as mad as a hornet, and shoved ye behind her.

"'Let the child alone, you sot!' she said.

"'I'll sot ye!' I yelled, and pushed her roughly into a chair by the stove.

"This roused all yer bad blood, small as ye were. Ye flew at me, peltin' me with yer little fists that couldn't have hurt a flea. Ye called me 'a bad, wicked man,' ordered me to 'let Margery alone, or ye'd tell——'

"Ye never finished that sentence, for every word had put me in a worse rage, and I grabbed a stick of wood from the hearth, flung it at ye, and ye dropped without a word, for it hit ye square in the head.

"My girl gave a shriek I'll never forget.

"'Oh, ye drunken wretch!' she cried. 'I'll hate ye all my life if ye've killed my darlin'.'

"She gave me a push and sprang toward ye, but she never reached ye, for I grabbed her by the throat—frightened at what I'd already done, and the heat of the room had made a madman of me—and choked her till she grew purple in the face, and then threw her from me. She stumbled, caught her foot in a rug, and fell. I laughed as she went over. Her head hit on the sharp corner of the stove with a sound I'll never forget till I die, and then she, too, lay still and white on the floor afore me."

CHAPTER XXVII
JACK'S STORY CONTINUED

When the man had reached the part of his story recorded in the preceding chapter, he was greatly agitated for several moments, as if the memory of that dreadful time was even now, after the lapse of more than twenty year, more than he could bear, while Geoffrey, too, felt as if he could hardly sit there and listen to the remainder of the fearful tale.

"The horror of it all sobered me a'most as quick as if I'd been struck by lightning," Jack at length resumed, pulling himself together with an effort. "I don't know how long I stood there, lookin' down on them two that I believed I'd sent out o' world without a moment's warning. Then I slunk out o' the house, hardly knowin' what I did, and went and hid myself in the barn. I must have gone to sleep, or fell into a stupor from the liquor I'd drank, for I didn't know anything more till the roosters set up such a crowing that nobody could have slept. I never could tell ye what the horror of that wakin' was, sir, and it's a'most like livin' it over again to tell it," groaned the man, with a shudder. "It was only about two in the mornin', but the moon was shinin', and it was most as light as day. I crept out into the yard and listened; there wasn't a sound except those roosters, and every crow sounded like a knell o' doom in my ears, and made my flesh creep with fear.

"I stole up to the house and looked in at the kitchen window. I couldn't help it—something drove me to it, though I shivered at every step. There they lay, just as they fell, with the light still burnin', and everything just as I'd left it. But, while I stood there the little shaver stirred and moaned, and my heart leaped straight into my throat, near about, chokin' me at the sight. It gave me hope—p'raps after all I hadn't murdered 'em, and they might be brought to. I rushed in, took the boy up, and laid him on the bed in the bedroom just off the kitchen. He moaned all the time, till I got a wet cloth and put it on his head, when he grew quiet and dropped off into a stupor again. Then I went to her—my girl—Margery—the woman I'd sworn to love and take care of till I died, and who had done me nothin' but kindness ever since we first met.

"I lifted her up, but she hung limp and lifeless over my arm. I laid her head on my breast and begged her to come back to me, to call me her Jack once more, and say she'd forgive me, and I'd never lift my hand ag'in her ag'in, nor touch another drop as long as I lived. But 'twan't no use. She lay there quiet and peaceful enough, but there was that dreadful purple mark and cut on her forehead where it had hit the stove. She wa'n't cold or stiff as I thought dead people always were, but there wa'n't no sign of life about her either and I laid her down again, my heart a-breakin', and feelin' like another Cain, only worse, for I'd killed a woman, and she my own wife!

"Then I began to think what would happen if I was found there, and I grew frightened. I couldn't make up my mind to stay and confess what I'd done, and hang like a dog for it, so I got together a few things and all the money that Margery had in her own little box, and the boy's safe, and wrappin' him in a shawl—for I daren't leave him while there was a breath o' life in him and a chance of savin' him—I stole out of the house, without even darin' to give my girl a kiss after the ill I'd done her and made for a station a mile or more away.

"I had an awful time of it, for the boy moaned every minute of the time; but I told people on the cars that he'd had a fall and I was takin' him to a doctor. I traveled all day in the fastest trains, and got to a town just about dusk. Here I called a doctor to the boy. He doubted if he could save him; but he pulled through after five weeks of terrible fever and pain, though when he got up again, lookin' more like a spirit than like flesh and blood, he didn't know me or remember anything that had happened. The doctor said he was a fool, and always would be one."

It seemed very strange to Geoffrey to be sitting there in his right mind and listening to this dreadful story about himself. It seemed almost like a case of dual existence.

"As soon as he was well enough," Jack went on, "I felt that we ought to be gettin' out of that place; it was too near home to be safe, and the police were liable to get on my track any day. So I began my roamin'. First we went to Texas, where I got work on a cattle and sheep ranch. After a time I scraped together a little money, and started out to raise sheep for myself. It wa'n't easy to be with any one, lest somebody should come along who had heard about what I'd done, and I might get snapped up. The boy and me lived in a cabin by ourselves, away from everybody else, but I never let him out of my sight, and I grew that fond of him I would have died rather than let harm come to him, and I'd vowed I'd do the best I could by him as long as I lived, and get together something handsome to leave him, to make up as far as I could for the deadly wrong I'd done him. As soon as I could get enough together, I meant to take him to some place where they care for them that have lost their mind.

"My sheep turned out wonderful; in five years money began to come in right fast, and I might have kep' on an' been a rich man by this time, if it hadn't been that a man I knew came down that way about that time. I saw him first at the village, where I went to lay in a stock of provisions. He didn't see me, but I heard him say he was goin' to buy out a cattle ranch ten miles away, and that was enough to give me a scare and unsettle me. I feared I'd be recognized and seized as the murderer of my girl, and though life wa'n't much to me with the heavy conscience and the grief I had to carry around with me all the time, yet, for the boy's sake, I was bound to stick to it as long as I could—there was nobody else to take care of him, and I knew he'd fare hard without me.

"The man who owned the ranch next to mine had offered to buy me out the year before, so I went to him and told him I'd made up my mind to go North and see if the doctors couldn't do something for the boy, and if he'd take everything off my hands I'd sell out cheap.

"He took me up quick as a wink, and in less than a week the money was in my pocket and the boy and me were on our way to New York. I bought a small farm just across the river in New Jersey. There was a good house and barn on it, and I stocked it well, hired a good strong woman to do the inside work and a man to help me outside, and then settled down to a quiet life; for I didn't believe anybody would think of lookin' for me there.

"I took the name of 'John Landers,' and tried to make the boy call himself 'George Landers'; but he didn't know enough to learn it, and seemed to have forgotten how to talk at all; so I hadn't much to fear from his lettin' anything out. We lived here for almost five years more, and I got ahead a little every season. But, sir, the horror of that dreadful deed never left me for a minute. My Margery's dead face was always before me, and my heart heavy with its load of guilt and loneliness. If ever a man paid for an evil deed in torment, I paid for mine a hundred times over.

"But the worst of my troubles was yet to come. The world's a small place to hide in when a man has committed a crime. I went to town one day on business, and stepped into the post-office—which was in the same buildin' with the railway station—to send a letter for the woman at home, when I heard two men talking in a low tone of voice, and one of them spoke the name of Jack Henly.

"My blood ran cold in a minute. My back was to them, for I was payin' for the postage on the letter, and they hadn't seemed to notice me. I didn't hurry, frightened as I felt, but took my own time and listened.

"It was me they were after, sure enough; they had tracked me all the way from Texas to that place, but, somehow, couldn't get any farther. Nobody had heard of a man named Jack Henly, and no one answered to their description. It was no wonder, for I was greatly changed, looking like an old man, for my grief had whitened my hair, wrinkled my face, and bent my form. I walked straight by them on goin' out of the office, but they never suspected me. I'd got another scare, though, that I couldn't get over, and made up my mind that I'd quit the country. So I sold off my stock, drew what money I'd laid by in the bank—my farm I couldn't sell at such short notice—shut up my house, and, takin' the boy, went to New York, intendin' to take passage in a vessel goin' to Australia, where I meant to go to sheep raisin' again, since I had done so well in Texas, while I thought I needn't fear any man in that country. I took passage, and bought a comfortable outfit for both of us, but the vessel wan't to sail for a week, so I kep' very quiet in a room I'd hired on a by-street, fearin' those men might still be lookin' me up.

"But I let the boy play out, for he pined in the house, while I sat by a window to watch that he did not get out of sight. Wall, one day I must have fallen asleep, for I woke with a start, and lookin' out, couldn't see hide nor hair of the boy. I went to the door, but he wasn't nowhere in sight. I started out to find him, never thinkin' of danger then. I walked for hours, askin' people about him, but nobody could tell me anything of him.

"Three days I kep' this up, until I nigh about went crazy, and wore myself out with loss on sleep, travelin' about, and with my grief for the little fellow.

"On the last day before we were to sail, while I was rovin' about the streets in search of him, I ran against those two men again—the ones who were lookin' for me. I knew by their quick, keen glances at me that they had got a suspicion I might be their man, and I got out of their way in a hurry. I was discouraged about findin' the boy. I didn't dare to look for him any more. I was afraid to go to the police about him, lest they had been notified to be on the lookout, and should snap me up; so, half crazed with fear and grief, I staggered on board the vessel I was to sail in, crawled into my berth, and lay there till we were well out to sea.

"Wall, sir, my heart was broke. I thought I never could hold up my head again, and I wouldn't have turned over my hand to have saved myself from goin' to the bottom; for I got to lovin' that poor little chap with my whole soul, and I didn't know how to get on without him.

"But we had a good passage. I was hale and hearty when we landed, and seemed likely to live my lonely life for many a year. I went into the interior, bought a sheep ranch, and set myself to do the work of three men; nothin' else would ease the pain and worry that was eatin' my heart out.

"Well, sir, to make a long story short, I've been on that sheep ranch ever since, until about six months ago, when a longin' seized me to come home and take a last look at my own land. I've grown to be a well-to-do farmer; I've plenty of money, and no one to spend it on or leave it to, unless I give it to you, Master Geoffrey, now that I have found you. Heaven be praised for that, and that you've got your mind back! I've been to New Jersey, found my place there neglected and all out of repair, but still a thrifty little farm if 'twas well taken care of. I've been to Texas for a look at my old ranch there. The man that bought it got rich, sold out, and then went North to live on his money. Then I came on here to see the place where I first found my Margery, and it was nigh this very spot—just there by that clump of spruce, where I was hid when you came—that we plighted our troth. Ah! my girl! my girl!"

The poor man broke down completely here, and sobbed like a child, and Geoffrey's eyes were full of tears, too, as he witnessed his emotion and realized what he must have suffered during the checkered life that he had led.

He had been deeply touched by the faithfulness and devotion which he had exhibited in his care of him during all those years while he was such a helpless burden, mentally, on his hands.

He saw that the man was naturally honorable and kind-hearted, and that he would never have been guilty of the crime which he had just confessed, but for the misfortunes that led him into evil company and to the use of intoxicating drinks.

"I'm a broken-down old man, sir," Jack said, after struggling hard for self-control, "or I never should blubber like this; but this place brings back those old days when my conscience was free—when life was bright and full of hope before me and my girl, and it seems more'n I can bear. It's wonderful, though, that I should run across ye here! Oh, sir, I did ye a woeful wrong, in my anger and jealous fit, when ye were a child. I've no right to expect it, but 'twould comfort my poor old heart more'n I could tell ye, if I could hear ye say ye don't lay it up ag'in me."

Geoffrey turned frankly toward the humble suppliant beside him.

"I do not, Jack," he said, heartily; "you were the victim of drink, and were hardly accountable for the deeds of that night; you condemn yourself more than you really deserve, for if you have told me everything just as it occurred, your wife did not die by your hand—her death was caused by an accident."

The man shook his head sadly.

"No, no," he said; "I can't get it off my conscience that it was murder: for if I hadn't laid hands on her she might have been living to-day."

"Still it was not willful or premeditated," Geoffrey persisted. "However," he added, "I freely forgive you for your share in my misfortune, if that will be any comfort to you."

"Thank ye, sir; thank ye; and if there is a God, I thank Him, too, that I've been allowed to set eyes on ye once more, and in yer right mind, too," was the fervent response.

"I reckon," he continued, after a moment of thought, "it might be called the work of Providence that I lost ye there in New York, for if ye'd gone with me to Australia, I doubt that ye'd ever been cured, and I'm right sure ye'd never been the gentleman that ye are. I'd thank ye to tell me about the good man that befriended ye."

"I will, Jack, presently, but I first want to ask you a few more questions about the past."

"All right, sir: anything I can tell ye, ye shall know.

"Well, then, I'd like you to describe the man who was my father," Geoffrey said, gravely.

Jack turned to look upon the young man beside him.

"The best description ye could get of him'd be to go and look at yerself in the glass," he said, studying Geoffrey's face and form, "for ye're as nigh like him as another man could be, when I first saw him after he brought that pretty little woman to live here. He'd been off to meet her somewhere, and he'd shaved off all his heavy beard, had his hair trimmed up in the fashion, and wore a dandy suit o' clothes."

"His name was Dale, you say? Are you sure that was his true name?" the young man asked.

"I couldn't take my oath as to that, sir, but everybody here knew him as Captain William Dale, though I don't know how he came to be a captain. She used to call him 'Will,' in a way that made his eyes shine enough to do ye good."

Geoffrey's eyes lighted at this.

It was evident that Captain Dale had truly loved the girl whom he had brought there, whether she had been his legal wife or not.

"Do you know what her name was before he married her?" he asked.

"No, sir; that is one of the things I can't tell ye; even Margery never found out that. They was both very shy of talkin' about themselves afore folks, and nobody ever knew where they came from, either."

"Did they never have visitors—was there no friend whoever came to see them?"

"No, sir; and they didn't seem to want anybody; she was just his world, and he her'n. My girl used to think it was kind of strange, though, that they never got any letters; but she never did, and never writ any, either."

"Did she seem happy?" Geoffrey asked, in a hushed tone, as if this was ground he hardly liked to trespass upon.

"As chipper as a bird," Jack returned; "and she could sing like one, too. Many's the night the boys have stolen to yonder house to listen while she sang and played to the cap; he had a pianer sent up from Santa Fe; and she was always bright and smilin'; she was like a streak o' sunshine in a dark place, for there wasn't anybody like her anywhere about."

Geoffrey felt his heart yearn wistfully for this sweet and gentle woman, who had been his mother, and who had brightened that wild and dreary place with her presence for one short year.

Still the mystery regarding his father, and her relations to him, seemed as dark as ever.

If he could not learn whence they came, it would be impossible to trace his history any farther, and a feeling of depression and discouragement began to settle upon him.

It seemed as if those two lovers had hidden themselves there, cut themselves adrift from all previous associations, and then lived simply for and in each other.

"Did Captain Dale's mine here pay him well?" he asked.

"No, sir, it did not; and that is something that always seemed strange to me," Jack said, reflectively. "He couldn't much more'n paid expenses here, but he never seemed to care, and I've always had a notion that he had an interest in other mines."

"What other mines?" Geoffrey inquired, eagerly.

"I couldn't say, sir; he was very close, and never talked business afore his help."

"What made you think he had other claims?"

"Well, after the first month or two he used to be away considerable—not long at a time; but he went often, and was always so chipper when he came back, I reasoned 'twas only good luck could make him so."

"What arrangements did he make with you when he left me in your wife's care?"

"There wa'n't any bargain," Jack said. "Margery was that fond of ye she'd been willin' to kep' ye for nothin' rather than let ye go; but the cap was always generous—he gave her two hundred dollars to start with, besides a handsome present on her own account, for what she did for his wife while she lay dyin'. Then, for the first two years he came once in six months to see ye, and always left a good round sum for ye—there wa'n't nothin' mean about Captain Dale—and when he didn't come he sent it."

"Did he never mention where he spent his time?" Geoffrey asked, "or speak of ever taking me away with him?"

"No, sir, never a word; the most he ever said was that he should put ye to some school as soon as ye were old enough." ·

"Did he—did he appear to be fond of me?" Geoffrey inquired, hesitatingly, a hot flush rising to his cheek.

"That he were, sir; it was as much as ever he'd let ye out of his arms from the time he came till he went, though he never staid very long, and I've seen the tears a-standin' in his eyes when he parted from ye."

"How long before—my accident was his last visit?"

"It must have been more'n a year, if I remember right; but the money came regular, and Margery seemed happier when he didn't come—she was always afraid he'd take ye away from her. I've often wondered what he did when he came again and found ye gone—it must have been a mortal blow to him," Jack concluded, and then dropped into a fit of musing.

CHAPTER XXVIII
GEOFFREY VISITS THE SCENE
OF THE TRAGEDY

"Where do you intend to go from here, Jack?" Geoffrey asked at length, breaking a silence of several minutes, during which both had been busy with various thoughts and emotions.

"To California, sir. I'm bound to have a last look at all the places I've ever been in, though it'll be a sad day that lands me there. My poor girl and I saw many happy days on that little farm just out of San Francisco. I didn't own it, we only hired it, for we hadn't money enough then to pay for a home; but I'd gladly give up every dollar I've earned since if I could only have my girl back again," Jack concluded, with another heart-broken sob.

His grief and remorse were painful to witness. His face was almost convulsed, great drops came out upon his forehead, and he trembled with emotion.

"I believe I will go to California with you, Jack," Geoffrey said, after a season of thought. "I do not believe it will be exactly safe for you to go there by yourself, to visit your old home. Suspicion might be aroused immediately, and you would be liable to get into trouble; but no one would think it at all strange if I should return to make inquiries regarding my old nurse."

"Wall, but everybody knew we went off together," said Jack.

"Very true; but if unpleasant questions were asked, I could explain that you escaped to Australia, while I was cared for by friends in New York; all of which would be true," Geoffrey responded.

"Thank ye, sir; ye're kinder to me than I deserve; but even if I knew they'd snap me up, I reckon I should go. I can never rest till I know where they've laid my girl," Jack returned, with a heavy sigh.

"You shall," Geoffrey answered, "we will find out all there is to know; but I particularly wish to learn if my father ever visited the place after we left. If he did he probably left some address so that information could be found, in case any trace of us was discovered."

Jack appeared to be very grateful to have his path thus smoothed for him, and the next morning the two men left the mining village and proceeded directly to San Francisco.

Before leaving, however, Geoffrey had cut several slips from the ivy that grew all about his mother's grave, and inclosing them wrapped in wet paper, in a small tin box, mailed them to Gladys.

"My darling," he wrote, "if you can coax any of these to live, pray do so, for my sake. I have a particular reason for making the request, which I will explain when I return," and Gladys had three of them nicely rooted before she returned to Brooklyn, at the end of the season.

Geoffrey and his companion reached the small town, near which Jack Henly had once lived, and only a few miles from San Francisco, about noon one warm August day.

They had their dinner, and rested for several hours, then when the day grew cooler, Geoffrey started out alone to visit Jack Henly's former home, and to try to discover the grave of his wife.

He found the place without any difficulty, a small house and barn standing in a lonely location, about two miles from the town, while there were only one or two other dwellings in sight. There was no sign of life about the place, and the buildings were fast falling into decay. Weeds and vines and wild flowers grew all about the yard, and everything looked desolate and forlorn.

Geoffrey shivered as he stepped up to a window and looked into that small kitchen, and recalled the dark deed which had been perpetrated there.

He did not believe the place had ever been inhabited since; it had a look of having been shunned, and perhaps regarded as a haunted house. He wondered how Margery had been found, and what measures had been taken to discover the author of the crime.

He did not remain there long; it was not an attractive spot, and there were no means of learning anything that he wished to find out.

He resolved to visit some of the neighbors, and try to ascertain what had been done with Mrs. Henly's body, and if Captain Dale had ever visited the place since the tragedy occurred.

The nearest neighbor was at least a quarter of a mile away; he could just discern the roof and chimneys over a little rise of ground to the south.

He mounted his horse again and rode toward it, coming, in a few minutes, to a large and comfortable farmhouse, where peace and plenty seemed to reign.

He found the farmer just driving up his cows from pasture. He was a man apparently sixty years of age, with a kind and genial face, quick and energetic in his movements in spite of his three-score years.

Geoffrey saluted him courteously, introduced himself, and asked if he could spare the time to answer a few questions.

The man called a boy to attend to his cows, then invited Geoffrey to dismount and come with him to the wide, pleasant veranda, where they could converse at their leisure, assuring him that he should be glad to give him any information he might possess.

Geoffrey accepted his invitation, and then entered at once upon the business that had brought him there.

"I am in this locality chiefly to ascertain something of the people who once occupied that house over yonder," he said, indicating Jack Henly's deserted dwelling, "and thought my best way would be to apply to some one living in the neighborhood."

The farmer's face fell at this. Evidently the subject was not a pleasant one to him.

"You couldn't have come to a better place to find out what you want to know, sir," he replied, "for I've lived here for the last thirty-five years, and I can tell you all about that sad story—at least all that anybody hereabouts ever knew; though it isn't a cheerful subject."

"I am very fortunate, then, in having come to you," Geoffrey said, in a tone of satisfaction. Then glancing at his watch, he added: "I find it is later than I thought, and as I would like to get back to town before dark, I will ask you to relate in your own way all that you know about the family, and I will restrain all questions until you get through."

"Well, sir," began the farmer, "the Henlys came here nigh about twenty-two or three years ago, and we thought we were fortunate in having such thrifty neighbors as they seemed to be. There were only three of them, Jack and his wife, and a baby only a few months old, that the woman had taken to nurse, its mother being dead. Everything went along smoothly, and they appeared to be doing well for four or five years, when Jack got into bad company and began to drink. Before this he and his wife seemed to think a great deal of each other, and in bad weather he would help her about the house, while in good weather she would work with him out of doors. In this way he gained time to do many odd jobs outside, and made considerable money by so doing.

"After Henly got in with his wild companions, we now and then heard that things were not very pleasant between him and his wife, but no one ever dreamed how serious the trouble was until the terrible tragedy burst like a thunderbolt upon us. My wife and Mrs. Henly had been great friends from the first; and had got in the way of borrowing little messes from each other, as neighbors often do, when they came short and could not get into town to buy what was wanted. So one afternoon my wife said she was out of tea, and would run over to see Mrs. Henly for a little while, and borrow enough for supper.

"It didn't seem as if she'd been gone long enough to get there, when she came flying back as pale as death, wringing her hands and seeming half frightened out of her senses. I rushed to the door to meet her, when she fell into my arms in a dead faint. When she came to she was so unnerved by what she had seen that we had hard work to get the truth out of her, but we finally made out that upon reaching Henly's she had knocked on the door. No one answered, and she stepped in, as she had often done, when she saw Mrs. Henly lying on the floor, a terrible bruise and gash on her forehead. My wife was so frightened and shocked that she dropped her cup on the floor, where it broke in a dozen pieces, and then, with a scream, turned and ran, as fast as her trembling limbs would carry her, toward home. I called my son and one of my men, and we started at once for the place. We found the woman lying as my wife had described her, only instead of being dead, as she thought, she was now rolling her head from side to side and moaning as if in great pain."

"Not dead!" interrupted Geoffrey, in a startled tone.

"No, sir, praise the Lord! not dead. We lifted her and laid her on her bed just off the kitchen, when I sent my man for a doctor, and my son back home to bring his mother, while I got some water and bathed the poor woman's head. My wife was too sensible to nurse her own feelings when she found she was needed, and that her friend was not dead, and she came immediately to do what she could for her.

"When the doctor came he said it was doubtful if the poor thing could live; the blow on the head had been a fearful one, and it was a wonder that it had not killed her outright. Besides that, there was the print of three fingers on her throat, showing that there had been a struggle with some one, and pointing to foul play.

"Of course when we found that Henly had decamped taking the boy with him, we suspected him of having done the deed, and the authorities were at once set on his track. But nothing has ever been heard of him or the child from that day to this; at least not to my knowledge. His wife had a tough time of it. We had her brought over here, and my wife and daughter took care of her through a three month's illness, and when she did get up again she was but the shadow of her former self."

"Did she get well?" Geoffrey exclaimed, amazed.

"Yes; she recovered her health, though she was not as strong as she had been, and her head was apt to trouble her at times. But her heart was broken over the disappearance of her husband and the boy. It was a long time before we could make her tell how she had been injured, and then she excused Henly. She said he had come home the worse for liquor, and did not know what he was about. She said he must have been frightened, believing he had killed her, and then taken the boy and fled. I suspect there was something more to it, but that was all we could ever get out of her."

"Ah!" thought Geoffrey, "she shielded him from the suspicion of having murdered me also, and she must have suffered torture on my account as well as his."

"As soon as she was able to get about," resumed the farmer, "she insisted upon going away altogether from the place. She could not go back to her home and live there alone, she said, and she wanted to search for her husband, to let him know that he had not killed her, as he must believe. I imagined, too, that she couldn't bear to meet the boy's father when he should come again and find that he had disappeared. She sold all her household goods, offered a reward of a thousand dollars—having deposited that amount in a bank in San Francisco for the purpose—to any one who should find her husband or secure any definite information regarding him, and then she left the place herself. We have never seen her since, nor heard what became of her."

"Did she leave no address?" Geoffrey inquired. "If not, how could she expect to be communicated with in case any tidings of her husband were obtained?"

"I believe a personal of some kind was to be inserted in certain papers in the leading cities of the country by those who had charge of the affair," replied the farmer, "but I guess it has never been printed. Their house has never been occupied since. A good many people believe that Henly murdered the boy also, and concealed the body somewhere on the farm, so the place has had the reputation of being haunted, therefore we have never had any neighbors there."

"Since Mrs. Henly was not murdered, I am at liberty to set your heart at rest upon that subject," Geoffrey responded. "The boy is alive and well. I am that boy!" The farmer started from his chair and stared at him in open-mouthed astonishment at this electrifying statement.

"I can't believe it," he said, at last, and bending to look more closely into his visitor's face, "and yet you said your name was Huntress."

"Yes, my name is Geoffrey Dale Huntress," Geoffrey replied, with a smile at his host's astonishment.

"That was the child's name, Geoffrey Dale—it must be true; do tell me how you happen to come back here after all these years?" the farmer urged, in an eager tone. Geoffrey felt that he was warranted in so doing, since Margery Henly had lived, and there was no longer any need of concealment on Jack's part.

"Jack escaped all pursuit," he said, "wandering from place to place; went to Texas on a sheep ranch for a few years, and finally turned up in New York, where I became separated from him, and could not be found. Just about this time he became convinced that the officers were on his track—they must have been those who were working for Mrs. Henly's thousand-dollar reward—and he was so frightened he suddenly shipped for Australia."

"Poor fellow," said the farmer, sympathetically, "he must have suffered keenly. But this is the strangest part of the whole story. I never imagined that we should get the sequel to that tragedy over yonder. Was the man kind to you? I used to think he was not over fond of you when you were a little fellow."

"No one could have been more kind than he was, as long as I was with him," Geoffrey said, gravely, as he recalled all that Jack had so recently told him.

He thought, too, as long as Margery had kept the secret of his having been nearly murdered also, it would be best to still preserve silence upon that point.

"It was my own fault," he continued, "that I was lost, for I wandered away without his knowledge, and he was not able to find me, although he labored faithfully to do so, until driven to desperation by the belief that he was being tracked."

"How did you learn that he had sailed for Australia, if you were lost before he went?"

"I learned that later," Geoffrey briefly replied.

"And what became of you?"

"A philanthropic gentleman became interested in me, adopted me, and has given me a good education."

"Well, well, well! wonders will never cease! It's a strangely romantic tale, young man. But how about your own father?" questioned the farmer.

"That is a mystery which I came here to try to solve," Geoffrey returned, looking troubled, for he seemed to be no nearer the solution than ever. "All that I really know about my father is that he was called Captain William Dale, and that he at one time owned shares in some of the mines of New Mexico, where my mother died. I have been there trying to gain some trace of him, but without success. Then I came on here, hoping to learn something of him through people who had known the Henlys. I thought it probable that he would come here, sometime, to see me, as he had previously been in the habit of doing, and, finding that I had disappeared, would leave his address so that he could be informed if anything was learned of my fate."

"He has been here," the farmer replied; "he came only about two months after Mrs. Henly left. I saw him and conversed with him. He appeared to be overwhelmed with grief upon learning of your strange disappearance. He instituted inquiries, offering a reward of five thousand dollars for your recovery, living, or one thousand for positive proof of your death, and under these circumstances I have often wondered why some clew to your fate was not ascertained."

Geoffrey did not think it strange. He knew that no one would have recognized in the poor little imbecile whom Jack Henly had cared for, the bright, happy child who had been Margery's joy and pride.

He was touched, too, by the evidence of his father's interest in and love for him, and yet it seemed inexplicable; for, if the man whom he had met at Saratoga was his father, and he was anxious to find him, as the farmer said, why should he have avoided him as he had done.

"But did he leave no address?" he eagerly questioned.

"There was something a little queer about that," said the farmer, "for he did not give any, really. I asked him where a communication would reach him, and he replied that anything directed simply to Lock Box 43, Santa Fe, would be all that was necessary."

Geoffrey's face fell at this.

He was terribly disappointed, for he had confidently expected that he would find something tangible through this man, by which he could trace Captain William Dale.

"Lock Box 43, Santa Fe," he repeated, thoughtfully, "and that was all?"

"That was all; but perhaps the man didn't want his name known all over the country, in connection with this tragedy here," suggested his host.

"That is so," Geoffrey returned, brightening, but he said to himself that he would yet know who had held that post-office box in Santa Fe twenty years ago, if it was in the power of man to discover it.

"Has he ever been here since?" he asked, after a pause.

"Yes, twice; and the last time he remarked, 'I shall never see the child again—I believe he is dead.'"

"What was the date of his last visit?"

"It was about ten years ago, and I have never seen him since. I am very sorry, Mr. Huntress, that I can tell you no more," said the man, evidently feeling for his visitor's discomfiture, "and it really must be a great trial to you to have such a mystery enshrouding your parentage."

"It is, but—it must be solved sooner or later," Geoffrey said, resolutely.

He arose to go as he spoke, thanked the farmer heartily for his kindness in telling what he wished to know, then mounted his horse and rode back toward the town, greatly perplexed and somewhat disheartened.

"Lock Box 43 is a slender thread to lead to much, but I'll follow it until it breaks," he said to himself, as he went on his way.

CHAPTER XXIX
AN UNEXPECTED MEETING

The sun had long since gone down, and darkness was rapidly settling over the country, as Geoffrey pursued his way, grateful indeed that he had such good news to take back to Jack, but well-nigh discouraged on his own account.

It had been agreed that he should learn all he could about Henly's old home, and where Margery was buried, and that Jack should himself revisit the place after nightfall, upon his return, since he did not dare to make his appearance there by daylight.

The road to the town lay through a heavy growth of timber, and, as Geoffrey came into it, the darkness was so intensified that at first he could hardly distinguish the way, when, suddenly, his horse gave a startled snort and shied one side, nearly throwing his rider from the saddle.

"Gently, gently, sir," he said, reassuringly, as he quickly recovered himself. "What is the trouble, my boy?"

He glanced searchingly about him, and saw a muffled figure sitting upon a rock under the shadow of a great tree.

Geoffrey's hand instinctively caught the handle of the revolver that he always carried when traveling, and then he rode directly up to the figure.

"Who are you?" he demanded, "and why are you sitting here alone in the darkness?"

"Do not fear, sir," responded a quiet, honest voice. "I am only a woman on my way home from town, and sat down here to rest for a moment."

"I beg your pardon, madame, for accosting you as I did," Geoffrey returned, apologetically, "but I confess I was startled, as well as my horse, for a moment. Are you not afraid to be traveling this lonely way at this time of the evening?"

"No, sir, I am not afraid. I know every step of the road, but I am not so young as I was once, and it tires me to walk," the woman replied, with a weary note in her voice, accompanied by a heavy sigh.

"Have you far to go?" the young man asked.

"No, only to the second house from here—to Farmer Bruce's."

"Ah! You are going to Mr. Bruce's. I have just come from there. I will turn about and see you safely to the house; or, if you could manage to sit on a man's saddle, you shall ride, and I will lead my horse," Geoffrey said, kindly; for now that he had been accustomed to the dim light he could discern that the woman looked worn and weary, and his sympathies were enlisted for her.

"No, no; thank you, sir, I will not trouble you," the woman returned. "But tell me," she continued, rising and coming toward his side, "is Farmer Bruce still alive? Is the family well?"

Something in her anxious tone and her agitated manner, as well as these questions, sent a sudden thrill through the young man's heart.

He bent and looked searchingly into her face, which was upraised to his.

"Yes, Farmer Bruce is living. You said you were on your way home. Do you belong to the family?" he asked.

"No—I—I used to live near them; I have come for a visit," was the confused reply.

Geoffrey bent still nearer to her, when the woman suddenly uttered a startled cry, and laid her hand upon his arm.

"Oh, sir! who are you?" she cried. "I am sure you must be Master Geoffrey. You are so like your father. I should know you anywhere, and I never could forget the boy I loved. You are Geoffrey, aren't you? and don't you remember—Margery?"

She ended with a sob, and her hold tightened on his arm as if she feared to lose him.

Geoffrey had half-suspected her identity when she had inquired so eagerly about Farmer Bruce; but it was a shock to him, nevertheless, to find his suspicions thus verified, and he felt that, if he should never learn anything more definite regarding his father, he should feel more than repaid for his journey hither, just to have found Jack and Margery, seen them restored to each other, and the shadow removed from their lives.

He seized the trembling hand that lay upon his arm, and shook it heartily.

"Yes, I am Geoffrey, and I do remember Margery," he said, in a glad, earnest tone.

The poor, long-suffering, wandering creature dropped her head against his horse's neck, and burst into a passion of tears.

"Heaven bless you, Master Geoffrey, for owning it at last—my heart's been well-nigh crushed since you denied it, and ran away from me in New York," she said, brokenly, between her sobs.

"Denied it, and ran away from you in New York!" repeated the young man, astonished.

"Yes, sir; sure you haven't forgotten that day when you bought the roses of me, and I asked you if you wasn't Geoffrey Dale? You told me no—your name was Everet, and you didn't know anything about Jack, nor about any of the other things I talked of."

A light broke upon Geoffrey's mind.

She had seen Everet Mapleson, and made a very natural mistake; she had believed him to be the child she had loved and cared for, and it was no wonder she was pained by his refusal to recognize her.

"I never bought any roses of you in New York, Margery," he said, kindly. "I have never seen you until now since I was a small boy of five years."

The woman looked up at him amazed.

Geoffrey smiled frankly into her upturned face.

"The young man whom you met was a Mr. Everet Mapleson; we were in college together, and we look so much alike that we are often mistaken for each other," he explained.

"Ah! dearie, my heart is lighter now you've told me this," Margery said, with a long-drawn sigh. "I was cruelly hurt when I thought you wouldn't own me, and I was so sure, too, that you could tell me something about Jack—can't you tell me where he is? Where, where have you been all these years, Master Geoffrey. Ah, I feared that cruel blow that Jack gave you had killed you, and I'd never see you again; but poor man! he'd never have lifted his hand against you if he'd been himself. Heaven pity him! wherever he is, if he's living at all."

She had rambled on in this disconnected way without even waiting for a reply to any of her questions, and Geoffrey felt the tears rise to his eyes, as he realized something of the burden that lay so heavy on her heart, and had made the long, long years so dreary and oppressive to her.

He dismounted from his horse, and taking her by the arm, said, gently:

"Come back to the rock, Margery, where you were sitting, and I will tell you all you wish to know. It is a long story, and you will be weary with standing."

She looked up appealingly.

"One word, Master Geoffrey. Jack——"

Her trembling lips refused to utter another word, and the young man thought he might as well tell her at once about her husband and set her heart at rest.

"Jack is living and well, and—within a mile of you at this very moment," he said, in a cheerful tone.

"Oh, dearie! Heaven reward you for those blessed words," Margery murmured; then her head sank upon her breast, and, tottering weakly forward, she dropped upon the rock where Geoffrey had first seen her, and fell to sobbing like a tired child.

Geoffrey waited until she had grown somewhat calmer, and then told her, as briefly as he could, something of his own and Jack's history during the last eighteen years.

She never interrupted him during the recital, but seemed to drink in every word, as one perishing from thirst would drink in pure, life-giving water.

When at last he had told her all, she lifted her face, and, while she wiped the streaming tears from her eyes, she exclaimed:

"Ah! Master Geoffrey, I feel almost as if I was drawing nigh to heaven, after all the waiting, the wandering, the loneliness, and misery, to find my Jack again, and know that he has been true to his love for me all the time. Poor fellow! his fate has been harder than mine, after all, for he's had to carry a burden of guilt with him; but it is all over now, thank Heaven! You will take me straight to him?" she concluded, eagerly.

"Of course I will," Geoffrey replied, heartily, "he is waiting at the public house in the town for me; waiting for me to come and tell him about his old home, from which he fled so many years ago, and about a certain grave, which he has imagined has lain lonely and neglected all that time, and which he was to go to visit, under cover of the darkness, upon my return."

"Poor man! poor man!" sobbed Margery, all unmindful of her own long suffering, in her sympathy for her erring husband, "but, praise the Lord, there's no grave for him to weep over, and he can walk the earth once more and fear no man."

She arose and drew her cloak about her preparatory to going back to the town with her companion.

Geoffrey insisted that she should ride, while he walked beside her and guided the horse.

He saw that she was very weary, as well as weak, from her recent agitation, and not fit to walk the long distance.

She demurred at first, but he would listen to no objections, and she permitted him to put her into the saddle, and then they started on their way.

Geoffrey questioned her about her life during the past eighteen years, and he marveled, as he listened to her story, at the woman's unwavering devotion and love for the man whose hand so nearly deprived her of life.

She told him, as Mr. Bruce had already done, that, as soon as she was able, she had sold off all her household goods and the farm-stock, and realized over a thousand dollars. She deposited all but enough for her immediate needs in a bank of San Francisco, where she already had some money laid by, and instructed a lawyer there to use it as a reward for the discovery of her husband.

She then began her own tiresome pilgrimage to search for him herself. She roved from one large city to another, stopping some time in each, now taking in washing and ironing to support herself and earn money to continue her search in the next place where she should go; going out as a servant in other places, or selling flowers or confectionery upon the corners of the streets for the same purpose, while she eagerly scanned every face she saw in the hope of somewhere and sometime coming across either Jack or the boy; she had never believed, as others did, that the latter was dead. She felt sure that Jack must have discovered some sign of life about him, and taken him away with the hope of having him restored.

In this way she had visited every large city in the United States. She had been in different mining districts also, thinking that perhaps her husband might have gone back to his old business, hoping thus to hide himself more securely. She had even been in Canada and other British provinces, but had never met with the least encouragement in her search, until that day when she had seen Everet Mapleson in New York and believed him to be Geoffrey. Her disappointment and grief, at his persistent denial of all knowledge of her, had actually prostrated her for the first time during all her tireless search, and she had not been able to leave her bed for several weeks, which accounts for young Mapleson's inability to find her.

At length, during the last few months, she had relinquished all hope; but an insatiable longing seized her to visit her old home once more, and the kind family who had befriended her in the hour of her sore need. After that, she meant to draw her money from the bank in San Francisco, and with it purchase a right in some home for the aged, where she could peacefully spend the remainder of her life.

The woman was not old, being only about forty-five years of age, but her sorrow and the laborious existence she had led had aged her far more than even another decade could have done.

She could tell Geoffrey nothing more regarding the identity of his father than he already knew. She had never seen him since his last visit to her home, more than a year previous to the tragedy, and she had never known any other address than the one of which Mr. Bruce had spoken. He had told her to send a letter to "Lock Box 43, Santa Fe," if anything should ever happen to his boy, and she wished to summon him.

But she had gone away without communicating with him; she had been eager to get away before he could come again, for she had not courage to meet him and tell him the dreadful story about his child, which she alone knew.

"Margery," Geoffrey said, gravely, after she had concluded her account, "have you never thought that there was something very strange in the fact that my father should have been so reserved about himself, and kept his only child so remote and concealed from all his friends?"

"Yes, Master Geoffrey, it did strike me as queer, at times; but I reasoned that perhaps he hadn't any very near friends, for he talked of putting you to some school as soon as you were old enough to go away from me."

"Do you think that everything was all right between him and my mother?"

"How right, sir?" the woman asked, with surprise.

"Do you think that they were legally married? Did you never see or hear anything while you lived with them, to make you suspect that they might not be husband and wife? It is a hard question for a son to ask, but the secrecy, with which my father has seemed to hedge himself about, has led me to fear that there was some grave reason why he could not, or would not, have me with him and openly recognize me. Why was he unwilling to have you use his name if you had occasion to write to him, but instead gave you a blind address, which no one could recognize, and to which, doubtless, he alone had the key?"

"Good lord, Master Geoffrey, never have any such thoughts entered my head before!" Margery exclaimed, in a tone of startled amazement. "I never saw a man fonder of his wife than Captain Dale was of your mother; and he had reason to be fond of her, too, for she worshiped the very air he breathed, and was always so sweet and merry that a man would have been a brute not to have loved her. But——"

"Well?" queried Geoffrey, eagerly, the hot blood surging to his brow, with a feeling of dread, as she stopped, a note of sudden conviction in her tone.

"Well, I do remember, once, that she did not seem quite happy, but I have never given it a second thought until now," Margery said, reflectively.

"Tell me about it," the young man commanded, briefly.

"They had been out for a walk one night after tea, and it was quite dark when they returned. They stopped a moment on the steps, before coming in, and I was at an open window up stairs just above them. Your mother had been crying—I could tell by the sound of her voice—all at once she turned and threw her arms around the captain's neck and sobbed:

"'Oh, Will, I wish you would, for my sake and—for our baby's sake.'

"'I will, my darling,' the captain told her, 'it shall be done just as soon as I can turn myself, but it would ruin me to do it now. Have patience, my pet, and it will be all right in a few months more, at the furthest.'

"She didn't say another word, only uttered a tired kind of sigh, kissed him softly, and then they went in. But I never thought much about it afterward. I didn't know but what she had been coaxing him to leave the mines and go back to where they came from, for I'm sure it couldn't have been nice for her to live there where there wasn't hardly another woman fit to associate with her," Margery concluded, thoughtfully.

But Geoffrey believed his gentle mother had been asking for something far more important than a change of residence; that would have been of comparatively little consequence to her, loving his father as she did. He imagined that she had been pleading to be recognized as Captain Dale's lawful wife, so that her child might have honorable birth.

He sighed heavily, for the farther he went in his search the darker and more perplexing grew the way.

CHAPTER XXX
A STARTLING RECOGNITION

Reaching the public house where he had left Jack, Geoffrey quietly drew Margery into the small parlor, where he made her lay aside her bonnet and cloak, put her into a comfortable rocker to rest, and then went out to break the glad tidings of her existence and return to her husband.

He found him sitting alone on the porch outside the bar-room—nothing ever tempted him inside such a place nowadays—looking wistfully out toward the east, where the full August moon was just rising above the horizon in all its splendor.

"Well, Jack, has the time seemed very long to you?" Geoffrey asked, in a cheerful tone, as he sat down beside him.

"It has, sir; I've had hard work to wait. I've a strange hankerin' after the old home to-night. If I could only wake up and find I'd been dreamin' all these years, and the old place just as it was, with my girl waitin' at the door for me, I'd almost be willin' to give up my hope o' heaven. But when I think it's only an empty house—a cold hearth-stone, and—a grave somewhere nigh, that I'm goin' to find, I feel a'most like givin' up the battle."

The man's head sank upon his breast in a disconsolate way, while it seemed as if he had no heart to ask Geoffrey anything about the trip from which he had just returned.

The young man waited a few moments, hoping he would question him; but as he still remained absorbed in his own sad thoughts, he at length remarked:

"Well, Jack, I found Farmer Bruce."

"Ay! then he's alive yet; he must be nigh on to sixty," the man replied, looking up now with a gleam of interest.

"I should judge him to be about that; but he's hale and hearty, and seems like a very kind-hearted man, too."

"A better never lived!" Jack affirmed; "many's the good turn he and his wife has done me, and—ah!——"

A shiver completed the sentence, as if those by-gone days were too painful to dwell upon.

Geoffrey pitied the poor fellow from the depths of his heart, and yet he hardly knew where to begin, or how to break his good news to him.

"Shall I tell you what Mr. Bruce told me, Jack?" he at length asked.

The man nodded, and, by the light of the moon, his companion saw a gray pallor settle over his face, which seemed to have grown almost rigid in its outlines.

Geoffrey began by telling him how Mrs. Bruce had gone over to borrow some tea of Mrs. Henly, the day following Jack's flight; how she knocked and there came no response, when she stepped into the kitchen and found Margery lying on the floor, and becoming so frightened at the sight, she had turned and fled back to her home, with hardly more than a glance at the prostrate woman.

"Farmer Bruce," he went on, "at once went back to your house, taking his son and a hired man with him. They lifted Margery and laid her on her bed, and then John Bruce rode off with all his might after a doctor——"

"Doctor! What could they want of a doctor?—a coroner, ye mean," interrupted Jack, in a thick, hoarse voice.

"No, a doctor, Jack—she needed one; she didn't need a coroner."

"Ha!"

The man started wildly to his feet as the hoarse cry burst from him; then he sank back again, pressing his hands hard against his temples and staring about him in a half-dazed way, as if he had not comprehended what he had heard.

"Master Geoffrey, don't—don't tell me no more," he pleaded, in an agonized tone. "I can't bear it; they didn't need any doctor to tell them that she was dead—just tell me where to find her grave. I'll go and take one look at it; then I'll make tracks again for Australia; I can't stop here."

The man's tone was so despairing, his attitude so hopeless, and his words so heart-broken, that Geoffrey had hard work to preserve his own composure.

"But, Jack, there—there isn't any grave," he said at last.

Jack lifted another vacant look to the young man's face.

"No grave! no coroner! a doctor!" he muttered, then suddenly he seemed to comprehend, and was galvanized into life.

He sprang up; he seized Geoffrey by the shoulder.

"Boy! boy!" he cried, in a strained, unnatural voice, "ye can't mean it! ye can't mean that she didn't die! that—that I didn't kill her after all! Tell me—tell me quick! if ye've brought me such blessed truth as that, I'm yer slave as long as I live."

He was terribly agitated. He shook as if he had suddenly been attacked with violent ague, and Geoffrey could see his broad chest rise and fall with the heavy throbbing of his startled heart.

"Sit down, Jack," he commanded, rising and putting him back into his chair; "you must be more calm, or I cannot tell you anything. Margery was not dead, but she was dreadfully hurt, and was ill for a long time, so ill that for more than a month they thought every day that she must die."

"And—she—didn't——"

The words were almost inarticulate, but Geoffrey understood him by the motion of his lips.

"Don't tell me," he continued, catching his breath in a spasmodic way, a look of horror in his eyes, "don't tell me that she lived to be—like as you was."

"No, no, Jack, she got well," Geoffrey replied, but his own voice shook over the words.

"O-h! my girl!"

Jack Henly slipped from his chair, falling upon his knees beside his companion, while his head dropped a dead weight against his arm.

"Look here, my man," Geoffrey now said, with gruff kindness, though he was nearly unmanned himself, "this isn't going to do at all. You must brace up, for there is a long story to be told yet."

He lifted him to his feet by main force, drew his arm within his own, and compelled him to walk up and down the porch two or three times. Then he seated him again, and began at once to tell poor Margery's story.

The man listened as if spell-bound; he scarcely seemed to breathe, so intent was he to catch every word. He did not move, even, until Geoffrey mentioned meeting the strange woman in the wood, when he looked up, a wild gleam in his eye, a cry of joy on his lips.

When Geoffrey repeated what she had told him about her traveling from city to city, searching for her husband, working at whatever her hand could find to do, to earn the money necessary to keep up her tireless quest, he could control himself no longer. Great sobs broke from him.

"My girl! my girl! I never deserved it of her! Where is she, Master Geoffrey? tell me and I'll creep on my knees to her feet and ask her forgiveness!" he wildly cried.

"Jack, she is here!"

"Here! Where?" and he glanced about him in fear and awe.

"Here, in this very house! waiting, longing to see you! to ease your conscience of its burden, and tell you that she freely forgives everything!"

"Can she?" the trembling husband breathed in an awed tone.

"Come and see," Geoffrey returned, and taking him by the arm, he led him toward the parlor where Margery was anxiously awaiting him, her patience nearly exhausted by the long delay.

Reaching the door Geoffrey opened it, pushed Jack inside the room, then shut the two in together.

"Jack!"

"Madge! my girl!"

The glad, fond cry of the wife, restored at last to her long-sought loved one, the pleading, repentant intonation of the erring husband, were the only sounds that he caught, as he turned away, and with tears in his eyes, went out alone into the quiet summer night leaving them in their joy.

Two hours later, Jack came to seek him, but he walked like a drunken man, weakly and unsteadily.

His unexpected happiness was almost more than he had strength to bear, and he seemed weak and shaken as if from a long illness; but on his rough and weather-beaten face there was a look of peace and joy that Geoffrey never forgot.

"Master Geoffrey," he said, in an humble tone, though there was a ring of gratitude and gladness in it; "it's all right at last, thank God! I'll never say there ain't a God again. I can face the whole world, now that my Madge lives and loves me the same as ever. I can breathe free once more, since I know her blood ain't on my hands—oh! it's too good a'most to be true!" he continued, drawing a long, full breath, "and bless ye, sir, all I've got in the world wouldn't pay ye what I owe ye."

"Jack, you owe me nothing," Geoffrey responded, grasping him heartily by the hand. "I do not forget who cared for me during the first few years of my life, and if I have helped in any way to restore peace to you and happiness to Margery, I am more than paid already."

"Thank ye, sir; but won't ye come in and sup with us—that is if ye haven't had something already."

Jack pleaded with an air of humility.

"No. I've been too busy with my thoughts to care anything for eating, and I'll join you with pleasure," Geoffrey answered, cordially.

He returned to the parlor with Jack, where he found Margery with a beaming face, and the landlady laying the table for three.

It was two hours later before they separated for the night, and during that time many plans for the future were discussed by the reunited couple.

Neither Jack nor Margery felt inclined to remain in the West, where they had suffered so much, and where there would be constant reminders of the painful past, and it was finally decided that they should proceed at once to the farm which Jack still owned in New Jersey, and if Margery was pleased with the place they would settle there and spend the remainder of their lives upon it. The next morning they went to pay Farmer Bruce a visit, and inform him of the happy ending to all their trouble.

The following day they went to San Francisco, where they drew Margery's money from the bank, in which it had remained so long, and a snug little sum it was, too, having accumulated for so many years. A week later they all turned their backs upon the Pacific coast and set their faces toward the East. Geoffrey accompanied them as far as Cheyenne, Wyoming, where he took leave of them, as he was going southward into New Mexico again. But he promised to pay them an early visit when he should return to Brooklyn.

While these events were transpiring in the far West, an interesting incident occurred in the far East—in no other city than Boston—which has its bearing on our story and properly belongs here.

On a bright, beautiful summer morning, in the month of July, a lady entered a handsome drug store on Washington street, and asked permission to look at a city directory.

She was a finely formed, brilliant-looking woman, elegantly dressed, and bearing herself with the ease and self-possession of one accustomed to the most cultured circles of society.

A portly gentleman, with a wealth of white hair crowning his shapely head, and wearing gold-bowed spectacles, stepped from behind his desk as the lady made her request, and politely laid the book before her. As he did so, and his keen glance fell upon her face, he started slightly, but was far too well-bred to betray his surprise at her appearance, if he experienced any, and immediately returned to his post at his desk.

But he managed to place himself where he could see his visitor, without being himself observed.

The woman turned to the D's in the directory, and ran her neatly gloved finger slowly down the line, pausing here and there as a name appeared to attract her special attention.

After carefully searching several pages, she turned back and began to go over the same ground again, while a faint line of perplexity and annoyance appeared between her finely-arched brows.

This second search seemed to be as unsuccessful as the previous one had been, and for the third time she reviewed the list of names under the letter D. It was useless, however; the name she sought was not there. She stood musing for a few moments, then opening her pocket-book—an elegant affair of Russia leather with clasps of gold—she took from it a card to which she referred.

"The name is surely not in the directory," she murmured.

There was a moment of silence, then the distinguished-looking gentleman behind the desk stepped forward again.

"Did you speak to me, madame?" he inquired, blandly.

The lady started and looked up quickly, the color on her cheek deepening a trifle at his query.

"I did not know that I spoke at all," she replied, with a brilliant smile, which revealed two rows of white, handsome teeth, every one of them her own.

"I beg your pardon," said the druggist, with a bow and a backward step, as if to beat a retreat again.

Madame made a motion with her faultlessly gloved hand to detain him.

"I was looking for the name of August Damon," she said, her eyes wandering again to the directory; "but I do not find it there."

"Ah! some one whose residence you wished to find in the city?" the gentleman remarked.

"Yes. I imagined I should find him here," said the lady, thoughtfully.

The druggist drew the book toward him, ran his eyes through the names under the D's.

"The name is not here," he said at last, as he raised his glance and fixed it with keen scrutiny upon that beautiful face before him.

Madame tapped her foot impatiently and somewhat nervously on the floor.

"I am greatly disappointed," she said.

"You are sure that you have the correct name—you have made no mistake?" the gentleman inquired, glancing at the card in her hand.

"Yes: but you can see for yourself," and she passed it to him, with a smile.

It was a common visiting card, yellow, and defaced with age and handling, and it bore the name of "August Damon," written with ink in a fine, gentlemanly hand.

"Do you know that your friend resides in Boston, madame?" the pharmacist asked, as his keen eyes fixed themselves again upon her countenance.

"They—used to; it—is some years since I last visited the city, and it is possible they have removed to some other place. They must have done so," she concluded, with a sigh, "or I should surely have found their name in the directory."

"Were Mr. and Mrs. Damon the parties to whom you gave your child, Mrs. Marston?"

The question was very quietly, very politely put, but it was like the application of a powerful galvanic battery to the woman on the other side of the counter.

A shock—a shiver ran through her entire frame.

She grew deadly white, and for a moment seemed ready to drop to the floor.

Then she rallied.

"Sir!" she said, with a haughty uplifting of her proud head.

"Madame!"

"I do not understand you."

"Did you not? Shall I repeat my question?" was the quiet query.

She made a gesture of impatience.

"You have made a mistake," the lady returned, but her eyes were searching the druggist's face with a lightning glance, while that deadly paleness again overspread her own.

"Nay, madame," was the bland rejoinder; "I am one of the few men in the world who never forget either a face or a name! Mrs. Marston, surely you have not forgotten Doctor Thomas Turner who waited upon you at the — — House one bitter night in the winter of 18—."

CHAPTER XXXI
A RETROSPECTIVE GLANCE

It was indeed Doctor Turner, although twenty years or more had changed him greatly.

They had given portliness to his form, turned his dark brown hair to a silvery whiteness, and seamed his face with many a line of thought and care.

He now wore, too, a full beard, which was also very gray, although not as white as his hair, while the gold-bowed spectacles, which had become a constant necessity, added to the strangeness of his appearance.

He had given up his practice some ten years previous, and was now the sole proprietor of the handsome drug store on Washington street, already mentioned.

But, although Doctor Turner had spoken with the utmost confidence in addressing the lady before him, charging her with her identity, he was nevertheless somewhat staggered when she looked him calmly in the eye and replied, without a tremor, in her full, rich tones:

"You are mistaken, Doctor Turner—if that is your name—mine is not 'Mrs. Marston,' and never was."

"I know that your true name is not Mrs. Marston and never was," the physician replied, after a moment's quiet study of his companion; "but you are nevertheless the woman whom I attended at the — — House on the date I have mentioned. You are very little changed, and I could not fail to recognize you anywhere."

The woman's face grew crimson, then startlingly white again; her eyes drooped beneath his steady gaze, her lips trembled from inward excitement.

"You have a remarkable memory," she murmured, and stood confessed before him.

"No better than your own, madame, if I had changed as little as yourself. Time has dealt far less kindly with me. Not a thread of your hair has silvered, your color is as fresh, your face as fair as on the day of our last meeting. Pardon me," continued the doctor, with a deprecating gesture, "for reminding you so abruptly of the past, but I have never ceased to feel a deep interest in the mysterious case to which I have referred, and I could not refrain from renewing the acquaintance."

"With what object?" queried madame, with cold dignity.

"I cannot say that I have any definite object in mind," responded the physician, suavely; "possibly I imagined I might be on the brink of a discovery. However, that is neither here nor there; if you are desirous of finding the gentleman who adopted your child, it may be that I can assist you, if, after you confide in me your reasons for seeking him, I shall deem it advisable."

Mrs. Marston started slightly at this.

"Do you know August Damon?" she asked.

Doctor Turner smiled.

"Madame," he said, "did you imagine that the gentleman who took your babe would be any less cautious than yourself in such a transaction? You were known as Mrs. Marston, but frankly confessed that the name was an assumed one. Your object was to find the child a good home and then drop out of sight altogether, so that those who took it should never be able to identify you afterward. Did you suppose it was to be a one-sided affair, that you were to have all the power and advantage in your own hands?— that if you withheld your true name they would give you theirs?"

Mrs. Marston, as we must still call her, flushed hotly.

"Then Damon was not the true surname of those people," she said, in a crest-fallen tone.

"No, madame."

"What was it?"

Doctor Turner did not reply for a moment.

Finally he said:

"Mrs. Marston, pray do not let me keep you standing; come into my private office and be seated; we can converse much more comfortably there and be free from intrusion, if customers should come in."

Mrs. Marston shivered slightly, although the day was an unusually warm one. She did not wish to talk over the long-buried past, and this recognition had been a bitter blow to her; but her curiosity regarding her child's fate was so great that she could not resist the physician's invitation, and she followed him to a small room beautifully fitted up as a consulting office, at the rear of the store.

Doctor Turner politely handed her a luxurious chair, and then seated himself opposite her.

"It is doubtless a great surprise to you to find me situated as I am," the physician remarked, by way of opening the conversation; "but some years ago my health gave out under the strain of a large and constantly increasing practice, and I was forced to relinquish it, although I still receive some office patients."

Mrs. Marston merely bowed in reply to this information, her manner indicating that she cared very little about Doctor Turner's personal history.

She glanced at August Damon's card, which she had recovered when Doctor Turner relinquished it.

"You were going to tell me the real name of the person whom this card represents, I believe," she said.

The druggist smiled, yet bit his lip with vexation at himself for having intruded his own affairs upon her, even for the purpose of making her feel more at her ease. He might have spared himself that trouble.

"That will depend entirely upon your motive in seeking them," he replied.

Mrs. Marston flushed again.

She was an exceedingly high-spirited woman, one could perceive at a glance, and it galled her beyond expression to have any one make conditions for her like this.

"How can it matter to you what my motives are?" she demanded, imperiously.

"A physician has no right to betray the confidence of his patients," calmly responded the doctor; "and unless you have some urgent reason for your request, I shall not feel at liberty to give you the information you desire."

"Are you their physician?"

"I was, for a time. I was first called to the child not three days after it had been given to them."

"How could you tell that it was the same child? Babes of that age look much alike."

"Do you suppose that a man in my profession could be so lacking in observation as not to recognize a babe at whose birth he had officiated, and in which so much of unusual interest seemed to center?" queried Doctor Turner, with a slight curl of his lips. "I knew her the moment I saw her; but they do not know, to this day, that I had even a suspicion that she was not their own flesh and blood."

"You never told them?" said Mrs. Marston, quickly.

"Madame," returned the gentleman, with dignity, "need I remind you again that an honorable physician never betrays the confidence of his patients. You confided in me to a certain extent, and I knew that you wished to drop entirely out of existence, as far as your relation with the child and its adopted parents were concerned. I knew also that they wished its adoption to remain a secret—consequently my lips were sealed."

The lady's eyes drooped and all the haughtiness vanished at these words.

"Thank you, Doctor Turner, for your consideration for me, and I am glad, too, that one so conscientious has been intrusted with the care of the child," she said, earnestly. "Is—she still living?"

"Yes, and as beautiful a young lady as any one would wish to see."

Mrs. Marston's face clouded, and a sigh escaped her red lips. Her companion thought it one of regret and yearning.

"Has she been well reared? Has she had advantages?"

"The very best that money could procure or fondest affection could suggest. Mr. August—ah—Damon——" the doctor caught himself just in season, for the gentleman's true name had almost escaped him, "has become a rich man, and no parents could have done more for the welfare of their own child than they have done for yours."

"Are there other children?"

"No; that is, they have none of their own, though I believe they have been giving a poor boy of great promise a home and an education during the last eight or ten years."

"Does she—the daughter—know that she is an adopted child?" Mrs. Marston inquired.

"I cannot say positively as to that," Doctor Turner replied. "She did not know it a few years ago, and I imagine she has never been told. I hope not, at all events; it would be better for her never to know it," he concluded, with significant emphasis.

"Yes," returned his companion, "I suppose it would. But you have not yet told me the name."

"And you have not told me your motive in wishing to learn it."

"I do not know that I have any special motive, other than a curiosity and a natural desire to know how my child is living, and how life has dealt with her," the lady answered, musingly. "I was traveling this summer and thought I would take Boston in on my route, ascertain, if I could, the residence of the people to whom my babe had been given, and perhaps obtain a glimpse of her."

"That is your only motive, your only reason?" the doctor asked, bending a searching glance upon her handsome face.

"It is."

"Then pardon me, madame, if I tell you that I do not consider it of sufficient importance to gratify your desire," Doctor Turner returned, gravely. "I can understand and sympathize with you—it is but natural that a mother should yearn for her child, even after a separation of more than twenty years; but I know well enough that Mr. Damon would not have withheld his true name from you unless he desired to cut you off from all future knowledge of the child whom you had given him. You also wished to drop entirely out of their orbit, to leave no trace by which they could ever find you, to learn the secret you were so careful to preserve, and they have only aided you by concealing their own identity. If you should put yourself in their way and try to see their daughter, they could not fail to recognize you, as I have done, and it would greatly disturb their peace; while if anything should occur to arouse the young lady's suspicions that she does not really belong to the parents whom she so fondly loves, I am sure it would cause her a great deal of unhappiness, while it might result in inquiries and discoveries that would be embarrassing to yourself."

Mrs. Marston sat proudly erect at this, her eyes flashing warningly.

"Such inquiries might be embarrassing, it is true, but they could result in nothing that would bring discredit upon either the child or me," she said, with conscious dignity.

"I do not question that, madame, yet it would seem to be the wiser course to let everything rest just as it is," said the physician, thoughtfully.

"Perhaps you are right," responded his companion, with a sigh, "but I would like to see her."

"Allow me to ask, Mrs. Marston," Doctor Turner resumed, after a minute of silence, "is your husband still living?"

The woman flushed, a startled, painful crimson, to her brow; then she straightened herself haughtily.

"Yes, my husband is living," she icily replied.

"And, excuse me, but having been your medical attendant, I feel something of an interest in the case—how was he affected by the—the loss of his child?"

Doctor Turner knew that he was trespassing on dangerous ground, but, under the circumstances, he felt that he might be pardoned for asking the question.

"I do not feel that you have a right to interrogate me thus," Mrs. Marston responded, with some excitement, "nevertheless, I am somewhat in your power, and——"

"Madame," interrupted the physician, with an air of pride, "you need not go on; if a little bit of your life is in my keeping, I assure you it is in the keeping of a conscientious man. Whatever I may possess regarding any patient, I could never use it in a dishonorable way."

"I beg your pardon," his companion said, instantly disarmed and secretly ashamed of her sudden anger. "I am very quick, and you touched a sensitive nerve. Doctor Turner, my husband never knew of the birth of that child, and he can never know of it.

"You look at me with horror," she proceeded hastily, as she met his astonished gaze, "as if you imagine that I must have been guilty of some great crime; but I have not, unless giving away my babe was one. I was a lawful wife, as I convinced you at the time, and the child had honorable birth; but there were reasons which made it absolutely necessary that I should conceal my maternity from every one who knew me. I did, from all but my sister, who has since died."

"Ah! then the lady who was with you at the time was your sister. I could not believe her to be simply a maid," the doctor interposed.

Mrs. Marston bit her lips with vexation at having thus thoughtlessly committed herself even in so small a point.

"Yes," she said, after considering a moment, "she alone knew my secret, and I believed it safe from all the world until I stumbled upon you to-day."

"It is safe even now," the physician hastened to assure her. "Believe me, I shall never betray it—you may set your heart wholly at rest upon that point."

"Thank you—I am very grateful for your past silence, Doctor Turner, and your assurance of future secrecy. I am not a heartless woman, nor devoid of maternal affection," she went on, her lips quivering painfully. "I could have loved my baby as fondly as any mother ever loved her child, if I had been allowed to open my heart to her; but I could not. I had to steel it against her. I never dared even to allow myself to kiss her until the moment they took her away—for fear that I should begin to love her and refuse to part with her. I cannot tell you why—I can never explain it to any living being. I am hedged—I have always been hedged about by circumstances that made it impossible, and as long as I live I must carry the secret locked within my own heart."

She stopped for a moment, overcome by the sad memories and emotions which this retrospective glance aroused, while the good doctor felt more genuine sympathy than he had ever experienced for her over that mysterious occurrence so many years ago.

"I will try to be content with what you have told me to-day," she resumed, presently, "although it was my intention, when I came here, to see for myself how my child had been reared. I am glad to know that she has been tenderly shielded by parental love—that life has been made bright and beautiful for her; may it ever be so, and perhaps, some time, in the great future, where there can be no secrets, I may be allowed to recognize and love the daughter which stern fate decreed I could not have in this life."

Tears actually arose to the physician's eyes at this little glimpse of the innermost sanctuary of the beautiful woman's heart; but he marveled more than ever at the terrible secret which must have well-nigh blighted her early life.

She looked up, caught his sympathetic glance, and was instantly the proud, self-possessed woman of the world again.

"And now, Doctor Turner," she said, rising and drawing her elegant lace mantle about her shapely shoulders, "I trust we may never meet again. If chance should throw us together in the presence of others, I beg, as a personal favor, that you will not recognize me without a formal introduction."

"I will not, madame; and for the sake of your peace of mind, I, too, hope that our paths may never again cross," he replied.

He accompanied her to the door, where they bowed politely and formally to each other, and then the handsome woman swept out upon the street, as composed and self-possessed as if she had merely been purchasing some trifling article for the toilet, instead of rolling away the stone from a sepulcher where, for more than twenty years, a corroding secret had lain concealed.

Doctor Turner went back to his private office, where he sat a long time, musing over the wonderful mystery which had stood the test of nearly a quarter of a century, and wondering if he should ever learn the solution to it.

"It was the most perplexing, yet romantic, incident connected with my whole life as a physician," he murmured. "If I could but get at the inside history of it I could write a book worth reading.

"It was almost too bad," he added, some minutes afterward. "not to tell her about Huntress—it is possible no harm would have resulted from the knowledge; but if there had I should have blamed myself. It was better not."

He watched the passers in the street for several days, hoping to get another glimpse at his visitor.

But he did not—he never saw her again.

CHAPTER XXXII
GEOFFREY FINDS A RELIC

Geoffrey Huntress arrived in Santa Fe late one evening, and in the midst of a driving storm, about a week after parting from Jack and Margery Henly.

He was glad to seek shelter in the nearest public house, which proved to be an adobe, and was kept by a goodnatured Spaniard and his wife, both of whom could speak English passably well.

Everything was in the most primitive style, yet comfortable, and the house was a most acceptable refuge from the raging tempest without.

Geoffrey slept well, and awoke to find a bright, beautiful morning breaking, and all nature fresh and attractive in its newly washed attire.

He ate heartily of the savory breakfast that had been prepared for him, and then started forth in search of the post-office to learn what he could regarding the history of Lock Box 43.

He was somewhat disappointed to find that the postmaster was a man only about thirty-five years of age, and, upon inquiry, learned that he had served in that capacity not more than five or six years.

Of course he knew at once that he could tell him nothing that he wished to know, and he began to fear that his journey hither had been all for naught.

"Who was postmaster here before you received your appointment?" he inquired, after making some general talk about the city.

"Old Abe Brown, sir, and I only hope I may be as lucky as he was; he held it for more'n fifteen years."

Geoffrey felt his courage rise at this information.

If he could only find old Abe Brown, doubtless he could tell him something interesting about Lock Box 43.

"Is he living?" he asked.

"Yes, sir, and hale and hearty, too," and going to the door, the obliging postmaster pointed out the rude dwelling which his predecessor occupied.

Geoffrey at once bent his steps thither, and was soon knocking at Mr. Brown's door.

"Come in," was the somewhat gruff, but hearty invitation, and pushing open the door, which was already ajar, Geoffrey saw an old man of perhaps sixty seated on a rude bench, weaving hats from a bundle of tough grass that lay beside him, while his wife, a woman somewhat younger, sat near him, sewing bands around and putting coarse linings into a pile of finished hats.

"Come in, stranger, come in!" repeated the man, as Geoffrey paused upon the threshold; "don't stand on ceremony, 'cause we can't, for we've got to get this case of hats off before dinner, and we'll have to work right smart to do it, too. Have a chair, sir; guess, though, you don't belong in these parts," and the old man gave the younger one a searching glance from a pair of keen eyes that gleamed beneath his shaggy, overhanging brows.

"No, sir, I do not belong here; I am a stranger," Geoffrey answered, as he entered the room and took the chair indicated. "I was directed hither to make inquiries regarding some circumstances connected with your services as postmaster several years ago."

"Eh!" ejaculated Mr. Brown, in an astonished tone, and suspending his employment to eye his visitor with an indignant glance, while his wife turned a pale, startled face to him.

Geoffrey smiled, as he realized that they imagined he had come in an official capacity.

"My inquiries are of a strictly private nature, and relate to a gentleman for whom I am searching," he explained to relieve their anxiety.

"All right; fire away then, lad," returned Mr. Brown, coolly resuming his work. "I thought if them chaps at Washington had sent any one down here at this late day to rake over old coals it was mighty queer, for there wasn't a single dis-crip-ancy from the time I went into the office till I came out. Old Abe Brown is honest if he ain't handsome," he concluded, with a merry twinkle in his eye.

"I do not doubt it, sir," Geoffrey replied, with a quiet laugh, "but I wish to ask you if you remember a man who hired Lock Box 43 for several years in succession during your term, and who had his letters, or at least, some of them, directed simply with that inscription?"

"Yes, sir, I do remember him—a tall, handsome chap, with blue eyes, and brown hair, and he had the finest beard I ever saw on a man, the first time I saw him; he had it all shaved off, though, after a while. I say, stranger,

I reckon he must have been something to you, for I'm bless'd if you don't look like him!"

The man drooped his hat upon this discovery, and leaned forward for a better view of Geoffrey.

"Go on, if you please," the young man said, briefly.

"Well, as I said, I remember him; I don't often forget anybody that I've ever had any dealings with," Mr. Brown resumed. "He was a generous fellow, too; had plenty of money, and scattered it right and left like a prince. It was a curious conceit, though, his having his letters sent just to the box— some of 'em; they didn't all come that way."

"No?" cried Geoffrey, eagerly. "To whom were they directed? What was his name?"

"Well, now," said the old man, again laying down his hat, and scratching his head meditatively. "I shouldn't wonder if you'd got me this time. I'm pretty good at spotting a face, but when it comes to names and figures—unless somebody happens to be owing me"—he interposed, with a sly smile, "I don't amount to much. 'Pears to me, though, his first name was William—William—hum! I don't know—William something; and there was a general or captain—I can't remember which—tacked on to it besides."

"Was his last name Dale, do you think?" Geoffrey asked.

Mr. Brown shook his head doubtfully.

"I couldn't swear 'twas, or 'twasn't," he said. "Somehow, that don't strike me as sounding just natural—I've a notion there was more to it."

"I am very anxious to know it, and would be willing to give a great deal to be sure of it. Could you find out in any way what it was?" the young man inquired, anxiously.

"I don't believe there's a single soul in Santa Fe to-day who was here as long ago as that, except my wife here. Maria, do you remember that handsome gentleman who used to have Lock Box 43?" the old man asked, turning to his wife.

"I used to see him now and then when I helped you, in the office, but I've forgotten his name, if I ever heard it," the woman replied, in a quiet tone. "But," she added, a moment later, as if some thought had suddenly occurred to her, "didn't you find something once that he lost?"

"Lor'! yes; so I did. But I'd never thought of it again if you hadn't mentioned it, and there's something marked on it, too. Perhaps that'll tell the young man what he wants to know."

Mr. Brown laid down his work, and rising, turned toward an old-fashioned secretary that stood in one corner of the room.

But he suddenly stopped, and looked searchingly at Geoffrey.

"I hope, if you find out what you want to know here, it ain't going to get the gentleman into any trouble," he said; "he was a good friend to me, and I should hate to do him an ill turn."

"You need not fear," Geoffrey answered, thinking it best to deal frankly with these honest people; "the man was my father—at least, I have strong reasons for believing so; he disappeared several years ago, and my object in coming to you is simply to try to get some clew that will help me to trace him."

"I'm afraid, sir, you've come to a poor place to find out very much," Mr. Brown remarked, and apparently satisfied with his visitor's explanation.

He proceeded to the secretary, opened one of its drawers, and took an old leather wallet from it.

Unstrapping this, he laid it open before him, and after searching some time in its various pockets, he drew forth something wrapped in brown paper.

This he carried to Geoffrey, and laid it in his hand.

"There you have it, and it's the best I can do for you," he said.

The young man quickly removed the paper, and found a portion of a golden charm or emblem; in the form of a knight-templar's cross; very handsomely enameled and engraven.

It had been broken diagonally across, the left and lower arms comprising the portion which the postmaster had found.

Geoffrey turned it over and found the name "William"—all but the last letter—engraved on the back, something after the fashion of the accompanying diagram.

The "m," and probably the surname of the owner was to be found on the other half of the cross, wherever that might be.

The young man sighed wearily, for if this was all the information which he was to obtain from his visit to Santa Fe, he would be as much in the dark as ever.

"Where did you find this?" he asked, at length, turning to Mr. Brown.

"On the floor, just under his box."

"Was he in the habit of wearing an emblem of this kind?"

"Yes, sir; he had a fine one on his watch-chain, but it wasn't like that," said Mr. Brown.

"Then how do you know that he lost this? It might have belonged to some one else."

"No; I am sure it was his, for I found it just after he'd been into the office to look after his letters, and there hadn't been another soul in the room for nigh an hour. I reckon it was one of them things like what he wore, that had been broken, and he tucked it into his pocket and it fell out when he took out his keys to unlock his box," Mr. Brown explained.

"That might have been the way of it," Geoffrey said, thoughtfully.

"I went to the door to call him back," the old gentleman continued; "but he'd got out of sight, so I put it away, thinking I'd give it to him the next time he came, and if you'll believe it, I've never set eyes on him from that day to this."

"Did he never come again?" Geoffrey asked, surprised.

"Yes, twice, though there was a good while between; but, as it chanced, I was away both times, and of course the boy I hired to help me and take my place at such times—the same one that's there now—didn't know him. The last visit he made he gave up his keys."

"How long ago was that?"

"That must have been as many as fifteen years ago, I should say; I can't just remember, though," replied Mr. Brown.

Geoffrey reasoned that probably his father had visited the place while on his way back from California, after he had been to make inquiries regarding his own mysterious disappearance, and having despaired of ever gaining any knowledge of him through Lock Box 43, had surrendered his keys.

"Did he ever reside here in Santa Fe?" he asked.

"I don't think he did, sir—he always looked as if he came from a distance, and he didn't come regular, either. I used to think he was up among the mines in the mountains."

"Did he receive many letters through this office?"

"At first he did, but not more'n three or four the last year or two, and I was to let them lay until they were come for. When he come last he said he was goin' to leave this country altogether."

"It is very strange," mused Geoffrey, as he sat turning over that little piece of gold and enamel.

"If it could but speak," he thought, "all my trouble and search would be over."

"Will you sell me this little relic?" he asked, at last, turning to the ex-postmaster.

"Bless you! no, sir. I shouldn't think of selling it to anybody; but if you're that man's son, as you say, it's yours by right, and you can have it and welcome."

Geoffrey thanked the honest old gentleman heartily for it and his kindness in answering his inquiries, and then arose to take his leave.

He picked up one of the hats that Mrs. Brown had just completed, asking if she could make him one and have it ready by the time he got around to Santa Fe again.

She said she would, and at his request named the price.

Geoffrey dropped a golden coin into her hand, remarking, with a smile, that she could give him the change when he came for the hat, or if he didn't come by the end of six weeks she would be entitled to the whole of it. He took this way to make these good people a little present without wounding their feelings, for he had no intention of ever returning to Santa Fe.

He was very much depressed by his failure to obtain any definite information regarding his father, and he found it hard to be reconciled to the fact that the ex-postmaster could not remember the name which it was so important he should learn.

He attached very little significance to the finding of the broken cross, for it proved nothing; still he put it carefully away, resolving to keep it as a curious relic.

But it was destined, insignificant as it seemed, to play an important part in the chain of evidence that was eventually to prove his identity.

It was the middle of September when he reached Saratoga again, where he found Mr. and Mrs. Huntress and Gladys, all impatient over his long absence, and overjoyed at his return. They had remained there far beyond the date they had intended, and they had only waited for his coming to go home.

They left immediately and arrived in Brooklyn the twentieth of the month, and were all delighted to be beneath their own "vine and fig tree" once more.

When Geoffrey told Mr. Huntress how fruitless had been his search, except for what he had learned from the Henlys, he replied, as he laid his hand affectionately on the young man's shoulder:

"For your sake, Geoff, I am sorry, for I know that you are sensitive regarding the subject of your parentage; but for my part, my boy, I am content, for I am free to own that I should feel a trifle jealous of any other man who should claim you and occupy the place of a father toward you."

All this was very pleasant to Geoffrey, but he knew that nothing would ever satisfy him until he could learn the whole secret; and he was now convinced that there was a carefully guarded secret regarding his birth.

The week following the return of the family to Brooklyn, Mr. Huntress came home from his office somewhat earlier than usual, and drawing Geoffrey into the library, he said:

"Geoff, you have had a good deal to say about business this summer; how would you like to get into something right away?"

The young man's face was instantly all aglow.

"First rate," he replied, eagerly. "I don't care how soon I begin to do something for myself. I've been an idler long enough."

"'An idler!' good gracious! Geoff, I wonder what your idea of work is, if you have been idle during the last four years!" exclaimed Mr. Huntress, with elevated brows.

"Well, I mean that I've been dependent long enough," Geoffrey corrected.

"Now, my boy, you couldn't hurt me worse than to talk like that. I have been paid a dozen times over, for all you have cost me, in the pride I've taken in you," his friend replied, reproachfully.

"My debt is a heavy one all the same, Uncle August—one that I can never pay—though I shall never cease to be grateful for your kindness. But about this business prospect, what is it?"

"Well, you see, the firm wants me to go to Europe," began Mr. Huntress, "to look after some of our interests there, which have been causing us some anxiety of late; but I have a perfect horror of the sea, and can't make up my mind to take the voyage. No one else can be spared, and so, if I cannot get a substitute, I suppose I shall have to screw my courage up to it somehow. Now, any man of ordinary intelligence can transact the business—the chief requisites are energy, honesty, and interest—and I want you to go in my place, Geoff. Your business career and your salary shall commence from the moment you give me your decision."

Geoffrey was all enthusiasm at the proposition, most delightful to him both as regarded business and the European trip, which had always been a coveted pleasure.

"I should like the trip, and more than all, I should like the business, if you think me competent to transact it," he said. "Here I have been racking my brains all summer to try to think of something to set myself about, and now it comes to me without an effort."

"You'll find that it will require effort enough before you get through," returned Mr. Huntress, smiling; "but it is a great relief to my mind to have you willing to undertake it. The only drawback," he added, growing serious, "is that Gladys may object to your running off in this unceremonious style, and for such a long trip; it would take five or six months to do all we want done."

Geoffrey's face fell at this.

In the enthusiasm of the moment over having some real business, he had not thought of this separation, and he knew well enough that Gladys would be very much opposed to it.

"True," he began, and then stopped.

"Gladys will surely oppose it with all her will," said Mr. Huntress, observing him closely.

Geoffrey made no reply, he was schooling himself to do his duty. He believed that he had no right to refuse this golden opportunity.

"I wonder," mused Mr. Huntress, a sly smile curling the corners of his mouth, "how it would do to let Gladys go with you; she has always been sighing for European travel."

Geoffrey sat erect in his chair, as if suddenly galvanized, and shot a look of astonishment at his companion.

"Uncle August! you know that wouldn't do at all, unless—Aunt Alice should accompany us," he said, in confusion.

Mr. Huntress burst into a hearty laugh.

"I imagine it could be managed without depriving me of my wife as well as my daughter. How would it do to have that young lady go along as—as Mrs. Geoffrey Dale Huntress?"

CHAPTER XXXIII
A WEDDING IN PROSPECT

At that moment a servant appeared at the door and was about to enter upon some trifling errand. Seeing the eager, intent look upon the faces of both men, she quietly withdrew, unobserved.

Geoffrey sat up, amazed.

"Surely you cannot mean that—that Gladys is to go as my wife?" he exclaimed, flushing hotly.

"And why not? You expect to marry Gladys some time," was the calm reply.

"Yes, I hope so, Uncle August; but I am not now in a position to properly take care of a wife."

"But we are going to pay you a good salary and defray your traveling expenses also, if you go abroad for us." said Mr. Huntress. "You will have to be away for several months, and I know that Gladys will grieve sadly over the separation. I have given the subject a good deal of thought; and I have talked it over with mother. Gladys wants a trip abroad, we want her to have it, too, and neither of us feels like crossing the ocean; therefore we have decided that the best arrangement, for all parties, will be to have a wedding and send you two off together on a bridal trip. Of course we shall miss our daughter—we shall miss you both for that matter; but the earlier you go the sooner we shall have you back again. What do you think of the proposition?"

"Nothing could give me greater happiness than to have my dearest hopes realized in this unexpected manner; but I had made up my mind not to claim the fulfillment of Gladys' promise to me until I could make a place for myself in the world, and provide a generous support for her," Geoffrey replied, with still heightened color.

"Nonsense!" began Mr. Huntress, and then suddenly checked himself. "No, it isn't nonsense, either," he added, "such a resolve was both a wise and a noble one, and worthy of you, Geoff. Under different circumstances I should feel that it would be wiser for you to wait until you were established in some profitable business. Somebody, however, must go abroad for the firm. I do not want to, neither of the other partners can leave, and so we have agreed to send some one in my place. Besides this, I am what would be termed a rich man, though I haven't as much as the Astors or Vanderbilts, and all that I have will some day belong to Gladys—except a little slice that I had made up my mind to lay aside for you—and she may as well begin to reap the benefit of it now. I want her to see the old country; she is just fresh from school, and in the right trim and mood to enjoy it; she would grieve and mope to have you go and leave her behind, so I want you to go together. I know that you would have a jolly time of it. So we will have a little knot tied beforehand, to make everything all right and proper, and then you may enjoy your honeymoon to your heart's content."

Geoffrey's heart was beating with great, heavy throbs of joy over these plans.

No thought of any such delightful scheme had for an instant entered his mind; indeed, he had feared that it would be a long time before he should feel that he had a right to ask Gladys to be his wife, and now every obstacle had been removed, and an easy path to the very summit of his hopes laid out for him.

"Well, Geoff," continued Mr. Huntress, who had been watching him while something of this was passing through his brain, "what lies heavy on your mind now? You look as somber as if I had been plotting to separate a pair of lovers, instead of giving them to each other with my fondest blessing."

Geoffrey looked up with gleaming eyes.

"I am anything but 'somber' over your proposition, Uncle August. I am simply trying to realize my great happiness," he said, in a voice that vibrated with joy; "but what will Gladys herself say to this plan?"

"Go ask her, my boy. I'll bet a big apple she won't say no," returned the gentleman, with a sly wink and a chuckle. "Hold on a minute, though, Geoff," he added, as the young man sprang to his feet to obey him, "I want to tell you a little more about the business part of the plan, before you get immersed in the lovely part of it. You've three months yet before you, as we do not want you to sail before the last of December, or the first of January— rather cold weather for a pleasure trip across the Atlantic, eh?" and he shivered at the thought; "but we can't have everything just as we want it. Another thing; owing to some details connected with our Boston house, you will be obliged to sail from that city instead of going direct from New York."

"We occasionally have some very pleasant weather in January; perhaps the fates will be propitious and give us a pleasant passage," said Geoffrey, smiling; "besides, I think I have heard that some of those Boston steamers are fully as comfortable and safe as those running from New York."

"Well, comfort yourself all you can, my boy. I don't envy you, however," retorted the elder gentleman, with a grimace. "Meantime," he continued, "we shall want you over at the office to receive instructions and gain a little knowledge regarding your duties on the other side."

"I do not care how soon you set me at work," Geoffrey eagerly replied, for he was longing with all his heart to become a man of business, and to feel that he was really doing something toward providing for his bride.

"I imagine that we shall all have enough to do if there is to be a wedding," said Mr. Huntress, smiling, "for mother and I want to marry our only daughter off in good shape, you know. There, that is all just now; you may go and find out how Gladys feels about it."

Geoffrey departed with a bounding heart, yet hardly able to realize the good fortune that had so unexpectedly fallen to his lot.

He found Gladys in the music-room, running through some new pieces which he had purchased for her the day before.

He went up to her, captured the two small hands that were evoking such sweet strains from the piano, and drew her to a small sofa that stood near.

"My darling, I have a *very* important communication to make to you," be said, bending toward her and fondly touching her forehead with his lips.

"'*Very* important?'" she repeated, archly. "You look as if it was very pleasant, too."

"It is to me, and I hope it will prove the same to you. What do you suppose our *paterfamilias* has been proposing to me this morning?" the young man asked, with a luminous face.

The beautiful girl thought a moment before replying, the quick color leaping to her cheeks.

"I *believe* I can guess it!" she exclaimed, clasping her hands with a gesture of delight. "Oh, Geoffrey, *is* he going to take us all to Europe? That *is* it!" she added, exultantly. "I know by your tell-tale face. How perfectly charming!"

Geoffrey smiled wisely.

"You have guessed too much and too little, my sunbeam," he said.

"What a paradoxical statement, my learned Bachelor of Arts! I expected better things of you," retorted Gladys, merrily.

"You have yet to find my statement true, in spite of the seeming paradox," he replied, with mock dignity. "Somebody is going to Europe—we are not all going, however."

"Oh, Geoff! you are not to be left at home, are you?" cried his betrothed, in a disappointed tone, her face paling at the thought.

"Guess again, my lady," he said, teasingly.

"Well, I know that papa would not go without mamma, and I am sure she would never cross the ocean without him, and they certainly would not take such a trip and leave me behind," responded Gladys, with a puzzled air.

"'Plato, thou reasonest well,'" quoted Geoffrey, an amused twinkle in his eyes; "and not to keep you longer in suspense, I will inform you that Uncle August has some business abroad, which, as he cannot make up his mind to the voyage, he thinks I can attend to, and he has proposed that I take you along with me. We are to have a six months' trip, combine business with pleasure, and get all the enjoyment we can out of it."

Gladys gave one startled, astonished glance at her lover's face as he concluded, and then her face clouded and her eyes dropped beneath his.

"Did—papa propose that to you?" she asked, in a low tone, a burning blush suffusing her face.

"Yes, dear. He said you had long wanted to go abroad, and he thought this would be a fine opportunity for both of us. Doesn't the idea please you?"

Geoffrey knew well enough what was passing in her mind, but he was so jubilant and so confident of the issue of the interview that a spirit of mischief possessed him to tease her a little.

"I should love to go abroad—I have always longed to go, as papa says," Gladys answered, gravely, and with still downcast eyes; "but—I do not think I can go without papa and mamma."

"Why?" returned Geoffrey, in a pretended surprise. "Uncle August thought, as you and I were both fresh from school, we should appreciate and enjoy the sight-seeing much better to go together."

"It would be lovely, but—Geoff, you know I cannot go—so," she persisted, with a crimson face, and a suspicious tremor in her voice.

He gathered her close in his arms, and laid her head against his breast.

"Darling, forgive me for teasing you," he said. "Of course, you cannot go—'so'; but, Gladys, will you go with me as *my wife?*"

He could feel the quick bounding of her heart at this unexpected proposition, and he knew well enough that she would raise no more objections to the trip abroad.

He then repeated the conversation that had passed between her father and himself that morning, telling her how surprised he had been at the plan, and how, at first, he had hardly felt it right to adopt it, considering his rather doubtful position in life. Still, he had reasoned, if he could save Mr. Huntress from a dreaded journey in the dead of winter, and if his services were to be worth the generous sum he had named as his salary, he might feel justified in waving his own scruples and in accepting the great happiness offered him, though he never would have dreamed of proposing such a measure himself.

"My Gladys," he said, in conclusion, "it is very sudden, and there is only a short time, before I must go. Will you come with me, or must I go by myself?"

There was a minute of silence, then Gladys raised her head, and laid her lips softly against her lover's cheek.

"Under such circumstances, you may be very sure that I shall not let you go alone," she murmured, with a happy little laugh.

His arms closed more fondly about her. He bent and kissed her lips, his face radiant with joy.

"Oh! my darling, who would have believed eight or nine years ago that such happiness could fall to the lot of the poor boy whom you rescued from a mob in the street," he said, in a tremulous tone.

They discussed their anticipated trip fully and freely after this, laid out their route, and formed many a pleasant plan for the coming years.

The whole family held a council that evening, and it was decided that preparations for the wedding should be entered upon immediately, and that the marriage should occur just previous to the sailing of the steamer on which the young couple would embark for Europe.

Mr. and Mrs. Huntress found it somewhat trying to contemplate the loneliness which they knew would follow the departure of their children, but they believed that the arrangement would be for their interest and happiness, and they would not mar their joy by giving expression to any feeling of sorrow or regret.

Geoffrey at once entered upon his duties, and with an enthusiasm and energy that promised well for the future; while Mrs. Huntress and Gladys busied themselves about the interesting mysteries of a wedding trousseau and preparations for the grand reception, that was to follow the marriage ceremony in Plymouth Church somewhere about the last of December or the first of January.

While all these events were transpiring in Brooklyn, Everet Mapleson was living in a state of depression and unrest in his beautiful home near Richmond.

After his trip to that mining district in New Mexico, where he had visited the grave and former home of Annie Dale, he returned immediately to Vue de l'Eau, where he remained, appearing very little like the free and easy student who had been so full of life and hope at the conclusion of his college course.

Colonel Mapleson and his wife returned from Newport about the same time, and both wondered what could have occurred to change their son thus in so short a time.

Mrs. Mapleson attributed it to his hopeless attachment to the beautiful girl whom she had seen at Yale, and for whom Everet had confessed his love; but she could not get one word from him on the subject, although she had tried to gain his confidence upon several occasions.

"Father," said the young man, coming into the library one morning, after the household had settled into its usual routine, "while you were away I visited the Hermitage, and made a singular discovery there."

"Ah! I imagined everything of a singular character had disappeared from that place when Robert Dale departed this life. What was the nature of your discovery, pray?" Colonel Mapleson remarked, looking up from the newspaper that he was reading, and removing his spectacles.

Everet described his visit to the place, told of his energetic blow upon the desk and its results, and then produced the package of certificates and the picture which he had found, to prove his statements.

"Well, this *is* a singular discovery, I confess," said his father, when he had finished. "Let me have a look at that picture."

He held out his hand, and upon receiving it he turned to the light to examine it.

"Yes, this must be a likeness of Mrs. Dale; it resembles her strikingly, although she was greatly changed, and this must have been taken many years previous to my acquaintance with her."

"Then you knew her?" said his son.

"Oh, yes; I've eaten many a fine cookie baked by her hands during my boyhood," replied Colonel Mapleson, musingly. "Poor Robert Dale! so he treasured his love for her as long as he lived!"

"And he has left all his money to her daughter," said Everet, touching the package of certificates that lay on the table.

"It would have been more to the purpose if he had given the family some of it while they were suffering the stings of poverty," Colonel Mapleson remarked, his attention still riveted upon the picture.

"Did you know the daughter?" Everet inquired.

"Yes; I had some acquaintance with her."

"Were they so very poor?"

"Well, they had a pretty hard time of it, I reckon, for a while; but I did not realize it at the time, for I was very young, only visited Uncle Jabez during my vacation; you know he sent me to Baltimore to school. Uncle Jabez gave them a cottage rent free, and gave them something besides to help eke out a small annuity that Mrs. Dale had, and that was all they had to live upon until they opened a small private school. After I came into possession of the estate I allowed them to remain in the cottage, the same as before, although they would not accept from me the money that they had received from Uncle Jabez; they were very proud."

"Then that cottage belongs to you?" Everet remarked.

"Yes."

"Has it ever been occupied since the Dales left it?"

"No."

"To whom does the furniture belong?"

"How do you know that it is furnished?" Colonel Mapleson asked, turning around and glancing sharply at his son.

Everet colored.

"I was riding by there, one day, and felt a curiosity to look inside the house— —"

"But the curtains are all drawn," interrupted his father.

"True; but I managed to get a glimpse for all that," the young man returned, lightly, although he did not care to tell just how he had learned that the house was furnished. "By the way," he continued, "there is some strange story about the disappearance of Mrs. Dale's daughter, isn't there?"

"Yes, I believe so; she went away somewhere to get a place as governess, and, as she never came back, people imagined there was some mystery about it."

"What is your theory regarding it?" Everet asked.

"My theory? I don't know as I have any; I was away traveling at the time. She may have gone as governess into some family, who afterward went abroad, taking her with them; or, what is more likely, she may have married and removed to some distant portion of the country."

"One would suppose that she would have wished to dispose of the furniture in her home before going away permanently," Everet observed.

"Oh, the furniture belongs with the cottage—didn't I tell you?" replied his father.

"No, you didn't," said Everet, dryly, and thinking old Jazeb Mapleson must have been pretty lavish with his money to have furnished the cottage in such a luxurious style for his poor relatives. "At all events," he continued, "it is strange that she did not communicate her plans, whatever they were, to some one whom she had known, isn't it?"

"Well, perhaps; but it seems to me that you are strangely interested in the fate of this girl, Ev," and his father turned about again and looked him squarely in the face, as he said this.

Again the young man colored.

"I don't see anything very remarkable about it, when I have just discovered a fortune for her," he replied, after a moment of hesitation.

"Well, no; there is something in that argument, surely," returned his father, in a tone of conviction. "How much does it amount to?" and Colonel Mapleson took up the certificates and began to examine them.

CHAPTER XXXIV
ROBERT DALE'S WILL BROUGHT TO LIGHT

He looked each paper carefully through, writing down the amounts represented, and finally adding them to find the sum.

"Well, it makes quite a handsome little fortune, when we take into consideration the fact that it has been accumulating all these years," he said, as he pushed toward his son the paper upon which he had been figuring. "And yet," he added, "I know that this cannot represent one-half of Robert Dale's fortune. What can have become of the rest?"

"He may have given it away during his life," Everet suggested.

"Possible: and yet I do not believe it," said Colonel Mapleson thoughtfully. "He was a strange character, as the hiding of these documents proves, and I am convinced there are more concealed somewhere else."

"I do not see what the man could have been thinking of, if he was in his right mind, to hide his property in such a way, without leaving some clew to it! How could he expect his heir would ever be benefited by his money, when what represented it was concealed in that secret compartment?" said Everet, impatiently.

"That is a question, and the act was only one of the many queer things that made the man what he was," replied his father.

"What will you do with these papers?" the young man inquired.

"I do not know what to do with them," returned the colonel, a perplexed frown on his brow.

"Who would inherit the property in case the direct legatee cannot be found?"

"I suppose I am the nearest of kin," said Colonel Mapleson. "It was so decided when the question as to who should inherit the Hermitage and land belonging to him, came up after his death."

"Then all this money will be yours also, if neither Annie Dale nor any of her heirs can be found?" said Everet, with suppressed eagerness.

"I suppose it will; but— —"

"But what?"

"I do not want it, Everet; I have enough without it. I would much prefer that the rightful heir should have it."

"I suppose you will advertise for Annie Dale, or for her nearest of kin?" Everet said, bending a keen look upon his father.

"I don't know. I shall have to think the matter over first—perhaps consult my lawyer about it," Colonel Mapleson replied, meditatively.

He fell into deep thought, and neither spoke for several minutes.

At length the colonel glanced up at the clock.

"Well," he remarked, with a sigh, "I have business to attend to, and I must be off."

He arose, gathered up the papers, carefully wrapping them all together, then, locking them into a drawer of his desk, he abruptly left the room.

Everet sat there for more than an hour afterward, his head bowed upon his hand, thinking deeply, his brow contracted, his whole face wearing a perplexed and troubled look.

At length, he, too, left the house, ordered his horse, and rode away in the direction of the old mill.

Reaching the Dale cottage, which was evidently his destination, he dismounted, fastened his horse, and then bent his steps around to the back door, intending to force an entrance, as before; and yet, if any one had asked the question, he could not have told why he had come there again.

But, as he was passing the window of the little bedroom, he was sure that he saw one of the curtains move.

"Aha!" he said to himself; "either a mouse or some human being was the cause of that. I do not believe there is anything inside that empty house to attract a hungry mouse, so I will be cautious in my movements, and maybe I shall make a discovery of some kind."

He slipped off his low shoes, stepped noiselessly upon the veranda, keeping out of the range of the window so as not to cast a shadow within the room, and crept close up to the low sill.

The curtain had been thrust aside a trifle, so that he could easily see the interior of the room, and he beheld that which riveted him, spell-bound, to the spot, and drove every drop of blood to his heart.

He saw his father sitting close beside the window, so close, that his lightest movement caused one of his arms to hit the curtain.

On the floor, before him, there stood an open trunk, of medium size, which, apparently, had been pulled from beneath the bed, and from which Colonel Mapleson had taken a portfolio, while he was absorbed in looking over a package of letters which it contained.

He was very pale, and his son could perceive traces of deep emotion on his face, which seemed to have grown strangely old during the last two hours.

The young man drew back, after that one look, the color all gone from his own face, and his lips strangely compressed.

Without making the slightest noise, he stole from the veranda, picked up his shoes, and hurried from the place.

Outside the gate, he paused long enough to replace his shoes on his feet, when he again mounted his horse, and rode quietly away.

Half an hour later Colonel Mapleson emerged from the front door of the cottage, and, after looking cautiously around, as if he was afraid of being observed, he passed quickly down the steps, out of the gate, carefully closing it after him, and then strode rapidly toward a thick growth of trees and bushes, behind which he had fastened his horse.

Springing into his saddle, he spoke sharply to the animal, and rode away at a brisk trot in the opposite direction from that which Everet had taken a little while before.

But at the end of a mile or so, he turned abruptly into another cart path, and, after nearly an hour's ride, came in sight of the Hermitage.

Dismounting, he led his horse behind the house into the dilapidated stable, where he would be sheltered and concealed from sight, if any one chanced to pass that way, and then he made his own way inside the Hermitage.

It was evident, from all his movements, that he had come there with some settled purpose, for he drew a hammer and chisel from one of his pockets, and then commenced a systematic examination of the room that had been Robert Dale's sanctum.

But it proved to be a rather discouraging undertaking, for there was very little about the room to suggest a place of concealment for anything of a valuable character.

There was so little wood-work about the house that there was not much chance for secret panels or closets. The doors were of oak—solid oak, for he tested them thoroughly with his hammer. The book-cases offered not the slightest evidence of any hiding-place; the desk he examined several times, finding the compartment of which Everet had told him, but no other, although he critically examined every portion of it.

The floor was of brick, paved in herring-bone patterns, but there was no indication that a single brick had ever been removed for any purpose whatever, although he inspected the whole surface with the utmost care. At last, wearied out with his fruitless efforts, he sat down in the chair before the desk, to rest and to think.

"I am confident," he muttered, "that the man must have made a will, and that there are other papers existing, representing a large amount of property. I believe he cunningly concealed them during his lifetime, thinking that when he came to die he would have warning enough to enable him to confide his secret to some trustworthy person."

He looked up at the ceiling; he closely scrutinized the window casings and the fire-place. But there wasn't a crack nor a crevice that promised a revelation of any kind.

Suddenly an idea struck him, and he hastily arose from his chair.

It was a stout office chair, cushioned with leather that was nailed to the frame. He turned it bottom side up. Nothing but solid wood met his gaze.

He set it upright again and passed his hand over the cushion. It was springless and to all appearance had never been disturbed since it was first nailed to the chair.

After thinking a moment, Colonel Mapleson took his jackknife from his pocket and deliberately cut the cover entirely off.

Only a scant layer of curled hair lay beneath, closely matted and filled with dust. He removed this, and instantly an exclamation of satisfaction escaped him, for there, in the bottom of the chair, he had discovered a square lid, so cunningly and smoothly fitted in its place that no one would ever have suspected it was there.

A tiny leather strap indicated how it was to be lifted from its place. He eagerly removed it, and, underneath, discovered a small japanned trunk about twelve inches square.

It was the work of but a moment to take it from its cunning place of concealment, where it had lain undisturbed for so many years, and set it upon the desk before him.

Then he sat down again, and gravely looked at it, while he actually trembled with excitement, and drops of perspiration stood all over his face.

It was strange that the unearthing of another man's secrets should affect him thus, and it almost seemed as if he shrank with a sort of superstitious terror from examining the contents of that inoffensive-looking trunk.

At length he raised the hasp, and threw back the lid. The first thing that met his eye was a document labeled, *"Will of Robert Dale,"* with the date, showing that it had been made only a few years previous to the man's death.

With a slight shiver of repugnance, Colonel Mapleson laid it unopened on the desk.

Underneath he found several bank-books and certificates, all in Robert Dale's name. Then, to his astonishment, he found a lady's kid glove that once had been white; a handkerchief, fine and sheer, edged with soft lace, and marked with the initials, "N. D.," worked in with hair. A little package, containing a few faded flowers, lay at the bottom of the trunk, and the secret of Robert Dale's hermit life, and of the disposal of his property, was a secret no longer.

An examination of the bank-books and certificates revealed the fact that many thousands of dollars would fall to Robert Dale's heir or heirs, whoever they might be, and that point doubtless the will would settle.

Colonel Mapleson replaced the contents of the trunk just as he had found them, until he came to the will, which he held irresolutely in his hands for a long time, and apparently absorbed in thought.

"Somebody has to know first or last," he at length muttered, with a long-drawn sigh, but, he shivered with a sort of nervous dread as he unfolded the document, which was not sealed, and began to read it.

It was very brief and comprehensive, bequeathing all that the testator possessed, unreservedly, to "Annie Dale and her heirs forever," and naming as his executor a certain man residing in Richmond—Richard Douglas, to whom alone had been confided the secret of the concealment of the will and other papers.

"Ah!" said Colonel Mapleson, "this accounts for their never having been discovered before. Richard Douglas was very ill at the time of Robert Dale's death, and was himself buried only a week later."

There was a codicil to the will, mentioning some later deposits which had been made in the name of Annie Dale, "certificates of which would be found beneath a movable panel in one end of the writer's desk, there being no room for them in the trunk with the others."

Colonel Mapleson looked greatly disturbed when he finished reading the document.

"It would have been better for me had a mountain fallen upon me, than the duty which this discovery imposes," he groaned, as he laid it back in its place and closed the trunk. "I must either do it, or commit a crime by withholding a fortune from the lawful heir."

He fell into a profound reverie, which lasted until the sun went down and the light began to grow dim and the air chill within that lonely dwelling.

An impatient and prolonged whinny from his horse at length aroused him from his painful musings, when he arose, and, taking the trunk with him, he left the house, brought forth his horse from his long fast, and started on his homeward way.

It was quite dark when he reached Vue de l'Eau, and, by exercising a little caution, he managed to effect an entrance to his library unobserved, where he immediately concealed the trophy which he had that day discovered.

While Colonel Mapleson had been engaged with his laborious search at the Hermitage, his son was earnestly pursuing investigations elsewhere.

After stealing noiselessly away from the cottage, where he had discovered his father within it looking over that trunk, he only proceeded as far as the old mill, where he again dismounted, and leading his horse beneath a shed that was attached to it, and which was so thickly overgrown with vines that it made a very secure hiding-place, he fastened him to a post, after which he climbed the stairs to the main portion of the crazy structure, and remained there, watching until he saw Colonel Mapleson leave the cottage, and when he was well out of sight he stole back to the mysterious little house, resolved not to leave it again until he, too, had seen the contents of that hitherto unsuspected trunk, and learned the secret of its being there.

He effected an entrance the same way that he had done before—by shaking loose the bolt on the kitchen door—made his way to the bedroom, lifted the valance of the couch and looked eagerly beneath it.

The trunk was there.

It was the work of but a moment to pull it forth from its hiding-place, but it was not so easy to open it.

He pried patiently at the lock for a long time before he succeeded in forcing it; but it gave way at last, and, with a thrill of expectation, mingled with something of awe and dread, he laid back the lid to examine the contents.

It was packed full of clothing.

There were dainty dresses of different materials—silk, and wool, and muslin. There were mantels and jackets, with underclothing, finely embroidered and trimmed with lace, besides many other accessories of a refined lady's toilet. There were pretty boxes filled with laces, ribbons, handkerchiefs, and gloves. There was a small jewel casket, in which there were a few but expensive articles of jewelry—a watch case, containing a small enameled and jeweled watch and chain, and many other articles in that closely-packed trunk.

But Everet cared for none of these things; he was hunting for, and at last he found, that portfolio over which his father had been so much absorbed, and he seized it with an air of triumph, for he believed it must contain the solution of the secret which of late had caused him many sleepless nights and anxious days.

CHAPTER XXXV
TWO LETTERS

The portfolio was not locked, and within it Everet discovered numerous letters, all of which were addressed to "Miss Annie Dale." Most of them were in ladies' handwriting, and a glance sufficed to show that they were from schoolmates and girlish friends.

There were also several essays, which had evidently been written by Annie herself, when she was at school, and these were carefully tied together with a narrow and faded blue ribbon. A package of little billets contained locks of hair of various colors and shades, fancifully braided and glued to the paper, each with the name of the donor written underneath. There were a few drawings, very neatly done, some of landscapes, others of flowers, ferns, and grasses, and one that brought a startled cry from Everet Mapleson's lips, for it was a faithful representation of that very house in the mining village of New Mexico, that he had visited only a few weeks since. The same hand had done this that had drawn the others, there could be no doubt, even if the initials "A. D." at the bottom had not testified to the fact.

"'A. D.,'" murmured the young man. "The puzzle is slowly unweaving itself. This trunk must have been brought here after she died; but *by whom*?"

His face was very grave and troubled, for disagreeable thoughts and suspicions came crowding thick and fast upon him.

He put the drawings carefully back into the pocket from which he had taken them, and then continued his examination of the portfolio. But he found nothing in the other pockets, save a goodly supply of stationery, and he finally came to the conclusion that if there *had* been any papers of importance in the receptacle they had probably been removed by his father that very day.

He began listlessly turning over the blotting leaves that were attached to the middle of the portfolio; there was now and then a half sheet of paper between them, but nothing else, until he came to the last two, when a scrap of paper with some writing upon it in a bold, masculine hand, fell fluttering to the floor.

Everet stooped and picked it up to return it to its place, but the instant the writing met his eye, the hot blood mounted to his brow, and he exclaimed, in a startled tone:

"At last I have found it!"

It was the *other half* of that letter, which had been torn in two, and which he had found caught in the writing-desk during his previous visit to the cottage. And this is how it appeared:

"Santa Fe, June 10, 18—.

NIE:

It is with deep pain andjust learned of the death ofse I know that this leavesannuity which was hersse and your future istle friend! I can sayn how vain andme; but, believe me, myyou, and were it pos-and strive to cheerI am now going to ask ae been friends during all ournot refuse me.

the cottage. Let it be stillas it has been in theany restrictions.

alone, for it wouldsecure some com-n yourself who will. Do not mind thethat we are relativesin this extremity.

ck sufficient forwhen I returnent arrangementI shall be veryyou.

our friend,

"William Mapleson."

Everet merely glanced at this, then taking his wallet from one of his pockets, he drew from it a folded paper.

It was the other half of the torn letter.

He laid the two portions together; the ragged edges fitted exactly, the writing was identical, and the epistle was complete, and read thus:

"Santa Fe. June 10, 18—.

"My Dear Annie:

"It is with deep pain and

regret that I have just learned of the death of

your mother. Of course I know that this leaves

you alone, and that the annuity which was hers

for life only must now cease, and your future is

unprovided for. My poor little friend, I can say

nothing to comfort you, for I know how vain and

cold words are at such a time; but, believe me, my

heart is with you. I sorrow with you, and were it possible I would come to you and strive to cheer you in this sad hour. But I am now going to ask a favor of you, Annie—we have been friends during all our life, and surely you will not refuse me.

"I want you to remain in the cottage. Let it be still your home for the future as it has been in the past—*it is yours* without any restrictions.

"You must not, however, stay there alone, for it would not be safe, and I want you to secure some companion—some one older than yourself, who will be a sort of protector to you. Do not mind the expense, Annie, for you know that we are relatives. I have a right to care for you in this extremity.

"Inclosed you will find check sufficient for your present necessities, and when I return I will make some permanent arrangement for you. Write me at once, for I shall be very anxious until I hear from you.

"Ever your friend,

"William Mapleson."

"I *thought* the writing was familiar to me. I suspected my father wrote it from the first, and yet his hand has changed very much since this was written. But surely there is nothing in this merely friendly epistle to warrant such dreadful suspicions as have nearly driven me wild during these last few weeks. I have believed the very worst—that it was *he* who enticed her away, and then betrayed her confidence. I know that he was in New Mexico at that time; I know that she went there and lived with some one for a year; and then that ring seemed to prove everything to me. Still, this is not a lover's letter; it is simply a friendly expression of sympathy and interest, and a desire to provide for a relative who had no one to rely upon. Heavens! will this mystery *never* be solved?" he concluded, rising and shutting the portfolio, but retaining the scrap of paper he had found.

He replaced everything in the trunk, closed it, though he could not lock it again, then pushed it back under the bed; after which he went quickly out of the house, feeling depressed and bitterly disappointed that he had discovered nothing tangible, either to prove or dissipate his suspicions.

As he stepped off the veranda, something white fluttered in the tall grass at his feet.

It was another letter.

A thrill went tingling all along his nerves, as he stooped and picked it up.

It was addressed to "Miss Annie Dale, Richmond, Va.," and bore the date of July 15th, of the same year as the other one already in his possession.

It was also in the same handwriting, and had been mailed from Santa Fe.

"This is one of the things that *he* came hither to secure, and he must have dropped it as he passed out," Everet murmured, as he sat down upon a step, drew the letter from its envelope, and began to read it.

"My Dear Annie," it began, like the other, "your reply to my former letter has hurt me keenly. I cannot bear the thought of your going out into the world alone to earn your own living. I hoped that you would be content to remain in your own home, and let me provide for you as a brother would do. But since you refuse—how cold and dignified your refusal was, too!—I am forced to break all barriers down and make a confession that for years I had yearned to make and dare not. Annie, you *must not* become a governess; I should be wretched to think of you in such a situation. If you will not let me take care of you there at home, in a friendly way, you *must come to me here*; for, darling, I love you. I have always loved you, ever since we played together, as children by the brook near the old mill, sailing our tiny ships side by side, and promised each other that, when we were older, we would be married, and make a voyage round the world together. Come and redeem that promise to me *now*, Annie, darling. Do not hesitate because it will involve the sacrifice of the fortune bequeathed to me, under certain conditions, for I cannot—I *will* not—marry my Cousin Estelle while I love another as I love you; and what is all the wealth of the world compared with our happiness? I am doing finely here in the mines. In a few years, at this rate, I shall be worth even more than I shall have to forfeit by this step, so I will gladly relinquish every dollar to Estelle for you, my darling.

"Annie, I believe that you love me—I have long believed it—and I have yearned to make this confession, and to hear a similar one from your lips, for a long, long time. Had I not been hampered by Uncle Jabez's will, and an unworthy vacillation on account of it, I should have told you this that last delightful summer we spent together. But I have passed the Rubicon now, so do not ruin all my hopes. I am sorry that I cannot come to you, my own love. But my presence is absolutely necessary here, and I cannot leave for such a long trip; but if your heart responds to mine—if you will come to me and give yourself to me, I will meet you on the way, at Kansas City, and from there I will take my little wife to her own home among the mountains of New Mexico, where we will be all in all to each other. You will not mind the isolation for a little while, will you, love, until I can make my fortune, when we will return again to our own dear sunny South? Annie, *will* you trust me? *Will* you come? If you do not, I believe my life will be ruined. Do not think, for a moment, that I shall ever regret Jabez Mapleson's money. I *shall* not if I can have you. Judge me by your own heart.

"Inclosed you will find the route you are to take, carefully mapped out, and the check that you would not keep before—my proud little woman! I feel sure that you can come with perfect safety alone as far as Kansas City, where I shall be surely waiting to receive you. Send a telegram naming the day and the hour when you will start.

"One thing more, love—say nothing to any one of your plans; leave that to me, to explain after we are one. Annie, you *will* not fail me. I could not bear it now, for I have set all my hopes upon you. I shall not rest until I receive your telegram.

"Ever your own, Will."

Everet Mapleson's face was as white as that of the dead as he finished reading this epistle.

"It is all true, after all," he said, with blazing eyes and through his tightly locked teeth. "It *was* he who enticed her away in secret, hiding her in that out-of-the-way place—literally burying her alive. I have been convinced of it ever since I found that ring with those initials—'W. M. to A. D.'—engraved within it, and yet I kept hoping it could not be proved. So she went to him—foolish girl!—believing that he'd marry her and give up his money; and she only lived one short year!

"Now Geoffrey Huntress' strange resemblance to me is all accounted for," he went on, after a fit of musing; "he is my father's son and—*my half brother*, and to him will belong all Robert Dale's fortune if he should ever learn the secret of his birth. Now I understand why he was given into Jack and Margaret Henly's care. It would have been very awkward for the heir of half Jabez Mapleson's fortune if that New Mexican escapade had leaked out. But I cannot comprehend how the boy became an imbecile—an accident, Mr. Huntress said—and I suppose those people got tired of caring for him and cast him off. No; that can't be, either, for that woman seemed terribly upset about it. It's all a wretched puzzle, anyhow.

"Zounds!" he continued, with sudden energy, "the governor is a wonderful actor. He never betrayed himself by so much as the quiver of an eyelid, this morning, when we talked about this girl's disappearance. I wonder what he will do about that money? Will he *dare* keep it? or will he try to find the boy and make it over to him in some roundabout way? No; I do not believe he will ever run any risk of having that New Mexican escapade revealed. He couldn't quite stand that, and my haughty mamma would never forgive him. He will keep the money, and say nothing. Geoffrey Huntress will *never* get his fortune, for *I* shall keep the secret that I have this day discovered closely locked in my own breast. Neither he nor my father shall *ever* learn through *me* that he is an heir of the houses of Dale and Mapleson.

"He loved her, though—I am sure he loved her!" he resumed, his eyes falling upon that still open letter. "This shows it in almost every line; and his face to-day, as I caught a glimpse of it through the window, as he bent over that trunk, looked as if he had just buried the dearest object of his life. It must have been hard to look at all her pretty fixings and remember that one short, happy year; for they were very happy, according to Bob Whittaker's story. That is the reason he keeps this house, and all in it, so sacred. Why couldn't he have married her, like a man? Money! money! I believe it is only a curse to half the people in the world."

He arose, folded the letter, and put it in his pocket; then going to the old mill, he unfastened his horse, mounted, and rode back to Vue de l'Eau, looking stern, and grave, and unhappy.

CHAPTER XXXVI
"HE IS NOT NAMELESS"

October and November passed without any event of special interest occurring in connection with any of our characters.

In Brooklyn, in the home of August Huntress, these were very busy days, but every member of the household was full of hope and happiness.

Gladys and Geoffrey saw but comparatively little of each other, except during the evening, for Geoffrey went early to the office in New York every morning, and did not return until dinner time at six; but both were looking forward to the thirtieth of December, the date set for their union with all the fond anticipations of young and loving hearts.

Their engagement was formally announced immediately after it was decided that Geoffrey was to go abroad, and cards for the wedding were issued by the first of December.

Congratulations poured in upon the young couple from all quarters, and, the winter being an exceptionally gay one, invitations abroad were numerous and pressing, their friends urging their presence, since they were to lose their society entirely during their long absence in Europe.

Everet Mapleson, while reading the fashionable items in a New York paper one morning, came across the announcement of this approaching marriage.

He bounded from his chair with a muttered imprecation.

"So soon!" he said, with a frowning brow. "They are in a great hurry, it seems to me; but perhaps the trip abroad explains it. Let me see—they are to be married on the thirtieth," he continued, referring to the paper again, "and will sail the next day on the Scythia. The Scythia? That is not a New York steamer—that sails from Boston; so, of course, they will have to leave New York immediately after their marriage to be in season for it."

He paced up and down the room, with bent head and sullen, thoughtful brow.

All at once he gave a violent start.

"I wonder," he muttered, stopping short in his pacing; "I wonder if it would be possible to manage it?"

He tossed back the disheveled hair from his forehead; his eyes blazed with some sudden purpose, his lips were set in a firm, livid line.

"*I shall try for it,*" he said, in a low, hoarse whisper. "I have everything to win or lose, and I will not yield without a desperate struggle."

Two hours later his portmanteau was packed, and he was taking leave of his father and mother.

They expressed great surprise over his sudden departure, and protested against his leaving home before the holidays, since they had made arrangements for a gay time at Christmas, chiefly on his account.

But he was resolute, and would not be turned from his purpose.

"There is to be a great wedding in New York on the thirtieth, for which I am booked," he explained, though he did not say who was to be married; "and I would not miss it for anything."

"Well, but you could easily reach New York in season for this wedding, even if you do not leave until after Christmas," his mother pleaded, for she was greatly disturbed to have him leave home at this time, while she suspected, from his gloomy face, who was to be married, and felt sure he was only heaping up misery for himself in going to New York.

"Perhaps I will come back just for your grand party at Christmas," he said, to appease her and be allowed to get off without further objections; "but I must run up North for a week or two, anyhow."

He reached the city on the morning of the sixth, and proceeded directly to the club, of which he was a member, and where he soon learned all that was going on among the *bon ton.*

During the following day he called upon Gladys' friend, Miss Addie Loring, from whom he meant to get all the particulars of the approaching wedding.

Miss Loring received him with evident pleasure.

"Where have you kept yourself all winter, Mr. Mapleson?" she questioned, brightly, as she cordially gave him her hand. "I feared you had deserted us altogether since leaving college."

"I have been in the South most of the time, but something, more powerful than home influence, constrained me to come to New York for a little taste of society and city life," Everet returned, in a tone and with a look that made the young lady's bright eyes droop consciously.

"Will you remain until the end of the season?"

"That depends," he replied, with a significant smile, which made her heart flutter strangely.

"New York is very gay this winter, and there will be plenty to entertain you for as long as you choose to remain," Miss Loring promised, with a charming smile. "I suppose," she added, "you have heard of the great wedding that is to come off on the thirtieth?"

"The great wedding! Whose?" Everet questioned, feigning ignorance, although the chief object of his call was to learn all he could about it.

"Why, that of your classmate and double, Mr. Geoffrey Huntress, and my dear friend, Gladys. I am astonished that you have not heard of it," said Miss Addie, really surprised that he should not have received cards for the marriage.

"Ah! So Huntress is going to marry Miss Gladys, is he? Pray, what *name* will he bestow upon the lady?" the young man asked, with a curl of his handsome lips.

"Why, of course, there will be no change of name—Geoff was legally adopted by Mr. Huntress, so that makes everything all right," returned Miss Loring, looking a trifle displeased at the slur that had been cast at her friend's betrothed.

"Then the groom-elect has never been able to discover the secret of his parentage?" Everet remarked, inquiringly.

"I think not."

"Are *you* pleased with this match, Miss Loring?"

"Of course I am—I think Geoffrey Huntress is a magnificent man," she affirmed, emphatically. "It would, doubtless, be a great comfort to him to have the mystery of his birth solved; but it doesn't matter, really—they love each other devotedly, and will make a splendid couple."

Everet winced under these last words, but deemed it wiser to keep his sneers and slurs to himself.

"I suppose it—the wedding—will be a very grand affair?" he remarked.

"Very; there are to be six bridesmaids, of whom I am to be the chief," responded Miss Addie, with animation. "They will be married in Plymouth Church."

"In *church*!" interposed Everet, with an eager look. "Will it be in the evening?"

"Yes, in the early evening—at five o'clock—and they will receive from six until eight. Mr. Huntress has spared no expense to make it a very brilliant affair. But I am surprised—I supposed, having been a classmate, you would have received cards for the wedding, Mr. Mapleson," Miss Loring concluded.

"No, I have not been honored. Will the happy couple settle in New York?"

"Really, Mr. Mapleson, you *are* behind the times," laughed his companion. "No, indeed, they sail the next day, at twelve, for Europe, to be gone for six months. Will not that be delightful? If the course of true love never ran smoothly before, it has done so in this case, for there has been nothing to mar it from the beginning."

Everet Mapleson's eyes gleamed strangely at this, and a spot of bright color leaped into his cheeks.

"On what steamer do they sail?" he inquired.

"On the Scythia, from Boston, owing to some business connected with that city. That is why the marriage and reception are set so early; they leave New York on an evening train, and will arrive in Boston early the next morning. Oh!" concluded the young lady, with a sigh, "I shall miss Gladys more than I can tell you."

"No doubt," Everet observed; and then, after conversing a few moments longer upon indifferent topics, having obtained all the points he wished, he arose to take his leave.

His chief object in calling had been to assure himself that he had not been misinformed regarding any of the details of the approaching marriage.

His next plan was to meet Gladys somewhere, if possible.

It was easy enough to do this, by securing invitations to the receptions among the *elite*, and a few evenings later he found her at a fashionable party on Lexington avenue.

She seemed lovelier than ever, with the rosy glow of perfect health on her face, her beautiful eyes gleaming with happiness, and her lips wreathed with smiles.

Her dress, on this occasion, was vastly becoming, consisting of a deep shade of ecru, embroidered with a delicate shade of blue intermingled with silver. Ornaments of silver in filigree, and set with diamonds, were on her neck and arms, while a graceful *aigrette* of blue and white was fastened in her hair by a star, to match her other ornaments.

She started slightly as she met Everet Mapleson's glance fixed upon her. He was so much like Geoffrey that it was almost impossible, even now, for her to distinguish them apart.

The next moment he was bowing before her, with extended hand.

"It seems a long time since we met, Miss Huntress," he said, in a tone which deepened the color in her cheeks, for it reminded her vividly of not only their last meeting, but also their parting.

But she thought best to ignore it all, and so returned his greeting with lady-like courtesy.

"I suppose you have been in your Southern home, Mr. Mapleson," she said. "I should think you would hardly like to leave its genial climate for our rigorous winter here."

"There are sometimes stronger attractions than a genial climate in winter," he replied, with an earnest look into her lovely eyes.

"Yes, New York is very attractive just now," she returned, determined not to appropriate his significant remark to herself, "Do you remain here long?"

"I think I may stay through *this month*," he answered, with an emphasis upon the last two words that brought the quick blood again to her cheeks, for she knew that he was thinking of her approaching marriage.

Still, she was willfully obtuse.

"What!" she exclaimed, archly. "Can you content yourself away from home during the holidays?"

"Yes—at least for *this* year. Miss Huntress, will you give my name a place upon your dancing-list?" he asked, glancing at the card that was suspended by a silken cord from her corsage.

Gladys opened and held it up before him, with a smile.

It was full, and she was glad it happened so.

His face fell, for his quick glance detected Geoffrey's name against several dances.

"I am too late, I perceive," he said, with a bow; "but, *perchance* I may be more fortunate before the month is out."

Something in his tone more than the words made her regard him closely, and a sort of chill smote her heart as she marked the peculiar gleam in his eye and the resolute lines about his mouth.

Some one claimed her just then, and, with a polite bow, she excused herself and left him, glad to get away from his presence.

The next time they met was more than a week later, at the opera.

Gladys was spending a few days with her friend, Addie Loring. It was to be her last visit before her marriage, and the two girls were making the most of it.

Mr. Loring invited them to accompany him to hear Parepa Rosa, and sent word to Geoffrey to join them; but he had an engagement for the first half of the evening, and could not; he would, however, join them later, he said in the note that he sent his betrothed.

Mrs. Loring was not well, and did not feel equal to going out, and so her husband had to be both chaperon and escort for the young ladies.

Everet Mapleson saw them the moment they entered their box, while it was not long before Miss Loring discovered his vicinity, when she bowed and smiled most cordially. A moment later she leaned forward and whispered to her father, who nodded assent, and then made a signal for Everet to come and join his party.

The young man needed no second invitation, and was soon seated between the two young ladies, gayly parrying Miss Loring's witty shots at his having come to the opera all alone, when there were so many belles and beauties who would have been delighted to share the pleasure with him.

Gladys drew herself a little apart. She felt uncomfortable to have him there, under any circumstances, while, too, she was interested in the opera, and it annoyed her to have those around her conversing, even though it was scarcely above their breath.

When the curtain went down, after the second act, Addie Loring raised her glass and began gazing about her.

Suddenly her face lighted, and, bending forward, she waved her hand to some one in the audience near them.

"Oh papa," she said, turning eagerly to her father, "there is Sadie Nutting! She must have returned on the last steamer. See! she is beckoning to me. Will you take me to her just for a few moments, while the curtain is down? I am sure Gladys and Mr. Mapleson will excuse us and entertain each other while we are gone, and we won't be five minutes."

Mr. Loring glanced at Everet, hoping he would offer to escort his daughter, for he was too comfortably seated to care to be disturbed.

But the young man had no such intention; this was just the opportunity he had been wanting, ever since he came to New York, and he meant to improve it, even though he should have only "five minutes." He said:

"Certainly, certainly," to Miss Loring, "go, by all means, to see your friend, if you wish," and he watched the father and daughter with a secret thrill of triumph as they went out, leaving him alone with Gladys.

She was greatly disturbed by the incident.

She could not blame Addie, for she knew that she was ignorant of her feelings toward Everet Mapleson; but she wished, with all her heart, that Geoffrey would come, so that she need not be alone with Everet.

The moment the doors closed upon Mr. Loring and his daughter, Everet turned smilingly toward his companion, and drew his chair nearer to her.

"Thank the fates, and that giddy girl, for this supreme moment," he began, in a low, passionate tone; adding: "Gladys, have you forgotten our last private interview at Vassar?"

Gladys looked up at him, both startled and indignant.

"I should be glad to forget it, Mr. Mapleson, if you would allow me to do so, for your sake as well as my own," she returned, with cold dignity.

"I do not *wish* you to forget it, Gladys," he returned, with increasing fervor, "for I love you a hundred fold more to-night, and I must unburden my heart to you, or it will burst."

"Mr. Mapleson!" Gladys said, half rising from her chair, a flash of anger in her eyes, "you shall not say such things to me; you know you have no right——"

"I *have* a right," he interposed, hotly; "a right because of my deathless love and my indomitable purpose to win yours in return."

"You cannot! how dare you?" Gladys began again, but he would not let her go on.

"I dare, because I *must* dare or *die!* oh! Gladys, I love you so! have pity on me!" he said, and his voice died away in an agonized whisper, showing how terribly in earnest he was.

The young girl was deathly pale now, and trembling in every limb; but she faced him with blazing eyes and curling lips, her perfect form proudly erect.

"You are no gentleman," she said, scornfully, "to say such words to one who, in less than two weeks, will be the wife of another man; to take advantage of me during the absence of my friends, and in a place like this force such a declaration upon me."

"I could not help it; I had no other time; you avoid me upon every occasion," he returned, the blood flushing his face hotly at her scorn.

"I have no choice; your looks, your acts all compel me to— —"

"I cannot help them—when I am near you I forget everything but that I love you!" he pleaded in excuse.

"Shame! Where is your sense of honor, that you persist in such language to the affianced of another?" she panted.

"Twice you have thrown that in my teeth," he retorted, fiercely, and fast losing control of himself. "Have you no shame, that you confess yourself the affianced of a nameless outcast?"

"He is not nameless, and you have no authority for calling him an outcast," retorted Gladys, proudly, all her spirit rising to arms at this attack upon her absent lover.

"Haven't I?" sneered the hot-headed young man. "Listen. I have been looking up Geoffrey Dale's pedigree, since I saw you last. I have traced him to his birthplace. His mother was a poor, but beautiful girl, without a home, without friends. She had a rich lover, who could not marry her without sacrificing a fortune, and he loved his money too well to do that, so he sacrificed the girl instead. He took her to a remote mining district, where, hidden away from every one who ever knew her, she lived with him for one short year, and died when her child was only a month old. That child was Geoffrey Dale; his mother's name was Annie Dale, and he has no right to any other, except the one that has been given him for charity's sake. You have a right to be proud of your betrothed, Miss Huntress."

"I am proud of him!" Gladys returned, in a firm, even tone. Astonishment at Everet Mapleson knowing so much about Geoffrey had contributed more toward calming her excited nerves than almost anything else could have done. "Yes, I am *proud* of him," she repeated, with a change of emphasis, "and you have told me nothing *new*, Mr. Mapleson. excepting that this young girl had no home or friends, and that the man who took her to New Mexico was rich, and willfully wronged her. Indeed, I know even more than you have told me."

"*More!* Do you know who his father was?" Everet Mapleson exclaimed, with a start.

"No, nor do I wish to, if he was guilty of the atrocious act you have named," Gladys returned, with withering scorn, "But the sin will some day recoil upon his own head: it can never change my regard for one who is innately noble and true."

"And you do not shrink from becoming the wife of one upon whom shame has rested from the hour of his birth?" demanded Everet Mapleson, regarding the beautiful girl with astonishment.

"No," she replied, steadfastly; "no shame rests upon *him*; that all belongs to the preceding generation; but I should shrink with loathing from the man who betrayed Annie Dale, as you represent, were he lord or prince—he is only worthy of my contempt, and I would scorn him as I would the veriest blackleg in this city."

The young man flushed hotly. It was not pleasant to listen to such words, believing what he did; they touched a sensitive spot.

"But this man of whom I have told you is a gentleman, nevertheless," he said.

"A gentleman?"

The words were uttered in the quietest possible tone, but the contempt which trembled through it was matchless, and made the young man wince as under a lash.

"Your distinctions are more nice than wise, Miss Huntress; but, mark my words, you shall never marry this man's illegitimate son!" he hissed, driven almost to a frenzy by her words, her look, and tone.

She turned upon him, her face colorless, but with eyes gleaming like two points of fire.

"You insult me, sir! You insult one who is a hundred fold more noble than yourself, by the use of such vile language. But," and she raised one daintily gloved hand to enforce her words, "were his name doubly tainted by the sin of others, it could not smirch the man I honor—the man I *love*. It will be the proudest day of my life when I wed Geoffrey Dale Huntress, *as I shall*, in spite of all that you have told me to-night, ay, even though you should do your worst, and proclaim it from every house-top in this city."

She was glorious, in her haughty pride and indignation, as she gave utterance to these loyal sentiments, and Everet Mapleson instinctively shrank before her with a sense of shame and humiliation. At that moment the doors behind them swung open, and Geoffrey himself entered the box.

CHAPTER XXXVII
A THREAT AND A WEDDING-RING

Gladys' first impulse, upon beholding her lover, was to spring toward him, denounce the man who had so insulted her and him, and demand to be conduced from his presence.

But her judgement told her that this would be very unwise; there must be no scene in that public place; there must be no quarrel between these two men, and perhaps it would be better that Geoffrey should never know that Everet Mapleson held the secret of his birth. She knew that he would never rest until he had wrung it from him, and that, she believed, would never be done without bitter feelings, and perhaps strife.

So, with a mighty effort, she controlled herself, drew her cloak about her shoulders to hide the heaving of her bosom, as she arose and turned a smiling, though still pale face, toward her lover.

"You have come, Geoffrey; I am *very* glad. You will recognize an old classmate in Mr. Mapleson," she said, as she moved her chair farther into the shadow of the draperies and made room for Geoffrey between herself and her other companion.

Everet regarded the girl with wondering admiration. He knew that she was laboring under intense excitement, and that it required no light effort on her part to conceal it. He understood her motives—that she wished to avoid a quarrel and a scene, and he thought her tact inimitable.

Geoffrey greeted his former college-mate courteously, which greeting Mapleson returned with a cold, rather supercilious bow. He was always conscious of his own moral inferiority when in Geoffrey's presence, and the feeling galled him excessively.

Geoffrey saw at once, in spite of Gladys' efforts to conceal it, that something had gone wrong with her, and he rightly guessed that Everet Mapleson had been the cause of it. He gently seated her, and then placed himself beside her, while Mr. Loring and his daughter returned at that moment, and the party settled themselves very comfortably for the remainder of the evening.

Everet devoted himself exclusively to Miss Loring, much to that young lady's secret delight; her father gave his attention entirely to the stage, thus leaving Geoffrey and Gladys to themselves.

"What is it, dear? what has troubled you?" Geoffrey asked, bending tenderly toward his betrothed, as he became more conscious of the difficulty she was laboring under to retain her composure.

Gladys stole one little hand confidingly into his, under cover of her opera cloak.

"Never mind, Geoff, now that I have you here; I will tell you some other time," she whispered, as she involuntarily turned her still flashing eyes toward young Mapleson, while a slight shiver ran through her frame.

Geoffrey's glance followed hers, and his face clouded.

"Has he dared——" he began, sternly.

"Hush!" she returned; "it is all past; he will never dare again."

She saw that Geoffrey needed but a word to make him demand an explanation of his rival, and she feared the worst from a meeting between them; so she resolved that she would not tell him what Everet had told her regarding his parentage; at least, not until after their marriage; perhaps, when they were on the ocean, where it would be impossible for him to take any aggressive measures until time had served to cool his anger, she might reveal to him what she had learned.

So she tried to smile and appear interested in the opera, while every moment she wished it would end so that she might be released from that terrible constraint.

It was over at last, to her intense relief.

Everet Mapleson escorted Miss Loring from the building, but when the party reached the sidewalk they found such a crowd before them that they were obliged to step back and wait for it to disperse before they could get to their carriage.

In doing this, Everet Mapleson had managed so that he should stand close beside Gladys, for he had determined to fire a parting shot at her.

He had been covertly watching her ever since their interview, and her attitude of trust and confidence toward Geoffrey had been almost maddening to him.

She was beautiful beyond comparison when she faced him in her indignation, defending her absent lover, and resenting the insult offered to herself; he had never seen her so spirited before, and it lent an added charm to her fascinations, while he was filled with impotent rage that he was powerless to awaken any feelings in her heart for him, save those of scorn and contempt.

"Why should *he* win?" he cried within himself, as he marked Geoffrey's air of tender proprietorship; "he who has not even a name to offer her, while I, who am heir to the proud escutcheon of Mapleson, and to a double fortune, perhaps a triple one, if he never discovers who he is, am able to excite nothing but aversion and contempt. I *swear* I will not submit to it, and I will find some way to part them, even now. *He* has crossed my path too many times. I have never forgiven him on the old score, and I will never forgive him for *being an interloper in my race.*"

All this was in his mind as he stood close beside the young bride-elect, while waiting for Mr. Loring's carriage, and some evil spirit possessed him to assail her again.

"Miss Huntress," he whispered, so close to her ear that no one could possibly hear him in the tumult around them, "doubtless you have heard that old saying. 'There is many a slip 'twixt cup and lip.'"

Gladys never noticed him by so much as a glance. She might have been some beautiful statue, and deaf to all sounds, for any evidence that she gave of having heard him. And yet he knew she could not have failed to catch every word that he had uttered.

His blood began to boil at being thus ignored.

"Do you imagine that I shall tamely submit to see another man win you, and he so far beneath you? *It shall never be!*"

Gladys turned at this, and looked straight into his eyes, and actually smiled—a smile that drove him almost to a frenzy; it was like a winter's sunbeam reflected from ice—sharp, dazzling, chilling.

"The *future tense* is not applicable in this case, Mr. Mapleson," she retorted, in as icy a tone, while the air with which she settled her small hand more firmly within her lover's arm plainly said, "I am *already won!*"

Everet Mapleson ground his teeth in baffled rage. It was evident that in an open battle Miss Huntress was too much for him.

"Wait," he whispered again; "the thirtieth may tell a different story; at all events, you are warned."

She did not deign to notice his threat, and, an opening now presenting itself, Mr. Loring led the way to the carriage, where, after assisting his companion to enter, Mr. Mapleson took his leave of the party and went his way.

Geoffrey was very much disturbed when Gladys told him that Everet Mapleson had again presumed to address words of love to her—for she had decided that this was all the explanation of the affair at the opera that she would give him at present—and it required all her power of persuasion to prevent him from demanding an apology for the insult.

"Let it pass, dear; pray let us have no trouble at this time," she had urged.

"But you are almost my wife, Gladys, and it is a terrible affront to me as well as to you," Geoffrey returned, hotly.

"He is so far beneath you, Geoff, morally, that I cannot bear to have you lower yourself enough to notice him, and believe me, he received a lesson that he will not soon forget," Gladys concluded, with a spirit and energy that both amused and delighted Geoffrey, who well knew what his betrothed was capable of when once thoroughly aroused, and he could imagine something of the scorn which the offender in question had called down upon his devoted head by his presumption. So he finally promised that he would not agitate the matter further, and he realized that it might result in a scandal that would prove very annoying just at that time.

It seemed, too, as if Everet Mapleson himself had no desire to come in contact with his successful rival, for he suddenly dropped out of society, and was seen no more during the interval between that occurrence at the opera and the thirtieth.

He was greatly missed, however, by many of the languishing belles, for he was esteemed "a great catch," and had been most industriously angled for by numerous anxious mammas, and scheming fathers with a doubtful bank account.

Miss Addie Loring, perhaps, really took his sudden and unaccountable absence more to heart than any one else, for she had secretly begun to entertain a tender liking for him.

During the last week before the wedding, that event became the chief topic of the day in the circle in which Gladys and Geoffrey moved, for the match was considered a most romantic one, and both parties were especial favorites, while for brilliancy and magnitude it was to be the affair of the season.

Gifts of every description poured in upon the young couple, for whom their friends seemed unable to do enough to manifest their regard for them.

"Mamma, I have silver and china enough to set up four establishments; what shall I do with it all?" Gladys laughingly remarked, one morning, after the arrival of numerous packages and cases. "While as for jewelry, *bric a brac*, and ornaments," she continued, "I shall never have room nor opportunity to display them all."

"You have been most lavishly remembered, dear," returned Mrs. Huntress; but she sighed while she smiled over the evidences of her daughter's popularity, as she thought of the care and responsibility which it would entail upon her in the future.

"It is very, very nice to be remembered by one's friends, and pleasant to know that one has so many," Gladys said, thoughtfully taking up a delicate vase, which rude handling would have crushed to atoms, but which she knew represented a large amount of money, "but if they would only give me some simple little token, just to show that they really care for me, I should not feel quite so overwhelmed. Perhaps I am too sensitive and notional, but I think the weight of obligation which is sometimes imposed upon brides is almost frightful, that is, unless they marry—as I am *not* doing—men who can enable them to indulge in similar extravagance in return later on."

"There is a good deal of sense in what you say, Gladys," returned her mother, "but these beautiful and expensive things represent branches of industries, and somebody must purchase them in order that certain classes of artisans may live. It is hard to know where to draw the line in these things. It would not be so questionable, though, if people would be really honest in their gifts and offer only what they could afford, instead of trying to outdo others from a feeling of vanity."

But, in spite of these practical discussions, there seemed to be no end to the accumulation of wedding gifts up to the last moment.

The wedding-day dawned, a bright, mild winter morning, and every hour was filled with preparations for the important ceremony that was to occur early in the evening.

Geoffrey saw but little of his betrothed that day, for he had many duties to attend to relating to their departure, and last instructions to receive regarding the business he had undertaken. But about two in the afternoon he came home to find Gladys just going to her room, from which she would not come forth again until she was prepared for her marriage.

"I am only just in time, I perceive, to take leave of *Miss* Gladys Huntress," he said, smiling fondly upon her, as he drew her into the music-room, and shut the door, for a few moments' private chat with her.

"You do not look more than sixteen," he continued, touching the light rings of hair that lay on her forehead, and smoothing the great satiny braid, that had been allowed to hang, like a schoolgirl's, down her back, until the hair-dresser should come, "and very little as if a few hours would make you somebody's—*wife*."

Gladys flushed at that last word, though a happy little laugh rippled from her lips.

"Perhaps I shall appear more matronly by and by," she said. "It is possible that putting 'Mrs.' before my name may make quite a change. How queer it will seem to be married and yet be Gladys Huntress still?"

Geoffrey's face clouded, and a pang shot through his heart.

"I wish it could be otherwise, darling, I wish I had an honored name to give you," he said, regretfully.

Gladys put up her hand and drew down his head until their lips met.

"Dear Geoff, forgive me," she pleaded, in a tone of self-reproach, "I was very thoughtless to make such a speech. I shall be just as happy to be called Mrs. Geoffrey Dale Huntress, as anything else; my pride will not consist in my name, but in my husband."

His arms closed about her more fondly.

He knew that she loved him with all the strength of her pure and noble nature—that she had chosen him from among the many admirers who would gladly have bestowed a proud name, as well as fortune, upon her, and that he ought to be content.

But he was not; it rankled, like a thorn in his heart, that he had no name to give her—that for want of one he was compelled to assume hers.

Neither he nor Gladys had ever been told of her adoption; both believed that she was August and Alice Huntress' own child, and, somehow, a feeling of obligation, that was almost degradation, would now and then assail him, that he was obliged to identify himself in this way.

"Geoffrey," Gladys continued, seeing the cloud still on his face, "do not allow so slight a thing to cast a shadow over our joy to-day. I am so happy— life looks so bright to me, that I am almost afraid it is all a dream, and I shall wake up to find it all gone from my grasp."

He could not resist her bright, tender face, nor the beautiful, trustful eyes as they were raised to his.

"My own love," he replied, his face clearing, "it is no dream to either of us—it is all a delightful reality, and anticipation of the happiness before us, during the coming six months, is like a poem to me. But," he added, "I suppose I must not detain you here—have you everything that you need or wish for to-night?"

"I believe so; but truly. Geoff, I wish it were all over," Gladys confessed, clinging to him. "Sometimes I have been sorry that we agreed to have all this fuss and excitement. I feel as if the occasion is almost too sacred for the gaze of the curious, and to be mixed up so with show, dress, and so many other petty details. If we could only have just a few of our especial friends with us, and say our vows quietly and solemnly, right here at home, I believe I should like it much better."

This had been Geoffrey's feeling all along; but it was Mr. Huntress' desire to have a brilliant wedding, and he could not find it in his heart to oppose any reasonable wish of one who had been so kind to him.

"Well," he answered, "we can comfort ourselves with one thought; the 'fuss and excitement' will not last long, then we shall have each other all to ourselves. But, darling, see here." He drew a tiny case from his pocket, and, opening it, disclosed a heavy gold circlet resting in its bed of velvet—"have you any idea how strong this little fetter is going to be?—only death will ever break the tie that it will cement."

Gladys bent forward to look at the mystic symbol, the vivid color surging to her brow.

"Oh, Geoff! what a heavy one; is it marked?" she said.

"Yes, and that is why I show it to you—it may not be marked in a way to please you," and he held it toward her for examination.

"Please take it out yourself and let me see—I do not want to touch it," she said, drawing slightly away.

He laughed.

"Why, you dear little goose! are you superstitious?"

"N—o; but somehow I do not wish to touch it until after *you* have put it where it belongs," she answered, softly.

He removed it from the case, holding it so that she could see the engraving on its inside surface, and she read, "G. D. to G. H. Dec. 30, 18—."

"G. D.!" she repeated, looking up questioningly.

"Yes," he replied, gravely. "Forgive me for referring again to an unpleasant topic, but I could not bring my mind to add another H. there. If I *have* a right to an honored name, and find it out sometime, then I will have the initial inserted—you see, I have had space left for it. Do you mind?"

"No, Geoff," Gladys returned, after a moment's thought, though her heart sank at his words, as she remembered what Everet Mapleson had told her, "you have done perfectly right to mark the ring as you wish, and, of course, no one save ourselves ever need know anything about it."

He put it away with a sigh of relief.

"I am glad that you approve, dear," he said, smiling, "and now mind that your glove is properly arranged, and no other ring on this, my especial finger; for this ring must never come off after I have once put it on, *unless* we find another initial to add to the others. Now, good-by, love, for the next three hours. I shall not see you again until we meet at church."

CHAPTER XXXVIII
THE WEDDING

Gladys went to her room with a sweet and tender gravity on her beautiful face.

Every passing moment made her feel more sensibly the sacredness of the vows that she was about to take upon herself, and the responsibilities she was so soon to assume.

"I know this great joy is far more than I deserve," she murmured. "I cannot understand why no shadow has ever been allowed to cloud my life, when so many are born to a lot of sorrow, trial, and toil. I will try to lift the burden from some hearts in the future; I will not live all for self, but reflect some of my own happiness, if I can, to brighten other lives less favored than mine."

Could any bride, on the eve of her marriage, have made a holier resolve than this?

Very lovely she looked, when she came forth from her chamber, in her spotless wedding attire.

Her simple, yet elegant dress, of white ottoman silk, was made *en train*, and its only garnishing was the voluminous vail, which covered her from head to foot, and was caught, here and there, in graceful draperies, with clusters of orange blossoms and lilies of the valley.

Unlike many brides, she was not pale, but a delicate and lovely color was on her cheek. Her eyes were brilliant and expressive with the deep and holy joy that filled her heart, and she was calm with that perfect content which an unwavering confidence and affection alone could give.

She rode alone with her father, who was to give her away, to Plymouth Church, where Geoffrey was to meet her. He was not there when they arrived, although he left the house some time previous to their own departure, and they waited for him in the vestibule, but somewhat anxiously, as it was already five minutes past the hour set for the ceremony.

At last there was a slight commotion about the door, and a voice was heard to say:

"He has come! All is well now!"

Gladys looked up as he came forward, and thought he looked a trifle pale and excited, but it might be because the light was dim, while her vail rendered everything a little indistinct.

He nodded and smiled reassuringly at her, however; they would not let him come near her, for her dress was all arranged to go in, and must not be disturbed, while her maidens were hovering about her like a band of fairies around their queen, and, with girlish superstition, they waved him off, saying he must not speak to her again until after the ceremony.

Mr. Huntress interviewed him regarding the delay, and then came and told Gladys it had been caused by a change in clergymen at the last moment. Their own pastor had been summoned by telegraph to a brother who was lying at the point of death, only a little more than an hour previous, and had been obliged to send a stranger—a friend who happened to be visiting in his family—to officiate in his place.

This was the only shadow that had marred the young bride's joy that day. She dearly loved her noble pastor, and was deeply disappointed not to have him pronounce her nuptial benediction.

But she had no time to express it, for Mr. Huntress gave the signal to the ushers to throw open the church doors, while the groom, followed by his attendants, passed down one aisle, and Gladys, on her father's arm and attended by her maids, went down another.

They all met at the altar, where the strange clergyman was already awaiting them.

Everybody wondered at the self-possession and the lovely bloom of the bride.

But the secret of it was that Gladys forgot herself and all her surroundings; forgot the crowd of witnesses behind her; the curious glances—the place— everything in the solemn moment and the vows she was plighting.

The clergyman, stranger though he was, made the service very beautiful and impressive, while the few words of kindly advice and congratulation which he uttered at its close, when he pronounced the young couple husband and wife, were exceedingly apt and well chosen.

Then it was over, and those two, before whom life seemed reaching out so fair and full of promise, passed slowly down the center aisle, every eye following them, while every lip seemed to have something to say in praise of them.

Gladys was very quiet as her husband put her into the carriage, for the solemnity of the service was still upon her. He, too, seemed in a like mood, for he only gathered the hand that wore his ring close within his own, and thus they sat, mute from excess of joy, during their drive home.

Very tenderly the young husband helped his bride to alight, led her up the steps, never relinquishing her hand until he placed her beneath the magnificent arch at the lower end of the drawing-room, where they were to receive the congratulations of their friends.

They had driven back very rapidly, and thus they had gained several minutes to themselves before the arrival of any others.

"My darling! my *wife!*" said the exultant young husband, as he stretched forth his arms to gather his beautiful bride to his breast.

Gladys looked up with a startled, searching glance. Something in his tone had struck strangely on her ears, although he had spoken scarcely above a whisper. She saw that he was still somewhat pale, but his whole face was lighted with triumph.

"Geoff——" she began, then the word suddenly froze on her lips, a bewildered look shot in her eyes, when all at once she started away from him, flinging out her arms with a wild gesture of horror and loathing, her face as white as her dress, her eyes almost starting from her head.

"Everet Mapleson! Oh! Heaven! how came *you here?*" she shrieked.

He strode up to her, the look of triumph still on his pale face.

"Because I have a right to be here—beside my *wife!*"

"Never! *never!*" she panted, wildly. "You have no right—I am *not* your wife!"

"But, my darling, you are. I have never left your side for an instant since we were pronounced, before God and man, to be husband and wife. You are mine, Gladys! by the laws of the land, as well as by the laws of God! You plighted your vows to me in the presence of hundreds of witnesses, and I shall claim you before all the world!"

She never moved while he was saying this. She stood looking at him with that wild, incredulous light still in her eyes, that deadly whiteness on her face, her arms still outstretched in that attitude of horror and loathing.

She was like a beautiful piece of sculpture that had suddenly been transformed from a happy, living being into pulseless marble by the blighting influence of some congealing wand.

"Can you not believe it, and be sensible?" Everet Mapleson—for it was really he—went on rapidly, for the sound of wheels from without came to him, and he knew that the room would be full in a few moments. "Do not make a scene. You are mine, and no earthly power can sever the bonds that unite us! I love you madly! I worship you! There is nothing I will not do to prove my devotion to you! I have given you a proud name; I have wealth, position, influence, and I am your slave if you will give me but a crumb of love upon which to feast my hungry heart. Gladys, again I implore you not to make a scene! Receive your friends as if nothing unforeseen had happened, and they will never suspect; and to-morrow we will go away over the ocean, and leave the world to get over its astonishment as best it can."

He paused, for the horror, the despair on her face, which grew every instant more terrible, filled him with fear and dismay.

She did not stir; she was as if frozen in that attitude. She simply stood staring into his face, her own as rigid as a stone, but with such suffering, such anguish, in that fixed gaze as he had never seen depicted in human eyes before.

Steps and voices sounded in the hall. He caught a glimpse of Mr. and Mrs. Huntress hurrying in, to be the first to congratulate their darling.

Another minute, and he knew there must come a fearful disclosure and explosion.

He moved a step nearer the motionless girl and attempted to take one of those outstretched hands in his.

His touch seemed to unlock those tense nerves and muscles as if by magic.

She shrank away from him with a low, shuddering cry, and then, without word or warning, fell forward, and would have dropped to the floor had he not caught her in his arms.

Mr. Huntress, who entered the room at that moment, sprang forward, with a cry of alarm.

"What is the matter?" he asked, his attention all concentrated upon Gladys, and never suspecting the dreadful trick that had been played upon them all.

"The excitement has been too much for her, I fear," Everet responded, in a low tone.

Mr. Huntress took the senseless girl from him, saying:

"Open that door behind you; we must get her away before that crowd comes pouring in. My poor girl! what can have caused this unusual fainting turn?"

Everet eagerly obeyed his command, and Gladys was borne into a small sitting room, and laid upon a sofa there.

The next moment Mrs. Huntress' anxious face appeared in the doorway.

"Oh, August, what has happened?" she cried.

"Gladys has fainted, from some cause or other. Go, Geoff" he continued, turning to Everet, "and send some one immediately for Doctor Hoyt."

The young man hastened to obey, glad to get away from the sight of that white, rigid face for a moment.

He found a servant in the hall, dispatched him for the family physician, and then went back to his post beside Gladys.

He was nearly as pale as the unconscious bride, for he knew that the truth must soon come out, and, hardened and dogged as he was, the prospect of the inevitable explosion was not a pleasant one.

Mrs. Huntress was on her knees beside her daughter, bathing her face with water, which she had poured from an ice pitcher standing near.

She had thrown back the delicate vail, and it lay all in a heap, like a fleecy cloud, about the pretty brown head upon the sofa pillow, while Mr. Huntress had torn off his gloves, and was chaffing the small limp hands with anxious solicitude.

"What could have been the cause of this? When was she taken ill?" he asked, half turning toward Everet, but still keeping his eyes fastened upon the face he loved so well.

"Just before you entered," Everet answered, in a clear, natural tone.

Mr. Huntress started, and turned a questioning glance upon him.

Their eyes met, and held each other for one brief moment.

Then Mr. Huntress dropped the hands he was chaffing, arose slowly to his feet, his own color fast receding.

"Geoffrey?" he said, in a doubtful tone, going close up to the young man.

"No, sir; *Everet Mapleson*, if you please." replied the young man, haughtily, as with a mighty effort he braced himself for the encounter.

"By Heaven, *it is!*" August Huntress hoarsely exclaimed, and recoiling as if he had been struck a heavy blow. "What—what is the meaning of this?"

"It means that your daughter has become *my* wife instead of marrying Geoffrey Dale, as everybody supposed she was going to do."

Mrs. Huntress sprang up with a faint shriek at this.

"No, no!" she cried, "that cannot be."

Then, as she peered closely into his face, and realised the truth of the fearful disclosure, she tottered feebly toward her husband, moaning:

"Oh, August! he has practiced a terrible deception upon us, and it will surely kill Gladys."

She was almost as helpless as the unconscious girl herself, and her husband was forced to put her into a rocker that stood near him, simply because he, too, was so weakened and unmanned by what he had heard that he was unable to support her.

But a terrible wrath began to rise within him; with it came a false kind of strength, and turning toward the wolf who had thus stolen into his household, he commanded, in a fearful voice:

"Young man, explain yourself!"

"Willingly, sir; the sooner the truth is out, the better it will suit me," Everet replied, haughtily. "I have loved your daughter for more than three years. Twice I have offered myself to her, and twice been rejected. When I learned of her engagement to the low-born boy whom you adopted, and whom I have despised and hated from the very first of our acquaintance, I vowed it should never be consummated. I worshiped her, and I resolved that I would win her at any cost. I have done so; she is mine, wedded to me this night, in the presence of yourself and hundreds of others, and I shall assert my claim in spite of you all. I hoped, in the excitement and confusion, and from my close resemblance to Huntress, that I should escape discovery until our departure from New York. If we had not reached the house quite so early—if the guests could have followed close upon us and kept Gladys' attention from being especially called to me, I think I could have warded off detection until we were well on our way to Boston. She seemed turned to stone when she did recognize me, and realized how she had been duped, and when I attempted to reason with her she swooned."

For a minute after Everet concluded, Mr. Huntress stood like one dazed by some fearful shock, his glance wavering between the still unconscious bride and the man whose victim she had become.

"It is a fraud!" he cried at last. "You have practiced a most damnable fraud upon us all; but I hope that you do not imagine for a moment that you can enforce your claim. The courts of New York will promptly annul the marriage."

"Allow me to suggest, sir, that you will first have to prove your point regarding fraud," Everet retorted, with quiet defiance. "Miss Huntress has been heard to affirm that she could distinguish between Geoffrey Dale and myself without any difficulty, and yet she went to the altar with me and pledged herself to me without a demur."

Mr. Huntress groaned.

"Was that strange clergyman a tool of yours?" he demanded, excitedly. "Was that all a clever device of yours also?"

"No. Strange as it may seem, he was substituted just as I related to you, although it proved a most fortunate circumstance for me; but the telegram which called your pastor from his home was *not* a *bona fide* one. I never should have dared to face him, who has so long known Geoffrey, for he would have detected the trick at once."

"Scoundrel!" said Mr. Huntress, between his teeth. "Where is my son?—where is Geoffrey?"

"I cannot tell you, sir. I *think*, however, he has also been invited out of town—for a few hours, at least," Everet returned, a little smile of triumph curving his lips as he became more accustomed to the situation and realized his power.

Mr. Huntress caught it, and a dusky flush mounted to his forehead.

"Leave this house instantly!" he commanded, unable to control himself any longer in the face of such effrontery.

"I could not think of it, sir," Everet quietly replied, and composedly seating himself by a window. "My place is beside my wife, and here I shall stay until she shall be able to accompany me elsewhere."

What Mr. Huntress would have done next it is impossible to say, but before he could even reply, the door opened and Doctor Hoyt entered.

"What am I wanted for? Bless me! what does this mean?" he exclaimed, glancing about him with undisguised astonishment, and perceiving the condition of the newly made bride.

"Gladys was taken ill immediately upon returning from the church," Mr. Huntress hastened to explain, suddenly bethinking himself that it would be wise to avoid a scandal, at least until he could take legal advice and see what hope there was of a release for Gladys from the hateful bonds that bound her.

"Ah, yes—a protracted swoon, caused by excitement or some sudden shock," said the energetic little doctor, with a professional air, as he took one of the limp, white hands that lay on Gladys' still breast, and felt for the pulse.

He could not find any, nor was there any movement about the heart, and he began to look very grave.

"She must be put to bed immediately, and there must be perfect quiet throughout the house," he said. "Huntress, you must explain this to your guests, and get them away as soon as possible. It is unfortunate, but I won't answer for the consequences if there is any confusion when she comes to herself. Here madame," to Mrs. Huntress, "get this finery off her head and loosen her corsage, and you, sir," to Everet, whom he supposed to be Geoffrey, "unlace those pretty number twos, and give the blood a chance to circulate in her feet."

His coming seemed to put life and confidence into the nearly distracted parents.

Mr. Huntress braced himself to encounter the crowd of wondering people in the drawing-room, and, going out, explained as briefly as possible the sudden illness of the bride, and the sympathetic guests, with a few well-bred expressions of regret, immediately dispersed, and in less than fifteen minutes the mansion was cleared and the stricken household left to itself, while not a suspicion of the fearful truth had got abroad.

CHAPTER XXXIX
WHAT BECAME OF GEOFFREY

Gladys lay so long in her swoon that not only her friends but the physician also became greatly alarmed lest she should never rally; the shock which had caused this suspension of animation might end in death.

Everet Mapleson, too, as he sat alone in that small room back of the drawing-room, was in a very unenviable frame of mind. He knew that if Gladys should die her death would lie at his door; he would really have been her murderer, and such a disastrous result of his reckless plot he had never contemplated.

He had fondly hoped, as he told Mr. Huntress, that, in the excitement and gayety of the evening, surrounded by friends and receiving their congratulations, he could easily play Geoffrey's part, and she would not detect the imposition until they should start off alone upon their wedding journey. He had practiced many little mannerisms that were peculiar to Geoffrey, changing his voice, as far as he could, to imitate his, and had not reckoned upon the keenness of love to discover the fraud so readily.

He had expected that Gladys would be very unreconciled and unreasonable at first, but he had hoped, when she realized that there was no help for the deed, she might resign herself to the inevitable, and that he would gradually win her love by the influence of his own for her and his devotion to her. He had been wholly unprepared, however, for the exceeding horror and loathing which she had evinced upon discovering him, and she had thoroughly frightened him by her rigid despair and the terrible lethargy which had followed it.

When they bore her away to her room he fain would have followed, his anxiety was so great upon her account; but as he essayed to do so, Mr. Huntress turned upon him in sudden fury.

"Stay where you are!" he commanded, "or, what would be better still, leave the house altogether."

"I shall not leave the house, sir," the young man answered, doggedly, and he resumed his seat, resolved to brave it out to the end, though a sickening fear was creeping over him that the end might be such as would make him wish he had never been born.

So the poor little bride was borne from his sight, her bridal robes were removed, and everything done for her recovery that love could do or professional skill could suggest.

Strange though it may seem, no one, save the physician, suspected the cause of this sudden attack.

Mr. Huntress had confided the circumstances attending it to Doctor Hoyt, because he felt that he ought to be informed in order that he might work understandingly, but not even a servant dreamed that their beautiful young mistress had been married to the wrong man.

"August, I am nearly wild about Geoffrey, as well as Gladys," Mrs. Huntress said, to her husband, as together they bent over the unconscious girl, anxiously watching for some sign of returning life. "Do you believe that wretch would dare to harm him?"

"No, indeed, dear. I feel sure that our Geoff is safe enough. I judge, from the fellow's words, that he has been decoyed to some place, where he was to be detained until the wedding was well over, and Mapleson well on the way to Boston with Gladys. Heavens! what an escape for the dear child!" he concluded, growing white over the contemplation of the young girl's sad fate if Everet had succeeded in keeping up the deception until after the steamer had sailed.

"But is it an escape?" Mrs. Huntress whispered, with quivering lips. "Can the marriage be annulled?"

"Certainly, Alice," her husband emphatically replied, "because we can prove the man a scoundrel and an impostor."

"It will make a terrible scandal," sighed his wife.

"Better that than that our dear one should be doomed to a life of misery. I will spend my last dollar to give her back her freedom and punish that audacious wretch," said Mr. Huntress, with firmly compressed lips. "Poor Geoff!" he added, after a pause, "I wonder where he can be; he must be in a terrible state of mind, wherever he is," concluded Mr. Huntress, with a weary sigh.

But they could not think of much save Gladys, while she lay in such a critical condition, and they hung over her with white faces and sinking hearts, while they anxiously watched the physician's every look and movement.

After what, to them, seemed an eternity of time, a faint sign of life began to show itself; the heart slowly resumed its motion, the pulse gave forth a feeble throb, a faint tinge of color flickered in the drawn lips, and the chest began to heave with the renewed action of the lungs.

"She will weather it," Doctor Hoyt said, under his breath, but in his brisk, decisive way, which instantly carried conviction and comfort to those parents' fond hearts.

But when she did come fully to herself, and looked up into those earnest faces above her, when reason and memory reasserted themselves, that same look of horror came into her eyes, that rigid settling of her features returned, and were followed by another swoon, although not so frightful or prolonged as the first one had been.

It was ten o'clock before the physician succeeded in arresting the tendency to fainting, and she came fully to herself.

"Geoffrey!" she moaned, as soon as she could speak, and looking around for the dear face, while a shudder shook her from head to foot.

Doctor Hoyt shot a warning look at Mr. and Mrs. Huntress; then said, in a reassuring tone:

"He is all right, and shall come to you when you are rather more like yourself. Now, drink this for the sake of getting a little strength."

He put a glass to her lips, and she drank mechanically.

Then, pushing his hand away, she struggled to a half-sitting posture, and looked fearfully about the room.

As her glance fell upon her wedding finery, which had been hastily thrown upon some chairs, she was seized with another violent shivering, and fell back among her pillows, covering her eyes with her hands, as if to shut out from sight and memory the fearful ordeal through which she had passed a few hours previous.

But the potion which the physician had administered was a powerful narcotic, which began almost immediately to take effect, and sleep soon locked her senses in oblivion.

Hardly had she begun to breathe regularly, and the weary watchers about her bed to hope that the worst was over, when the great clock in the hall below struck the hour of midnight.

At the last stroke the door of the sick-room swung softly open, and Geoffrey's face, pale, haggard, and anxious, appeared in the aperture.

It required a mighty effort on the part of Mr. and Mrs. Huntress to refrain from uttering an exclamation of joy at sight of him.

But the doctor held up a warning finger. Mrs. Huntress, who had half started from her chair, sank back to her post beside Gladys' pillow, while her husband, with a look of intense relief, stole quietly from the room.

We must now go back to the hour when the wedding party started from the house for the church.

Geoffrey, as has been stated, left a little in advance of the others, as he desired a few moments' interview with the clergyman before the ceremony.

Not a thought of foul play entered his mind as he drove away, neither had he a suspicion that a different carriage had been substituted for the one he had ordered, that having been suddenly and cunningly sent off to the station for an imaginary arrival on the evening express.

He was so absorbed in his own thoughts that he did not even observe the route the driver was taking, until he suddenly noticed that the speed of the horses had greatly increased and he was rolling along at a remarkable rate through quiet and almost deserted streets.

It was quite dark, but the street-lamps gave light enough to show him that he was a long distance from the place where he wanted to go.

He tried to lower the window beside him.

It was immovable.

He tried the other, but it was as fast as the first one.

He thumped on the front of the carriage, to attract the attention of the driver; but a crack of the whip was his only answer.

He shouted, commanding the man to stop, but the horses only went on the faster.

Driven to desperation, Geoffrey drew back, and, with one powerful blow from his foot, shivered one of the windows to atoms.

At the sound of the breaking glass, the coachman slackened the speed of his steeds.

"Driver, where are you taking me?" Geoffrey shouted, thrusting his head from the window. "I want to go to Plymouth Church."

"Oh! *Plymouth?*" replied the man, in a tone of innocent astonishment, as if he had been bound for some other church, and was surprised to learn that he had made a mistake.

Geoffrey was unsuspicious enough to believe this, yet he was very much annoyed.

He desired to see the clergyman before the ceremony, and he knew it was already past the hour set for his marriage.

"You have no time to lose," he shouted again to the driver. "I fear you have made me late, as it is; get me there as quickly as you can."

"All right, sir," came back the answer, while the carriage suddenly turned a corner, and the man whipped the horses to a run.

Geoffrey had no overcoat with him; he thought he should not need it, the day had been so mild, and he would be shut into a close carriage; but now the chill night air came in through the broken window, and he began to suffer with the cold.

On and on the carriage went, faster and faster the horses flew, until suddenly Geoffrey discovered, to his dismay, that he was rolling over an open country road, while the lights of the city were gleaming far behind.

Again he leaned forth and shouted to the driver to stop; that he was wrong.

But this time there came no answer, save the whiz and crack of the lash, and the sound of the horses' hoofs upon the road.

He began to fear that the man was intoxicated.

He called, he commanded, he threatened; all to no purpose, except to make the driver urge his horses to go faster and faster.

They were far out in the suburbs now, with the houses few and far between, and Geoffrey was nearly in despair.

What would the wedding party think, upon reaching the church, to find no bridegroom there? What would Gladys think? What would those hundreds of guests say when they should discover there could be no wedding? What would be the end of this dreadful adventure?

Could it be possible that the man who was driving was some insane creature, carrying him to destruction?

Every possible explanation, save the right one, flashed through his mind as he sat there, utterly powerless to help himself, yet almost crazed with anxiety and suspense.

He shouted himself hoarse, without eliciting the slightest response or attention.

He leaned as far out of the carriage as he was able, to look at the man on the box, but could only dimly distinguish a figure muffled to the ears in a huge ulster, but as motionless as a statue, except for that periodical swing of his right arm in wielding the whip.

Geoffrey dared not leap out, even though in his desperation he was strongly tempted to do so; he realized that such a hazardous proceeding might result in instant death, while there was no way by which he could climb to the top of the carriage to reach the driver; there was *nothing* that he could do but submit to the inevitable, and await further developments.

So, wearied out and thoroughly chilled by the keen night air, he first stuffed one of the cushions into the broken window, then sank back into a corner, and surrendered himself to his fate.

For three long hours he sat there and was driven at a rapid pace, knowing not whither he was going.

At last, to his infinite relief, the carriage stopped.

Taking instant advantage of this circumstance, Geoffrey leaped to the ground, and turning furiously to the driver, he demanded what he meant by bringing him there.

The man might have been a deaf mute for all the notice he took of either the young man's question or passion.

He neither spoke nor moved, except to quickly turn his horses about and drive rapidly back in the direction from which he had come, leaving his victim standing in the middle of a lonely road with not a house in sight.

For a moment Geoffrey was so bewildered that he did not know what to do; he had not the slightest idea where he was, only he was sure that he must be miles and miles from Brooklyn.

But his insufficient clothing but illy protected him from the cold, and he soon began to realize that he could not stand there long without great danger to himself.

He began to walk rapidly, and soon found himself ascending a hill, and upon reaching the top he saw, beneath him, the lights of a small village gleaming through the darkness.

Quickening his steps he reached it after ten or fifteen minutes, and, to his joy, discovered that a line of railway passed through it.

Following this he soon came to the station, where he found a sleepy-looking agent and telegraph operator, who regarded him and his immaculate dress suit with undisguised astonishment.

He inquired when the next train went to Brooklyn, and to his dismay learned that this was only a branch road, and that no train was due there for an hour. It was small comfort, too, to be told that it would be only a freight train with a passenger car attached—that it would stop at every station where there was freight to be delivered or taken up; that it would be a full hour reaching the main line, where he would have to wait another hour for a train to Brooklyn.

All this delay he knew would prevent him from reaching home before midnight, and then there flashed upon him, for the first time, a suspicion that he had been brought to that remote place by no intoxicated driver's freak, neither had he been the victim of a maniac's frenzy, but that his abduction had been deliberately and cunningly planned to prevent his appearance at his own wedding—to hinder, if possible, his marriage with Gladys.

But who could have perpetrated such a dastardly act, and what could have been the ultimate object? It did occur to him that Everet Mapleson might have had something to do with it, but he quickly abandoned that idea for, much as he distrusted and disliked him, on many accounts, he could not think anything so bad as this of him—little dreaming how much worse he had done—while, too, he believed he had left the city more than a week previous.

He was very cold, and he knew he could not be three hours more on the road without a coat or wrap of some kind to protect him; but how to procure it was a question he could not solve, for the station-master told him there was not a clothing store in the place.

While he was hovering over the fire in the ladies' waiting room, shivering with the cold, and feeling inconceivably wretched, a tall, portly woman entered, bearing a large gripsack in one hand, a heavy shawl and waterproof in the other.

She wore a long circular of some rough cloth, which completely covered her from her neck to her heels, a knitted hood upon her head, a pair of brown woolen mittens on her hands, and looked so warm and comfortable that Geoffrey shivered afresh.

His eyes fastened themselves instantly and enviously upon the shawl she carried.

A bright idea struck him, and, addressing her courteously, he asked her if she would sell it to him, explaining briefly that he had been on his way to a wedding in a close carriage, when accident threw him unprotected out into the cold.

"I will give you twenty dollars for that shawl, madame," he said, knowing well, however, that it was not really worth half that sum.

But she refused his offer—the shawl had belonged to a sister who had but just died, and she could not part with it; however, she would sell him the circular she had on, she said, for half what he had offered for the other wrap, and wear that herself.

This proposal pleased him even better than his own, for he would be far less conspicuous in the dark circular, and he never had felt better over a bargain, or experienced a greater sense of personal comfort, than when he gave up his ten dollars and wrapped himself in the shabby garment, just as the lazy train came puffing up to the station.

He found a seat near the stove, and strove to possess his soul in patience until he should reach the main line. The waiting at the junction, however, was even a greater tax upon his nerves, but it was over at last, and, boarding the Brooklyn train the moment it stopped, he was soon rolling rapidly toward home.

He reached Brooklyn only a little before midnight, called a carriage and arrived before his own door five minutes before the hour struck. He let himself quietly in with his latch-key, and, fearing he hardly knew what, stole up to Gladys' room, where he had observed a light, and seen shadows on the curtains before entering the house.

CHAPTER XL
AN ACCIDENT REVEALS AN HEIR-LOOM

"My dear boy!" cried Mr. Huntress, under his breath, as he stepped out into the hall beside Geoffrey, cautiously closing the door after him, and then seizing him warmly by both hands, "where on earth have you been, and what has happened to you?"

"The most mysterious and villainous thing that could happen," replied Geoffrey, with a gloomy face. "I have been kidnaped—carried miles and miles away—and it has taken me hours to return."

"I suspected as much," said Mr. Huntress, sternly.

"Then you haven't attributed my absence to any fault of mine, Uncle August?"

"No, indeed, my boy. I *knew* better."

"What made you suspect foul play? But first tell me about Gladys. How has she borne it?" Geoffrey asked, with a wistful glance at the door beyond which his darling lay.

Mr. Huntress shot an anxious look at him.

Clearly he had no suspicion of what had occurred during his absence.

"Gladys has suffered a great deal mentally, but she is sleeping now," he said, gravely, and wondering how he could ever tell him the terrible truth.

"It must have been dreadful. I can imagine the consternation of everybody when they discovered there would be no wedding," said Geoffrey, excitedly, while he began to pace restlessly up and down the corridor. "How awkward!—how wretched for my darling!—how uncomfortable for you and Aunt Alice! How did you manage? What could you do or say?"

"Come with me, Geoff, where we can talk without fear of disturbing Gladys, and I will tell you. I have something *very strange* to tell you, too," said Mr. Huntress, linking his arm within that of the young man and leading him to an alcove over the front entrance.

"Something strange," Geoffrey repeated, in a startled tone.

"Very. There has been a most villainous plot connected with this affair."

From Mr. Huntress' manner, Geoffrey saw that something of a very grave nature had occurred.

"What is it?" he demanded. "Tell me at once; I can bear anything better than suspense.

"Geoff, there *was* a wedding!"

"Uncle August!"

"But no one save ourselves and our good doctor, as yet, suspects that there was anything wrong about it."

"Are you crazy? What *do* you mean?" cried the young man, breathlessly. "A wedding? That could not be. Gladys could not have been the bride."

"Gladys *was* the bride, and every guest believes that *you* were the groom."

Geoffrey sank upon a chair, his strength all gone, while a dim suspicion of the horrible truth began to take form in his mind.

"What *can* you mean?" he gasped, hardly above a whisper, a deadly pallor on his face, an agonized look in his eyes.

"Be calm, my boy," said his uncle, laying his hand affectionately upon his shoulder. "A dreadful thing has occurred, but it was all a farce—a fraud, rather—which the law will set right in time, and Gladys may yet be yours——"

"Heavens! Uncle August, you are driving me mad! Explain! explain! I *cannot* bear these enigmas!" cried the poor fellow, springing to his feet in a fearful state of agitation, while a cold perspiration started out all over his face.

Mr. Huntress gently forced him back into his chair and began at once to tell him all that had occurred, from the moment of the departure of the bridal party from the church, up to the present hour.

Geoffrey sat throughout the fearful recital as if he had suddenly been turned to stone, and when at last it was concluded, there were several moments of dreadful silence. He seemed paralyzed, mentally and physically, by the blighting affliction which had overtaken him, and by the bold daring of the enemy who had thus ruined his dearest hopes.

Agony, however, at last broke the spell.

He arose, and stood pale and stern before his uncle.

"Where is he?" he demanded, in an awful voice, although it was barely audible, "where is that treacherous villain who has robbed me of my wife and broken her heart? Tell me, for there must be a terrible settlement between him and me. Where is Everet Mapleson, Uncle August?"

"*Here!*" responded a defiant voice close beside them, and, wheeling suddenly about at the sound, Geoffrey saw his rival standing between the parted draperies that separated the alcove from the main hall.

"I am here to answer for myself," he continued, in the same tone, while he looked as pale and resolute as Geoffrey himself, "but first I demand tidings of my—*wife.*"

That word was like a blow to Geoffrey, who staggered back with a groan of anguish.

But he quickly rallied.

"She is *not* your wife!" he said, fiercely; "a farce—an act of fraud, could never make her such."

"You are a trifle premature in your statement," retorted young Mapleson, with a sneer. "I do not deny that my purpose was accomplished by something of strategy, but it *was accomplished,* notwithstanding—Gladys Huntress was married to me to-night, and it is simply useless to contest the fact."

"You may have gone through the marriage service with her; but you personated me, and it was only a mock ceremony. Besides, there were certain preliminaries to be attended to—your intentions made known— your certificate to be properly filled; without these there could have been no legal marriage," Geoffrey returned, sternly.

Everet Mapleson smiled superciliously.

"All that you mention was most carefully attended to, sir," he said, with an air of triumph that was simply maddening to his listeners. "The clergyman was duly apprised of my intentions, and received a handsome fee, fifteen minutes before the arrival of the bridal party at the church; the ring had been purchased and carefully marked and now adorns the hand of the bride. Not a single detail has been omitted, I assure you, to make my position and my claim secure."

"Bah! your audacity is astounding!" said Geoffrey, contemptuously. "It was a barefaced fraud, and the marriage will never stand in law," persisted Geoffrey, firmly, but oh! with such a sinking agony in his heart.

"Prove it if you can," retorted Mapleson, arrogantly. "You will not find it an easy thing to do, however, for I shall make a desperate fight to thwart you."

"Wretch! how dare you attempt such a diabolical plot?" Mr. Huntress demanded.

"I was desperate enough to dare anything, sir," Everet replied, addressing him with more respect then he had yet shown. "With the love I bear your daughter I could not brook defeat. I vowed that I would win her at any cost, and but for my own indiscretion all this fuss might have been avoided. I was so elated by my success in having the marriage performed that I could not resist taking advantage of my position, and, in attempting to salute my bride after our return to the house, she recognized me. If I had done nothing to attract her especial attention to me, the next two hours might have been tided over well enough, and, once on the way to Boston, *en route* for Europe, I could have laughed at any outside interference."

Geoffrey shivered. It was dreadful to have to listen to these revelations, and to realize what a narrow escape Gladys had had, for he knew that if Everet Mapleson had succeeded in deceiving her until the steamer sailed, the shock of her discovery, when alone, and in the power of the audacious scoundrel, might have resulted in her death. Even now they might not be able to secure her release, and she would still have to remain his wife in the sight of the world, but no moral obligation bound her to him, and no power could ever compel her to live with him.

"Could you ever hope to gain any satisfaction in the presence of a wife who would loathe the very sight of you, and whom you knew would never cease to love another?" Mr. Huntress demanded, with curling lips.

"'Love begets love,' you know, and I imagine it would not have been such a hopeless task, after all, to win the heart of my wife, with such devotion as I have to offer her," Everet Mapleson flippantly replied.

Geoffrey's blood boiled as much at his confident, arrogant tone, as at his words, and almost before he had concluded, he walked straight up to him, seized him by the coat collar, wheeled him about, and marching him to the head of the stairs, pointed below and said, in a stern, authoritative tone, as he released his hold of him:

"*Go!*"

The young man was so taken aback by this summary act, that he did not even offer to resist until he reached the top stair, when he put out his hand and seized the railing.

He turned, with blazing eyes, and faced Geoffrey, but the expression which he saw upon his face warned him that he had no irresolute spirit to deal with.

"Go!" reiterated Geoffrey, inflexibly, "or I may be tempted beyond my strength and forget one of the 'thou shalt nots.'"

"*I will not!*" he returned, as resolutely, all his antagonism aroused. "Do you imagine that, after having struggled so desperately to attain the dearest hopes of my life, I will fly like a coward in the very hour of their achievement?"

But even while he spoke, with all the bravado of which he was master, he shifted uneasily before the terrible look in Geoffrey Huntress' eye.

Yet it aroused all the passion in his nature; the hot blood mounted to his brow, coursing in an angry tide through all his veins, and before either of his companions could suspect his intention, he swung aloft his right arm to smite his rival to the floor.

But the blow never descended. In his hot-headed anger he forgot the danger of his position, made a misstep, lost his balance, and fell headlong down the long flight of stairs, and then lay silent and motionless, while those two men above looked down upon him with white, startled faces, and hearts throbbing heavily with a sickening fear.

The stairs were carpeted and thickly padded, so that his fall had not been a very noisy one; yet the disturbance was sufficient to bring both Mrs. Huntress and the physician forth from Gladys' room, in a state of alarm and consternation.

"What is it? Oh, August, what has happened?" cried Mrs. Huntress clinging to her husband.

"That villain played the spy upon us, and in attempting to strike Geoffrey, lost his balance and fell," Mr. Huntress explained, adding, anxiously: "But pray go back and stay with Gladys; let her know nothing of this, even if she wakes, and we will take care of this fellow."

He led her back to the young girl's room, and was greatly relieved to see that she was still sleeping heavily, and had not been conscious of the confusion outside.

The doctor and Geoffrey, meanwhile, had sprung down the stairs, lifted the prostrate man, and carried him into one of the rooms below.

A careful examination convinced Doctor Hoyt that there were no bones broken, the thickly carpeted and padded stairs had doubtless been his salvation in this respect; if he had suffered no internal injury, he had surely escaped in a wonderful manner.

The force and shock of the fall had stunned him, but it was not long before he began to rally and look about him.

As he sat up, rubbing his confused head and trying to realize what had happened to him, Doctor Hoyt glanced curiously from him to Geoffrey.

Both were dressed in evening suits, both were very pale, and their resemblance to each other was something wonderful.

"I do not wonder that the scamp succeeded in his villainous scheme," the physician said, in an aside, to Mr. Huntress. "I never saw twins that were more of an exact counterpart of each other.

"Well, how do you find yourself now?" he added, in his abrupt, professional way, turning to Everet.

"I believe my shoulder is sprained," he replied, cringing with pain, as he attempted to move his left arm.

"Any peculiar faintness at the stomach—any internal pain?"

"No, I reckon not; I have hardly come to myself yet, though."

The doctor made another examination.

"You'll do," he said, as he completed it; "there are no bones broken or out of joint, and if there was anything very wrong inside it would begin to show itself. It's lucky for you that you haven't a dislocated neck. The next time you want to play pugilist don't choose a flight of stairs for your battle-ground. Now, if you'll take my advice, you'll make tracks for your hotel, give yourself a good rubbing all over with alcohol, and go to bed."

Everet glanced darkly at the man, and it was on his tongue to tell him that he should do no such thing; but he had been too thoroughly shaken up by his fall to feel in a very defiant state, and he realized, too, that he had received very good counsel, which it might be wise to heed.

Mr. Huntress, after hearing the doctor's verdict, had slipped quietly from the room, feeling greatly relieved; but he returned in a few moments with several small articles in his hand, which he had picked up in the hall and on the stairs.

There was a small pearl-handled knife, a Russia leather wallet, two or three pieces of gold, and some of silver.

These he handed to the young man.

"They must have slipped from your pockets as you fell," he said.

Everet received them without even a civil acknowledgment, and replaced them in his pockets.

"Does this belong to you also?" Mr. Huntress asked, holding out a small, glittering, peculiarly shaped object.

"Yes; thanks," he now had the grace to say, in an eager tone. "It is a pocket piece and an heir-loom; I would not lose it for a great deal," and he held out his hand for it.

Geoffrey glanced up carelessly at these words; then he stepped quickly forward, his eyes glittering, a strange expression on his face.

"Let me look at that, if you please," he said.

Mr. Huntress passed it to him, although Everet Mapleson frowned at the act.

If Geoffrey had been pale before he was ghastly now as he received that small object on the palm of his hand.

It was *half of a knight-templar's cross, which had been broken diagonally, and was beautifully enameled and engraven*!

He turned it over, holding it nearer the light to examine the back of it.

"Ha!" he exclaimed, with a violent start, while he glanced wonderingly at Everet, who was also regarding him with astonishment.

"Will you tell me how this happens to be in your possession?" Geoffrey asked, meeting his eye.

"Certainly," the young man returned, with mock politeness; "it belonged to my great-grandfather, who served in the revolution. He became a knight-templar just before enlisting, and was presented with that emblem by the lodge of master masons over which he had served as W. M. The date of the presentation, with my venerable relative's name, is engraved on the back, as you perceive."

"What became of the other portion of it?" Geoffrey asked.

"My father has it."

"Your father has it?"

"Yes," curtly responded Everet, annoyed by this questioning, yet impelled to reply by something that struck him as peculiar in Geoffrey's manner. "It was broken by accident," he added, "after my ancestor's return from the war, never having left his person during all that time, and he gave one-half to his son—'as a pocket piece,' he said—keeping the other himself. At his death his portion was given to my father, who had been named for him, and, when I was of an age to appreciate it, *my* grandfather's half was handed down to me."

"And your father—*you are sure*—has the other part of it now?" Geoffrey inquired, with pale lips.

"Yes," Everet said, with a shrug of his shoulders; "we have always regarded them as heir-looms, and have been careful not to lose them."

"*I* have a 'pocket piece' which *I* have been 'careful not to lose' since it came into my possession," Geoffrey remarked in a hard, dry tone.

He took something from one of his pockets as he spoke, laid it beside that other piece lying in his palm, and held it out for Everet Mapleson to see.

CHAPTER XLI
GEOFFREY LEARNS THE TRUTH AT LAST

It was that portion of a knight-templar's cross which old Abe Brown had given to Geoffrey when he was in Santa Fe the previous summer.

It matched Everet's exactly, and the two fragments formed a perfect cross as they lay together in Geoffrey's palm.

Everet glanced at it, then shot one quick, frightened look into Geoffrey's stern face.

"Where did you get it?" he demanded, in husky tones, and starting to his feet in great excitement.

"It was found in Santa Fe, where your father—where *my* father lost it."

"Your father?" cried Everet, in a startled tone.

"Yes, Everet Mapleson, you and I are—*brothers*!"

"It is a *lie*!" hoarsely shouted Everet, recoiling, yet knowing but too well that he spoke only truth; "do you suppose I would own——"

"*Stop!*" commanded Geoffrey, sternly; "do not utter words which you may have bitter cause to regret later. This broken emblem, which I thought so valueless when it came into my possession, now becomes the strongest link in the chain of evidence that proves my identity. Last summer I traced this man to Santa Fe, and there lost his trail. There was only this paltry piece of gold, with the name William engraven upon it, to show that he had ever been there. I believed that my father's name was William Dale, for I learned that a man bearing that name had lived in a certain mining district of New Mexico, where, as I was told, I was born and my mother had died. I found my old nurse and her husband, who related all they knew of her life there, and into whose care my father had given me after her death. They, however, did not even know *his* place of residence or address; letters, he told them, would reach him superscribed 'Lock Box 43, Santa Fe.' At Santa Fe I was given this piece of jewelry by a man who had been postmaster there many years ago, and who remembered the man that lost it, but could not recall his name. Upon it was engraven 'William,' which I had been told was my father's first name, and now I find the other half of the cross bearing that of Mapleson on it. Is your father's name William *Dale* Mapleson?" Geoffrey suddenly asked, as if the thought had just come to him.

"No," was the curt, scornful reply, although it was evident that the speaker was striving to conceal the agitation which Geoffrey's account had caused.

Geoffrey stood silently and thoughtfully observing the cross that lay in his hand and the name inscribed upon it.

He no longer had any doubt about his being able to solve the mystery of his birth, though he greatly feared that the solving would only serve to confirm his worst fears.

"Then," he said, in a cold, hard tone, "he dropped that of Mapleson and assumed that of Dale for purposes best known to himself, for I know now, as well as I wish to, that your father and mine are one and the same person. I know that he must have taken a beautiful girl to the mining region of which I have spoken—that she lived there with him as his wife under the name of Dale. *He* called *her* Annie. I have seen her grave, and those who knew them both claim that he loved her as his own life, and was broken-hearted when she died. Whether she had any *legal* claim upon him; whether *I*, the child who was born to them there, can claim honorable birth and an honorable name, are points which remain to be proved. Do *you* know aught of this story?" Geoffrey demanded of Everet, in conclusion.

The young man did not reply for a moment.

He seemed to be considering whether it would be best to conceal or proclaim what he had discovered, and denounce the man, whom he had so long hated, as the illegitimate son of his father.

Suddenly he threw back his head in a reckless way, an evil light in his eyes, a curl of scorn on his lips.

"Yes," he said, "I do know the story from beginning to end. I know that a girl named Annie Dale disappeared very mysteriously from Richmond more than twenty years ago; that she fled to her lover, who met her at Kansas City, and then took her to that mining village among the mountains of New Mexico, where she lived with him as his mistress, though nominally as his wife, until she died."

"That man was William Mapleson, your father?" said Geoffrey, in a tone that was terrible from its calmness.

"That man was William Mapleson, my father," repeated Everet, defiantly, though the blood mounted hotly to his brow as he said it, showing that he was not yet quite hardened enough not to feel something of shame over the confession.

"Did *he* give you the history of that exceedingly *honorable* portion of his life?" Geoffrey asked, with curling lips.

"No; I found it out for myself. I have never felt at ease with your resemblance to me: it has haunted me day and night," Everet replied. "A slight circumstance occurred to arouse my suspicions that there *might* be some natural cause for it. I began to trace the mystery, and followed it up until I learned the truth—that you were Annie Dale's child, and she was—what I have already told you. I suppose, in point of fact, that we *are*, in a certain way, related to each other," he went on, with a disagreeable shrug. "If, *under the circumstances,* you can derive any comfort from it, much good may it do you."

Geoffrey grew crimson, and, for a moment, his eyes blazed wrathfully at this taunt.

"Was Mr. William Mapleson at Saratoga during any portion of last summer?" he asked, struggling for self-control.

"I believe he ran up there for a few days when he came North to join my mother at Newport," Everet returned, wondering what the question could have to do with the point under discussion.

Geoffrey glanced significantly at Mr. Huntress.

"What was his object in registering there as William Dale?" he asked.

Everet looked up, astonished.

"He did not," he said, skeptically.

"He did. I met him one morning in Congress Park. He accosted me by your name, believing me to be yourself, and then became greatly agitated upon being informed of his mistake and told who I was. My suspicions were aroused, for I have always been on the alert to discover my parentage, and I begged an interview with him. He appointed one for five o'clock at his room, number forty-five, at the United States Hotel. I was punctual, but when I inquired for the gentleman who occupied room forty-five, I was told that he had left at noon. I examined the register, and found his name entered as 'William Dale, from Santa Fe. New Mexico.'"

"Then it must have been some one else," Everet affirmed, perplexed over the affair, and yet instinctively feeling that his father must have been concerned in it, though just how he was at a loss to imagine.

"That was the thread by which I traced him to Santa Fe, and from there to that mining village, where I learned the story of my birth and my mother's death; and this story will have to be sifted to the bottom," Geoffrey concluded in a resolute tone.

"Really, I do not see what use there will be in raising a row over the affair," retorted Everet, with a supercilious glare at the young man. "There are hundreds of men who have been rather gay and wild in their youth, and if there have been girls in the world who were foolish enough to accept their favors, it is nobody's business but their own, and worse than folly to rake it over. Colonel William Mapleson is a man who occupies an honorable position and bears a proud name. He is a high-tempered gentleman, too, and I warn you will brook no nonsense from any one."

Doctor Hoyt, who had been an interested listener thus far during the interview, turned abruptly on his heel, with an expression of supreme contempt at this speech.

"Honorable position—proud name, forsooth! Possesses more temper than morality, I should judge, if his son is a specimen of the race," he muttered, and then passed up stairs to ascertain if all was going well with his fair patient.

The haughty heir of the house of Mapleson winced visibly beneath the scathing words.

"Nevertheless," said Geoffrey, with deliberate emphasis, in reply to what he had said, "Colonel William Mapleson will have to answer to me, *personally*, for the wrong—if wrong there was—that he did my mother. Now, sir, we have had enough of this for to-night, and *you can go*! Shall I call a carriage for you, or do you prefer to walk?"

Everet burned to defy him in this, but he knew it would be useless to resist the resolute purpose which he read in every line of his stern face; so, after a moment's hesitation, he said he would walk; and, with a sullen scowl on his face, and wrath flaming in his heart, he left the house and bent his steps toward the nearest hotel.

Neither Geoffrey nor Mr. Huntress thought of retiring that night, though the physician soon after went away, saying Gladys would do well enough for several hours, and he would come around in the morning; while Mrs. Huntress caught a little sleep upon the lounge in her daughter's room. They sat together until morning, reviewing Geoffrey's life and laying plans for future action.

When morning dawned it broke upon a saddened, yet, withal, upon a thankful household. Saddened because of the terrible ending of all the bright hopes which they had cherished only a few hours previous, but thankful because Gladys awoke once more herself, and that no harm had befallen Geoff, as they feared, during his long absence from home.

But Gladys was very sad, and could not refer to the events of the night before without becoming greatly agitated; but her long rest had given her strength and more of self-control, while she had been greatly comforted upon being told that she need never look upon Everet Mapleson's face again unless she chose, and that an appeal to the law would soon free her from the hateful tie that bound her to him.

She nearly broke down again, however, when Geoffrey went to her, late in the day, and clung to him almost hysterically; but he spoke cheerfully, and tried to comfort her with brighter hopes for the future, although his own heart was terribly burdened by the great sorrow that had fallen so like a thunderbolt upon them both.

"Oh! Geoff," Gladys burst forth at one time during the interview, "must all Brooklyn and New York ring with this dreadful story!"

"No, my darling. Uncle August and I have been considering that matter, and we think that no one, save those of us who already know the truth, need learn anything of it. I am surprised that your father and mother were enabled to act so discreetly during all the confusion last night—not even a servant suspects anything wrong as yet," Geoffrey said, reassuringly.

"But will *he* keep still about it?" Gladys asked, with a shiver of aversion, as her mind reverted to Everet Mapleson.

"I think he will be very glad to, dear—at least for the present," Geoffrey said, confidently, "until he finds out just what steps *we* intend to take. It would be very mortifying to him to have his villainy discovered, and become a target for everybody to shoot at, because he failed to get possession of the bride he had strained every nerve to win, while we shall do our utmost as soon as I return."

"Return! Where are you going?"

"Ah! has not Aunt Alice told you? I am going South immediately, to try to get at the truth regarding my birth."

He then told her something of the revelations of last night, and she was greatly astonished and shocked to learn of his relation to the man who had so injured them both.

"Brothers, Geoff? Just to think of it!" she cried, wonderingly.

He smiled somewhat bitterly.

"I fear if what he says is true, that the house of Mapleson will not own me either as a son or a brother. However, I wish to know the truth, whatever it is, and then just as soon as I return we will try to have that wretched fraud of last night rectified."

"Can it be done without publicity, Geoffrey?" Gladys asked, anxiously.

"Yes, I believe it can be arranged so that very few will ever be any wiser for what has happened."

This was one of the things that Mr. Huntress and Geoffrey had talked of the night before, and the events of the next few days confirmed them in the belief that all scandal might be avoided.

The next morning Mr. Huntress went to the house where Everet Mapleson had been accustomed to stop, but he was not to be found there. He had left nearly two weeks previous—the day after he had met Gladys at the opera—they discovered later.

Afterward they learned that he had hidden himself in a little town a few miles out of the city, and there matured his plans, and hired his accomplice to assist in his miserable plot on the evening of the wedding.

Upon leaving the Huntress mansion, after his interview with Geoffrey, and the discovery that he knew so much of his history, he had stolen away to the nearest hotel, where, after thinking everything quietly over, he began to realize that he could never compel Gladys to acknowledge herself as his wife; he believed, too, that the courts would, upon learning the facts, annul the marriage.

"Oh! if I had only kept still, and got her away before the deception was discovered, my triumph would have been complete, and now I have lost everything." he groaned in impotent wrath; and yet he was so furious at Geoffrey that he vowed he would make a desperate fight against a divorce, if for nothing but to keep the lovers apart. But until they should take some decisive step he resolved to keep still and out of sight, for he also was far too proud to care to become the subject of a scandal.

It occasioned no surprise among the friends of the Huntress family when they learned that "young Mrs. Huntress" had not been able to sail for Europe, and that the trip was to be postponed for at least another month—possibly until spring.

Her physician also prohibited all callers and excitement, giving as a reason that her strength had been overtaxed, and she had barely escaped nervous prostration.

People did not wonder at this; it appeared very reasonable, for they knew the season had been very gay, that the young couple had been in great demand, and all this, together with the excitement and care of preparing for such a wedding, was enough to wear out any young girl.

So Gladys and her mother remained quietly at home, hedged about with these restrictions, while Geoffrey and Mr. Huntress went South.

Mr. Huntress had insisted upon accompanying the young man, for he was determined that full justice should be done the boy whom he had reared and loved as his own son. If Colonel Mapleson had wronged his mother he should at least tell the story kindly and courteously to her child; if he had inherited anything from her it would be his business to see that he had his rights.

The weary travelers reached Richmond late one afternoon. They found that Vue de l'Eau—Colonel Mapleson's estate—was a long distance from the city, and they would be obliged to hire some conveyance thither.

This was not an easy thing to accomplish, for the night promised to be very dark, the roads were muddy, and the weather unusually cold for that genial climate. But by offering a generous sum, for he was anxious to have the ordeal before them over as soon as possible, Mr. Huntress succeeded in getting a man to take them to their destination.

It was seven o'clock when they at last reached the home of the proud Southerner, and the two men alighted before the door with grave faces, and nerves that were none too steady, in contemplation of the interview before them.

"Yes, sar, Massa Mapleson's home, sah," the dusky-skinned servant replied to Mr. Huntress' inquiry, and then obsequiously led the way through the magnificent hall, which divided the stately mansion through the center, to a spacious and richly furnished library at its lower end.

"A. D. Huntress and Son," Mr. Huntress wrote on a card, and handed it to the servant to be given to his master, and then they sat down to await his coming.

Five minutes later—though it seemed as many hours to those impatient men—Colonel Mapleson appeared in the door-way, opposite August Huntress.

He was a tall, rather spare man, with a finely shaped head proudly poised above a pair of military looking shoulders, a massive brow, surmounted by a wealth of iron-gray hair, regular, handsome, yet rather haughty features, a keen, eagle-glancing blue eye, and an energetic manner.

Geoffrey recognized him instantly. It was the same man whom he had met in Congress Park at Saratoga.

"Ah! Mr. Huntress," remarked the gentleman, courteously, as his visitor arose to greet him; "glad to see you, sir—glad to see you!"

Then espying Geoffrey whom, having been seated on his right and a little back of him as he entered, he had not at first seen, he started, his face lighted with pleasure, and he went toward him with outstretched hand, exclaiming, heartily:

"Holloa! Everet! where on earth did you drop from? I supposed you still in New York having a gay time."

Mr. Huntress came forward at this, saying:

"You have made a slight mistake, sir; this young man is my son by adoption—Mr. Geoffrey Dale Huntress."

Colonel Mapleson recoiled, an ashen pallor overspreading his face at these words, a look of fear followed by one of dismay, then of conviction springing into his eyes, which were fastened upon that familiar yet strange face.

Then he staggered toward a chair, sank heavily into it, his head dropping upon his breast, while he murmured, in a tone of awe mingled with agony:

"At last! at last it has come!"

There was an awkward silence after that, during which the man appeared to be absorbed in painful thought.

Mr. Huntress broke it at last by remarking in a grave tone:

"I told you, Colonel Mapleson, that this is my son by *adoption*; we have recently learned that he is *your* son by the more sacred tie of blood, and our errand here to-night is to learn how *much* or—*how little* that may mean."

The man sat suddenly erect, as his guest concluded this speech, and looked almost imperial as he bent his keen, flashing eye full upon August Huntress, a firm purpose written on his face, and a look, also, which plainly told that he had never yet turned his back upon danger, trouble, or an enemy, and never would.

"You *shall* learn, that, sir," he said in a clear, proud tone; "*Annie Dale was my lawful wife, and he,*" extending a hand that trembled visibly toward Geoffrey, "*is our son!*"

CHAPTER XLII
FURTHER DEVELOPMENTS

Mr. Huntress was struck dumb with astonishment by this unexpected declaration; but Geoffrey sprang forward, clasped that extended hand, and exclaimed, in a voice that shook with emotion:

"Oh, sir, I can never express my gratitude for that blessed assurance!"

Colonel Mapleson's fingers closed almost convulsively over the young man's hand, while he turned his gaze upon him, searching his face with eager, hungry eyes.

"Geoffrey," he murmured, in a trembling tone, "you are my Annie's boy."

His lips quivered, a great trembling seized him, and he seemed on the point of breaking down utterly.

It was several minutes before he could collect himself sufficiently to speak, although he struggled manfully with his emotion.

At length he turned again to Geoffrey, to whose hand he had clung all the time, saying:

"How like you are to Everet, my other son. I mistook you for him when I first entered the room."

"So you did upon one other occasion, if you remember," Geoffrey returned.

The man made a gesture of pain.

"Ah!" he said, humbly, "you will forgive me, I hope, when I explain why I avoided you at that time. But this meeting has unnerved me. I find myself unable to either think or speak collectedly. Will you both remove your outer coats, and then, Geoffrey, tell me the story of your life—of your adoption by this gentleman, while I try to recover myself. But first tell me, have you both dined? Shall I not order something for you?" he concluded, with thoughtful hospitality.

They assured him that they had dined just before leaving Richmond, and needed nothing; and then, having removed their overcoats as requested, Geoffrey began his tale.

His face had brightened wonderfully during the last few moments; the expression of tense anxiety, of doubt and apprehension, had all faded from it, and he looked more like himself than he had done since the day of his interrupted marriage; it was such a blessed relief to know that no stigma was attached to his birth.

He told all that he had learned of his history through Jack and Margery Henly, and how he had so strangely come upon them while striving to follow up the faint clew that he had obtained of his father at Saratoga; of his having been found so helpless and forlorn in New York by Mr. Huntress; of the restoration of his mental faculties through his kindness and interest, and of the happy life that he had since led as a member of his household. The only incidents that he omitted were those in which Everet—his father's other son—had been concerned, and which he would not then pain him by mentioning, though possibly they might have to be told later.

Colonel Mapleson listened with rapt interest and attention throughout the whole recital, and appeared deeply moved during that portion which related to his mental infirmity.

When it was all told, he seemed to fall into a painful reverie; his face was inexpressibly sad, his attitude despondent, as if memories of the past, which had thus been aroused, came crowding thick and fast upon him, filling him with sorrow and regret.

Finally he aroused himself with a long-drawn sigh, and rising, went to a handsome desk which was in the room, in which he unlocked a small drawer, and taking a box from it, brought and laid it upon the table by which Geoffrey was sitting.

"I had grown to feel almost as if this portion of my life had been blotted out," he said; "at least until it was so suddenly recalled to me by meeting you at Saratoga last summer. But our mistakes rise up and confront us; our sins find us out when we least expect it. Open that box, Geoffrey, and draw what comfort you can from its contents."

Geoffrey's face flushed at being thus addressed.

He had come there with his heart full of bitterness toward the man who, he believed, had done his mother an irreparable wrong.

But now he found those feelings fast changing to pity and sympathy for him. His manly confession had more than half conquered him at the outset, while his tender memories of the acknowledged wife of his youth, and the fond inflection with which his voice was filled every time he uttered his own name, told him that some of his dearest hopes had clustered around those early days when he had been a wee infant, and stirred a tenderness within his own heart for his father which he had never imagined he could feel.

He untied the faded blue ribbon that bound the box which Colonel Mapleson had given him, with fingers that trembled visibly, removed the lid and found a thin, folded paper within.

He opened it. It was an old telegram addressed to William Mapleson, Santa Fe, New Mexico, and contained these words:

"I will come, Will. Start at ten on the eighth."

There was another paper underneath this, and his heart beat rapidly as he drew it forth.

A blur came before his eyes, a nervous trembling seized him, making the paper rattle in his grasp, for something seemed to tell him, even before he looked at it, what it was.

Yes, it was even as he had surmised, for there, in black and white, as plain and strong as the law could make it, was the certificate which proved the legality of the bond that united William Mapleson and Annie Dale, and dated only a few days later than the telegram which he had just seen.

They had been married in Kansas City immediately upon the arrival of Miss Dale, by the Rev. Dr. A. K. Bailey, of the Episcopal church.

A song of thanksgiving arose in Geoffrey's heart as he read this, for it proved that his mother had been an honored wife—that no stain had ever rested on his birth; he was the legitimate son of William and Annie Mapleson, and the burden of fear and dread, that had so long oppressed him, was rolled away from his heart at last.

There was something else in one corner at the bottom of the box—a tiny case of black morocco.

Geoffrey seized it eagerly, turned back the lid, and a small, heavy ring of gold lay before him.

His heart leaped anew at the sight of it; nothing had been neglected to do honor to the beautiful girl whom William Mapleson had loved.

He turned it toward the light and read on its inner surface; "W. M. to A. D., Aug. 12th, 18— —"

A heavy sigh, that was almost a sob, burst from him, though it was one of joy instead of sorrow.

"A fortune could not purchase these from me," he said, looking up with moist eyes, while he reverently laid back in their place the priceless treasures he had found.

A spasm of pain contracted Colonel Mapleson's face at his words, for he could well understand the feeling that lay behind them, and he could not fail to realize, too, something of the questionable position which his boy had occupied all his life.

He was very grave and thoughtful, and Mr. Huntress, as he watched him, could see that he was struggling with some weighty matter that lay upon his conscience.

At length he lifted his head, with a quick, resolute motion, showing that he had settled it, whatever it was.

"Mr. Huntress and Geoffrey," he said, glancing from one to the other; "I have a long story to tell you, and a hard one, too, for not a soul in the world save you two and the clergyman who performed the ceremony really knows that I was ever married before the present Mrs. Mapleson became my wife. I am bound to tell this story not only to you, but also to her; that, as you cannot fail to understand, will be the hardest part of my confession."

Both his listeners sympathized with him deeply. They could easily perceive how humiliating it would be to this proud man to make such a disclosure to his wife after having deceived her for more than a score of years; yet both knew that it was an act of justice which should be performed in order that Geoffrey might be acknowledged as a son and heir, and thus attain his proper position in the world.

"It is a painful story, too," the colonel went on, "for Geoffrey. I loved your mother with all the strength of my nature—as a man loves but once in his life—and when I lost her the world became a blank to me, while even now it is almost more than I can bear to speak of it. I cannot tear the wound open and live over all that experience more than once, and if you do not object, I would like Mrs. Mapleson to be present while I make my confession."

Mr. Huntress urged him to act according to his own wishes in the matter. As far as he was concerned Mrs. Mapleson's presence would make no difference, unless the situation should prove to be too trying for her.

"She must know it within a few hours at the farthest, and it will also be necessary for her to meet you; so it might as well be done at once. What do you say, Geoffrey?" Colonel Mapleson asked, turning to his son.

"Do just what you think will be for the best, sir," he replied; and his father immediately arose and left the room.

"Estelle," he said, going into his wife's boudoir, where she sat, handsome and stately, reading the latest magazine, "will you come down to the library for a little while. I have some callers to whom I wish to introduce you."

Something unusual in her husband's tone made Mrs. Mapleson drop her book and search his face.

He was white to his lips.

"Why, William, what ails you? Has anything happened to Everet?" she questioned, anxiously, her motherhood aroused for her child.

"Everet is well, so far as I know, but— —"

"Surely you are ill, or you have bad news?" she interrupted.

"No, I am not ill, although some business of a painful nature has upset me a trifle," he answered, knowing that he was looking wretched, and not attempting to conceal his agitation.

"You know I do not like to be mixed up with business transactions," his wife replied, with an impatient shrug of her shapely shoulders.

"But I particularly desire your presence while I make a statement to those gentlemen," Colonel Mapleson said, striving to speak more calmly, though the hand that was resting on the back of Mrs. Mapleson's chair trembled in a way to really startle her.

"Why, William," she said, facing him. "have you been getting into financial trouble at your time of life?"

"No; it is an error—a mistake made long years ago that I wish to rectify," he gravely answered.

"Who are these people?" she asked, still searching his face earnestly.

"A Mr. Huntress and his son from New York."

"Huntress!" repeated the lady, reflectively. "Where have I heard that name before?"

"Never mind now, Estelle; you can think of that some other time. Please do not keep me waiting."

He took her hand, laid it on his arm, and led her from the room, while she wondered to see her proud husband in that mood, for there was a gentleness about him, mingled with a humility and a deprecatory air, that was entirely foreign to him.

Not a word was spoken by either as they passed down the grand staircase. Colonel Mapleson was too absorbed in the painful duty before him, while "coming events" seemed already to have "cast their shadows" upon the handsome face and proud spirit of his wife.

A painful expression almost convulsed Colonel Mapleson's face as he paused irresolutely a moment before the library door.

But his hesitation was only for an instant.

The next he turned the handle, led his wife within the room, when he closed and locked the door to insure freedom from interruption.

Then he led his companion straight to August Huntress.

"Mr. Huntress, allow me to present to you my wife, Mrs. Mapleson," he said by way of introduction.

The lady glanced into the gentleman's face. Instantly her own froze into a look of horror; a shock went quivering through her frame like the blow of an ax upon a tree. She started wildly back from him, her eyes diluted, her lips apart.

"*August Damon!*" she gasped, and sank fainting to the floor.

CHAPTER XLIII
COLONEL MAPLESON'S STORY

Colonel Mapleson sprang forward to lift his wife, amazement depicted on every feature.

August Huntress appeared like a man suddenly deprived of his senses, and stood spell-bound, gazing with a look of awe upon the prostrate woman before him, whom he instantly recognized as Mrs. Marston, *the mother of Gladys.*

Geoffrey, after one astonished glance at this vivid tableau, started forward to assist Colonel Mapleson to bear his wife to a sofa at one end of the room.

"Shall I ring for assistance?" Mr. Huntress asked, rousing himself with an effort from his state of stupefaction, and reaching toward a bell-pull.

Colonel Mapleson turned sharply upon him, with a stern, troubled face.

"Did you ever meet my wife before, sir?" he demanded.

"I—I think I did, once—years ago," Mr. Huntress replied, shrinking from compromising the lady, yet forced to tell the truth.

"Where?" was the terse query.

"Perhaps," returned the gentleman addressed, while he met his host's searching gaze frankly and steadily, yet with conscious dignity; "perhaps it would be as well to give our immediate attention to the recovery of your wife, and allow her to make her own explanations when she is able to do so."

It was a polite way of telling him that he would say nothing more until Mrs. Mapleson gave him permission to do so.

Colonel Mapleson bowed acquiescence.

"Hand me a glass of water, if you please," he said to Geoffrey, and glancing toward a table on which there was a water service. "We will do what we can for her ourselves, without having any prying servants about. I do not believe my wife ever fainted before."

He sprinkled her face vigorously, bathing her temples, and chafing her hands, to restore circulation.

She began to recover almost immediately, and before the expiration of ten minutes was able to sit up, and called for water to drink.

Her self-possession returned at the same time, and looking up in her husband's face, with her usual brilliant smile, as she passed back her empty glass, she remarked:

"I hope, William, that you and your guests will excuse my sudden indisposition. It was a startling greeting, a sorry welcome to strangers. But you did not present me to the other gentleman."

She glanced inquiringly about for Geoffrey, who was standing a little back of her.

As their eyes met, she started, opening her lips as if about to address him, believing him for the instant to be Everet.

But her mind worked very rapidly, and she checked herself.

She remembered that she had seen a young man at Yale who strangely resembled her son, and that his name was Huntress.

This must be he. But what could he want there in her home? And why had his coming so disturbed her husband, who was usually the coolest and most collected of men?

The blood suddenly leaped to her temples, and then as quickly receded, leaving her very pale, as the answer throbbed in her brain: "A secret in *his* early life."

Colonel Mapleson was watching her every expression; he marked the quick color, then her pallor, while he wondered what secret of her past life lay in her acquaintance with August Damon Huntress.

He, however, introduced Geoffrey, whom Mrs. Mapleson greeted very graciously, remarking that she believed she had seen him at the last commencement of Yale, when he had taken his degree at the same time with her son, "whom," she added, with a covert glance at her husband, "you resemble to a remarkable degree."

Colonel Mapleson's heart throbbed heavily. He knew the moment had come when he must unvail a portion of his life which he had believed was buried in oblivion.

"Estelle," he began, taking a chair and turning his face a little from her, "my object in asking you to meet these gentlemen was because I have a confession to make to them, and—to you; a confession of such a painful nature that I felt I could make it only once, therefore I wish you to hear it at the same time."

Mrs. Mapleson glanced from him to Geoffrey. She was very quick, and immediately she recalled what Dr. Turner, of Boston, had told her only the previous summer; for it was she who had been his visitor that day; she who had been searching for August Damon's address in the Boston Directory. She remembered he had told her that the man for whom she was inquiring had adopted and was educating a boy of great promise, and now, in view of his wonderful resemblance to Everet, she began to suspect something of the nature of her husband's confession.

"It is the strangest thing in the world," she thought, as she turned her eyes upon Mr. Huntress, and realized who his children, by adoption, were.

"It is the strangest thing in the world," was echoed in Mr. Huntress' brain, as he met her glance, and, with a sudden heart-throb of joy, realized something that she did not.

"I will go back as far as my boyhood," Colonel Mapleson resumed. "You have heard me say, Estelle, that I was in the habit of visiting Vue de l'Eau, often spending weeks and sometimes months with Uncle Jabez when I was a boy. I think I could not have been more than twelve, when, during one of those visits, I became acquainted with a young girl just about my own age, who resided near here with her mother. I refer to Annie Dale."

Mrs. Mapleson gave a violent start at this; a light broke over her face, which instantly became crimson, then grew as suddenly white.

"We became very fond of each other," her husband proceeded, without noticing her emotion, "and we were together day after day, week after week, playing ball, hoop, battledore and shuttlecock, sailing our boats together on the stream which feeds the pond that used to run the old mill, riding horseback together—in fact, were scarcely separated from the beginning of my stay until its end. It was always the same every time I came; I always sought my charming little companion on the day of my arrival, and gave her my last good-by when I went away.

"This went on for several years, until I grew to love her with all the strength of my young heart, and I fondly believed she returned my affections, although she was so modest and shy that she never betrayed it, at least after she grew to womanhood, save by evincing pleasure and a sort of trustful content in my society.

"There came a time when I resolved to confess my feelings toward her and learn if possible if she returned them, but before the time for my visit arrived that year, Uncle Jabez died and everything was changed. This uncle," said Colonel Mapleson, glancing from Mr. Huntress to Geoffrey, "made a very singular will—a very *arbitrary and unnatural will*. He divided the whole of his property, which was very large, into two portions, one of which he bequeathed to me, the other to his niece, Miss Estelle Everet, who is now my wife—upon the condition that we would marry each other. He gave us until Miss Everet would be twenty-five to make up our minds; if we both refused to comply with his wishes at the end of that time, and each married some one else, the whole fortune was to go to a certain Robert Dale, who was first cousin to our uncle. If either of us died during that time, such an event would free the other party and he or she would inherit the fortune thus left; if either married during that time the same result was to follow. I was at that time in my twenty-first year, Miss Everet was seventeen.

"You can perhaps imagine something of my feelings upon learning the contents of this will. I had always expected to inherit a share of my uncle's property, for I was a favorite with him, and he had hinted that I was to be his heir; but I had never dreamed of being hampered with any such arbitrary conditions. I was very indignant. So was my cousin, for, although we had always been the best of friends, we felt that this was a matter in which we should have been left free to choose for ourselves. However, the property was divided between us, and we found ourselves independent. I was an orphan, and had been entirely dependent on my uncle; I had just completed my education, and was thinking of establishing myself in some business, when I suddenly awoke to the fact that I was rich and could live as I chose, provided, at the expiration of eight years, I would marry the woman my uncle had chosen for me. But I loved Annie Dale, and I knew I could not marry any one else while my heart belonged so entirely to her. I became so wretched and unhappy over my situation, while at the same time I could not make up my mind to part with my newly acquired fortune, that I could not come here to Vue de l'Eau to live, where I should have to meet her constantly: so I had the house closed and started off on a trip through the West.

"During my wanderings I went to New Mexico, where I heard the most wonderful stories regarding the wealth of the Morena Mines. A bright idea suddenly came to me. I would invest in them—I would throw myself in the business of mining during the next few years; if what I had heard was true I could easily double, perhaps treble, what money I put into them before I should have to give up my fortune according to the conditions of my uncle's will—the money thus earned would be legitimately mine. I could then make over to my cousin my share of Jabez Mapleson's fortune, and be in a comfortable situation to marry the girl I loved.

"Inspired with enthusiasm over this idea, I bought largely in the Morena Mines, and then bent all my energies toward the one object of my life. The first three years I was very successful, and if my luck continued, I knew that by the end of another three I might snap my fingers over Jabez Mapleson's will, and secure the wife of my choice. But just at this time a terrible temptation presented itself to me.

"Annie Dale's mother had been a widow for several years. Her husband was a cousin of my uncle's, and when Mr. Dale died, leaving his wife and child destitute, Uncle Jabez had given them the use of a small cottage on his estate and increased the small annuity, which Mrs. Dale possessed, to a sum that enabled them to live comfortably with economy. Afterward, when Annie grew older, they opened a small private school, and, having succeeded in securing all the pupils they could accommodate, they declined receiving further aid from him. They lived very poorly and meagerly, however, and it galled me to see their poverty; so, upon coming into possession of the estate, I took advantage of their absence on a visit at one time, and had the cottage thoroughly repaired and newly furnished in a style to suit myself. Mrs. Dale was almost inclined to be angry with me for this, saying it was far too elegant for their position in life; but the deed was done, and I laughingly told her it was only a poor return for all the trouble I had given her as a boy, when I tracked her spotless floors with my muddy boots, and depleted her larder with my rapacious appetite, as, day after day, I shared Annie's lunch.

"But I am getting away from the temptation of which I began telling you, which came to me after I had been three years in the mines. Annie's mother died very suddenly after an illness of only a week, and I did not learn of the fact for nearly two months afterward. I wrote at once to Annie, begging her to choose some elderly companion and remain where she was—to consider the cottage still her home and accept aid from me until I could return and make some permanent arrangement for her. I told myself that if I could only keep her there in seclusion for a couple of years longer, I should then be in a position to return and ask her to become my wife. But in a cool, dignified letter she refused my request, telling me that her plans for the future were already made, and that she was on the eve of leaving for Richmond, where she was going to remain with an old nurse, until she could obtain a position as governess in some family.

"For a week after receiving this letter I fought a terrible battle with myself. I could not endure the thought of that delicate girl going out in the world to toil for the bread she ate. On the other hand, if I yielded to my own desire, and asked her to marry me, it would doom her to a life of hardship almost as severe, for I could only make over my share of Uncle Jabez's fortune to my cousin at a sacrifice that would leave me almost a beggar. I could not force a sale of mining interests without losing nearly all that I had made during the last three years. I was nearly distracted, and I imagined a thousand evils and dangers that might result from Annie becoming a governess. Not only would such a life be a burdensome and disagreeable one, but, worse than that, she was liable to meet some one who would be attracted by her beauty and sweetness—some one who would win her, and thus I should lose her.

"The thought was unbearable, and I resolved upon a desperate measure. I wrote again to her, confessing my love—that I had always loved her, and begging her to come to me and share my life in the West. I told her that I would gladly give up fortune—everything—if she would become my wife; and I meant to, by another year, or as soon as I could sell to advantage. I told her, also, that I could not come on for her, as my interests at the mines would not admit of my being absent long enough for that, but I would meet her at Kansas City, Missouri, where we would be immediately married, and then proceed to our simple home among the mountains of Mew Mexico. I begged her not to say anything to any one where she was going until after our marriage, when I preferred to announce the fact myself. I sent her a route carefully mapped out, and a check ample for all her needs, begging her to telegraph me the day and the hour that she would start. You have the telegram she sent in reply there," Colonel Mapleson said, turning to Geoffrey, and glancing at the package which still lay on the table beside him.

"I have always kept that precious bit of paper," he resumed, "for its contents made me almost wild with joy when I received it. I set out immediately to join my dear one, reaching Kansas City only a few hours previous to her own arrival. I had everything arranged, however, and we drove directly from the station to the house of a prominent clergyman of the city, where we were married in the presence of his household, and three hours later we were on our way to New Mexico.

"But I knew it would never do for me to take my wife to the Morena Mines, where I was known by men who were also from the South, and through whom the knowledge of my marriage would soon travel back to Virginia. Only a short time previous I had bought out a man in another district, getting his claim for a mere song, and not a soul in the place knew me. I resolved to take Annie there, make just as pretty and comfortable a home as I could for her, call myself William Dale, going back and forth from one mine to the other, as my business demanded it, until I was satisfied to sell out altogether and return to Virginia, proclaim my marriage, and give Miss Everet the other half of her fortune. But when I confessed this to Annie, as of course I had to do in order to assume her name, she was very unhappy. She was not lacking in spirit either, and made me almost despise myself for the part I had played.

"'I would never have come to you if I had known this,' she said. 'I hate deception and double-dealing of whatever nature. You might have told me frankly how you were situated, and I would have waited and been faithful to you until you could have openly made me your wife.'

"'But you would not have allowed me to take care of you,' I replied.

"'No,' she answered, flushing; 'my pride would not have yielded to that, but I could have done very well for myself for a while, and waited patiently until it was right that we should be married.'

"I had a hard task to pacify her. She was determined at first that the whole truth should be confessed, saying she would not occupy a false position. But when I told her that it would ruin me to force a sale of my stock; that I should lose all the hard labor of the three years that I had spent there, and not even then be able to replace the money from Uncle Jabez's fortune which I had invested, she became more reasonable. I promised that if she would try and be patient and happy for a year, I would replace every dollar that was not my own, and have something handsome besides, as a capital for myself.

"I honestly meant to do all this, for I knew that I should never thoroughly regain the respect of my wife until I had redeemed my position and hers before the world."

CHAPTER XLIV
THE COLONEL'S STORY CONCLUDED

"Annie and I were very happy," Colonel Mapleson went on, after a momentary pause, "during the year that followed—happy in spite of a little cloud that had arisen so soon after our marriage, for our prospects were very encouraging. I was doing finely. Every month my profits were increasing, and thus the time of our emancipation was growing nearer. If I could only replace what now no longer properly belonged to me, Annie said she would be content to remain in that mining country as long as I desired. She was willing to live simply, even frugally, if I would only do right, acknowledge our marriage before the world, and not have to hide like a couple of criminals.

"Our joy was increased tenfold when, a little before our first anniversary, a bright, handsome boy was born to us."

Again Mrs. Mapleson started and shot another glance at Geoffrey.

"That explains it all," she murmured.

"Yes, Estelle," replied her husband, who caught the words, "that explains why this young man resembles Everet to such a wonderful degree. They are both thorough Maplesons. My wife," he continued, a sudden pallor nettling over his face, and speaking now with visible effort, "began to recuperate almost immediately after his birth, her color and strength returned, her spirits seemed as light as air, and she was as happy as the day was long, in the possession of her new treasure, while she was the most devoted little mother imaginable. She named her baby, herself. 'Geoffrey Dale Mapleson,' she said he was to be called, 'only we shall have to drop the Mapleson for a while, I suppose—only a little while longer, Will,' she pleaded, as she twined her arms about my neck and drew my head down close to the little one lying beside her.

"'My darling,' I told her, 'in six months, at the farthest, you shall go back home as Mrs. William Mapleson. We will call it our real wedding journey. Estelle shall have her money, then we will come back here for a few years longer, after which, if all continues to go well, we shall have no cause to regret Jabez Mapleson's fortune.'

"I shall never forget the look of joy on her face when I made that promise, and all during the evening she was as gay as a child, and more lovely than I had ever seen her. The next morning I was obliged to leave her for a couple of days. I had to go to the other mines, then to Santa Fe to make a deposit. My darling clung to me as I bade her good-by. Our boy was just two days old then.

"'My Will, my Will, somehow I cannot bear to let you go this time, even for a day, and two will seem an age!' she said, as she kissed me again and again. Then she laughed at her own childishness, told me playfully, though with tears in her eyes, to begone before she repeated her folly.'"

A groan burst from the lips of the narrator at this point, and it seemed as if he would not be able to go on.

Mr. Huntress and Geoffrey both shifted their position, for they could not bear to look upon his agonized face as he thus laid bare this sacred page of his heart.

Mrs. Mapleson buried her face in her handkerchief, while every now and then a shudder ran through her frame.

"She never kissed me again; she never called her 'Will' again; she never *knew* me again," Colonel Mapleson went on, in a hollow tone, "for she took a cold that very day and was raving with delirium when I returned. She grew worse and worse, and in two weeks was—dead. My bright, beautiful wife, whom I loved better than my own life, for whom I was willing to give up fortune, position, *everything* that I had hitherto held most dear, lay a lifeless thing of clay—gone from me like a breath, leaving me broken-hearted and with my reason nearly dethroned."

It was truly pitiable to witness the man's emotion and his struggle for self-control.

His frame shook like a tree swayed by the wind; his lips and his voice trembled so that it was difficult for him to articulate, while his broad chest heaved convulsively with the anguished throbbing of his heart.

"Well," he said, after a while, "I must not dwell upon that sad time, and I scarcely know how I lived during the week that followed. We buried her in a quiet spot beneath a mammoth tree, not a stone's throw from our home, where she used often to sit on a warm summer's day with some dainty bit of work in her hands. You have seen her grave, you say," he interposed, turning to Geoffrey. "Does it look sadly neglected and overgrown? Is the stone defaced or the name obliterated by the storms of so many years?"

"No, sir," his son answered, looking up with moist eyes, for he had been deeply moved by his father's story and his evident suffering in telling it; "the fence that surrounds the little lot has fallen somewhat to decay, but a luxuriant growth of vines hides all that. The stone still stands upright in its place and the name 'Annie' is as distinct to-day as it ever was."

"I have never been there since we broke up our home," resumed the colonel, with a heavy sigh. "The girl, Margaret, who had served my wife most faithfully ever since our marriage, married, as you know already, a man by the name of Henly. They were going to California to live, and she said she would take care of my boy until I could make some better provision for him. I knew not what else I could do, so I accepted her offer. I broke up my home, gave away what I could not sell of the furniture, and we left the place, the Henlys taking you, Geoffrey, to California, where I planned to visit you when I could. I returned to my interests in the other mines where I tried to drown my grief by working as a common miner. But time, instead of healing my wound, only made it rankle worse. I grew bitter and antagonistic; the happiness of others maddened me; the fortune I had before been so willing to release, for the sake of her I loved, I now vowed I would keep out of spite for my loss. I resolved to keep my marriage a secret. I would keep all my wealth, and as my boy grew older he should have the benefit of it, even though I should never be able to acknowledge him as mine. But I was restless, I could not remain long in one place at a time, and I wandered from place to place trying to drown my sorrow in excitement. Four times, after an interval of six months between each, I visited the Henlys. My child was growing finely and doing well every way, so I decided to let him remain where he was until he should be old enough to go to school; then something impelled me to come back to my home. I put my affairs all into the hands of an agent, and six years from the time of my leaving Vue de l'Eau found me here again once more assuming the duties of its master. A few weeks later I met my cousin, Miss Everet. Estelle," with a glance toward his wife, "do you mind my telling it all?"

"No," was the brief, low response.

"She appeared very glad to renew the acquaintance of former years, although no allusion to our uncle's will was at that time made by either of us.

"She had grown very beautiful, had been much in society, and possessed charming manners. One day, during a call upon her, she playfully remarked that it was her birthday and she had not been the recipient of a single gift.

"'You should have mentioned that fact before,' I returned, 'but perhaps it is not too late even yet, for some remembrance of the day. Tell the number of your years and you shall have a rose for every one.'

"I knew well enough, but I would not appear to know.

"'Twenty-four,' she replied, and her face clouded as she said it.

"I could tell well enough what she was thinking of; in one year more she would be twenty-five, then Robert Dale could claim her fortune, and a life of poverty would lie before her.

"Instantly the thought arose my mind, 'Why has my cousin never married?' I did not believe that she had remained single out of any regard for me, or from any desire to fulfill the conditions of our uncle's will; indeed, she had expressed herself so indignantly at the time of its reading, that I imagined she would always be adverse to any such union. Still, it seemed strange that a young lady so attractive, and eligible in every way, should have remained single, when I did not doubt, indeed I knew, she might have chosen from among a half-dozen men whose fortunes were even larger than her own.

"'Perhaps,' I thought, 'she has become bitter and antagonistic—is bound to enjoy her money until the last moment, and then pass it over to me.' I did not want it—the thought was very disagreeable to me. Perhaps she loved a poor man, and was intending to make the most of her time; perhaps, I reasoned, she has been saving her income all these years, and will marry when her twenty-five years are past; maybe she is even waiting to tire me out and get the whole for that purpose. But there appeared to be no one of whom she was fond. I noticed that she treated all gentlemen alike, even receiving my visits and attentions with no more pleasure than those of others.

"'Why not marry her if she will have you?' was the thought that shot through my mind, as I started out to get the roses I had promised her. 'I will not give up my fortune to that miser without a struggle. I might ask her to be my wife, and then, if she refuses, I have fulfilled the conditions of my uncle's will.' But, at first, a feeling of horror came over me, at the thought of giving to another the place which my Annie had filled, and I angrily repudiated it. I avoided my cousin's society for a time after that, almost hating myself for contemplating for a moment a marriage with her for mercenary reasons. But when she chided me gently for my neglect, seeming to feel actual pain on account of it, those questions returned to me with even greater force than before, and I resolved to try to learn her mind upon the subject.

"I knew that I should lead a wretched existence in this great house, with no woman to brighten it with her presence, and, perhaps, after a time, if she should consent, I might confess the great temptation and sorrow that had come to me, and perhaps she would pardon it, and be willing to receive my boy and give him a mother's care. As soon as I reached this conclusion, I made no delay about putting my fate to the test.

"We were one day talking about my estate here, and of some improvements I was intending to make, when I suddenly said:

"'Estelle, Vue de l'Eau has no mistress. I wonder if you could regard the conditions of Uncle Jabez's will any more favorably now than you did at the time of his death?'

"She flushed hotly, and shot a quick, keen glance at me.

"'I believe we were mutually antagonistic to it,' she replied.

"'People grow wiser as they grow older,' I remarked; then boldly asked: 'Will you marry me now, Estelle?'

"'Do you think it right for people who do not love each other to marry?' she questioned.

"'Is that equivalent to telling me that you do not love me?' I inquired. 'I will be frank with you, my cousin,' I continued. 'I confess that I have not the affection for you that young lovers generally rave about; but I admire you; you are beautiful, cultured, talented, and I am free to own that you are far more attractive to me now, than you were in those old days when we were both so bitter and indignant. If no one else has won your heart, I will do my best to make your future pleasant. We have only one more year of grace; we must consider this subject and reach some decision before it expires; so what say you, cousin mine?'

"She thought a moment, then lifted her head with a resolute air, and said:

"'Yes, I will marry you, William, if you are willing to take me just as I am, without very much heart to give you, but willing to do my best to make you a good wife; I believe it will be the wiser course for both of us.'

"Thus our engagement was made, and we were married the following month. I have endeavored to keep my promise to my wife to make her life a pleasant one, and until now," with a sorrowful glance at the bowed head and shivering form of his proud wife, "I believe that we have been comparatively happy in our domestic relations; at least, I have known more of quiet content than I thought it would ever be possible for me to attain. I have kept this secret—the only one I ever kept from her—until this hour.

I did not have the courage to confess it after our marriage—I kept putting it off until after my son, Everet, was born, a little less than a year after our marriage, and when I saw how my wife's heart was bound up in him, I could not bring myself to it.

"Later, when I went to see how *my* boy was thriving, intending to make some other provision for him, when I learned of that tragedy in the Henly family and that both the man and boy had disappeared, I was almost glad I never had spoken of that sad episode in my life, although I spared no expense to try to trace my child.

"Estelle, this is my confession; you have heard the whole, and know the extent of my deception. So many years had passed that I had grown to believe that it would never be unvailed until that day when all secrets are to be made known. This young man, whom I introduced to you as Mr. Huntress' son, is *my* son, whom I believed lost to me forever; but he was led, *most strangely led* to the discovery of his parentage, and came hither to-night to claim acknowledgment. By the way, Geoffrey, I never knew either when or how I lost that portion of the knight-templar's cross you found. I missed it shortly after my last visit to Santa Fe, but never expected to recover it again. You shall keep it, my boy; it has always been regarded as a pocket piece for luck; may it ever prove to be such to you. My only reason for having the Henlys' letters simply directed to 'Lock Box 43' was to prevent my identity being discovered. I could not give them my real name, and did not like letters addressed to William Dale to come to the same box, so I just gave the number.

"About my visit to Saratoga last summer," the colonel continued, after a short pause, "I have to confess to something that I never experienced before, either in times of peace or war, a feeling of cowardice. I was on my way to Newport to join Mrs. Mapleson, and took a notion to run up to the Springs, which I had not visited for years. On the train from Albany to Saratoga an elderly gentleman accosted me, expressing great pleasure at meeting me once more, and inquired most kindly after my wife. He was a man whom I had known during that short happy year that I had spent in that mining village, and who had known me only as Captain William Dale. He, too, was going to Saratoga and begged the privilege of accompanying me to the hotel where I intended stopping. At first I hardly knew what to do. I could not bear to undeceive him regarding my name, for it would have required explanations too painful to make to a stranger, so I finally thought it would not matter if I registered for once in my assumed name; therefore I wrote it and named my place of residence as Santa Fe, since he knew that I used to do business there. A strange fate I thought it, which threw you in my way under just those circumstances. You remember how I took you for Everet, at first; but I was terribly shocked when it dawned upon me who you were, and I fully intended, at the time, to keep my appointment with you for that afternoon. But when I came to think it all over quietly, to realize all the revelations that must be made to my wife, my son, to yourself, I was nearly crazed; I knew from your appearance that you had been well cared for, that life was bright and prosperous with you, and it seemed as if I could not rake over all the past, and in the midst of my frenzy I packed my valise and left on the noon train. I have bitterly regretted it since, for my heart longed after its own; I have been ashamed that I, a Mapleson, should have turned my back and fled from any circumstances. I have repented of my folly, too, because a duty has fallen upon me, since then, which made it imperative that I should find you; but of this I will speak again later.

"What is it, Estelle?" he asked, as a heavy, shuddering sigh from his wife smote his ear; "has my story been too much for you? I fear it has. Perhaps I have been selfish and thoughtless in bringing you here before strangers to listen to all this, but it had to be told, and this interview must have taken place between us all. Forgive me for wounding you, and let me take you to your room; perhaps, though, you never will forgive me for the deception which I have practiced upon you."

He went up to her and laid his hand upon her shoulder with more of tenderness than he was in the habit of manifesting toward the proud, handsome woman. But she put him from her with a passionate gesture, in which, however, there was a pathetic air of appeal.

She arose and stood before him, her face almost convulsed with agony.

"Oh!" she cried, wringing her hands, "if you had only told me all this when you asked me to marry you; or, if I had been true to my womanhood, how much we both might have saved each other! Forgive you for your deception? oh! William, I have been tenfold more guilty than you."

CHAPTER XLV
MRS. MAPLESON'S CONFESSION

Colonel Mapleson regarded his wife as if he thought she had suddenly taken leave of her senses.

August Huntress' heart was stirred with compassion for the beautiful and imperious woman, for he realized full well the trial that lay before her, and could understand how humiliating it must be to have her sin find her out at this late day, when she had believed it buried forever.

All these long years she, too, had treasured her secret, believing that no one save the strange physician who had attended her at the birth of her child, and those two who had adopted it, knew anything of that episode in her life, and that she had so successfully concealed her identity at the time that it could never be discovered.

"What can you mean, Estelle?" demanded Colonel Mapleson, as soon as he could collect himself sufficiently to speak.

Then, as he remembered how she had greeted Mr. Huntress, how overcome she had been at sight of him, he glanced sharply toward him and knew instantly, from the look of sympathy on his face, that he must be in some way associated with that mysterious deception of which his wife had spoken.

"I mean," the wretched woman returned, in a voice of despair, while she sank weekly back into her chair, "that the secret which you have kept concealed from me during all our married life cannot compare with what I have withheld from you; you simply hid the fact of an earlier marriage and the existence of a son, while I committed a *monstrous crime* to conceal a like secret from you."

"Good heavens, Estelle!" cried her husband, starting back from her with a look of horror at her appalling statement. "I cannot believe it," and he, too, sank into the nearest chair, overcome with consternation, and actually trembling with dread of what was to follow.

Again he looked suspiciously at August Huntress, while a hundred thoughts flashed through his brain.

He fully believed that he must have been connected in some way with the crime of which his wife spoke.

Had she married him clandestinely, timing those early years while he had been away in the mines of New Mexico, and then deserted him to wed the other half of Jabez Mapleson's fortune and preserve her own? Had they met and loved each other in their youth? Was that the reason why Estelle had been so indifferent to all other suitors; why she had told him she had "not much heart to give him," when he had asked her to marry him? She had called him "August Damon" when brought face to face with him, in a tone which betrayed that she had everything to fear from his presence there, and she confirmed this by fainting at his feet.

But there were only sorrow and compassion written on Mr. Huntress' face as he witnessed the proud woman's humiliation; there was no vestige of any latent affection, no anger or harshness, such as there would have been if she had wronged him or played him false; there was no look, save one of regret and sympathy, as for one who, he knew, had committed some great sin that had at last found her out and must be atoned for.

"What does she mean? Do you know?" Colonel Mapleson asked, huskily, as his visitor—perchance feeling the magnetism of his glance—turned his eyes from the bowed form of Mrs. Mapleson to the mystified husband.

"I—know something, but not all," he answered, reluctantly.

"Then you *have* met my wife before?"

"Once, and only once, as I have already told you."

"Where—under what circumstances?" demanded the colonel, with considerable excitement.

"Pardon me," returned Mr. Huntress, with dignity, as it suddenly occurred to him what his host's suspicions might be. "I prefer that Mrs. Mapleson should herself tell you that, since it is more her secret than mine. Perhaps, however, it would be better for Geoffrey and me to retire to some other room while she speaks with you alone," and he half arose as he spoke.

But Mrs. Mapleson threw out one clenched, jeweled hand, with an imperative gesture, to check him.

"No," she cried, a quiver of agony in her voice; "if any one has a right to hear my confession, my story, you have," and at this, Geoffrey turned a startled face upon the man whom he had always regarded as honorable and irreproachable—one of nature's noblemen.

"Oh, the curse of gold!" the unhappy woman went on, wildly. "What will it not tempt one to do? The love of it blunts natural affection and honor, and warps the reason. It leads one to deceive, to scheme, and to sin for the possession of it. What blind fools men and women are to sacrifice so much—love, a lifetime of innocence, purity, and happiness, for the sake of a little paltry yellow dust! If I could but live over my life, how gladly would I endure poverty, and toil, and self-denial, to secure a quiet conscience and a heart free from its burden of sin and dread! Oh, such a life as I have led is but a miserable failure from beginning to end!"

Colonel Mapleson began to be alarmed at his wife's increasing excitement, while her remorse and her ominous allusions drove him almost distracted.

He arose, and, going to her side, took her trembling hands in his, saying:

"Estelle, if you cannot calm yourself, I shall insist upon your going to your room; you will surely be ill if you yield so to nervous excitement. Whatever this matter is that seems to weigh so heavily upon your mind, I can wait until you are in a better state for its recital. Come, let me take you up stairs," and he gently tried to force her to rise.

But she wrenched her hands from his clasp.

"No, no," she cried, with a shiver; "I will not carry this dreadful burden on my heart another hour! For more than twenty years I have borne the brand of an inhuman monster on my soul, and I wonder that it has not transformed me into something so repulsive and loathsome that every one would shrink from me in fear and disgust. I have often looked at myself with amazement to think it was possible for any one to conceal so effectually the corruption and wretchedness and duplicity of one's nature. I believe I have realized, as no one else ever did, what the Saviour meant by a 'whited sepulcher full of dead men's bones.' William!" turning upon her husband, with a wild, glittering eye, and searching his face with a glance of pitiful appeal, "I expect that you will despise and hate me, that our son will loathe me, when you learn what I have to tell you."

The scene was becoming very painful, and Mr. Huntress, pitying her from the depths of his heart, arose and walked out of her sight, feeling that he could not look upon her agony, while Geoffrey sat spell-bound, dreading the impending disclosure more than he could express.

Colonel Mapleson, feeling as if he must do something to calm her excitement, went to a closet, poured out a glass of wine, and brought it to her.

"Estelle, drink this," he said, kindly, as he put it to her lips, though his hand shook so that he could not hold the glass steadily.

She hastily swallowed it, and then pushed him from her; it seemed as if she could not bear him near her while her sin was unconfessed—until he should hear and judge her, and she could know what her doom was to be.

For more than twenty years he had been her husband. He had always been kind and chivalrous in his treatment of her. At first she had been proud of him for his honor and manliness, then her pride had gradually developed into a strong, deep affection, which, however, she had never allowed herself to parade before him, because of his unvarying reticence toward her. She had tried to be a good wife to him, to win his respect by her faithfulness to duty, her devotion as a mother, and his admiration by preserving her beauty and shining a star in the society they frequented; and now, after succeeding for so long a time, it drove her nearly crazy to think that perhaps the confession of her early folly would undo all this and breed contempt for her, or worse—his pity.

His own deception seemed very trivial compared with hers, for a cruel fate alone had prevented him from acknowledging his wife and child whom he had fondly loved and would have cherished as long as they had been spared to him, while she had deliberately planned to abandon her delicate babe and cast it unloved upon the care of strangers.

The wine which she had drank, however, served to steady her nerves, and to give her strength for the trial before her, and after a few minutes she raised her white, drawn face, saying:

"Sit down, all of you, for my story is not a short one, though for all our sakes I will make it as brief as possible.

"You will remember, William, that after I came into possession of my half of Uncle Jabez's fortune, I went abroad. I had always had an intense longing to see Europe, and when the means to do so were at my disposal, I resolved to gratify that desire. You know, too, that as a family we had always been poor. It had been a continual struggle with us to secure even the necessaries of life, and the battle with poverty had been a most bitter one to me. Now, I was bound to get the most I could out of life, to make up for the deprivations of my youth. I indignantly refused to marry as my uncle desired, for I, as well as you, considered that he had no right to make any such stipulations in disposing of his money; but I was young, I had seven years before me in which to enjoy my wealth, and I said I would spend every dollar of my income in being happy and making up to my family for the hardships of previous years. So I settled a comfortable income on my father and mother, and then, taking my sister Nellie for a companion, I sailed for Europe to gratify my taste for travel and sight-seeing. We both spoke French and German fluently, for we had been faithful students, and fitted ourselves for teaching; both were self-reliant and courageous in spite of our youth—our conflict with our unfavorable surroundings had made us so—therefore we felt competent to travel by ourselves without a chaperon, who, we felt, would hamper our movements. Some of the time we had a guide, but in England, France, and Germany we were able to go about quite independently. It was perhaps a daring thing to do, but Nellie was somewhat older than I, and very self-possessed and dignified in her bearing, and we never met with the slightest inconvenience from being without an escort. We had a very pleasant time together; we had plenty of money, and did not need to stint ourselves; Nell loved art, and I music, so for a year we put ourselves under the best of masters, and gave ourselves up to these accomplishments, and had our fill. But I am getting somewhat ahead of my story.

"While we were in London, a few months after reaching England, we met a literary gentlemen, a Mr. Charles Southcourt, who paid me considerable attention, and to whom I was very strongly attracted. We met often, too, upon the Continent, for he, also, was traveling in search of material for his writings, and our routes frequently crossed each other. Finally, during my second year abroad, he confessed his affection for me, and asked me to marry him. He was brilliant, handsome, talented, but poor. Had he been rich I would not have hesitated a moment, for I loved him; but I knew, far too well, what poverty was to be willing to relinquish my fortune and the handsome income it brought me, the luxuries and pleasures it yielded me, to say nothing of depriving my parents and sister of the comforts and advantages they were enjoying, and I refused him. He knew that I returned his affection—he had not dreamed of being rejected—and demanded the reason. I told him frankly. He then informed me that all pecuniary difficulty could soon be removed, for there was a prospect of his soon receiving a responsible appointment somewhere in the far East, which would secure him an ample income which, with what he should realize from his writings, would enable him to provide for the comfortable support of my family, and secure to me every luxury which my own fortune was then giving me. Would I become his wife if he secured this appointment? he asked. I told him yes, and I believe if it had not been for depriving my delicate and aged parents and sister of the comforts they were enjoying—if I had only had myself to consider, I should have willingly thrown up my fortune, and become his wife, whether he secured the appointment or not.

"Full of hope at having won my consent, Charlie returned at once to London—we were at that time in Rome—to bend all his energies to secure his coveted position. Two months later, Nellie and I returned to Paris, where we were again joined by Mr. Southcourt, who was jubilant, for he said he was sure of his appointment, and he showed me a letter, from a person high in authority, which seemed to promise it beyond a doubt.

"About this time we received a letter from home telling us that papa was failing; the physician feared the worst, and we were told to hold ourselves in readiness to return at once if he should continue to grow worse. Mamma wrote that she could not bear to shorten our pleasure, but she knew that our own hearts would bid us come if they found that he could not rally; that was, however, merely a warning to prepare us; she would write again if there was any change for the worse.

"I told Nellie that we must go home at once; something might happen to make papa's disease terminate suddenly, and he would die before we could possibly reach him, if we should wait to hear from mamma again. Nellie agreed to this, but Mr. Southcourt was very unhappy over our decision; he could not bear the thought of separation; he said something might occur to make it final, unless I should marry him at once and give him the right to call me his wife before I left; in that case he would let me go and feel sure of me. At first I would not listen to this proposal. I knew but too well that if my marriage was discovered, the income from my half of Uncle Jabez's property would be stopped, and my sick and dying father be deprived of everything that had now become so necessary to him. But Charlie was so sure that he should get his appointment, when he would at once settle one-third of his income upon my parents; he was so hopeful over his book, so importunate, and distressed at the thought of my leaving, while Nellie also thought there could be no risk, that my scruples and better judgment were overcome and I yielded, upon one condition—that our marriage be kept a profound secret until he actually secured his position. He agreed to this, because he said he knew I should scarcely reach home before he would have the wherewithal to enable me to make over my share of Uncle Jabez's fortune to my cousin, without missing it, and so we were privately married in Paris just before leaving for London.

"Upon our arrival there, we found that a steamer had just sailed, and no other would leave for three or four days. The very next morning we received another letter from home saying that papa had rallied and was so much improved, mamma regretted she had written so discouragingly before, and told us not to think of returning until we felt entirely ready to do so. I was so happy in my new relations that I was only too glad of this respite, for the prospect of a separation from my husband was as painful to me as to him. Three short, blissful weeks after that we spent together, and then there came a startling cable message, bidding Nellie and me to return instantly."

Mrs. Mapleson paused and struggled with herself at this point; evidently her task was a bitter one, and almost more than she was able to accomplish.

"I cannot tell you of that parting," she finally resumed; "it was almost like parting soul from body, and I shall never forget the look that was on my Charlie's face as he stood on the pier at Liverpool and watched the vessel that bore us away out of sight.

"We reached home just in season to be recognized by papa, to receive his dying blessing and his bidding to care tenderly for mamma, and then he was gone. Our mother was utterly prostrated by his death and the watching during the long weeks of his illness, and for months she, too, seemed to be upon the borders of the grave.

"Meantime, I heard regularly from Charlie, and every letter told me of some delay regarding the decision upon his appointment, but it was sure to be all right in the end, he said, and he would let me know the very moment it was decided.

"You can easily realize that those months were anxious ones to me, for I feared, as the guilty always fear, detection, while, too, the deception I was practicing was inexpressibly galling to me. Mamma rallied after a time, and for a little while we thought she would recover, but the improvement was not lasting, and it soon became evident that consumption had fastened upon her.

"It was nearly five months since my return, and I began to be very unhappy, for there was still no favorable news from my husband. One day I was sitting alone in my room writing to him, and feeling very much depressed, when Nellie suddenly burst in upon me, her face all aglow, and bearing a telegram in her hand.

"'Estelle, what will you give me for good news at last?' she cried, gayly, and holding the telegram above her head, out of my reach.

"'I will give you a hundred dollars, Nell, if it is good news,' I answered, springing up to take it from her, my heart beating high with hope, for I felt almost sure that the message could contain nothing else.

"I tore it open with trembling eagerness, only to find these words within:

"'Lost; appointment given to a man named Wilmot. Will write particulars.'

"It was a dreadful blow! Nellie had read the message over my shoulder, and for a moment we were both so paralyzed that we could only look into each other's face in dumb agony. Then I remembered nothing more for a week, while for a month I did not leave my bed. During this time Charlie wrote, bitterly regretting that he had sent me the message, but saying he had promised to let me know as soon as the matter was decided, and on the impulse of the moment, his judgment blunted by his own disappointment, he had cabled what afterward he realized must have been a cruel blow to me. He said that money had bought up the position, while he had been so certain that the influence at work for him was stronger than any amount of bribery could be. 'Still,' he cheerfully concluded, 'he would try for something else, and do his utmost to relieve me from my embarrassing position.'

"All this, however, was poor consolation for me; I could not confess my marriage and go to him a beggar in his poverty, even though my heart longed for him with all the strength of its deep and lasting love. My mother failing, slowly, but surely, was dependent upon me for every comfort that she possessed and besides this I could not make up my mind to put the ocean between us when I knew I should never see her again if I did. My husband had spoken of my 'embarrassing position,' but he did not dream one-half the truth, for I had concealed from him the fact that I was soon to become a mother."

CHAPTER XLVI
MRS. MAPLESON'S STORY CONCLUDED

"Estelle!" exclaimed Colonel Mapleson, in a shocked, yet sympathetic tone, "of all the romances that I have ever read or known, this is the strangest!"

"Yes," Mrs. Mapleson continued, "I had persistently refrained from telling my husband my secret, and Nellie alone knew it. At first I only meant to reserve it until he should come for me, as he was to do immediately upon securing his position. I was sure that, if he knew, he would instantly demand my return to him, and an open acknowledgment of our union, and so I kept putting it off, until now, that I had received that fatal news, it was too late. I could not send for him to come to me, for then the secret must come out with all its direful results, while I knew he could not take care of me in a strange country when he was so unsuccessful in his own. I was almost insane for a time, for I saw no way out of my difficulties. My mother was so feeble that she demanded the constant attendance of a nurse, and the most expensive luxuries, to prolong her life. Where would the money come from to furnish all these, if it should become known that I had violated the conditions of my uncle's will? Where, too, would the money come to meet my own expenses of maternity, and to care for the little one that would soon be mine? All too late I realized the terrible mistake that I had made in yielding to Charlie's importunities, although I loved my husband most tenderly.

"'What *shall* I do?' I cried, in despair, to my sister, one day, when all these facts, and the terrible fate awaiting their revelation, had been reviewed for the hundredth time.

"'I'll tell you what I've thought of Estelle,' Nellie answered, gravely. 'It seems a dreadful thing to do—heartless, dishonorable, and everything else that is bad—and yet I see no alternative. We *must* manage some way to keep your money—at least, so long as mamma lives: *we must not let her suffer*, though I'd work my fingers to the bone rather than do such a thing for my own sake. William Mapleson does not need your fortune; he has enough already. Robert Dale, that miserable old miser, would only 'hide it in a napkin,' if *he* were to get it. So we may as well have the benefit of it, at least until Charlie is able to do something for you. Now for my plan. You have had a long illness; you are drooping, failing; you need, *must* have, a change. Mamma is quite comfortable just now, and, with the nurse to attend her, does not really need any one else. But that she may not feel lonely without us, we will send for her old friend, Miss Willford, to come for a long visit, and then *we* will go off on a trip for your benefit.'

"'Oh, Nell, will *you* go with me?' I sobbed, in a burst of relief and gratitude.

"'Indeed I shall. You did not suppose I would send you off alone, I hope,' she answered, and then she further unfolded her plan.

"We would pretend that we *both* needed a change, after the confinement of the last few months. No one would then suspect any secret reason for our going. We would travel a while, keeping as secluded as possible, and finally go to some large city—Boston we finally decided upon, as we had never been there, and knew not a soul living there—where we would remain until after the birth of my child. Then we would give it into the care of some one, paying well for it, until my husband was in a position to claim me; and then, as soon as I had regained my strength, we would return home, and no one would be the wiser for what had occurred.

"This plan gave me new courage. All my former energy returned, and I immediately began my arrangements for my proposed trip. Mamma and her nurse both favored it, and Miss Willford was sent for. I wrote my husband of our plans—or as much regarding them as we told anybody—telling him how to address his letters; and then Nellie and I went away, without exciting the suspicion of any one regarding our real object. We went first to Philadelphia, where we remained in secluded lodgings for a few weeks, giving our names as 'Mrs. Marston and maid, Nellie Durham'—Nellie preferring to act in that capacity. Then we proceeded to New York, where we stopped a while, finally going on to Boston, where my little girl was born."

Geoffrey turned abruptly around and faced Mr. Huntress as Mrs. Mapleson reached this point in her story. Never until that moment had he suspected that Gladys was not his kind friend's own daughter. But he knew that he had formerly resided in Boston. He remembered that Mrs. Mapleson had addressed him as August Damon, and how she had been overcome upon meeting him. He remembered, too, how, when he had proposed leaving the room while she made her confession to her husband, she had said "if any one had a right to hear her story, he had," and putting all these things together, it flashed upon him that Gladys might have been that little girl who was born, under such peculiar circumstances, in Boston.

Mr. Huntress met his inquiring glance, and smiled faintly; but he was very pale and sorrowful.

It had not been an easy matter for him to sit there and listen to that story, and to have it revealed that Gladys was not his very own. He had always hoped to be able to keep the secret of her adoption.

"Is it true, Uncle August?" Geoffrey questioned.

Mr. Huntress nodded gravely.

"How very, very strange!" said the young man, with a perplexed face.

Then his countenance suddenly brightened!

He leaned eagerly forward, laid his hand on Mr. Huntress' knee, and whispered, excitedly:

"Then *he*—Everet Mapleson, is *her half-brother, and that marriage was nothing but an illegal farce!*"

"That is true—I have been thinking of that very thing," returned Mr. Huntress, grasping the hand upon his knee with cordial sympathy, "and though it has been very hard to have the fact revealed, that our dear girl was not quite our own, yet my joy at having that great trouble so easily wiped out of existence, counteracts all the pain."

"What is it?" Mrs. Mapleson asked, wondering at their eager whispering and excited manner.

"I will tell you later, madame," Mr. Huntress replied. "Pardon the interruption, and pray go on."

"William, the worst of my story is yet to come," Mrs. Mapleson resumed, turning with a pathetic look to her husband.

He reached forth one hand, and laid it affectionately upon hers.

"Do not think me so hard, Estelle," he said, in a low, kind tone; "I do not forget the 'beam' that was in my own eye, and I have no right to criticise the 'mote' in yours, especially when you have been so great a sufferer, and your hands were so tied by your dependent mother and sister. Your heart was all right—you would never have concealed anything but for the force of circumstances."

"Oh, wait; you have yet to learn that my heart was not all right," she moaned, dropping her head upon her hand. "My baby was a beautiful child—I realized that the first time I looked upon her, but I did not dare to let my love go out toward her, for I knew that I must give her up, at least for a time. And yet, what to do with her was a very trying question. At first

I thought of putting her into some institution, requiring some pledge that she should not be given away within a specified time. But I found I could not do this, so I advertised for some one to adopt her, promising to give five hundred dollars with the child. I received numberless letters in reply, but only one out of them all really pleased me, and this was signed 'August and Alice Damon.'"

"Ah! now I understand," interposed Colonel Mapleson, glancing quickly at Mr. Huntress, and looking intensely relieved.

Then his eyes wandered to Geoffrey.

"How wonderful! that those two should have found a home in the same family!" he murmured.

"I appointed a meeting with Mr. and Mrs. Damon," his wife went on. "They came, and at once I knew that they were the very people to whom I would confide my little girl, in preference to all others. But you gave me an assumed name," she said, pausing, and turning to Mr. Huntress.

"Not an assumed name, madame, but only a part of my real name, which is August Damon Huntress," that gentleman explained.

"Why did you withhold your surname from me?"

"Madame, I knew well enough that *your* name was not Marston. I felt sure that no mother would give away her child, as you were doing, and reveal her identity. On the other hand, I did not wish the identity of the child preserved. I did not intend that you should have any advantage over me. If I took her, I meant her to be mine wholly, without running any risk of having her taken from me, or of ever learning that she had been abandoned to the care of strangers. Consequently, I gave you the name of Damon."

"Well," said Mrs. Mapleson, with a sigh, "as it happened, it made no difference, but if I had suspected it at the time, you would not have had my child, for I meant to keep track of her. *I meant to have her again* just as soon as my husband and I were reunited."

"But you told me," began Mr. Huntress, with an amazed, horrified face— —

"I know I did," the lady interrupted. "I promised you that I would never trouble you—would never even ask to see her. I pretended to give her to you unreservedly, although, you remember, I would not subscribe to any legal form of adoption. I allowed you and others to think me a heartless, unnatural monster for the sake of gaining for my little one a good home and loving care until I could see my way clear to demand her restoration. It was dishonorable—it was a wretched deception, but it was all a part of that terrible secret that had to be guarded at whatever cost. But I had to pay dearly for it, as you will soon realize.

"My sister and I left Boston, both of us in better spirits than we had been since leaving England, for we believed that everything had been so successfully concealed there was not the slightest danger of discovery. We came back to our home to find mamma more comfortable than when we left her, having had a bright, cheerful visit with her old friend, while she appeared delighted with the improvement which our trip had made in us. But she lived only one short month after that. She took a sudden cold, which brought on a hemorrhage that terminated her life in a few hours.

"More than this," Mrs. Mapleson went on, hurriedly, while she pressed her clasped hands over her heart, as if to hold in check its painful throbbings, while she related the saddest event of her whole life, "on the very day that she was buried a bulky package was brought to me, postmarked 'London.' It contained considerable manuscript, a Bank of England note for one hundred and fifty pounds, my marriage certificate, and—a letter. The letter told me—oh, William!" she burst forth in a quavering voice, "you *knew* that your Annie must die. You had to face the dread fact before it really came, and you were somewhat prepared for it; but I—I had no warning; the shock fell like a thunderbolt to crush me! My Charlie was dead long before I knew it. He had been in his grave nearly a fortnight when the terrible news came to me. The letter was from a friend of my husband, and stated that he had met with an accident that must result fatally, having been—crushed—in a falling elevator."

The poor woman appeared hardly capable of going on. It seemed as if all the agony of that dreadful time was revived by this recital.

"He had only a few hours to live," she went on, at last, "and, though he could not hold a pen to write me one line, he made up that package with his own hands, telling his friend that it was to be forwarded to Miss Estelle Everet. You see, he kept my secret even while dying, and would not send me one of the fond messages of which I know his heart must have been full, for fear of betraying me. He said that I would take charge of the publishing of the manuscript, if I thought best to give it to the world, for the expenses of which he inclosed the Bank of England note. That, however, was only a blind, for the manuscript was in such a crude state it could not be published, and he had simply taken that way to send me, without exciting suspicion, the only existing proof of our marriage, and what little money he possessed.

"My fond, faithful Charlie! He deserved a better fate and a better wife. Of course, after that, there was no fear of discovery, even though I mourned with the bitterness of despair over my lost hopes. My mother's death was excuse enough for my grief, though people said I laid it to heart more than they imagined I could. For a long time I felt as if life was little better than a mockery. Mine certainly thus far had been a miserable failure. My husband dead, my child lost to me forever—for, of course, I could never claim her now—what was there in the world for me to live for?

"After a time I grew bitter and reckless. I told myself if I could not have the blessings that usually crown a woman's life, I would make the most of the fortune that I still possessed; I would travel—I would see the world—I would not deny myself a single wish or whim. My sister and I started off again. We went to England first, where I found my husband's grave, but did not dare even to mark it with any expression of my love. We went to Egypt and Palestine, joining a party of travelers thither, and after spending another year in roving we came back once more to America.

"Three months after our return, Nellie, too, sickened and died, and I was left utterly alone in the world—alone with my ill-gotten wealth and splendor. What was my money to me then?—like the apples of Sodom; and yet I experienced a grim sort of satisfaction that the income of Uncle Jabez's property was still mine, that I had outwitted the world and the lawyers or executors of Uncle Jabez's will by my art and cunning. But only a little more than a year remained before I should be twenty-five, when, if my cousin and I were both unmarried, Robert Dale would have our fortune. I grew rebellious at the thought. I had nothing but my money to live for now, and my money I wanted to keep. I had sacrificed truth, principle, and all the noblest elements of my woman's nature for it, and I was willing to make almost any sacrifice now to retain it.

"Just about this time you returned, William, and," a burning blush now suffused the face of the proud woman, "I welcomed you with secret joy, and instantly made up my mind to marry you if you would have me. I made myself agreeable to you with that sole object in view. You know how well I succeeded, although you did not dream that I was scheming for that, and I did not experience a qualm, since I did not deceive you regarding the state of my heart toward you; my acceptance of you was as frank as your proposal for my hand. Neither of us professed any love for the other: we simply decided that it would be a wise union, and that we could be a very comfortable couple. A strange, heartless arrangement, I suppose the world would have said could it have read our motives, but it would have seemed even more strange if the experience of our lives had been revealed. I was hardened and reckless then, for I felt that fate had used me very badly. I have not deserved the quiet, peaceful years—quiet and peaceful but for the stings of conscience—that have been my lot since. I have been growing happier during all that time, growing to——"

She broke off suddenly, flashing a quick, pained glance at her husband, while the blood again mounted to her brow.

"During all these years," she continued, presently, "I have never learned anything regarding my child, save once. Last summer, after Everet left me at Newport, to come home, I was comparatively alone there for a few days, my friends, whom I was expecting to meet, not having arrived, and a sudden impulse seized me to go to Boston and try to learn something about my daughter. I had always kept the card you gave me, Mr. Huntress, and I imagined if you were still in that city I could trace you through the directory.

"Upon my arrival I stepped into a drug store on Washington street and asked for the directory, to begin my search. You can imagine something of my amazement and consternation when I found myself face to face with the physician who had attended me at the birth of my child. He also recognized me, although I tried to deceive him regarding my identity. But he insisted that he knew me, and finding denial useless, I appealed to him for information regarding my child. He said he knew the man well who had adopted her—that he had been for years the family physician; but he would not give me his name or address."

"That must have been Dr. Turner," said Mr. Huntress, looking astonished; "but how could he have known that we adopted the child? We never told him that she was not our own."

"True; but he was called to attend her for some slight ailment only a few days after you took her, and recognized her; he would not, however, violate your confidence nor his sense of honor by telling me anything by which I could trace you or the child. He comforted me greatly, though, by assuring me that she was a beautiful and talented young lady; that she had received every advantage, and was surrounded by the fondest love and care. I remember now that I have seen her," Mrs. Mapleson said, with starting tears, "and my heart yearns strongly for her as I think of it. I saw her at Yale when my son graduated; she was with you," turning to Geoffrey, "and she is truly a lovely girl. Mr. Huntress, you have held your trust sacred, and I am deeply grateful to you."

CHAPTER XLVII
AN UNEXPECTED RETURN

"Surely, Estelle, your lot has been a hard one," Colonel Mapleson gravely remarked, after an oppressive silence; "your sufferings have been keener than mine, and I can only wonder how you have concealed them so successfully during all these years."

"I promised that I would try to make you a good wife, and I have striven to be agreeable and companionable to you. I knew if you suspected that I had any secret sorrow, you would imagine it was because I was unhappy with you, and so I have done my best to appear contented with my life."

"Done your best to *appear* contented," repeated Colonel Mapleson, with some bitterness, but in a tone that reached her alone.

His wife looked up quickly, and a bright flush dyed her face again.

She reached forward, and laid her hand upon his arm.

"I *have* been content, William," she said, under her breath; "it was only a *little* while that I had to *strive*—while my grief was so keen and fresh. But let us not talk of this *now*," she concluded, with a glance toward their visitors.

Colonel Mapleson sighed; then he said, with an anxious look at her face:

"Estelle, I am afraid all this excitement will prove too much for you, and you had better go to rest; but, first, come and speak to my son, will you?"

His tone was pleading, and his unusual gentleness touched her; it told her that he felt more of sympathy than blame for the errors of her past. She arose with a sense of relief, such as she had not experienced during all her married life. Her burdensome secret—that terrible barrier that had always stood between her and her husband—was at last all swept away. She could not tell whether it would create an impassable gulf between them or not, but at least she had nothing now to conceal.

She went to Geoffrey with him, prepared to welcome him as her husband's first-born, with all the cordiality of which she was mistress.

"My boy," said the colonel, holding out his hand to him, "can you own your father after all that you have heard?—can you forgive the deception of my early years—my moral cowardice in turning my back upon you at Saratoga—and let me have the satisfaction of repairing, as far as may be, the hardships of your youth? My debt of gratitude to your other father"—with a glance at Mr. Huntress—"I can never repay."

Geoffrey warmly grasped that extended hand.

"You have made my heart more glad than I can tell you, sir," he said. "I can forget—I can overlook everything, now that I know my mother was your loved and honored wife. I came here fearing the worst—fearing that a dreadful stigma rested upon my birth—that I was not entitled to an honorable name."

"You are entitled to much more than that, Geoffrey," Colonel Mapleson returned, smiling, although his lips trembled and his eyes were full of tears; "there is a handsome fortune awaiting your disposal."

"A fortune!" said the young man, wonderingly.

"Yes, inherited through your mother from that very same old miser—Robert Dale—of whom you have heard so much this evening."

"How can that be?" Geoffrey asked, while Mrs. Mapleson uttered an exclamation of surprise.

"You shall know very soon; but first shake hands with my wife," his father responded, presenting Mrs. Mapleson.

"You are, indeed, very much like my son," she murmured, as she gave him her hand; "and, believe me," she added, with touching humility, "I am rejoiced to have you restored to my husband, even at the expense of the trying confessions and revelations of this evening."

Geoffrey respectfully raised her hand to his lips, and the act conveyed, far better than words could have done, the sympathy he felt for the suffering which she had endured.

She then bade Mr. Huntress good-night, after which her husband led her from the room.

He accompanied her to her own door.

"Good-night, Estelle," he said, gently, "I hope you will go directly to bed and try to sleep."

She turned suddenly—that proud, imperious woman, who, for more than twenty years, had repressed every sign of affection for him—and threw herself upon his breast.

"Oh! William, say that you do not quite hate me for what I have told you to-night!" she cried, in an agonized tone.

Her husband looked astonished at her act; then his face softened, his eyes lighted with sudden joy.

"Why, my wife? I believe you almost love me after all! Do you, Estelle?" he eagerly questioned; "do I possess any more of your heart now than I did when you married me, or has it been a continual struggle all along to be a good wife to me?"

She was sobbing like a child, now; the haughty, indomitable spirit that had upheld her so long was subdued at last.

"I have not dared to let you see how much of my heart you have won; you know you told me you did not entertain a lover's affection for me, and I would not force mine upon you," she confessed, with her face still hidden upon his breast.

He folded his arms more closely about her.

"And *I* have imagined that *you* were holding *me* at arms' length during all our life," he said, laying his cheek softly against her still glossy hair. "Estelle, we will be lovers all the rest of our lives, for, my wife, you have become very, very dear to me—I did not realize *how dear* until now. We will not look backward any more, but forward; we have both erred greatly in the past, and it would ill become either of us to criticise the other. Tell me, shall we drop the vail of charity over it all, and begin to live our real life from this hour?"

For the first time in her life, she put her arms about his neck, and voluntarily laid her lips against his cheek.

"I do not deserve this, William," she said, humbly, "but you have made me happier than I ever expected to be again."

He returned her caress with great tenderness, then said:

"I must not keep you standing here, dear, nor our guests waiting below; but I will come to you again later."

He opened the door for her to pass in, then closed it, and returned to his visitors, brushing aside some truant tears as he went.

His face, however, lighted with pleasure as he again entered the library, and looked into Geoffrey's noble, manly face, and realized that he was really the son of the beautiful young wife whom he so loved years ago.

But the young man himself was very grave.

He felt that he stood in an exceedingly delicate position.

He had come to Colonel Mapleson, believing that he had wronged his mother, and willfully abandoned him when a child; he had meant to denounce him for it, and reveal also the villainy of which his other son had been guilty.

But he had found a father ready and eager to welcome him, ready to acknowledge the wife of his youth, and to give his son the place that rightfully belonged to him; and now it seemed almost cruel to expose the wrong of which his half-brother had been guilty. He could not endure the thought of coming between the two in any way; of destroying the confidence of the father in the son.

Something of this Geoffrey and Mr. Huntress had been considering during Colonel Mapleson's absence from the room. They had about decided to say nothing of the affair of the interrupted marriage, until they had seen Everet, and acquainted him with the facts which that night had revealed. Perhaps, they could arrange to hush up the matter altogether, if the young man proved to be amicably inclined or reasonable; at all events, they had concluded not to mention the affair that night—to, at least, give it a little more thought first. In explaining about the broken cross, Geoffrey had simply said that they had seen the other half in Everet's possession, and that he knew nothing of their visit to Vue de l'Eau.

It seemed as if a great weight had been lifted from Colonel Mapleson's heart when he returned.

He drew a chair near his guests, and began at once to enter more into the details of the past. He gave them a full history of his eccentric relative, Robert Dale; told of his long-concealed fortune, when and how it had been discovered, together with the will which bequeathed the whole of it to Geoffrey's mother.

"This, of course, now becomes yours," he concluded, turning to the young man, with a smile. "Quite a fine property, it is, too, amounting, with the accumulated interest, to upward of one hundred and fifty thousand dollars. Besides this, you will inherit one-half of what I possess, the other half going to Everet."

"I could not take anything from this estate, sir," Geoffrey said, suddenly growing crimson.

"Why not?" questioned his father.

"Because you married contrary to the conditions of your uncle's will, so, in that case, I do not feel that I have any real right to any of it. If your marriage had been discovered, you would have had to forfeit all to your cousin, Miss Everet."

"You are very conscientious," replied Colonel Mapleson, gravely.

Then he suddenly looked up, with a wise smile.

"It has not occurred to you, I perceive," he added, "that you could claim every dollar that Mrs. Mapleson and I possess. We both violated the conditions of that will; consequently, our fortunes rightly belonged to Robert Dale, and you, being his only heir, would inherit it all."

Geoffrey looked amazed at this. Such a thought had not occurred to him; but now he could not fail to see the force of his father's argument.

"I do not want it—I could not take it; I shall have more than enough from what will come to me from my mother," he said.

"There are few people in the world who would not take all they could get," replied Colonel Mapleson, feeling a certain pride in this noble renunciation of his son. "But, taking everything into consideration, it seems to me that matters are somewhat complicated with us. I suppose Mrs. Mapleson's daughter—your adopted child, Mr. Huntress—will come in for her share of her mother's property."

August Huntress flushed.

A painful struggle had been going on in his mind ever since his meeting with Mrs. Mapleson.

He could not endure, for a moment, the thought of ever having Gladys know anything about her birth. She fully believed herself to be Mr. and Mrs. Huntress' own child, and he knew it would be a rude shock to her to learn that she was not, and to be told the facts regarding her parentage, and he meant to prevent it if he could.

"Colonel Mapleson," he said, speaking very seriously, "I hope that Gladys will never learn that she is not really my child; I never wish her to receive anything from Mrs. Mapleson."

The colonel's face fell.

He knew that his wife's heart was yearning after her child; at the same time, he could understand and appreciate Mr. Huntress' sensitiveness upon the subject; while, too, the young girl could not fail to be painfully shocked upon learning the sad, even cruel, history connected with her birth.

"I think it would be a great disappointment to my wife not to be allowed to claim the relationship," he replied, thoughtfully.

"I have no doubt of it, sir," returned Mr. Huntress; "but could she not better bear the disappointment than to have her child made unhappy, after all these years of content, by learning that those who have hitherto occupied the place of father and mother are nothing to her by the ties of blood? She has not a suspicion of the truth, and I am confident that no one, save Doctor Turner and ourselves, has the slightest knowledge of it, so that it never need be revealed. Mrs. Mapleson promised solemnly never to claim her, under any circumstances; she gave her unreservedly to us, and I cannot feel willing to have our relations disturbed. As far as any property which she might inherit from your wife is concerned, I would not give it a moment's consideration. I have an abundance, and Gladys will have it all by and by. I did intend to make a division between my two children," turning with a smile to the young man by his side, "but since Geoffrey is now so rich, he will not need it. However, it will amount to about the same thing in the end, as they will soon have all things in common, I trust."

"Ah! is that so?" Colonel Mapleson inquired, with a brilliant smile and a nod at his son.

"I hope so," Geoffrey answered; "and I, too, think it would be wiser to keep the truth regarding Gladys' birth still a secret. Its revelation can do no one, save Mrs. Mapleson, the least possible good, and I doubt if even she would not regret a disclosure that would result in so much unhappiness to others."

"I believe you are right," Colonel Mapleson said, after thinking it over for a few moments. "I reckon it *would* be the better plan to allow things to remain just as they are."

"I beg you will not consider me selfish or unfeeling in this matter," said Mr. Huntress, earnestly, but greatly relieved by this decision. "I sympathize deeply with Mrs. Mapleson, but I feel that she could not suffer a tithe of what my wife and daughter would endure to have their relations disturbed, not to mention my own feelings in the matter."

"I understand," his host responded, heartily, "and I know it is but right and just that the one should yield in order that the many may be happy, and I believe that my wife will see it in the same light when she comes to consider it. But," turning again to Geoffrey, "when is this wedding to occur?"

The young man colored and glanced at Mr. Huntress, for he hardly knew what to say in reply to this.

"Well, I—the day is not set yet. I was anxious to have my relations with yourself settled, and—we——"

It was an unusual occurrence for Geoffrey Huntress to lose his self-possession under any circumstances; but just then he felt himself to be in a very painful position, for every moment he shrank more and more from revealing his half-brother's wretched plot, and he was greatly relieved by a little stir in the hall at that moment, which attracted Colonel Mapleson's attention from him.

The next instant the library door was flung open, and Everet, himself, pale and travel-stained, stood before the astonished group.

"Ha!" he cried, catching sight of Geoffrey. "So you have stolen a march on me! trying, I suppose, to browbeat the governor into confessing that romantic liaison of his youth."

"*Everet!*" exclaimed his father, turning sternly upon him, an angry flush mounting to his brow, at this rude intrusion; "what do you mean by rushing in here like this, addressing my guests in such an abrupt way, not to mention your exceedingly disrespectful language regarding myself?"

"Your *guests*! Why don't you present them to me, or are you a trifle delicate about introducing Annie Dale's son to *me*?" retorted the young man, in a nervous, unnatural manner.

"Silence, sir!" thundered Colonel Mapleson, looking perfectly aghast at this strange behavior on the part of his usually courteous son. "What do *you* know of Annie Dale?" he continued; "and why do you speak of this young man in that sneering way?"

"I know a great deal about Annie Dale and the suspicious life she led in a certain mining district for a year," Everet retorted, with reckless scorn.

He had been wrought to the highest pitch of angry excitement by finding Geoffrey and Mr. Huntress there before him.

"I know," he went on, "how she was enticed away by the promise of a marriage which never took place, and how she afterward died—doubtless of a broken heart—leaving a nameless brat to inherit her shame."

"Everet! you have suddenly taken leave of your senses! I believe you *are* in the delirium of fever," returned his father, regarding his now flushed face and glittering eyes with alarm. "But have a care over your words. How on earth you have become possessed of such strange notions is more than I can account for."

"I can easily enlighten you. I have a couple of letters in my possession that were written by Annie Dale's lover, which will prove all that I have hinted at; and I found a very pretty ring, too, last summer, during my travels—not a *wedding-ring*, either, mind you. I doubt if she ever had that— which was lost, on the very spot where she had lived and died."

He drew both letters and ring from one of his pockets, as he spoke, and flung them upon the table, before his father.

Colonel Mapleson recognized them at once, while he was amazed by the fact of their being in the possession of his son. One of the letters he remembered losing after a visit to the cottage where his Annie had once lived, and he had been greatly disturbed over the fact; but the other, and the ring—which his dear wife had lost one night while sitting on the porch in their mountain home—he could not understand how he came by them.

"You found that ring?" he asked, amazed.

"Yes. I visited a certain cottage among the mountains of New Mexico last summer, and while standing upon one of the steps leading up to the door it gave way, and underneath I found this ring."

"Ah! we never thought of looking *under* the step," said the colonel, musingly. "It was a little loose for her finger just then, and, slipping off, rolled away out of sight, and we thought it very strange that we could not find it. Yes," he continued, taking it up and regarding it tenderly, "Annie Dale never had her engagement-ring until the day of her marriage, when this was put on her finger as a *guard to her wedding-ring*! Annie Dale was my loved and honored wife, Everet, and Geoffrey, my son and hers," indicating the young man by a motion of his hand, "will show you the certificate of our marriage, and the ring with which she was wed!"

"*Your wife!* Annie Dale *your wife!*" Everet repeated, starting back, amazed, all his color fading again at those words, and shocked into more respectful speech by the unexpected acknowledgment.

CHAPTER XLVIII
PEACE AT LAST

"Yes, Annie Dale was my wife!"

Everet bent a sullen look upon Geoffrey.

"Then *he* is *not* a——"

An imperative gesture from his father silenced the obnoxious word that trembled on his lips.

"Geoffrey Huntress, as he has hitherto been known," he said, "*is my son*, honorably entitled to my name, and an equal share with yourself of all I possess—a son whom I long mourned as dead, but whom I have most gladly welcomed to my heart and home this night, upon learning who he was."

"Would you have done so had you not been forced to it?" Everet rudely demanded.

"Everet, you are very disrespectful to-night," returned his father, with a frown, "I cannot understand why you should manifest such a spirit of hostility. But we will not talk more of this now; you shall have the details of the story of my early life later. I trust, however, that your sense of what is right and just will prompt you to some acknowledgment for your discourtesy toward your brother."

"*My brother!*" retorted Everet, aroused afresh at the word; "he has been nothing but a stumbling-block in my path ever since I first saw him; he humiliated me before friends in a way that I have never forgiven; he thwarted me in my hopes at college and in many plans—all but the last one," he concluded, with a taunting laugh, turning defiantly toward Geoffrey, who was regarding him with more of sorrow than of anger.

"What do you mean, my son?" demanded his father, who saw that something was very wrong between them, and was almost in despair over his inexplicable conduct.

"Has he not told you how I cheated him out of his wife?" Everet asked, supposing, of course, that that wretched story had been rehearsed.

"Cheated him out of his wife!" repeated Colonel Mapleson, growing pale, and glancing apprehensively from one to the other.

His son gave vent to a short, nervous laugh, but feeling considerably crest-fallen at having so recklessly betrayed himself, since he saw that nothing had been said about his miserable plot.

Mr. Huntress here interposed, seeing that the truth must come out, and explained in a few brief sentences what had happened.

Colonel Mapleson sank back white and nervous, as he listened, realizing, almost at the outset, the terrible thing which his son had so nearly accomplished.

"Do you know what you have done, Everet Mapleson?" he said, in a solemn, impressive tone, when his visitor concluded, and the young man was startled and awed in spite of his bravado. "You have been upon the brink of a fearful precipice; you have very nearly committed a dreadful crime, for which I could never have forgiven you, for which you would never have forgiven yourself; the girl whom you have sought to make your wife is your sister."

The young man grew pale, but more at his father's tone than from any conviction of the truth of his statement. But he rallied after a moment.

"What stuff are you telling me?" he retorted, contemptuously.

"It is no 'stuff;' it is sternest truth; Gladys Huntress is an *adopted daughter*."

"Ha!" and now Everet Mapleson seemed suddenly galvanized. "Did Annie Dale have another child?" he demanded, with hueless lips.

"No; but she is your *mother's* child, by a former marriage."

"Great Heaven!"

There was no defiance or recklessness in his manner now. He sank breathless upon a chair, a horrified look upon his face, a shiver shaking him from head to foot, perspiration starting from every pore.

"My mother's child! *Impossible!* Who told you?" he questioned, hoarsely.

"Your mother herself! She was unexpectedly brought face to face with Mr. Huntress to-night; she recognized him and fainted. Upon recovering she confessed to a former marriage, and said, in order to conceal the fact, she had been obliged to give away her child—that Mr. Huntress was the man who adopted her."

Colonel Mapleson then went on to explain more at length something of the occurrences of the evening, but he was interrupted in the midst of his recital by Everet throwing himself prostrate upon the floor, while a heart-rending groan burst from him as he fell.

When they raised him he was unconscious, and a small stream of blood was trickling from his mouth.

He was carried at once to his room, a servant was immediately dispatched for a doctor, while his anxious friends used what remedies there were at hand for his relief.

When the physician arrived he said his patient had evidently been suffering from a severe cold for several days, and that this, with weariness of body and a sudden shock of some kind, had brought on the hemorrhage, while there were also some indications of a brain trouble, and a severe illness would doubtless follow.

Mr. Huntress and Geoffrey proposed going away early the next morning, but Colonel Mapleson, who seemed greatly unnerved by the excitement of the previous evening, begged them to remain for a few days at least, as he could not bear to give up Geoffrey again so soon after being reunited to him.

They had not the heart to leave him in his trouble after that, and consented to remain long enough to learn what the prospect of Everet's recovery would be.

But he grew steadily worse, and raved in the wildest delirium, recognizing no one, although there was no return of the hemorrhage. At the end of four days Mr. Huntress decided that he must go home, but Geoffrey concluded that it was his duty to remain with his father until the crisis in Everet's illness should be passed, for Colonel Mapleson seemed to lean upon and to experience much comfort from his presence.

He proved of the greatest assistance in the sick-room, where he attended Everet most faithfully, and endeared himself to the whole household by his gentleness and courteous bearing.

At the end of three weeks the fever turned, and Everet was pronounced out of danger of any further brain trouble, although it would be a long time before he would fully recover from the weakness of his lungs.

Geoffrey withdrew himself immediately from the sick-room as soon as the patient recovered consciousness, realizing that his presence might be annoying to Everet, and retard his convalescence; although he remained at Vue de l'Eau for another week, at the earnest request of both Colonel and Mrs. Mapleson.

Then he felt that he could not stay longer away from Gladys, and he returned to Brooklyn, taking with him the knowledge of his father's firm and lasting affection, and Mrs. Mapleson's respect and friendship, together with the handsome fortune which he had inherited from Robert Dale, and which Colonel Mapleson had transferred to him.

It had been agreed by all parties that Gladys should never be told the secret of her parentage, although Mrs. Mapleson had wept bitterly when she consented to remain all her life unrecognized by the child for whom her heart yearned inexpressibly.

She could but acknowledge, however, that it would be for her daughter's happiness, and she was willing to sacrifice her own feelings to secure that.

She had been greatly shocked upon learning of Everet's wretched plot, and the narrow escape he had had from committing a fearful crime, and she had pleaded with Geoffrey, when parting with him, to forgive her son for the injury he had done him, saying she felt sure that he would deeply regret it, when he fully came to himself.

Geoffrey assured her of his full and free pardon, and actually expressed the hope that he and his half-brother might some time come to regard each other, at least with a friendly, if not with brotherly, affection.

His return was a very joyous one.

Gladys had been assured by her father, long before this, that she was free; that no tie bound her to Everet Mapleson; that the events which had occurred upon the night set for the wedding had been simply a farce, the result of fraud of the worst type, which rendered the ceremony illegal.

She was almost like her old, bright self when Geoffrey arrived, although not quite so strong as formerly, for she had suffered a fearful shock, and it was not surprising that its effects should yet be visible.

Only a few days after Geoffrey's return, Mr. Huntress' beloved pastor and his wife were invited to dine with the family, and later in the evening, when the servants were all below—everything having been confidentially explained to the reverend gentleman previous to his visit—Geoffrey and Gladys stood up in the drawing-room and were quietly made one, while only those who were acquainted with the private history of the young couple ever knew of this second ceremony, their fashionable friends and the world all believing that the real marriage had occurred at the time of the brilliant wedding before described.

No one was surprised that the European trip was postponed until warmer weather. "A sea voyage in the dead of winter was a thing to be dreaded; besides, Mr. and Mrs. Huntress had finally decided to brace up their courage and go with them, if they would wait until spring."

They sailed about the middle of May, and had an unusually smooth passage. They spent a whole year abroad—a year of delight, and such as few experience in this world, and then returned to Brooklyn, where Mr. and Mrs. Geoffrey Dale Mapleson set up their own establishment on Clinton avenue, not a stone's throw from their former home.

The change in Geoffrey's name, together with the discovery of his parentage, had been very easily explained, and then, of course, everybody said "they always knew that he and Everet Mapleson must have the same blood in their veins; but it was really a very romantic circumstance— Geoffrey having been injured and carried off by his nurse's husband in a fit of drunkenness, and never discovering his parentage until now."

The next fall, after the young couple's return from Europe, Colonel Mapleson and his wife paid them a visit, and it was noticeable that a great change had come over the strangely-wedded pair.

The stately and soldierly colonel was devotedly attached to his beautiful wife, who had acquired a peculiar gentleness and sweetness, in place of her former imperious manner, which made her tenfold more attractive. It was evident, too, that she was strongly attached to her noble husband.

When she was presented to Gladys, she folded her closely in her arms.

"My dear," she said, with a thrill of tenderness in her tones that moved the young wife strangely, "I hope we shall be very good friends, for, although Geoffrey is not my own son, *I want to regard you both as my children!*"

Tears sprang into Gladys' eyes.

She lifted her face and kissed the lovely one bending above her.

"I am sure I shall love you very, very dearly," she said.

And she did. A tender friendship was begun during that visit, which grew stronger and more devoted with every year, and when, at length, two little twin girls were born to Gladys, she named one Alice and the other Estelle.

"For our two mothers," she said to Geoffrey, with a fond smile.

Colonel Mapleson was very proud of his Annie's boy, but his happiness would never be quite complete, he said, until there could be perfect harmony between his two sons. He hoped that time would bring even that to pass, for Everet had shown great remorse over the deception that he had practiced upon Gladys, and he finally made an humble, though manly, confession to her, and entreated her pardon for the injury he had done her and her husband.

But it was not until Geoffrey was called to the death-bed of his father, three years after his marriage, that they really became friends.

The making of Colonel Mapleson's will brought it about, for he consulted his sons about the matter. Geoffrey refused absolutely to be named in it, except simply to receive an affectionate remembrance from his father, and this attitude excited Everet's wonder.

"Why do you do this?" he asked, coldly, and regarding his brother with suspicion. "You are my father's elder son, and entitled to half of his fortune."

"I do not wish it, believe me," Geoffrey answered. "I have enough as it is. I can never tell you," he added, earnestly, "how much more to me than fortune, or any other inheritance, is the *name* that I can legally claim from our father. Let that be my share—indeed, I *will not* have anything else."

Everet stood, thoughtful and silent, for several moments. Then, with an evident effort, he looked up in Geoffrey's face, and said:

"I know that you might have *all*, had you chosen to take it, and in that case *I* would have been a beggar. You have led me to believe—and not by this act alone, either—that there is at least one truly noble, unselfish man in the world. If you do not utterly despise me, will you henceforth recognize me as a friend?"

He extended his hand as he spoke, but it shook visibly, and he was very pale. It had not been an easy thing for this proud young Southerner to make such a confession and appeal.

Geoffrey grasped it warmly, his manly face all aglow with sincere joy.

"Not only my 'friend,' Everet, but, my *brother*, in name and in truth," he answered, heartily; and thus a life-long bond was established between them, which strengthened with every succeeding year, while the desire of Colonel Mapleson's heart was granted him ere he closed his eyes upon all things earthly.

A little later, Addie Loring, who during all this time had refused many an eager suitor, became the mistress of Vue de l'Eau, where she reigned the center of a happy and peaceful household.

She often visited her girlhood's friend at the North, and entertained her, in turn, in her Southern home, where the elder Mrs. Mapleson was supremely content in the presence of her child and grandchildren, even though they were ignorant that no other bond save that of mutual love and sympathy united them.

Mr. and Mrs. Huntress were also very happy in the
many years to enjoy them—years which brought with

"Old age serene and bright,

And lovely as a Lapland night."

Mr. Huntress retired from active business soon a
Europe, resigning his place in the firm to Geoffrey, w
ability as a business man, and was as energetic and
had his fortune still to make, instead of already bein
handsome competence.

Gladys, true to her vow upon that wedding-day,
sadly, and yet which, they all felt, had been wisely ov
time between the duties in her own home and the wo
burdens of others, "reflecting some of the happiness o
those less favored;" thus laying up treasures for hersel
lasting than either silver or gold.

"Who soweth good seed shall surely reap;

The year groweth rich as it groweth old,

And life's latest sands are its sands of gold."